I0688736

SIREN'S SON

THE TRITON SERIES BOOK TWO

EMORY GAYLE

To all you butterflies – whether you have discovered your wings or
not. You are beautiful.

I

KYLAYA

CLOAKED IN BLACK OF NIGHT, I couldn't make out anything around me. Nothing. Nothing but…me.

Lit from within, my powers flowed. Glowing warm and comforting in the endless darkness, they were a sign that I wasn't in the world that Jett and I had built. The safe place where we would meet and fall in love. This wasn't that place.

A beacon in the darkness, I stood. Energy coursed through me, as the inky clouds of night churned and moved in the air around me.

My heart gave a solid thump in my chest.

I need to get out of here.

As if the darkness heard my thoughts, it started to converge.

Panic stabbed through my veins as I watched it get closer. There was nowhere to run. My feet moved, but I didn't go anywhere.

No escape.

My powers raced through me unable to come out. No matter how hard I pulled, they remained inside. Every fiber of my being was screaming at me to *move*. There was something wholly unnatural in that space with me. Something that I had never experienced in my dreams before.

A scream cut from me as darkness filled in the space around my feet and slowly crawled over the top of my foot. Like sharp ice, it's oily tendrils slid up my skin; cutting and freezing me as it wound tightly around my body.

Another scream tore at my throat.

Run! Do something!

A hand slammed down on my arm. Startled and scared, I fought against it. Its grip tightened and pulled hard, yanking me backward.

I was taken from pitch black and thrown into light. My eyes slammed shut against the brilliance. Lifting a hand, I tried to shield myself from the blinding light and see where I was - and, more importantly, who had brought me there.

The touch of a hand on my back startled me once again. I twisted around in a snap, ready to defend myself.

"Jett!" I exclaimed in relief. I threw myself into his arms and exhaled, "Thank the gods!"

My heart was swinging wildly from my rib cage, half from the terror of the darkness and half from being in Jett's arms again.

Safe.

He stood silent and still as I hugged him tightly.

"Where are we? Did you see that black stuff?" I asked, as I pulled back.

He didn't answer, but looked down at me with eyes that glowed a brilliant violet, unlike anything I had seen them do before.

"You okay?" I asked.

"I'm fine," he said and smiled widely. I gasped and staggered back. Needle sharp teeth were revealed between his lips where his beautiful smile should have been. A grin deepened on his face at the look of horror on my face.

"What? Do I have something in my teeth?" he asked, pointing to his face. I didn't know what to say, I just stood there and stared at him. "No? Maybe it's just my face in general?" I stared, silent and still. "Okay," he continued, "how about this one, then?"

He raised his hands up and rubbed his face. When he brought his hands down, Jett's round deep eyes, sandy blonde hair, and strong jaw were replaced by the sharp features of Mazz and his short black hair.

"Better?" he asked. Jett's deep voice was gone, with Mazz's taking its place.

"I-" I stuttered and shook my head, taking another step back.

"Hmm, still not the right one, huh?" Mazz uttered and shook his head violently. Mazz melted away and the rugged features of Sam took his place. My jaw dangled open as I watched in silent horror. "Still no? *Fine*," Sam scoffed. This time he didn't move.

Green bled into his skin from his temples as Sam's short thick hair sprouted from the top of his head and cascaded down his shoulders in heavy wet locks of deep green. Blood seeped into his eyes turning them red and then black. I suppressed the urge to turn tail and run, as I realized who it was that had infiltrated my dream.

"Midira?" I whispered, as if saying it out loud would make it come true.

"*Queen* Midira, let's not be disrespectful," she scolded. She slid across the floor in a deep green dress with a death-drop of a neckline.

I was reminded of the last thing that she had said to me when she visited me in the bathroom. Appearing to me from the water in the sink - one of her many tricks - she took one more opportunity to threaten me…and spill a little secret that would change one of the guys' lives forever.

One of them was her grandson.

I hadn't said anything to them. How could I? We had enough on our plates without me blathering on about visions of Midira saying one of them was her grandson. I didn't even know which one she was talking about, not that it mattered. That information wasn't going to go over well no matter who it was.

"You *are* lovely," Midira purred like a drowning kitten. "You would have made an excellent Siren. I can see why he loves you," she said, tipping her head down and levelling her eyes with mine.

I turned my face, breaking eye contact with her.

"I will *never* be one of you."

"We'll see," she smiled.

That was it, I was done. I grabbed her face, placing my palms on her green skin and I pulled. My powers could suck the energy from any magical being, at least I was pretty sure they could. It worked on a couple of gods, it had to work on the Siren queen. I closed my eyes and braced myself for the surge of power from her.

Nothing came.

Laughter broke from her lips, cutting through the air like shards of glass.

I opened my eyes and looked straight into hers.

"This is a *dream*, KyLaya. Your powers don't work here." I shoved her away and staggered back.

"An *excellent* Siren," she said, smiling. My temper raged as my hand went instinctively for the dagger at my side. My fingers wrapped around the hilt. I smiled right back at her and aimed; bringing my arm back I let it go with deadly accuracy.

The knife sank through her ribs and into her heart. She staggered back, dropping her eyes to the weapon lodged in her chest.

But, it wasn't her eyes that looked back up at me.

"No!" I screamed and ran forward.

It wasn't Midira who I had killed.

It was my father.

KYLAYA

"NO!"

I shot straight up in bed.

Oh shit. That was a bad one. A really bad one.

Grasping my face in my hands, I rubbed it hard. I'd been having the worst dreams since I had seen Midira in the bathroom of Jett's place days ago. They didn't seem to be getting better; if anything, they were getting worse. The other night I dreamed I had killed everyone in the house and then myself – which was when I woke up.

The nightmare clung hard to me as I staggered out of bed. Not even a hot shower, which usually made me feel alive again, could revive me. I was thinking of my father more and more the longer I was away from him. I hadn't been separated from him since I was a child, not once since KyLena disappeared. After my sister was taken he never travelled without me - no matter what kind of a trip it was. My heart ached thinking about him in an eternal sleep - waiting for someone to wake him. He had no idea what was going on, or that I was technically missing. Maybe, that was for the best. He would lose his mind if he knew where I was and what I was doing.

I shook my head, willing my thoughts away from my father, as I sat down on the bed. Jett's room had become another home to me. I almost thought of it as my room. My towel was wrapped tightly around me as I tried to clear my mind. I just wanted everything out.

But it wouldn't go.

Midira told me that one of the guys was her grandson. One of them was Siren royalty, and he had no idea.

No one did.

But me.

Damn me.

"Hey, you okay?" Raya said as she paused at the door looking a me. "You were up a lot last night tossing and turning. You almost kicked me right out of the bed," Rayna teased, as she fluffed and folded her clothing into a neat pile beside the bed.

"I'm sorry," I apologized. "I've been…having nightmares." We had been sharing a bed since that night in Stenen. With the town on fire and all the people that lived there taken, we thought it was a good idea to stay in one house together. Jett and Jasper's was the best choice.

Even though I was grateful for another girl in the house, I'm not sure she felt the same about me. It had become very apparent that she had feelings for Jett. At least, she did until I came into the picture.

I had to give it to her though, she wasn't taking it out on me. She had been friendly and kind, but I could see the hurt in her eyes whenever Jett touched me. She was far stronger than anyone gave her credit for.

"What's the plan for the day?" she asked as she slipped a sweater over her head.

"Not sure," I said absent mindedly looking down at my hands.

"Hey, you okay," Rayna asked stepping around the bed toward me.

"Huh?" I asked looking up at her.

"Okay, what's going on? You look like death…no offense," she said, watching me carefully.

"None taken. I just…I miss my father," I answered, not wanting to lie.

"Oh." She looked down at her clothing and grimaced. "Eros hasn't really been helpful with that has he?"

"Nope," I sighed. Eros was supposed to be looking for a cure for my father's state. He hadn't shown his godly butt around the house since Stenen. To say I was frustrated with the lack of help from our friendly neighborhood god was an understatement.

"What do *you* want to do?" she asked me. I looked up. I hadn't thought about it.

"I don't know what I *can* do," I admitted. Rayna's eyes lifted to the ceiling in thought as she pulled her lips to the side. An expression I had learned was her thinking face. Her gaze dropped down to mine.

"The Fates would know how to heal him," she answered. My heart stopped.

"They would?"

"I can't see why not," she answered with a shrug.

"I – I…gosh, I hadn't considered that! Thank you!" I said with a smile. My mind was full of questions and, for the first time, hope.

"Glad to help," she said, walking to the door. As she opened the door she stopped and turned to me. "KyLaya."

"Please, just Ky. There are very few people who call me by my full name and they are all old aristocratic sobs back home."

"Ky," Rayan began, "I know that this thing with Jett has made things a bit…awkward between us. I'm sorry for that. I just hope you know that I do want to be your friend. If you need to talk, I will listen." With a gentle smile she left the room.

I was dumbfounded. How she could manage such kindness was beyond me. There were many girls in Triton that gave me major stink-eye over my engagement to Mazz, and their feelings for him were so much shallower than Rayna's were for Jett. Some were openly hostile with me, at least they were until I became Prime. I admit to not liking Rayna when I found out how she felt about Jett. Not that I worried about Jett leaving me for her, but I just didn't like the feeling of someone else around that had such history with him. I got over it though. In the days that had passed since Stenen, Rayna's intellect and calculating nature made her someone I instantly respected. She was smart and had integrity, which meant that she wouldn't be a party to debasing herself in an attempt to gain Jett's affection.

I liked her.

Jett's cozy sweater was just what I needed to feel comfortable and warm, as a chill ran down my back. A droplet of water fell from my lightly towel dried hair and ran down my chest, bringing a shiver over me.

Leaving the room, I walked the three steps to the kitchen. The summer sun was already in the sky, shining brightly through the lightly curtained window. At the wooden kitchen table sat Mazz and Sam. Mazz's sharp eyes lifted to me and a warm smile tipped his lips.

"Morning, sleepy head," he said with a low chuckle. As always, his black hair was styled and he looked as regal as ever. How he managed to do that in a t-shirt and jeans was beyond me.

"What?" I asked at his laugh. He pointed to my head. My hands flew to my head and I ran to the bathroom. My hair was all over the place. Usually it was calm and smooth after washing it, now it stood up, folded and flipped over itself. A frizzy disaster. *Great.*

I ran my fingers through my hair, taming it as best as I could. I was seriously short on all the amenities that I had back home and I hated to admit how much I missed them. I couldn't say that I was missing my heels, though. Hugging Jett's sweater tightly around myself, I smiled.

Yeah, he's not getting this back.

Jett's sweater was huge on me. It reminded me of being little and trying on my parents' clothes. Again, I was reminded of my father and how much I missed him. My hands stilled as I looked at my reflection.

Would he even recognize me anymore?

Gone was the polished daughter he knew. I looked…haggard. Well, for Triton standards. Still, it wasn't all bad. My clothes were more comfortable. I took considerably less time fretting over loose hairs and imperfect make up. It was freeing in a way.

I was still smoothing out my hair when I emerged from the bathroom.

"Better," Mazz grinned.

"Thanks," I said with a half-smile. "Where's Jett?"

Mazz's smile immediately fell. I knew it was hard on him to see me with someone else, but that wasn't going to change.

After years and years of dreaming of each other, Jett and I were finally united. It was still surreal at times, but I was so incredibly happy with him. A part of me that had been missing was put into place, at last. I finally had Jett. Nothing was going to change that. Mazz was just going to have to get used to it.

"He had to run into town," Sam answered. "Said he needed to check something. He should be back soon."

I heard a moan and a groan from behind me, and turned to see where it came from. Jasper stumbled from his room and into the kitchen. Looking like a beast emerging from its cave, his hand cupped over his eyes. I could have sworn I heard him *hiss* at the light. His dark blonde hair in a messy array on his head, and sleep clinging to him so hard, he was barely aware of anything or anyone else in the room.

"Caffeine," he grumbled. Sam chuckled low, and slid a cup of steaming tea toward Jasper.

The two of them were just about the cutest couple I had ever met. I was envious of their easy companionship and the way that they knew what the other needed before they had to speak. Not to mention Jasper and Sam were some of the kindest men I had ever met.

"Whoa," I uttered, looking at Jasper as he stumbled his way over to the table.

"Shh," Sam shushed through a grin. "Don't wake the bear. When he's ready, he'll come to you." Jasper sat down heavily at the table next to Sam and leaned his head heavily on his hand, smushing up his face.

"Aww, my poor baby," Sam sang and wrapped an arm around him, rubbing Jasper's shoulder.

"Shut up," Jasper mumbled and sipped his tea. His eyes were nothing but slits as he slowly started to come around to the land of the living.

I giggled as Jasper snuggled up to Sam. Sam's smile was everything.

"Can I talk to you?" Mazz asked before I could grab a chair for myself.

"Sure," I answered.

Sam watched the two of us leave the room. Catching my eye before I went out the door, he mouthed "good luck" to me, and then turned his attention back to Jasper.

Mazz lead the way outside. Even though he had come unprepared for a trip, he was still looking Triton good – though, I could see the polish starting to dim on his overall appearance. Somehow, it suited him and I wasn't sad to see it go. The Hasp in him was cracking and that wasn't a bad thing for him. As much as I respected his father, Hasp was always really hard on Mazz - forcing him to endure more, work harder, and grow up faster. As a result, Mazz could be cold to anyone that wasn't…well, me. He didn't have a reputation as the kindest person around Triton. But, I knew the *real* him. The sweet, funny, and loving brother that I could never be without.

The sun was far more awake than Jasper, shining bright and warm on my skin, even at such an early time. Mazz lifted his face to the sky and took a deep breath. I could have sworn, for a second, that even *he* was enjoying the air.

Not sticking around the house, where there were many ears to listen in on our conversation, Mazz took the path to the garden. I could tell by his gait that he wanted to have a serious talk. His shoulders were up, his hands were in his pockets. His whole body looked tight and ready to spring. I knew without asking what his problem was.

Me.

"Okay, Mazz. Let me have it," I said, stopping in front of a tree, resting my back against the hard, rough bark and crossing my arms.

"What?" he asked, trying to look like he had no idea what I was talking about.

"Don't act all innocent. I can read you like a book. What's the matter?" I asked. His lips pressed into a thin line as he crossed his arms, rocked back on his heels, and dropped his gaze to mine.

"We have to go home, Ky. You have to return to Triton."

"I know, Mazz," I answered, narrowing my eyes at him.

"Do you?" he asked, turning on me. His eyes were like fire and I knew I was about to get an earful. "You sure don't act like it! Seems to me that you are pretty content throwing away your responsibilities and hanging out here with *him*!"

"*What?*" I gasped, truly astonished that he had the gall to say that to me.

"Don't even act like you don't like being here with *him*. I'm ashamed-"

"Whoa! Stop right there before you say something that will get you punched in the face," I threatened. "How *dare* you insinuate that I am lounging around here while my people suffer; that I am not taking my responsibilities seriously and that I don't care to return home! I would think that you would know me better than that! You big jerk!"

"*I'm* the jerk?" He shouted, pointing to himself.

I nodded staring hard at him.

"I came looking for you because I was worried sick that something had happened to you! Instead, I found you practically in the arms of another guy-"

"Who rescued me from being killed by a Siren and nursed me back to health!" I said pointing at him.

"Sure, but you were all healed up-"

"In time to have to battle it out with a freaking *god*, Mazz! You make it sound like I've been in bed with Jett this whole time."

He stood straight and backed up. I crossed my arms and glared at him. Mazz started to pace. "Look," he began, "it's just...I..."

"What, Mazz? What!" I yelled. "You want to make me look like an ass that doesn't care about my father and people? Well, congratulations! You're doing one heck of a good job!"

"That's not it, Ky," he said, dragging his hand across the back of his neck.

"Then what *is* it?" I asked, praying that he wasn't going to say that he was jealous. I didn't know how to handle that.

"I just want everything to go back to the way it was," he admitted, his shoulders sinking. I looked at him and sighed.

"Mazz, there's a part of me that wants to go back, too. To when things made sense. When we weren't fighting and awkward as all Hades. But, we can't - and I'm not as sad about that as you are."

"Because you have Jett," he said and looked at me.

"Yes," I answered honestly. He backed away from me nodding solemnly.

"You would trade our friendship and your father's health, for *him*?" he said, narrowing his eyes on me.

"That's not what I'm saying!" I barked back.

"Really? 'Cause that's what it looks like."

"How can you *say* that? You know how important my father is to me. You know how much our friendship means to me. How can you look at me and say that?" I asked him, tears threatening at the corners of my eyes. I couldn't believe I was hearing this from him. Of all people, he knew me, *really* knew me. What he said *hurt*.

"I'm saying it because I don't know what else to do to get you to see the consequences of what you are doing!"

I had no words. I was hurt and confused, and feeling guilty. I didn't know where my heart was supposed to be.

"You have a life at home, Ky. Don't give that up for some guy!"

"I'm not-"

"You are!"

"Fine! I'm a horrible person! Is that what you wanted to hear? I'm selfish and self-centered and don't care about anyone but myself!"

"Ky-"

"Not to mention that I'm heartless and not above ditching everything I know for some random guy. Yup! That's me!" I yelled at him.

"Okay, that's enough," Mazz uttered.

"Well really, Mazz, don't you see? My heart is split! No matter what I do, I hurt someone! I hurt myself!"

"Last I checked, your family and your duty came above whatever it is you have with Jett," Mazz uttered. "What's it going to be, Ky? Him…or me?"

"Don't make me answer that question," I threatened, turning from him. "You won't like my answer."

Mazz nodded once, bit his lips and stepped back from me. "The Ky I knew would never turn her back on her family. Never," he whispered.

"I'm not turning my back on my father, Mazz," I said, my temper picking up again.

"Whatever you have to tell yourself, Ky," he answered.

I just about punched him. It took all the strength I had not to beat the crap out of him, right there. I had never been so frustrated and angry in all my life.

"You're being such a jerk, you know that?" I said to him. He grinned.

"Okay, Ky. Paint me in whatever color you want, but the truth is these are *your* actions that you have to face. I'm just the one pointing them out to you."

"You're being petty because I don't love you the way that you love me."

I gasped at my own words. His eyes snapped to mine. I didn't mean to say it, but there is was. Mazz looked like I just slapped him.

"I'm sorry," I uttered. His jaw tightened as his eyes held on to mine. My heart broke, right there. I could see it in his eyes. The trust. The friendship. Broken. He turned and walked away.

"Mazz!" I called, but he didn't even look at me. I ran after him. He had been my best friend for as long as I could remember, I couldn't lose him. I couldn't. No matter how hurt I was, or he was, we had to work it out. "Mazz, stop! Please!"

He didn't.

I ran in front of him and shoved him. "Stop, damn it!" I yelled.

He didn't say anything, just crossed his arms and bit his lips. I could feel the anger rolling off of him.

"I'm sorry," I said. He didn't look at me. "Mazz, I don't know what to do. I don't. I don't want to hurt you. I don't want to fight with you. I want things to go back to the way they were."

"That's not going to happen, Ky," he uttered.

"I know. I do know that." I picked at my fingers, unable to bring the words to my lips that I was thinking. Mazz sighed and glared at me, but he waited. "I love you, Mazz. I have since we were kids, but I can't love you the way that you want me to. I know that's not what you want to hear, but I can't fake that for you. I won't do that to you. It would all be a lie and you deserve better than that. I love Jett. I have for a long time-"

"You just met the guy!" he yelled.

"No, that's not true," I answered.

I had never told Mazz about Jett. How could I? It sounded crazy. Dreaming of someone for years and hoping that they were real - it was insane. Not to mention that I had been falling in love with the man from my dreams. How could I tell my fiancé that?

"I haven't been honest with you," I said, stepping toward him. His brows shot up as he looked at me. I took a deep breath and summoned my courage. I didn't know if it would help to tell him, or just hurt him more. I was terrified to find out.

"Jett and I have met before," I said.

"What? When? How?" he demanded.

"It's a long story," I said. "Sit with me?" He didn't say anything. Taking a few paces back and forth, he fought his own internal battle as he made up his mind. I sat in the grass - and waited and hoped. In the end, he took a seat next to me under the trees.

I stared down at my fingers, trying to figure out how to start this very overdue conversation. It wasn't elegant, but I opened my mouth and let it all out. The dreams, Jett and me, and the world where we found each other every night when we slept. I told him everything. All of it.

His expression was stoic and distant.

"That's why you two are so..."

"Close? Yes," I answered for him.

"Why didn't you tell me, Ky? All this time you had this other person in your life and I didn't know," he asked. His brows furrowed deeply and his jaw clenched as he shook his head.

"It was still a dream. I was afraid if I told you, you'd think I was insane. I didn't want it to ruin our friendship. You're kind of a jealous person, and I knew if I told you there was another guy that I was friends with, you'd be upset. What Jett and I have is different than what you and I have."

"But, you were going to *marry* me until you found out that he was real," he said.

"Yes, I was. I never thought for a second that he was anything other than a dream. It was the same for him. In our minds, we had this weird relationship and connection that only existed in our dreams. I never imagined that one day we would meet. That we *could* be together. When we found each other…everything just clicked into place. The ramifications of that *click* were something that we were not prepared for."

"You mean you never thought about it," he said, standing and starting to pace again.

"It was an impossibility. Jett only existed in my dreams. You were my reality."

"Now, I'm not?"

"You *are*, Mazz. But, I can't ignore my heart. There has always been a part of me that's been missing. For a long time, I thought that it was when KyLena left. Then I thought it was when father got sick. Now, I realize that Jett was that missing piece. Everything just fits, Mazz."

Mazz's eyes were on me, unblinking, unemotional. It was unnerving.

"I have no idea what you are going through, Ky. None. However, I do know what it's like to have feelings for someone and know it will never work out. I wouldn't wish that on anyone, let alone my best friend. I can't believe that you kept all this from me, Ky," he said.

"You would have had me assessed, Mazz. Admit it," I said.

"Possibly," he admitted.

"Uh-huh," I nodded.

"I'm sorry," Mazz said.

"What?" I blurted.

"I'm sorry you had to go through that. I'm sorry I wasn't there for you."

"You didn't know, Mazz."

"Still, you should have known that I would support you. I wasn't what you needed me to be. I'm sorry. Plus, I haven't exactly been making it easy on you here. At the heart of this, you are my best friend and I want you to be happy. I always thought that I was the only one that could make you truly happy. Now, I see that's not the case."

"Mazz…"

"I'm not saying it doesn't hurt, but I understand better and that helps…a little." Then he pulled me in for a side hug.

In that moment, I knew we'd be okay. It would take time, but we would get there. We had to. I couldn't lose him.

Mazz sighed heavily and I hugged him tighter. I knew this was a lot for him. He was like his father; he liked a scheduled world where everything had its place and purpose. That was so not the world we were living in anymore. Our relationship aside, we'd been dragged into a fight with the gods, and were completely in over our heads. Jett and I were all of a sudden on the god's hit list; for what, we didn't know. Deimos and Phobos, Ares' sons, were after us; and, Ares himself, according to Eros.

Eros was one of Ares' other sons with Aphrodite. Eros most definitely took after his mother. He was kind and gentle, for the most part, with wild bright blonde locks and icy blue eyes. He didn't reek of death like his brothers, nor did he look it.

Our encounter with Deimos and Phobos, in Stenen, had revealed a power within me that I could never have imagined. Somehow, I could consume the essence of a god; taking on their knowledge and powers. We didn't know any more about it than that. All I knew was something deep inside me called to the power of the gods. It wanted, needed, it more than anything I had ever experienced before.

It scared me. *A lot.*

I could still feel Deimos in my veins. The anger of his emotions flared when I was frustrated and it took all of me to calm the rage that spiked so easily. He was not a happy guy and he was *strong.* Really strong.

"Hey, you."

His deep voice wrapped me in a warm embrace, and sent a tingle down my arms.

"Hey," I answered, turning and welcoming Jett in with a smile. He took one look at Mazz's arm around me and I could see the muscle in his jaw flex. I looked at Mazz and he reluctantly removed his arm from me. I stood.

Since Mazz showed up, Jett had been extra grumpy around him and extra protective around me. I understood why, but I wanted them to get along. I just couldn't see that happening…like ever.

"You okay?" he asked me, eyeing Mazz, as I stood.

"She's fine, *Jetstream*," Mazz answered. Jett's nostrils literally flared as he glared back at the house. If I could guess, Jasper had something to do with the nickname.

Jasper was Jett's older brother, though he didn't always act like it. It was Sam, Jasper's husband that was the mature one in that relationship.

I felt his fingers lace with mine and I looked up. Jett's vibrant violet eyes met mine and already my pulse was racing. Just looking at him had me craving his lips on mine. It was insane how attracted I was to him. Years of talking and building our friendship as children led us to slowly develop feelings for one another. Seeing him in real life for the first time was literally a dream come true. Every day since then I woke excited to see him.

"I see you have been talking to my brother," Jett grumbled. Mazz smiled his perfectly devilish smile and I wanted to kick him in the butt.

"Mazz," I warned.

"What? They said it was his favorite name!" Mazz replied lifting his shoulders in feigned innocence.

"Whatever," I answered. "You two have to figure out how to get along. I have a feeling we're going to be stuck together for a while."

"Not if we do as I say and go home," Mazz said, standing and facing Jett.

"She's not going anywhere," Jett said.

"You aren't the boss of her, last time I checked. She's the *Prime* of Triton and she needs to return to her people!" Mazz argued.

"She's doesn't *want* to go," Jett said taking a step to Mazz.

"Really? She hasn't said that to *me*," Mazz answered.

"*She* is standing right here!" I pointed out, stepping between the two of them.

Jett turned to me, his brow furrowed and then his jaw clenched.

"Is that true, Laya? You want to leave?" he asked, turning his anger on me.

"Don't get pissy with me, Jett," I warned him. "I want to see my father!"

"Oh," he said backing down. "Why didn't you say something to me?" he asked, "I would never deny you your family."

"I know that," I said softening at his new tone. "I miss him and I'm worried about him."

"You see? We should go home," Mazz said placing his hands on his hips. Jett glared at Mazz, but eased when his eyes met mine.

"Is that what you want?" he asked me.

"I…I am worried about him, but I don't want to leave you. Not when we have half of Olympus looking to lay waste to us," I said.

"Why don't I come with you, then?" Jett asked.

"What?" Mazz and I said at the same time.

"I'm not going to say that it won't be dangerous, but I don't think that you should go alone," Jett said.

"Are you serious?" I asked, hope filling me.

"Yes," he replied with a smile.

"I – oh my gods! Thank you! I won't let anything happen to you," I said, grasping his hand tighter.

"I know that," he smiled and placed a kiss on my forehead. "But, I don't plan on getting arrested."

"You really would come home with me?" I asked, in awe of him. I knew what that meant. The idea must have been terrifying for him. His people were scared of the Mer. Being the offspring of Sirens, called Sirenites, they had been forced into hiding from Mer for a very long time. The Mer harbored some serious hate for anything related to Sirens. If Jett was discovered, it would mean being arrested or worse.

"Of course," he said, lowering his face to mine. I could feel his lips next to my ear and a rush of warmth spread through me like wildfire. "I would do anything for you," he whispered to me.

A thundering in my chest sent pulses of wicked pleasure through me. What the man did to me was incredible. He barely touched me and already my insides were on fire. I lifted my eyes to him as he pulled away from me. One look in his eyes and I knew he was feeling the same thing as I was. It took every bit of self-control I had not to grab him and *really* kiss him. Even in front of Mazz.

"Wanna go for a walk?" Jett asked, his eyes not breaking from mine for a second.

"Love to," I answered. "We'll talk later, okay Mazz?"

"Sure, Ky," he said with an edge to his voice, and walked away.

My heart sank. I never wanted to hurt him. Breaking my gaze from Jett, I watched Mazz walk away. His shoulders were slumped under an invisible weight. A weight that I put there. Jett squeezed my hand and I looked back at him.

"He'll be okay, Laya," Jett said as we walked toward along the line of trees by the garden.

"Will he? I hurt him - bad. I hate it."

Jett pulled me around behind the shed and out of ear and eye shot of the house. It had become pretty congested in the house with Jasper and Sam sharing a room, me and Rayna sharing Jett's room, and Jett and Mazz sharing the living room. We were basically walking on top of one another and tempers were up. Jett and I hadn't had much time to ourselves and we were really in need of it.

"Give him time. He'll come around. You mean too much to him," Jett said, as he brushed a chunk of my hair behind my shoulder.

I sighed and nodded.

"How are you dealing?" Jett asked me as we stopped behind the little storage shed. I wanted to just let it all out, tell him everything. All about my dreams, my father…but I couldn't.

"*Me?* How are *you* dealing? I feel like we have invaded your home in the worst way," I countered, steering the conversation away from me.

"I'll be fine. I'm worried about *you*. These new powers of yours…" he didn't finish.

"Right," I nodded. "I wish I had some answers, but I'm at a loss myself. They just came out of nowhere. It's like, all of a sudden, I have this urge to take - and I do. I have little to no control once I start. I don't know how to stop, and that…scares me," I admitted, remembering what it was like to take Deimos's power and then a bit of Eros's as well.

"Well, hopefully, Eros will have some answers for us when he gets back. Until then, just try not to suck all the life out of me and we'll be good," he teased. I didn't see the humor in it and he could tell. "What?" he asked, taking a step back from me. "Have you *wanted* to suck the life from me?"

"No! No, I haven't, but I-"

"What?" he asked, coming closer to me; searching my eyes for an answer. I had thought a lot about the consequences of this new power of mine. The need to pull power from others. The want for that feeling within me again. I knew what I was.

I was an addict.

I knew it. I felt it. Something within Jett called to me when we were close to each other. A part of me wanted to take it for myself. So far, I had controlled that part of myself, but I feared a day when I wouldn't be able to and what that would mean. I didn't want to hurt him.

"What if I do?" I asked. "What if one day I *can't* stop myself and I turn on you? What if-"

"Stop," he interrupted, gripping my arms in his strong hands and stooping to look me directly in the eye.

"I don't want to hurt you," I whispered.

"You won't. I *know* you won't," he said.

"You can't say that. You *don't* know. *I* don't even know," I countered.

"I *do* know and I'm not worried. At all," he answered, looking deep in my eyes and bringing his hands gently to my face.

"Yeah, well. You're an idiot," I said back.

"*Wow*. Try to tell a girl that you have absolute faith in her and you get insulted," he nodded, taking a step back and placing his hands on his hips with a grimace scrunching up his face.

"I'm sorry. I just…I don't trust *myself*. How can *you* trust me?" I asked, throwing my hands up and allowing my fears to get the best of me.

"I know you, Laya. I know who you are deep down, even when you don't."

"I-" I had no words. He blew me away. I dropped my head against his chest as he came close again.

"You're not going to scare me away, Laya. I'm not going anywhere," he uttered into my hair.

"You sure about that?"

"Absolutely. Besides, I'm not a god; so, there's nothing I have that you can even take," he said and I could feel the smile on his lips as he kissed the top of my head.

"But, what if"-

"Don't stress over 'maybes' or 'what-ifs' they will drive you insane. Take one day at a time; one problem at a time," he advised.

"Right. One problem at a time. Which one should we tackle today?" I asked, not even knowing where to start.

"How about the fact that I haven't had a decent kiss from my girlfriend in a couple of days? Anything you can do about that?" he asked, lifting my face and tracing a line from my cheek down my jaw with a light touch. Grinning, I looked up into his beautiful amethyst eyes.

"I think so," I said nodding, as I wrapped my hands around his neck. His hands rested on my hips as he gently pulled me to him.

He was so much taller than me I had to get up on my toes to meet his face. He dropped down to me and softly placed a kiss on my lips. It was sweet. It was soft. It was perfection.

It *so* wasn't enough.

The feel of his lips on mine awakened a hunger in me every time I was close to him. I needed him more than I had ever needed another being. Pressing against him, a low sound emanated from him as he responded to my touch. His mouth worked against mine, and I could feel a coiling in my core. A rush of velvet moved over me as his fingers worked their way up my ribs. I moaned against his lips.

Gods, the guy can kiss...

He flashed, his power moving us too fast for the eye to catch. I found myself with my back against the shed with Jett pressed against me. A low sound tumbled from his full lips when I tipped my head up to him. A quick flick of my tongue had his hand tightening around my hips. I flattened against his hard chest, feeling the strength of his muscles working under his shirt. My heart jolted and sent a stream of hot liquid through me when his hands found the bottom of my shirt and his fingers glided across my skin.

I was panting through our kisses and aching to feel his hands on me. Really on me. I brought my hands down his back, feeling the hard cords of muscle tighten, until I got to the bottom his shirt. He moaned against my lips. My fingers softly swept a line across his skin at the top of his jeans from the center of his back around to his abs, across the indents on his hips. He shuttered and his breath hitched. It was such a high knowing that I could do that to him. Then he suddenly stopped and flashed away from me.

"What? What is it? Did I do something?" I asked him, placing a hand on my swollen mouth, still feeling him on my lips.

"No! Of course not. I just..." he heaved a breath that had his shirt pulling at his sculpted chest, showing off his amazing body, and just had me wanting him all over again.

"Just?"

"I don't want to move too fast with you," he admitted. "I think, given our situation, that it would be easy to go all the way quickly; but I want to wait, Laya. I don't want to rush any part of this." He walked back to me. "I want to enjoy every part of you...slowly," he uttered next to my ear.

"You couldn't make it any harder for me to not pin you to this wall," I answered.

"Me? Do you have any idea what you do to me, Laya? You undo me," he said and my heart sang. "I don't know where the self-control comes from to stop myself. I honestly don't."

"Well, I know a little bit about that. I'm not saying that my self-control has been that great," I admitted. "One of us should maintain a level head, I suppose."

"Sure. Why does it have to be *me*?" he chuckled and leaned his head against mine. I laughed quietly too.

"I love you," I whispered.

"What?" Jett's eyes were huge as he stared at me.

Oh gods, did I? No, I couldn't have. Could I? I started to full on panic. *I didn't just say it. Please tell me I didn't just blurt "I love you"!*

"No. I – I didn't say, well I didn't *mean* it," I began, but he just stood there and stared at me.

"You didn't *mean* it?" he asked, watching me closely.

"Yes, I do! I mean, I don't...kind of?" I roared in frustration and embarrassment. How did that just slip out like that? I was thinking it, but I didn't mean to say it!

It's too soon! He's going to freak!

I mean...I did love him. I did. My feelings had slowly grown over the last couple of years. Now that we had met, they took off and weren't looking back. I hadn't truly realized how far they had got until that moment, though, and the shock of it was just as real for me as it was for him.

I can't believe I just freaking blurt-

"I love you too, Laya."

"What?" My heart stopped as I looked at him.

"I love you," he said again, taking my hands in his and looking intently in my eyes. My pulse was out of control. "I've been aching to tell you, but there just never seemed to be a good moment. I have loved you since I was a kid. First as a friend, but now…I simply cannot imagine my life without you."

"Oh, my gods," I uttered and a laugh bounded from my lips. I bit my lips to try to control the huge grin spreading across my face. I couldn't believe it. *He loves me!* For a moment I thought that I might die from the amount of joy building in me. I squealed and jumped into his arms, pressing a kiss to his lips.

"Say it again," he said to me.

"I love you, Jett."

He kissed me again and again…and again…

JETT

THE WORDS from her mouth were liquid honey – they couldn't have tasted any sweeter. I had been wanting to say it for so long. But, how do you confess that you are in love with someone that doesn't exist. My heart beat hard and fast in my chest as I pressed her to me. Her small frame fit against me perfectly, like we were made for one another.

I could feel her pulse racing and knew that she was just as affected by my words as I was by hers.

Love.

Something that I never thought that I would get to experience. For years I had envied Jasper and Sam's relationship. Their unending support and commitment. The person that they could share anything and everything with. I wanted that, too. With Laya I had that. We had been sharing since we were kids, but there was always the dream-stoppers to close the door on intimacy.

Now, with her in my arms, I could feel my chest expand and my world make sense. She was always meant to be here, always meant to be with me. I looked down as her brilliant blues looked up at me. A kick in my chest and my heart was off again, sending bursts of electricity dancing through my veins with pleasure and pain laced in them.

Gods, she didn't know what she did to me. She had no clue.

I leaned down and placed my hands on her cheeks.

"I love you," I whispered, just to see her smile. She graced me with one and I was a goner.

"You-" but she was cut off when Mazz started to shout for her from the house.

"What does that guy want *now*?" I grumbled.

"Be nice," Laya warned. "He's still my friend."

"Ky!" he shouted again.

"Well, you'd better say something before he gives himself a hernia yelling for you," I scoffed.

"Jett!" Rayna called.

"That would be *your* unrequited love shouting for *you*," she pointed out.

"Don't start," I warned her pushing her with my hip. She smiled and we walked out from behind the shed.

"What on earth is the problem?" I yelled at them. Rayna and Mazz both ran to us, as Jasper and Sam tumbled out of the house.

"What is with you guys?" Laya laughed, but in that moment the slough that housed our portal to Triton *exploded*.

Water shot into the sky like a geyser, and from the portal came a sight I will never forget…Sirens.

Holy shit balls.

Over a dozen Sirens filed out of the portal, dressed in battle gear and all carrying a dagger, tipped in poison. The Sirens hadn't seen us yet, but that wouldn't last long.

"That's what!" Rayna hissed at me as she and Mazz raced up to us and we all piled behind the trees. "Our marks started to burn and the two of you had disappeared on us."

"We just wanted a moment alone," Laya pointed out.

"Nice," Mazz uttered. Laya leveled a good glare at him and he turned from her.

"Rayna?" I said, pulling Laya behind me as the first five Sirens saw us and started coming our way.

"I see them," she said.

"Do you have a weapon?" I asked her. She reached to her back and lifted her shirt. Tucked into the back of her pants was a dagger.

"Nice," I smiled. She smiled back.

"You can't be too careful, especially now apparently," she added. "Mazz-"

"I'll be fine, don't you worry your pretty head about me," Mazz said to me.

"Oh, I won't," I answered. "Laya, you stay here."

"Ha!" she laughed and drew a dagger from her back too. She smiled at Rayna, who nodded in approval. She turned her eyes on me and shrugged. "What? We have the same taste in weapons," Laya explained.

"Just stay here, where it's safe," I said to her. She drew back her arm and threw the dagger with deadly speed. I heard a thud and turned. A Siren laid dead on the ground just behind us.

On the ground, with Laya's knife buried through her eye to the hilt, the sneaky Siren had dropped dead the moment the dagger hit her. Laya crossed her arms and looked at me expectantly.

"I'm sorry, you were saying?" Laya said as she gingerly walked over to the Siren and retrieved her blade.

"Fine. Be *careful*," I conceded and laid a hard kiss on her.

"Always," she said, flipping the blade in her hands and sending it flying at another Siren. It hit her in the chest, right between her ribs and into the Siren's heart. She dropped to the ground with a thump. *Damn, Laya.* I had never seen someone that accurate with their blades before and it was all kinds of sexy to see her skill in battle.

I couldn't help myself, I grabbed her and kissed her hard again. The feel of her against me was still fresh in my mind and, though we were being descended on by a swarm of Sirens, I couldn't help the urge to wrap her in my arms and plant her against the side of the shed again.

"Jett!" Rayna shouted. I turned and there was a Siren coming at me. My power shot down my arms and out my palm before I even thought about it. A pink line of crackling energy hit the Siren in the chest. She fell with a scream. Behind her, there were more - lots more.

"Jett!" Jasper shouted.

"Get him in the house!" I yelled at Sam. Sam nodded and manhandled Jasper back into the house as he beat against Sam's shoulders. Jasper wasn't a fighter and I knew damned well he would end up getting killed because he wanted to help. Sam had a few tricks up his sleeve when it came to Sirens. I knew Jasper was safe with him.

I heard a battle cry and flipped my attention to the swarm coming for us. Rayna was facing off against three Sirens. Her blade was flashing in the sun, glinting as she slashed the air and sliced through a Siren's throat. She was a fierce fighter in the water, but on land she was even better.

Mazz must have found my stash of weapons in the house as he stood on the porch and drew an arrow to my bow. I had to hand it to him, he was deadly with that thing. Shooting arrows was not a skill of mine, I just never got the hang of it, but Mazz was a pro. His focus was razor-sharp and he didn't miss, dropping any Siren that came near Laya. I couldn't fault him that, so I let it go.

A dagger soared through the air and a sickly thud sounded just behind my right shoulder.

"Wake up, Jett!" Laya called to me. "She nearly had you!" I reached out a hand and a blast of pink light shot from it, colliding with the chest of a Siren that had come up on Laya.

"You should talk," I chuckled. She smiled slyly at me and then turned back to the fight, but this time she didn't wander far. I was glad. With Laya closer to me, I could protect her. Though watching her fight, I had to admit, she didn't need much for protection. She was every bit as strong and fierce as Rayna, but more graceful and with a power that radiated beneath her skin. She was stunning.

"Loverboy, duck!" Mazz shouted as an arrow sailed by my ear. Too close to my lobe.

"Watch it!" I shouted back at him.

"Me? You're the one daydreaming, not me," he answered back.

I flicked a wrist and a line of light whipped out, slashing into the legs of four Sirens that were converging on Mazz. They all ended up on their backs as my power slithered around their bodies, constricting tighter and tighter until their last breaths sounded.

"You're welcome," I said to Mazz as I walked by.

"Yeah, I had them," he answered with a glare.

"Sure, you did," I replied.

"Will you two knock it off before I knock you both into next week! You're embarrassing yourselves," Rayna barked at us as she swept out with her blade, slashing a Siren in the abdomen. The Siren doubled over; Rayna stood, plunged the knife into the base of the Siren's neck, and twisted it. The Siren fell in a dead heap. Rayna threw her hair over her shoulder and exhaled with a nod.

That a girl.

Mazz's eyes were wide as he watched Rayna go after another group of Sirens without hesitation or a moment to collect herself. Shaking his head, he ran after her and helped take out the Sirens. I turned, looking for Laya.

Not too far away from Rayna and Mazz, my eye caught Laya taking on a Siren. The Siren wore a different colour on her battle gear, signaling that she was a higher rank than the others. My heart stopped.

The Siren's eyes were bulging out of her head and her skin was a deathly pale. Even though Siren-born Sirens had many different colours of skin, this Siren was pale peach and looked a moment from death. I would have been happy, but that's when I saw Laya's hand. She had it firmly gripped around the Siren's neck…and she was pulling power from her.

I could see the fever taking over. The intoxicating draw that Laya couldn't fight.

"Laya, stop!" I shouted.

She turned her head, her eyes unseeing…and smiled.

KYLAYA

THE SIRENS had burst from the portal in a startling explosion of metal and mayhem. My eyes grew three sizes as they searched the area for us. I had hidden the dagger in the back of my pants yesterday. Rayna had offered it to me. I gladly accepted the generous gift. I didn't want to be caught without anything to defend myself with ever again. The night with Deimos and Phobos was not going to happen again. I would have given anything for my daggers that night.

Zeroing in on my first target, I aimed and sent the knife flying. It landed exactly where I wanted. I smiled and turned to Jett, whose expression would have been hilarious if he wouldn't have just been treating me like some damned damsel in distress. I was not some helpless mermaid in need of saving, thanks.

"The look on his face," Rayna chuckled.

"I know," I said as we walked toward the Sirens.

"I would be up for some tips after this. I'm good at hand to hand, but my aim at a distance isn't the best," she mentioned as she jabbed her knife forward, dodging an attack with grace and swinging around with her blade. The Siren didn't see the hit coming as Rayna cut deep into her side. The Siren hissed in pain and anger and turned her glare on Rayna. Rayna stood.

"Come on, sweetheart. Give me your best," Rayna called.

Wow. That took guts.

The Siren screamed loud enough to make me cover my ears, but not Rayna. She dropped low, kicked a foot out and made crunching contact with the Siren's knee. Collapsing to the ground, the Siren failed to maintain a hold on her knife. Rayna kicked it away and kneed the Siren in the face, bringing her completely down. When the Siren tried to get up, Rayna shot her knife deep into the chest of the Siren, whose scream died quickly on her lips.

"Nice," I uttered and nodded in appreciation of her skill. She would have made an excellent addition to the Guard. Reqet, the Guard's leader, would have loved her.

Rayna turned her attention away from me as another Siren charged her. That was when I was struck from behind and tossed to the ground. My training kicked in at the last second and I managed to roll to a fighting stance, ready to engage the Siren that had got to me. What I was not ready for was what the Siren was…or rather *who*.

The eyes were out of my nightmare and for a moment I was frozen. Black irises, as dark as night looked at me and I knew in an instant who I was looking at.

"Midira," I gasped. The Siren was nothing like the woman that I saw in my dreams, but there was no mistaking the eyes, I knew those eyes all too well.

"Hello, KyLaya. I was hoping that I would get to see you in person. Well, close to in person," she said as she drew her knife and faced me.

"I can't say that I'm happy to see you," I answered, still unmoving.

"Ouch. That would hurt - if I cared," she answered, narrowing her eyes on me.

"This isn't really you is it?" I said, pointing to her body with my knife.

"No. Lucky for me, I have a healthy supply of Sirens that love to have me use them. This is a shell, nothing more," she explained, picking at the battle gear in disgust.

"Why are you here?" I asked, taking a step back from her as she advanced on me.

"Why? I came to see my grandson, of course," she said. "You *have* told him about me, haven't you?"

I narrowed my eyes at her. Of course, I hadn't told him…whoever *he* was. I didn't know which of the guys was related to her and it wasn't something that I wanted to go around announcing either.

"Not exactly," I answered.

"Oh, damn. Was hoping for more of a reception than that," she pouted, placing a hand on her hip.

I was confused. There was no way that she was there just to see her grandson when she came with a battalion of Sirens hell-bent on killing us. It was in the moment, when I had stupidly stopped to think, that she sprang. Moving with a speed that only came from some supernatural talent, she shot up to me.

Her dagger flashed in the light. I blocked her strike with my own, throwing my arm out. The clang of steel on steel was loud but not louder than the scream of frustration from Midira.

"You are faster than I gave you credit for," she said, pushing her dagger towards me.

I dipped down, throwing her weight off and sending her pitching forward. I reached out an arm and caught her legs, tripping her up. She fell to her chest on the ground. Her dagger knocked from her hand, out of reach. I grasped mine hard and dove at her.

It took her no time to flip on her feet and regain her bearings. When I brought my dagger down, she grabbed my wrist and slammed it into her leg, jarring my hand. The pain shocked me and I dropped my one weapon. I found myself grappling with the queen of the Sirens.

She threw a knee up, knocking me square in the jaw. I saw stars for a moment and was pinned under her as she mounted me. My arms were under her knees and completely useless. She smiled down at me. If I hadn't been trained on how to battle in this position, I would have full out panicked. But, I didn't.

Throwing my hips up, I bucked Midira. Losing her balance, she fell forward, just enough for me to grab her leg and roll. I took her down to the ground, removing myself from such a defenseless position. She screamed and jumped on me again.

I could see my knife, but it was still too far away to grab. A blow landed on the side of my face and then to my ribs. I bent over, the wind knocked right out of me. Something hard slammed into my back, knocking me to the ground.

Rolling to try to get out from under the attack, a foot landed a perfect kick to the underside of my jaw and darkness closed in. If I didn't get up, I was going to lose the fight and my life. Without thinking it over, I reached out and grabbed Midira's ankle. All I need was the smallest amount of skin to pull from. Just a spot to get the connection I needed.

But there was nothing. The Siren's battle gear covered every part of their body in thick material. Another foot landed in my stomach. I moaned and coughed; trying to breathe through the pain I rolled to my side, gripping my stomach.

"Not as strong as I would have thought. Disappointing," Midira chided.

"You've seen nothing of my strength," I cursed. Summoning my power, I let it flood my body. I could feel it working its way through my veins and muscles, waking and healing them as it went. I was on my feet in a flash. Midira's eyes widened when I snapped out a hand and gripped her around the neck.

"Go ahead," Midira laughed. "This is only a shell, remember? You can't hurt *me*."

I smiled. "Think again."

I pulled.

The surge of power came right through her connection to the Siren and into me. It was her. It was Midira herself, not the Siren. There was a scream, but it was from the other end of the connection.

I had her.

I had...*power*.

The part of me that called out for it drank deep. It satisfied something within me that I didn't understand. A part that scared me. A part that was...*very* strong.

Pulling hard, I drank in more. The screaming echoed in my head as I drowned myself in Midira's power.

So angry. So spiteful.

I could hear her hate in the back of my mind. I could see the destruction that she planned. The lives that she would end. The downfall of all Mer. It was all there.

The world around me disappeared as the rush from my addiction took over. There was nothing but pleasure.

A flash of pink blossomed behind my eyes.

The connection was broken and Midira was thrown from me.

"What the..." I muttered, as I looked at my empty hands.

Midira laid on the ground a few feet away screaming in pain. A large gash opened across her shoulder and down her arm. She held the wound and scrambled to her feet. Her eyes stuck to me, as I tried to shake the disappointment of being torn from her.

Jett flashed to my side.

"You okay?" he asked.

"I'm *fine!*" I answered. Midira's power buzzed along my spine. In the back of my mind, I could hear her. I hurt her, there was no mistaking that - just didn't know how much.

Midira stumbled to a stand, a pained smile broke out over her lips.

"Well, if it isn't my grandson come to play with his grandmother after all these years," she said.

It was like a punch to the gut.

Jett. He was her grandson.

Jett looked at the Siren with a furrowed brow.

"What are you talking about, Siren?" he said, placing himself between me and Midira.

"That's no ordinary Siren, Jett. It's Midira," I explained. His eyes narrowed on her as a streak of light shot down his arm and at her. Midira twisted out of the way just in time to avoid Jett's blast.

"Come now," she huffed. "You wouldn't kill your dear old grandmother, would you?"

"My what?"

I looked helplessly at Jett. There was no sheltering him from it. No way I could save him from it now. No matter how desperately I wanted to.

"Your sweetheart, here, has been keeping a little secret from you," Midira said, smiling at me. Jett's eyes flew to mine. I couldn't look at him.

"How disappointing," Midira scolded, shaking her head.

"Shut up," Jett said to her and looked at me again. "What is she talking about, Laya?"

"I-"

"My dear, we're *family*," she said with a smile that stilled my breath.

"Family?" Jett repeated.

"You're my grandson," Midira said and leaned close to us. "*You.*"

Jett's eyes grew about ten sizes. "No," he uttered.

"Oh, *yes*," she replied, laughing and nodding.

"No. It's not possible. No," Jett said again.

"I have been looking for you for a long time. I must say, you have turned out better than I could have hoped for. But you will be more. *Much* more."

Jett shook his head and stumbled back. Midira's head shot back as a loud laugh cracked from her. Jett, just stood there, stunned and shaking his head.

I could feel her power buzzing in my veins. It called out to me, wanting more. Needing more. The angrier I got, the worse the need became.

The look on Jett's face hurt. He was in pain.

Shooting forward, faster than I had ever moved before, I slapped my hands to her cheeks and pulled. Her power hit me hard. I drank it in deeply once again. Filling the need that was screaming within me. I knew that I wouldn't be able to kill her or even take all her power before she cut off the connection, but hopefully, it would put her on her ass for a while.

Her scream pierced the air and plunged through me like a knife; but the energy I pulled dampened the blow of it as the sweet feeling of her power filled my veins. Midira brought her head level with mine, swallowed her scream and looked in my eyes.

"He's not the only one," she whispered and smiled.

My jaw tightened and I swallowed hard. A pink light flashed. Midira fell over, dead at my feet; a large hole ripped into her chest. I turned around. Jett stood behind me. His eyes unfocused as he looked at the body of the Siren that Midira had used as a shell. Lifting his hands up, he looked at them and then me.

"Jett…" I began, but he shook me off and flashed away.

At the death of Midira, the other Sirens turned and ran for the portal. Mazz and Rayna took off after them, taking out as many as they could before they dove into the water.

A deep ache spread in my chest, knowing the pain that he must have been in. I felt like I had betrayed him and I had no idea how I was going to fix that. But, it was Midira's final words that echoed in my head.

He's not the only one…

JETT

I NEEDED TIME.

I was no fool. I knew that Midira could have been lying about being my blood. For the life of me, I couldn't see the end game of saying that, though. *Why?* I had wrestled with the part of me that was ashamed of my heritage. The part of me that had struggled with how I was conceived and whose blood ran in my veins. For years, I battled with that. I had finally put it behind me; and then I find out that not just any Siren was part of my blood, but the worst of them all - Queen Midira of the Sirens.

Fuck. Me.

I could feel her presence before I saw her.

Laya.

I flashed away. It was a jerk move, but I couldn't handle her. I didn't deserve her. I wasn't worthy of her. Never thought I was to start with; now, I knew it. The blood of the Siren Queen. The evil that creature had done ran in my veins. It made me sick. There was this deep-seated need to reach into my body and pull everything that was hers out of me. But I couldn't. No matter how much I hated it, she was a part of me.

I looked out at the sea of golden wheat in front of me, against the endless blue sky.

I love this time of year.

We should have been gearing up for harvest. The wheat was turning and ripening early with all this weather. That's what we should have been doing; but, taking the crop off was the furthest thing from my mind.

The day was beautiful, warm, and calm. It was the perfect prairie summer day; but, even weather like that did nothing to lift my spirits.

It wasn't until I heard footsteps that I realized I had lost track of time. I had no idea how long I had been sitting where I had flashed to.

"Jett."

I turned at the sound of her voice. Bright blue eyes met mine and my heart backflipped in my chest. *Laya.* She had found me.

"Don't. Just…don't," I said, standing and walking from her.

"Damn it, Jett! Talk to me!" she yelled.

"What do you want me to say to you, Laya?" I barked back, harsher than I should have.

"I don't know - but flashing from me isn't going to help anything," she pointed out. She was right. That didn't mean I had to like it - or listen.

"Where are the others?" I asked, trying to change the subject.

"Cleaning up. After Midira was killed the Sirens all ran back to the portal. Rayna and Mazz took out a few more. Only two got away as far as we can tell. The bodies are being burned as we speak," she explained. I nodded, unable to look at her.

"I'm so sorry, Jett."

I looked at her. Her beautiful face was scrunched up and there were tears in her eyes.

"What are *you* sorry for?" I asked.

"I didn't tell you. I knew, and I didn't tell you."

"You *knew* I was Midira's *grandson*?" I asked, rather loudly. *How could she not tell me?*

"I – well, no. I knew that *someone* was, but I didn't know who," she answered.

"When did you find out? Why didn't you say anything to me?" I asked.

"It was about a week ago; and, I didn't say anything because I knew it would hurt all of you to know that one of you was related to that witch. We were already dealing with a lot. I didn't want to add to that. I…I should have said something. I know that now. I'm sorry," she said. I looked at her and shook my head.

"It doesn't matter. I mean it would have been nice to have a heads up about information like that, but I'm not upset with you, Laya. I'm not," I explained.

"Then what's wrong?" she asked, walking slowly toward me; like I was a wild animal who was ready to run at any second. Maybe I was.

"What's *wrong?*" I said, heaving a sigh and running my hand through my hair. "How would you like to find out that the person that you hated more than anything in the world was your blood? Your *family?*" I took two steps and stopped. Frustrated energy ran through me hard and fast.

"I- well, yeah, that would suck," she admitted. I nodded and choked out a laugh.

"But…that doesn't change anything about who you are to me, Jett."

"Don't say that." I was done running from Laya, but I wasn't ready to face the repercussions of what this would mean for us. It was one thing for her to love me as a Sirenite. The blood of the queen Siren? That was *different*.

"What? The way I see you, the way I feel…nothing has changed." She crossed her hands over her chest.

"That isn't true," I answered, turning from her. There was no way that the Prime of Triton was going to stay with someone from Midira's bloodline. No way.

"What in Hades? How can you say that?" she cursed, throwing her hands out.

"You can't tell me that being the grandson of the most hated Siren of all time doesn't affect the way you feel about me. You can't. I *know* it does."

"Okay, well, I'm just going to push past how insulting that is to me and go on to tell you that you are being an ass."

"Come again?" I asked, staring at her. Was she seriously just insulting me?

"You're being an *ass*. You think that I am so incredibly self-centered and *shallow* that just hours after telling you I *loved* you I would take it back because I don't like your *Grandma?*"

"Yes – wait, no. That's not what I meant," I said.

"Sure, sounds like it to me. I don't give a crap what blood runs in your veins. I'm not in love with your damn blood, Jett. I love *you*. If you can't see that, you're an idiot. Worse, if you think just because Midira's blood is a part of you it changes who you are - you are more of a fool than I could have ever thought."

"You know…this is all just a bit to handle. Okay? Sirenites know that they have pretty shitty heritage growing up, but we work to get over that and move on. This is different! It's Queen Midira for Poseidon's sake!"

"I get that! I do. But, do *you* get that none of that changes who you are? Do you get *that?*"

"I…no."

"Why in Hades not?" she shouted. My temper hit high with frustration and pain.

"Because, I'm *ashamed!* Okay? I'm ashamed to have blood that is anywhere close to Midira's!" I admitted rather loudly. Her eyes grew wide. I pressed my lips into a tight line and turned from her. A hand settled gently on my shoulder. Her eyes were soft as she walked around me.

"Jett, you are the kindest, strongest, most loving and loyal person that I have ever met. *That* is who you are. It doesn't matter what blood is in your veins. The choices you make are what defines you - not your heritage."

I had no words. My heart beat heavy as I looked at Laya. How could she still love me knowing what I truly was? How?

"I don't deserve you," I uttered pulling her to me.

"Of course not, but not because you have Siren blood. You're just damn lucky to have me," she said and looked up into my eyes, smiling.

"No argument here," I answered. She stood on her toes and placed a kiss on my lips. It was sweetly soft and tender; and, it radiated a love that I didn't feel worthy of.

I knew I would spend my life trying, though.

KYLAYA

THE REST OF THE DAY was spent cleaning up the farm from the mess of the fight. I never thought I would have to clean up bodies, but that was what I found myself doing. It wasn't fun.

"That's the last of them," Rayna said and she stepped away from the pit where we had piled the dead Sirens.

"Let's just hope that no one comes by and sees this. We look like serial killers," Jasper said, throwing gasoline on the heap.

Rayna laughed. Dark humor; but, considering the situation it was warranted.

"What tipped you off that they were coming?" I asked Rayna.

"My mark started to burn. Mazz's started to burn too. It's hard to explain, but there is this kind of knowledge that is starting to wake up in me. I know things that I never did before."

"Really?"

"Yeah. I just *knew* that there were Sirens on the way. Not gods or something else. Sirens."

"Nice."

"It's freaking me out to be honest," Rayna said and brushed her hands on her pants.

"Oh, I'm sorry. Why? If you don't mind me asking," I added, looking at her.

"There's this part of my mind that's opening up. It's like having a memory locked up and now having access to it. Every day something new pops into my head that wasn't there before. It's useful, don't get me wrong, but I can't help feeling like I have this other side to myself that I never knew was there. It's just…unnerving. I feel like I've lived another life that I had no memory of until now," she explained.

"Wow. I can't imagine what that's like for you. I'm sorry, Rayna."

She shrugged and looked away.

"Is Mazz experiencing the same thing?" I asked. He never said anything to me about that.

"Yeah. We think it's part of the mark and whole 'guardian' thing," she said.

Why wouldn't he tell me? "I see."

"We're…figuring it out," Rayna said as she tossed a lighted match into the pile. Flames ignited immediately. The three of us stood there for a moment as the fire climbed higher. One of us would have to monitor it for a while to make sure that the fire didn't catch and burn the whole place down. Fire spread easily in the long grass and fields that were as far as the eye could see in this prairie landscape – so I was told.

A strong set of arms wrapped around me. I leaned my head back against Jett's chest.

"How are you doing?" I asked him. He didn't answer as his arms tightened. Things weren't resolved for him with finding out who his family really was. There was a chance that they never would be. I couldn't imagine what he was going through, but I knew to the very depths of my being that it didn't matter that Midira was a part of his family. Jett was who he made himself to be, not what his blood was. I just wished that he would see it that way.

"Dealing?" I asked, turning in his arms to face him. He looked down with those deep amethyst eyes and kissed me gently on the forehead.

"Dealing." His voice was low but steady. I tightened my arms around his chest, needing to comfort him.

"Midira's a bitch," Jasper uttered. Jett's and my attention were snapped up in a flash. We both looked at Jasper with wide eyes.

"What?" Jasper responded. "It hasn't crossed your mind that she could be lying about all this? She's manipulative and *evil*."

"I'm well aware of that, Jasp. I just don't see what the purpose would be to do that. What's her end game?" Jett asked

"To mess with you? Make you doubt everything? To try to get us to turn on you? Who knows! She's crazy," Jasper answered.

I agreed with Jasper. We didn't know if she was telling the truth or if it was a manipulation – but we needed to find out. How we were going to do that was beyond me.

"How are we supposed to figure that out, Jasp?" Jett huffed. "It's not like we can just walk up to Stronghold, knock on the door, and ask for a DNA test," Jett fumed, voicing my thoughts exactly.

"True. But I know one person that knows a thing or two about where Siren children come from," Jasper answered.

"Who?" I asked.

"Pearl, of course," Jasper answered.

"*Pearl?* You think she knows if Jett's a royal Siren?" I asked him.

"She's our best bet!" Jasper said.

I looked at Jett. Did he even want to know for sure? I watched Jett's eyes dip to the ground. His hands rested on his hips as he wrestled with wanting to know or not. Jasper and I locked eyes.

"Okay," Jett said finally and flashed to the house before we could blink.

"He's in!" Jasper said with a celebratory fist pump.

"Why are you so excited?" I asked him.

"Jett needs this. One way or another, he needs to know who he is. He has since we were kids."

"I think this is a mistake," Rayna added.

"Why?" Jasper asked.

"What if he finds out something worse; something that he can't get over," she asked. Jasper waved a hand.

"What could be worse than finding out you're Midira's blood?" Jasper asked and started to walk to the house. A tight knot in my gut told me that there were worse things out there and Rayna was going off of her new intuition. I looked at her. Her eyes were focused on the ground.

"You okay?" I asked her. She jumped at the sound of my voice, her eyes blinking away whatever was going on in her head.

"I don't know, Ky. There are warning bells going off in my head like crazy, but I can't seem to figure out why. I need to talk to Mazz," she said and took off to find him.

That can't be good.

JETT

IF THERE WAS A WAY to find out if what Midira said was true, I was going to do it. I needed to know. I couldn't put a finger on why, but there was a drive in me to find the answer. There was something that I was missing - had always been missing. This whole thing with Midira could explain why I had always thought I needed to know more about where I came from.

I ran up the steps to the farmhouse, taking the whole thing in a jump, and launched through the door. Sam was sitting at the kitchen table twisting his family ring on his hand and staring hard at it.

When Sam had returned to Stenen long ago, he came without his family. He was adopted by his fosters, the Sirens and Sirenites that adopted babies that were rescued from Mer. We'd never seen the family that raised him to teenage age. Even when Sam got married to Jasper they weren't there. He never talked about them and we respected that it was a subject to stay away from.

Sam's eyes lifted to me as I came in the door.

"Whoa! Where are you off to in such a rush?" he asked, sitting back and placing his hands on the table; breaking the train of thought he was on.

"Pearl's," I answered and reached for the truck keys dangling on the cabinet key hook.

"What? Right *now*? Why?" he asked.

"If anyone might know if Midira is telling the truth – she will."

"You sure you *want* to know?" he asked me. I stopped in my tracks and looked at him.

"Why are you asking me that?"

"Since I have known you, you have had a deeper need than any other Sirenite to find out your heritage. What is this answer going to do for you, Jett? Is it going to change anything about who you are?" he asked.

"This has nothing to do with *who* I am. I need to know why the hell Ares is hanging around trying to draft me as a part of his weirdo band. This could have something to do with that. Have you forgotten that Deimos and Phobos took our people? I want to know why and where they are. Damn it, Sam. If any of this is tied to me, I need to know!" I yelled at him.

"Okay, fair point. Just make sure you don't sink into that Sirenite pit of despair you often do. It took a year for you to get out the last time you fell in. Don't forget that," Sam warned.

"I'm not going to do that again," I answered, getting my back up. I didn't like to be reminded of the funk that I was in a few years ago. Being in a community of Sirenites and Sirens was something that should have helped me deal with my heritage, but no matter how hard I worked, I couldn't shake the shame and horror of who my parents were. Was my mother some violent Siren? Who was my father? I don't know why, but it really bothered me.

"Good. Glad to hear that, 'cause you have a wonderful girl who will get dragged into it with you," he added.

"Right," I answered with a nod. *Laya.* I couldn't bring her down with me. My anger was legendary during that time. Jasper took the brunt of it last time, but even he has his limits. I almost lost my brother. I wouldn't do that again to him – and I refused to do that to Laya.

"Well, when do we go?" Sam asked standing.

"*We* don't. *I'm* going…now," I said walking to the door.

"Whoa, Jett. Hold on," Sam said running and blocking the door.

"What?" I asked Sam.

"Nothing," he shrugged, placing his hands in his pockets casually. "Just wanted to hold you off long enough for them to tell you that you weren't going alone," he said and stepped aside as Laya and Jasper walked in the door. Their eyes met mine and both flashed to the keys in my hand.

"Oh, no you don't," Laya yelled, levelling a grade 'A' glare at me.

"You're not going anywhere without me," Jasper said.

"Us," Laya said and elbowed him.

"Right. Us," he said with a nod as he crossed his arms.

"This is something I need to do on my own," I said to them.

"*Bull shit*," Sam coughed. When I glared at him, he patted his chest and shook his head.

"Look, Jett. I know how much this means to you. We all do. But, like it or not, we're coming with you," Laya said.

"I don't need a bunch of babysitters with me, thanks," I answered, twirling the keys in my hand and walking for the door.

"Oh, hell no! I am no one's babysitter - least of all yours," Laya said, narrowing her eyes at me and stepping in front of me, blocking the doorway with her small frame.

"That's not what I meant," I said to her. She walked straight at me. I closed my eyes, seriously expecting a punch in the face. When her lips landed on mine, I froze. Her arms circled my neck and I melted.

When she broke her embrace, I looked into her eyes and the fire was gone from them.

"We're coming," she said, looking at me.

"Damn it. *Fine*," I conceded. Laya looked up at me and smiled triumphantly.

"Dang!" Jasper exclaimed. "I'm totally using that the next time I want something!"

Laya giggled.

"Yeah, that's not going to work on me, Jasp," I said. He winked at me and I shook my head.

"Let's go," I huffed as I walked out the door with Laya's hand in mine and trailed by Jasper and Sam.

JETT

"PEARL really has a beautiful spot, KyLaya. You'll love it," Rayna said from the back seat.

The gravel crunched under the tires as we drove down the backcountry roads to Crystal Lake. Laya sat beside me. Her eyes on the road and her hand gripping the handle of the door tightly. It occurred to me that she wasn't used to driving in a vehicle. I reached over and squeezed her hand. Her beautiful eyes darted to mine and a smile graced her face.

"She knows more about the Sirens than anyone around here," I said.

"She's got some serious tricks up her sleeve to boot," Mazz added. "Never met anyone like her."

"I'll second that," I added, actually agreeing with Mazz for once.

Mazz and Rayna came with us, too. I wasn't happy about that, but I was outvoted as they came with built-in Siren and god alarms. They rode with Laya and me in the truck. Sam and Jasper followed in Sam's truck.

"You really think that she'll know the answers you're looking for?" Laya asked, watching me.

"No idea; but, she's our best bet," I answered, not wanting to get her hopes up, or mine. Even Pearl had her limitations.

Soon the gravel roads turned to pavement as we hit the highway. In a few minutes, the great gates of Camp Crystal came into view as we turned off the highway to the lake.

"Whoa. I didn't see these the night I came," Mazz uttered.

"They are quite the sight," Rayna said.

"What is she keeping in there?" Laya asked as she stared at the great gates. Two massive iron gates over twenty feet tall guarded the entrance to the camp. An intricate design with the initials "C.C" wound through their design. The gates were a gift from the Sirenites as a thank you for all that Pearl had done for our people. They were a beautiful piece of ironwork that took years to make. We were dang proud of them, even if they were a little extreme for their use.

The road to the camp was walled in tall trees and wide bushes. Wander off the road there and you would be lost almost immediately. The forest was *thick*. A treed canopy reached over us in a green array of colour. Sunlight poked through like rays through a strainer, creating a speckled pattern on the road and hood of the truck.

I could already smell the water from the lake. Fresh. Clean. Pure. I couldn't help the contented smile that pulled at my lips.

The Siren side of me wanted in the water so badly that we were already racing down the road before I realized I had poured on the gas. Laya's eyes were wide as she took in our surroundings zipping past her open window. I laid off the gas and I watched a sigh escape her. She had been holding her breath. When a lazy smile spread across her face, I knew she just caught her first scent of the lake.

At the end of the road, the trees parted to reveal a large expanse of grass.

Camp Crystal welcomed us in.

The freshly cut grass scented the air, mixing with the water to create an intoxicating perfume that was just about enough to make me forget why we were there.

The open green space was filled with four buildings that stood between us and the lake. To the far right was the largest of the buildings - a massive hall. With its state-of-the-art kitchen, it was the gathering place for the campers. A place where they can eat and socialize. It didn't match the rest of the buildings on the beach, though. Next to the hall was the Main Office. Pearl ran the camp from there. It was a large log cabin painted in dark brown with white trim. I came last summer and helped give it a new paint job. It was still looking good. Flags adorned every corner of the building and potted flowers were arranged all around the base.

Next to the Main Office was the storage shed and then Pearl's cabin, both were smaller log buildings painted in the same dark brown with white trim. I pulled the truck up behind the Main Office and turned it off. I looked at Laya, whose eyes were on the lake.

"Pretty isn't it?" I said.

"It is," she answered simply.

I smiled. The lake had a power all its own, but it came from Mer. I knew she sensed it, there was no denying its pull; even for the Sirenites.

"Jett!" Pearl called, as she hopped down the steps of the Main Office right to the truck.

"Hey, Pearl," I answered.

"What brings you here? Is everyone okay?" she asked looking past me. Her brows pinched as she scanned the truck.

"We're fine, Pearl," Mazz answered.

"Sirens attacked us at the farm," Rayna added.

"What? Sirens? At your *farm*?" Pearl uttered, looking between all of us as Jasper and Sam walked up from their truck.

"They poured out of the portal like ants," Jasper answered.

"Gods," Pearl whispered. "And you all survived?"

"Hey, we do have *some* skills," I pointed out. Pearl smiled and nodded.

"Of course, you do. Come grab a chair out front and we'll talk," Pearl said.

I took Laya's hand as we walked out to the beach where Crystal Lake opened up in all her glory. She was small but stunning. Fresh, clean water lapped up onto the shore. I could smell the lake all around us and my water powers called to it. I knew there was Mer power in it, but that didn't stop my Siren side from aching to dive into its depths.

A hand squeezed mine.

"It's really pretty," Laya whispered as she stood beside me, looking out at the water.

"Yup, it's a favorite spot for all of us in the area - human and Sirenite alike," I answered.

We grabbed an assortment of random-looking beach chairs that Pearl had tucked under her stairs and made a circle on the beach. The air was warm and the water smelled amazing as we took a seat.

"What's going on, Jett?" Pearl asked as she lowered herself gracefully into her green plastic lawn chair.

"Well…" I began. We filled her in on the fight at the farm. Rayna and Mazz talked to Pearl about their new abilities, which was an earful for me, as I had no idea that they were gaining the knowledge and power they were. Rayna had said nothing to me. Lastly, I told her about Midira.

"I was hoping that you might know if Midira was telling the truth about who I am. Am I really her grandson?" I asked Pearl.

She leaned back in her chair, sighed and closed her eyes.

"I promised, a long time ago, that I would keep this a secret - it has been a burden for a long time. However, I see that keeping it no longer serves a purpose. The time has come."

"What secret, Pearl?" Laya asked. I leaned forward so much I nearly fell from my chair.

"Okay, this is going to be somewhat of a shock, but there is no use keeping it from you anymore. Your lives depend on it," Pearl said.

"You mean that you know why the gods are after us?" Laya asked.

"Jett. I know why they are after Jett. Not you, my dear. Sorry."

"Why?" Jasper shouted. Everyone turned to him, but he just kept looking at Pearl.

"I don't even know where to start," she said shaking her head, dropping her gaze to the ground. "Umm. Okay, you know how you were taken away from your mother and put into the care of the Nereids after you were born," she began.

"Yes," I said. "All Sirenites are taken to the Nereids, the protectors of the bodies of saltwater, after they are rescued from the Sirens. It's the last stop before coming to Stenen. Like a safe haven."

"True, but…you were different. Where the Nereids usually look after a Sirenite baby for a week or two tops, they cared for *you* for *years* before bringing you here."

"What? Why?" I asked.

"To throw the scent off of you. You don't age while you live with the Nereids. So, you remained a baby for the years that you were with them. It threw your timeline off. Where they would have been looking for a child, you were still a baby. It was a way to protect you…and your brother," she explained, glancing up at Jasper.

"Me?" Jasper asked.

"Yes, *you*." Pearl looked at the two of us and grabbed our hands. We looked at each other and then back to Pearl. "You are real, true, blood brothers; but, more than that, you are *twins*."

"*What?*" Jasp and I shouted.

"That's not possible. Jasper is years older than me!" I argued.

"You were born to the same mother at the same time, but Jett was taken to the Nereids while Jasper was taken to Stenen. It protected you because they were looking for twin babies, not a single baby. Instead, you looked like any other Sirenite that arrived at Stenen."

"But…" Jasper uttered and looked at me. We had always looked alike - a lot alike - but twins?

"I know it's a lot to take in, but it's the truth. It's why she's after you," Pearl said.

"Midira," Sam grumbled.

"Yes," Pearl answered. "She's looking for her grandsons."

Silence.

"We're…we're…" Jasper uttered, unable to formulate a full sentence. Not that I blamed him.

"Yes. You are. Midira had one daughter, Celia. She is your mother."

"Midira has a *daughter*?" Jasper asked.

"Is she still alive?" I asked.

"Yes, but-"

"Didn't she ever look for us? Why hasn't she ever come to see us? Where is she?" Jasper asked.

"It's complicated, Jasper," Pearl said waving a hand.

"She didn't want us, Jasper," I said. "She doesn't care. She's a *Siren*." Jasper's face dropped.

"Well, that's simply *not* true," Pearl said, looking at me. "She doesn't know you exist," Pearl said hesitantly.

"Come again?" Jasper said, his brow furrowed as he looked at Pearl.

"How can the mother of a child not know it exists?" I asked.

"Midira and your father used her. Once you were born all memory of the two of you was erased from her mind. She doesn't remember carrying you or giving birth to you. I'm sorry," Pearl explained.

"Why would they bother to erase her memory? Wouldn't it have been a great honor to bear the next generation of Siren royalty? Didn't she want to help her mother get more power?" Laya asked.

"No. Celia wasn't like her mother or any other Siren for that matter. She wouldn't help her mother hurt others. Midira knew that if she wanted more in her bloodline, she would have to force her daughter into giving birth…and that's what she did."

"Forced? What do you mean forced?" I asked.

"She was raped," Sam whispered. Pearl nodded.

"Brutally," Pearl said, dropping her head. Sam took Jasper's hand. Laya turned her sad eyes on me.

"I'm so sorry, Jett," she whispered.

"We always knew that we came into the world through a union that wasn't loving, but…this is…" I couldn't finish. The product of a savage rape. That's what I was…Jasper too. I didn't know how to take that.

"Who was he?" Jasper asked, coming around faster than me.

"Oh, my dears," Pearl hesitated.

"Just tell us, please," I said. Pearl took a breath and then nodded.

"It was Ares," she said.

"*Ares* raped our mother," Jasper repeated.

"Yes," Pearl affirmed.

Silence.

Ares? Ares! Ares is my…no that's not possible. No. No!

"The union of Midira's bloodline and that of a god was prophesized to produce a power beyond that of the gods," Pearl explained. "Ares believed that he could control that power, absorb it somehow; so, he sought out a union. Midira only gladly agreed and offered up her daughter."

"How do you know all this?" Mazz asked.

"She was my friend," Pearl said.

"Midira?" Jasper blurted.

"No! Celia, her daughter," Pearl clarified.

"You were friends with Midira's daughter?" Sam asked.

"Yes," Pearl confirmed with a smile.

"How could you be *friends* with someone like her?" Rayna asked.

"As I said, she wasn't like the other Sirens. Let me explain. You need to know what your mother was like. I can't have you believe she is even a shadow of her mother."

"Go on," I said.

"Thank you," Pearl said and took a deep breath. "As you know, there are two kinds of Sirens. The Siren-born - which are born to a Siren at Stronghold, the Siren city. They are the most violent and evil of the Sirens. Then there are the Mer-born Sirens - the ones that are born to a Mer family and raised Mer until they are *turned* Siren. Mer-borns are seen as less than nothing to the Siren-borns in Stronghold. The Siren-borns use them as slaves. They humiliate, beat, and torture them. Celia was sickened by the world that she was surrounded by and refused to play any part in it. For that, she was an outcast and an embarrassment to her mother. She suffered a great deal of bullying and abuse at the hands of the other Sirens and her own mother. She had almost given up when she met a little Mer-born girl who changed her world. That little girl was my sister."

"Your *sister*?" Laya repeated.

"Yes," Pearl said. "Opal turned Siren at an unusually young age. She was just a child when her eyes changed from Mer blue to Siren violet, the sign of the Siren taking over within her. We tried to hide her, but we were found out and reported. I'll never forget the day the guards showed up at our home and pulled her from my mother's arms, screaming and crying. The Mer's fear of the Sirens has created an evil within them that they don't see. She was just an innocent little girl."

Pearl paused and forced out a shaky breath. No one spoke while she reined in her emotions and continued. "Opal, my sweet little sister, was taken from us and cast out of Titus Prime; left to the sea or the Sirens, whichever found her first. For her, it was the Sirens that got to her first. She was taken to Stronghold and put into slavery there. Celia found her at the mercy of some of the Siren-borns, who were about to use her for torture practice. She saved her. Celia took Opal home and hid her from the other Sirens and her own mother. She saved my sister from a life of slavery and torture at the hands of the Siren-born. Caring for her like a sister, she protected her and befriended her. My little sister would have lived in a hell beyond anything we could possibly comprehend if not for your mother."

"Where is your sister now?" Jasper asked.

"In the end, Opal was discovered by Midira," Pearl shared, her eyes shifted to her hands as she clasped them in front of her. "Mirdira flew into a rage. Celia was to take the throne - how could he be so soft? So weak? To teach Celia a lesson, to show her what it was to be a real Siren, and to make sure that she never made the same mistake again - she killed my sister in front of Celia. Opal was brutally tortured to death and Celia was forced to watch until her last breath left Opal's lips. It broke Celia."

"My gods," Laya whispered.

No words came to me. I was in shock.

"Celia felt responsible for Opal's death. She wrote to me to let me know about my sister. You see, she had manipulated her way into a Siren squad that would seek out newly turned Sirens. When she came to the city, she would leave letters from Opal in a hiding place for me. Through Opal's letters, I learned about Celia and all the kindness and love she showed my sister. I knew that Opal would not have wanted Celia to feel responsible for her death and neither did I. For a long time, Opal knew safety and love. I knew how much that meant to her and I made sure that Celia knew that too. Even after Opal died, Celia and I wrote to each other. She became like a sister to me. I was the only one that she could talk to, or confide in. When she became pregnant the letters still came. She told me all about the rape and the plans of Midira and Ares. She knew what was going to happen to her and her baby, and she told me everything. Midira didn't know about the letters. She didn't know about me. No one did."

"I – gods, Pearl," I said sitting back in the chair, shocked to my very core.

"I know this is a lot. I'm sorry to just throw it out at you like this, but you are owed an explanation after all this time," Pearl said, leaning forward in her chair, looking at Jasper and me.

"Didn't she ask you about us? Didn't you tell her?" Jasper asked.

"No. I swore I wouldn't. Ever," Pearl explained. "Celia is an exceptionally smart Siren. If I told her about you two, she knew she would look for you. That would have put you in danger of being found by Midira and Ares. She knew she couldn't protect you from them, so she made me swear to keep you a secret. She loved you two deeply. You were the only light in her life during a very dark time. It broke her to lose you. For that reason alone, I am glad Midira wiped her memory."

"So, how did we end up in the Nereids hands? Surely, Midira and Ares would have been anxious to get us," I asked.

"True, but I was able to tip off the Nereids to their plan. With the help of Celia, they were able to infiltrate Stronghold and sneak you out," Pearl answered.

"Where is our mother now?" Jasper asked. I looked at Pearl. She hesitated.

"You're not going to tell us, are you?" I said. Jasper looked desperately at Pearl.

"She doesn't know who you are and she won't believe you. It will be traumatizing for you all. Please don't ask me to put her through that. She's been through too much. It would hurt her. I can't, I won't, do that to her," Pearl reasoned.

Silence spread through the group as Pearl's words started to sink in.

Midira's grandson.

Ares' son.

That's who I was. That's who Jasper was.

At least the two of us were blood brothers. That was something.

I didn't know what to do with myself. Part of me wanted to take Laya and flash away from everything, the other wanted to take out Ares for hurting my mother so badly. I couldn't imagine the horror that she had lived through.

"Why is Jett granted a guardian and Jasper isn't? Ares being their father makes them both demigods. That's not a normal thing for a demigod to have," Sam said.

"No, it's not," a voice said from behind us.

"Eros!" Laya shouted, jumping out of her seat and embracing the god.

Standing tall behind Laya's chair the guy looked like he was coming straight from a bodybuilding competition and forgot to put his shirt on. Jeans. Bare feet.

What does this guy have against shirts?

"Hello, KyLaya. I'm so glad I found you. There is a fog over your location," Eros looked at Mazz and Rayna. "Good job, you two. Your range is getting bigger every day. You should be proud."

"Thank you," Rayna said with a smile and looked at Mazz.

"It's been…a lot, but we're navigating it," Mazz added.

"You've done your predecessors proud," Eros said. Mazz and Rayna both smiled.

I stood and walked away from the group. Questions flew as Eros spoke, but I couldn't hear any of it. My mind was flying in all directions.

Growing up, Sirenites didn't think about who their parents were. The Sirens that gave birth to us were forgotten. The men that sired us weren't even a thought. To my knowledge, no one had ever learned who their parents were…until now. For some reason, I had always struggled with not knowing; but after all that, I wasn't sure if knowing was any better.

What do you do when you find out that you are the product of a savage god's plan to impregnate an innocent woman?

"So…twins huh?" Jasper's voice caught me off guard.

"Yeah," I muttered.

He looked uncomfortable. Jasper *never* looked uncomfortable. I dropped my shoulders and looked at my brother. Blood or no blood shared between us, Jasper would always be my brother. This wasn't going to change that or make our bond stronger. It was just…new information. "I guess that explains why you are so immature for your age. We're actually the same age," I joked.

"Ha. Sure. I – um…" Jasper stopped and looked at me.

"Yeah, I don't know how to take any of this either," I said, knowing where he was going. "Midira's grandkids…what the crap are we supposed to do with that information?" I said shaking my head.

"Midira? How about *Ares*? We're freaking *demigods*, Jett!" Jasper exclaimed.

"Whoa, we don't know that. I mean-"

"What are you talking about? Our father is a *god*…what does that make *us*?" Jasper asked, looking intently at me.

I froze.

I couldn't be.

I wasn't…*no*, I shook my head.

"I – nope, it's not possible," I said. There was no way I was a demigod. No way. Jasper paced at my side, hands on his hips.

"Look, I'm not going to argue with you. I know this is a lot to take in. I just…"

"What?" I asked.

"We're *brothers*, Jett. I know that things haven't been easy for us over the last few years, but you're my blood - for *real*. We're in this together. I hope you know that. Wherever this leads, I'm with you," Jasper said.

I didn't know what to say. When Jasper put his arms around me and brought me in for a hug, I didn't deny him.

My twin brother. Twin. *Twin.*

Just a few days ago my biggest worry was the storage shed for the new tractor. Now, I'm a son of the Siren Princess and the god of war. *How did this happen?*

"Thanks, Jasper," I said, pulling back from him. "You'd have a pretty damn hard time getting rid of me, even before all this. You've always been my brother, blood or not."

"Ah, geez! You know how to make a guy tear up!" Jasper said dramatically, wiping at his eyes. I chuckled and shoved him.

"Jett?" her voice was soft and tender. I turned to Laya and wrapped an arm around her, pulling her against me. "You okay?" she asked.

"I will be," I answered. "Kind of mind-blowing finding out we have parents like that. I never thought of anyone other than Louise and Brock as my parents."

"It takes more than blood to make a family, Jett. Louise and Brock raised you. They loved you. They're your real parents. Midira and Ares don't make you who you are, you decide that. Don't forget that."

"Yeah," Jasper said with a nod. I chuckled.

"I suppose having the same blood as Jasp can't be too bad," I said.

"You know it!" Jasper smiled. I turned to Laya.

"Ares might be my father, but I have no interest in getting to know that part of my heritage. Like, none at all," I said with a wave of my hand.

"Ouch," Eros uttered as he dropped into our conversation.

"Oh, come on," I said back to him. Eros was nothing like his father, Ares. He took after his mother's side, Aphrodite.

"What? Can you blame me for wanting siblings who aren't psychopaths?" Eros asked.

Laya laughed at my side.

"I guess not," I answered honestly, considering what bloodthirsty murderers Deimos and Phobos were.

"We're half-*brothers*. Don't tell me that isn't exciting for you," Eros said, smiling from ear to ear.

"*I'm* pretty happy about it," Jasper interjected. "You seem to have come out normal. Well, more normal than your brothers."

"They take after Ares," Eros said. "Which makes me wonder how the two of you have turned out so well having Siren *and* Ares' blood in your veins. No offense, but there's a lot of anger and rage in those bloodlines," Eros pointed out.

"Celia. That's *all* Celia," Pearl added. "She was so unlike her mother. It's *her* blood in your veins, not Midira's. Remember that."

That warmed my heart. Even if our mother didn't know that we existed, she loved us for the time that we were with her. That's saying something. I couldn't help but wonder where Celia was. Was she happy? Did she have other kids? Did we have brothers or sisters that we didn't know about? Another question about my life that would go unanswered.

"I have so many questions about our mother. I want to know her," I said to Laya.

"Of course, you do. She was innocent in all this. I don't want to use the word victim-"

"She is a victim. She was raped and forced to bear children. I can't imagine what she went through. My gods. How could a mother do that to her own child?" I said, thinking of the absolute misery Celia must have faced because of Midira.

"Please, Pearl. Can't you tell them anything about their mother?" Laya asked. Pearl's mouth tightened as she stared at the ground.

"Very well, I understand your need to know. I can't tell you much, though," Pearl conceded.

"Anything!" Jasper returned. "Is she still alive? Where is she? Does she have other kids? Did she escape? I want to know!" Pearl held up her hands to stop Jasper and get him to breathe. I shook my head at him.

"No filter," I chuckled.

"Celia did escape her life with the Sirens. Even after her mind was wiped of your birth, she knew that she needed to leave. Outside of her mother's reach, she found peace and even happiness."

"Good. She deserved that," Sam said.

"And more," Pearl added.

"Well, this has been interesting but, I have some information about what is going on with our KyLaya and my *brother* Jett," Eros said with a smile and a nod to Jett.

"Too soon," I uttered, still unable to fully comprehend that Ares was my father.

"Alright," Eros pouted. "As I said I would, I have been able to find out that the Fates are indeed in the Mariana Trench this time of year. They know we are coming…because they know everything, but I sent word ahead. We just have to get there," Eros explained.

"The Fates?" Pearl asked, looking at us.

"After the fight against Deimos and Phobos, we knew that we needed some answers about why the gods were hunting us down. I suppose we have solved one of those mysteries," I said. Pretty sure that Ares was looking for Jasper and me because we were his sons.

"Well, you two supposedly have a power within you that is greater than the gods," Pearl said. "That was why you were conceived. Be careful, they will be looking for you."

"We don't have that power," I answered.

"Unless that power is good looks, then…one of us has it," Jasper added. Sam rolled his eyes, but a smile crept across his face. Jasper winked at him flirtatiously.

"Powers are funny things," Eros said. "Depending on the god, the power, the circumstances, there are many reasons why you might not have wakened them yet. If the Fates determined that you were going to have this great power, you will. There's no point running from it."

"I'm not interested in any great power," I said.

"It doesn't matter," Laya uttered and looked up at me. "I don't want mine, but no amount of wishing is going to get rid of it. The best thing we can do it learn to control it so those around us are safe."

"You are no danger to any of us," I told her and kissed her forehead.

"What I am saying is that we need more information," Laya went on. "Why does Ares want all this power from you and Jasper, and what *exactly* is the power that I have? There's still too much that we don't know. I don't like being in the dark like this," she said.

"She's right," Mazz added. "There's more to this than what we are seeing. Rayna and I have been catching glimpses of…well, we aren't sure what it is exactly." He looked at Rayna.

"It's big. Whatever it is," Rayna said. "We can sense it. There's this urgency we feel to do something, we just don't know what we are supposed to do. By talking to the Fates we're hoping to get some clarity about what we are seeing and sensing. Plus, Ares has my family. I want them back. The Fates will know where they are."

"So, in other words, we're going," Jasper said. "All of us."

"Oh no," I said shaking my head. "You're staying here where it's safe. I'm not taking you into the Trench."

"Last time I checked you weren't the boss of me, brother," Jasper said, looking me in the eye and crossing his arms. "Like it or not, we're coming. If this trip gives us any insight into what's going on, we all need to know. That includes Sam and me."

Laya looked up at me and I could see the grin she was trying to hide as she bit her lips. I sighed. I didn't want to take Jasper with me. He wasn't trained to fight. He would end up getting hurt or worse. Demigod or not, I didn't want to see him in danger. However, I was no fool. I knew he was coming - if that meant that he stalked us the entire time.

"Well, clearly it doesn't matter what I have to say," I huffed. Laya hugged me and I could feel her laughter against my chest. "You're no help," I grumbled at her. She lifted her beautiful face to me and damned if she didn't steal my breath.

"Looks like you're stuck with them," she said with a smile that made my heart sucker punch me.

"Looks like it." I dropped down and kissed her. She softened in my arms and fit against me. A little moan from her almost had me forget that there was anyone else on that beach with us. When she pulled back, her cheeks were flushed and I could see her pulse racing on her lovely neck.

A chill erupted over my skin. We all knew what lay in wait for us in that Trench. There was a reason the Fates chose that spot. No part of me wanted to bring the people I loved most into a place like that, but we didn't have a choice. The Fates would have all the answers that we were looking for and we desperately needed answers.

"Let's go," I said, holding tight to Laya. She sighed and nodded.

Here we go.

JETT

"FOR THE LAST TIME you are NOT bringing a suitcase!" I yelled at him.

"We don't know how long we'll be gone! You don't expect me to stay in the same clothes and underwear the whole time, do you?" Jasper yelled back at me, as he threw another shirt into the open suitcase on his bed.

"You have your backpack. It's big enough for your *essentials*," I argued.

"*My* essentials are much different than yours, Jett. There are some things that I simply can't live without."

"Try." I slammed the door to his room, grumbling as I went, and stalked back to the kitchen.

"That's about the fourth argument today, Jett," Laya said to me, as I took a seat next to her at the old kitchen table. After some debate, we decided it was a good idea to come back to the farm and pack supplies that we would need for our journey. We'd never been to the Trench, so we really had no idea what we were in for. What I did know was bringing anything was better than bringing nothing. Unfortunately, that meant that we were packing for a trip - which was not something that Jasper and I did well together.

"Oh, yeah," Sam said. "They do this every time they go on a trip. Jasper insists on packing for a year and Jett packs like he's staying for an afternoon. They argue right up to leaving the driveway who is right. You'll get used to it," Sam explained. Laya shook her head, a smile pulling at her lips.

"Shut up, Sam," I huffed.

"Now, don't take it out on Sam," Laya warned.

"I'm not!"

She looked up at me and tilted her head.

"Fine. Sorry, Sam." I conceded.

"Wow," Sam gushed. "She's staying," he said, pointing to Laya. Her smile grew three sizes and a red blush bloomed on her pale cheeks. Little did Sam know; I wasn't planning on getting rid of her - ever.

"I suppose I'll keep her around," I answered. Laya shoved me and I chuckled.

"You're lucky to have me," she said, with a side look.

"Don't I know it," I said, which made her blush deeper. I leaned over and pressed my lips to hers. Soft. Warm. Perfect. I still wasn't used to the feel of her. It was all so new and damned exciting. Really, *really* exciting.

"Umm, hello?" Sam interjected. I realized that I hadn't stopped kissing Laya. I leaned back, my lips tingling. Laya sat back in her chair and sighed with a smile.

I cleared my throat as Sam rolled his eyes. "What were we talking about?" I asked. Laya giggled softly and covered her mouth.

"Get a room," Jasper barked as he came in the kitchen. Leaning down, he placed a kiss on Sam's lips and proceeded to pour himself a large cup of tea.

"Is his majesty finally packed?" I asked him. Jasper turned and levelled a first-rate death glare at me.

"I'll take that as a no" I answered for him.

"How am I supposed to pack everything I may need in that tiny bag?"

"If *I* can do it, *you* can do it," Rayna said as she appeared from the room she shared with Laya. "I'll show you some tricks to help get the most out of your bag. I learned some great tips when I went backpacking last year."

"At last, someone that *gets* me," Jasper said as he guided Rayna into his room and closed the door.

"Have you guys seen Mazz?" Laya asked.

I shook my head, not that I was really looking for the guy. He was a constant reminder of the life that Laya had back home and her engagement to him. While I knew for certain that her feelings weren't anything more than sisterly toward him, I knew for a fact that his were. What I hated the most was that, really, he was a stand-up guy. He took on a god to try to protect Laya. I couldn't fault him for that. He was open to Jasper and Sam, which was not something that I thought that a Mer would be. And, to top it all off, he had Pearl's stamp of approval. That went a long way with me. Pearl wasn't one to befriend easily or lightly. She might come across as the kindest person on the planet but, trust me, you did *not* want to be on her bad side.

"What time are we taking off?" Laya asked.

"In an hour," I answered and watched the furrow in her brow deepen.

"I'd better find him," she said. She stood from the table and walked out the front door.

I watched her until she was out of sight. Her long hair swayed in rhythm with her hips. Her ass looked too good in the jeans that Rayna had given her...*damn*. A smile pulled at my lips thinking about having her backed against that shed again.

"Don't you look the smitten kitten," Sam said with a smile.

"Whatever," I replied with a shake of my head.

"I'm happy for you. It's taking everything in me not to hug you right now," Sam gushed.

"I appreciate your self-control," I answered.

"Yeah, I know," he said with a deep laugh. He stopped and looked down at his mug. "How are you handling all this?"

"All what?"

"Oh, I don't know, how about you being Ares' kid? A demi-god? The fact that KyLaya could suck all the power out of you? That."

"I'm handling it."

"Sure," he said slowly. "Look, Jett, I have known you since you were a kid. I know when you're not okay. If *I've* figured it out, KyLaya will too.

I didn't answer, just stared at the table.

"Right now," he went on, "you two are distracted around each other. Call it puppy love or whatever, it won't last forever. You'd better come clean with what's bugging you before she figures it out and corners you on it; or worse, it comes out and blindsides her. You don't want to hurt that girl."

"I'm perfectly fine," I said to Sam. He narrowed his eyes at me. Reaching across the table, he grabbed my arm.

"Don't-" but it was too late. I could feel his power enter me. An overwhelming urge to talk, bubbled up from my gut. Compelled to dump everything that had been plaguing my mind, I suddenly found myself airing my fears to him without the slightest hesitation.

"We could all be pawns in some god's chess game and never know it. I mean, look at what happened to Celia. She had no control over giving birth - what hope do we have? Where is it all leading? What if the Fates tell us something horrible? What if this power in me is terrible? Violent? What if I hurt someone? What if I hurt Laya? And then there's Laya. She can steal a god's *powers*! You think that they're going to just let her walk around with that little ability? No. No, they will come for her. They all will. I know it. I can't lose her. I can't."

Sam let my hand go. The world crashed down on me under the weight of everything that I had blurted out. I lunged across the table and grabbed him by the collar of his shirt.

"Don't you *ever* turn your powers on me again, Sam. Do you understand?" I threatened.

"You needed to let it out, Jett," he said unapologetically. "It would have eaten you. Fears are normal. You should face them with her, not hide them from her. She's stronger than you give her credit for."

"My fears and feelings are none of your damn business," I said and pushed him away from me.

"You need to talk to her, Jett," Sam repeated.

"Leave it alone, Sam, for your own good. I'm serious. Leave it alone," I warned as I pushed my chair back and walked out the door onto the deck.

The clean air hit my lungs like cool water on a hot day. I took a deep breath in, trying to calm myself. All of my fears and worries had been forced to the surface and were now running around in my thoughts; dragging up all the feelings that came along with them. I felt bombarded with uncertainty.

Damn it, Sam. Damn you and your infernal intuition.

Worst of all - he was right. It *was* eating at me. Our people's goal for so long had been to hide and remain off the gods' radar. Now, I found myself at the center of the attention that I had fought so hard to stay away from.

It wasn't just that. The "why" was driving me crazy. If I knew anything about the gods it was that there was always a *plan* – even a plan for the *plan*. What we were seeing was only a part of the picture.

There was an end game for them. We just needed to find out what it was.

Wherever this was all going to lead, I knew one thing for certain - and it was the *only* thing keeping me grounded - I *loved* Laya.

There was nothing and no one that was going to change that. No matter what, I wasn't leaving her. We had finally found each other. I wasn't about to let that go.

With that thought, I took a deep breath and went to finish packing the last of our supplies.

KYLAYA

"MAZZ?" I called, as I walked the path by the trees alongside the garden. "Where are you?"

No answer came, so I kept walking. I knew he wouldn't have left. He wouldn't leave me. I knew that without a doubt in my mind.

"Mazz?" I called again.

"Here!" an answer came from down by the portal. I turned and walked down the hill to where the portal lay hidden under the slough. The Siren fire burned behind us in the garbage pit.

"What are you doing?"

Mazz was standing facing the murky water, his arms folded across his chest. His brow furrowed deeply as he looked at the water that hid the portal to Triton.

"I'm trying to figure out how the Sirens would have found the portal," he answered, pointing to the water. "*I* don't even know where this is on our side. I've been working with Pearl for a couple of years now and she hasn't shown me or given me the slightest hint where to find this. How on earth did the Sirens find it?" he asked looking at me.

"I don't know," I said, looking at the water. "Maybe they got the location from one of the Sirenites that Ares took?"

"Could be," he mused. His lips thinned as his eyes stayed steady on the water.

"What are you on to? I know when you've found a thread that you want to pull at. What is it?"

"Have you had any weird dreams lately? Visions? Anything?"

"How did- how did you know?" I asked, my heart starting to race thinking about all the violent nightmares that I had been having. Not to mention Midira being a visitor to my dreams, too.

"Damn. I was afraid of that."

"What's going on? Why are you asking me that?"

"Pearl talked to me about Midira's ability to infiltrate people's dreams. She can manipulate young Mer into going with her through their dreams. I think – I think that's what happened to KyLena," Mazz explained.

"My sister? You think that Midira convinced KyLena to go with her?" I asked. That made sense in the scariest way. When she disappeared, there was no evidence of a kidnapping. Nothing about a young Mer that she could have run away with. There was just nothing. It was like she just got up and left. If she was convinced to leave on her own by Midira...

"Whoa. That's...that changes everything."

"It does," he said sternly, nodding.

"What's wrong? There's more. What is it?" I asked, looking up at him.

"Midira typically only has access to you in your dreams, unless..."

"Unless what?"

"Unless she has your blood, or in your case...your sister," Mazz uttered.

"What?"

"With KyLena, she can reach you when you are awake, Ky. She can have conversations with you that you may not even remember."

The day in the bathroom. The first time Midira talked to me. It flashed in my mind and my knees nearly buckled. She was using my sister to get to me! Oh, my gods! KyLena!

"You think that Midira took Lena? Really? Are you sure?"

"I don't know for sure, but you need to be careful, Ky. If she's started to get to you, her connection will only get stronger the more that she does it."

"Shit," I cursed. "She's spoken to me a couple of times, Mazz." Panic slammed into my chest, knocking the air right out of my lungs. I was putting everyone at risk. If Midira could get into my mind while I was awake, who knows what she would do to me or *through* me.

Gods, when did my life get so complicated?

"Rayna and I are working on blocking her. With this new knowledge, we have learned how to hone our powers. We're getting better every day. I'm pretty sure that we're now strong enough to block her from getting to you during the day. It's at night that we have trouble. There's power and magic to the night that we're having a really difficult time with."

"Well, thank you for all you are doing to keep us safe, Mazz. Really, it's amazing what you guys are doing."

"Just part of the job," he smiled.

"Are *you* okay? Do you feel different?" I asked, happy that he was finally opening up to me about his knowledge and powers as a guardian.

"I feel…new, somehow. It's been coming on stronger every day. I think it's being close to you that is bringing it out. I see everything more clearly. Rayna is feeling it too. We've been talking a lot and comparing notes. Our minds are changing. We can perceive things we never could before. It's no wonder that Mistress Hol was so good at her job in the vaults at Triton, she probably had every scroll in the place in her head the whole time."

"With all this information, do you know what is going on with Midira and Ares? What their plans are? What about my powers? Do you know anything about them?" I asked.

"If I did, I would have told you. I promise. The memories, the information, isn't always clear. Sometimes it is a feeling. Sometimes an image. I am starting to learn to trust it."

"Would Midira have been able to get information from me without me knowing?"

"I believe so. Once she is in your mind, she can access your memories…like when Jett brought you through the portal for the first time," he answered.

"Well, how do I *stop* her!" I yelled. It was freaking me right out to know that she had been in my head and I didn't even know it.

"That's what I'm here for, remember?" Mazz said, threading an arm over my shoulders with a smile.

"I'm sorry I haven't been there for you more," I said looking up at him. "This must have been…I don't even know what it must have been like."

"It's okay. I haven't exactly the easiest person to talk to lately." I didn't answer. "Look, Ky, I have been thinking…a lot."

"Overthinking things?"

"Maybe," he said with a smile.

"At least one thing hasn't changed," I laughed. Mazz nodded.

"I understand my feelings better now," Mazz said. "I *know* them better, I suppose. I do love you. I will always love you, but I should never have put it on you to share those feelings for me. You have always been honest and open about how you saw our relationship. I had no right to expect differently just because I changed my mind. I'm sorry," he said.

"You know I love you. That will never change. I can't imagine my life without you! Seriously, I can't. You are family. You always have been; you always will be."

"Thanks, Ky. I needed to hear that."

"Does this mean that you're going to be civil to Jett now?" I asked. He smiled and grabbed me in a hug.

"Of course not," he grinned and squeezed me tighter as I tried to battle out of his arms. A low chuckle broke from his lips as I finally squirmed free and shoved him.

"Thanks a lot, Mazz," I laughed, unable to stop the smile from appearing on my lips.

"With all this new knowledge, I have thousands of new insults that I haven't used! You aren't really expecting me to keep all those beauties silent, are you?"

"Oh, good grief," I scoffed and crossed my arms, looking away from him.

Mazz chuckled and placed his hands in his pockets, the way he always did when he knew it was time to be serious. "I will do it for you, Ky."

I turned back to him. His eyes were earnest as he gave me a half-smile and shrugged.

"You know I can't stand it when you're mad at me. Plus, I miss my best friend," he added. "Things haven't been the same since…you know, and I hate it. I need 'us' back. Now, more than ever. If that means having to get used to Jett…then I will do it."

"Wow, you said his actual name. You *are* serious."

"Of course, I am," he said with a nod. "We haven't had a fight this bad since the teddy bear fiasco," he pointed out. I laughed.

The Teddy Bear Fight was the biggest, worst argument that we ever had. Mazz tore the head off my favourite toy bear. It had been a special gift from my father. A land toy that I cherished above all others. My most prized possession.

Mazz was a young, energetic, and clumsy, kid; which spelled trouble more often than not. One day, while we were playing in my room, he pulled a sword out that his father had given to him. It was incredibly sharp and he wasn't supposed to use it for anything other than training; but he snuck it into my room that day to show me his "moves".

As he was wielding the sword - showing me the vast range of movement he had with it - he took a swing that was too wide. The sword crashed into my floating shelf, slicing right through it and the objects on it. He killed a jewelry box, a conch shell, and, most heartbreakingly, my stuffed bear. The teal striped bear had been a gift from my father when I was a baby. It was softer than anything else I had and I loved it more than any of my other toys. It looked ratty and stained, but it was everything to me and came everywhere with me. Mazz had swung so hard and so wide that the head was cut right off the bear. I stared in wide horror as I watched my bear's head roll away from its body.

I. Was. *Furious.*

He was lucky that I didn't skewer him with his damned sword. I screamed at him so loud that our parents ran in from my father's room, where they had been meeting. By that time, I had lunged at Mazz and tackled him to the ground. I was pulled off, tears falling down my face, and swinging like a wild animal. Mazz apologized but I just screamed at him all the more.

We were both punished. Mazz, for sneaking out his sword - and me, for giving him a black eye.

At the time, it was the most earth-shattering thing that could have happened to me. Now, Mazz and I look back and laugh. He was much more careful with my things after that.

"I haven't thought about that in years," I said, a smile creeping across my face. "We really had it out then, didn't we?"

"We sure did."

"I hated you. But, I hated being separated from you even more," I admitted.

"Me too. Even though you gave me a black eye," he added.

"You deserved it," I said back.

"It was an accident!" he yelled at me and we both started laughing.

"Are we good?" I asked him, watching him closely. He looked away and thought.

"Yeah, we're good," he answered with a single nod. I wrapped my arms around his waist and squeezed.

"Thank you," I said.

He didn't answer as we stood there and enjoyed some peace. The minutes ticked away, inching closer to our departure time. I looked around the farm at the tall trees and the golden fields and felt a loss that I wasn't expecting. I was going to miss it there.

When Mazz was ready, he linked his arm in mine and we walked back to the house together.

JETT

"RIGHT, well, if you're sure you're going through with this," Pearl started, "the entrance to Mer is at the bottom of the lake. It leads to Titus Prime. It is the closest portal we have to The Trench."

We were back on the beach with Pearl, almost exactly twenty-four hours after we'd found out about Celia and Ares. Jasper was *finally* packed – thanks to Rayna's help and some of Sam's personal charm. Our packs weighed heavily on our shoulders and clanked as knives and daggers knocked against each other. If anything went down, we were armed and ready for it.

My attention was drawn away from Jasper's bag, which looked a lot bigger than I remembered, when the Main Office door banged shut. A figure came bounding down the stairs that I had never seen before. My eyes narrowed.

"Oh! Right!" Pearl said shaking her head.

"Who's *that?*" I asked, pointing to the tall guy that was now making his way across the beach to us.

"That's Darrien, my…nephew," she said with a smile.

"Nephew?" I asked. Other than the sister that she just told us about, I didn't think that she had any family. But, then again, she didn't tell us about Opal until yesterday. It was possible she was keeping other family under wraps too. Pearl was a mystery at the best of times.

"Well, twice or three times removed," she commented with a shrug. The guy walked over eying me and Pearl. Stark black hair, styled at the top. I could tell just by the way he held himself that he was military. Even though we had never met any of the Triton soldiers or guards personally, we had watched them enough. They moved a certain way, talked a certain way, and had the same straight-as-a-stick posture;

coupled with swagger that shouted *I can kick your ass*. Darrien was no exception; but unlike most that I had seen, he wasn't condescending.

"Darrien, this is a good friend of mine. Jett," Pearl said with a smile on her face.

"Nice to meet you," Darrien said and reached out a hand to shake mine. The guy was as tall as I was, if not taller. He had a firm grip to his shake, but he wasn't rude. When he looked me in the eye though, I saw a flash of uncertainty and knew instantly that he had seen my Sirenite-violet eyes. To the Mer, Sirens were the epitome of evil. Anything that was related to them was hated with the same ferocity. That included me and the rest of us. Immediately, I was on edge.

She brought a damned Mer here. Why?

His green eyes flashed to Pearl. She smiled and nodded. Darrien released my hand and stood back, crossing his arms over his chest and eyeing me.

"What brings you guys here?" he asked.

"I don't see how that is any of your business," I snapped back not liking the question; as if he had some kind of claim on the camp.

"Okay," Darrien uttered and looked at Pearl.

"What are *you* doing here?" I asked him.

"Helping Pearl. Unlike you, the reason I'm here isn't a national secret," he said with a sarcastic grin.

"Ha!" Pearl laughed. Darrien looked at her and broke into a playful grin.

"What's going on here, Pearl? You've never mentioned having a nephew," I asked, looking this Darrien guy over. "Who is this guy - for real?"

"She doesn't have to answer any of your questions," Darrien said, stepping in front of Pearl, as if he needed to protect her from me. *Me!* I could feel the hum of my power in my gut as my temper flicked higher.

"Hi! I'm Ky," Laya said, stepping between me and Darrien, and flashing an innocent smile at him. Darrien broke his glare at me and looked at her. His shoulders relaxed as he turned his attention to Laya.

"I'm Darrien," he said, reaching a hand out and shaking Laya's.

She looked over her shoulder to me and frowned.

"What?" I asked her. She shook her head.

"Rayna! I'm Rayna," Rayna offered, having come in closer as well. She reached out to shake his hand. He took it.

"Nice to meet you," he said, and shook her hand.

"Well, *hello*! I'm Jasper," Jasper said as he grabbed Darrien's hand a little too excitedly.

"Sam," said Sam with a nod as he elbowed Jasper.

"Ow," Jasper cried and looked at Sam. Sam lifted a brow at him and Jasper kissed him on the nose. Sam smiled reluctantly.

"Oh, my gods," I groaned. They were all making fools of themselves in front of this guy. *Unreal.*

"Darrien has been here helping me get the camp ready for the summer," Pearl said.

"It needed work," Darrien said with a smile to Pearl.

"Oh, whatever," she said and shoved him playfully in the shoulder.

"If you needed help, Pearl, I would have come and helped," I said, feeling a little offended that she didn't ask me in the first place, as I was usually the one that helped her get things ready.

"You had enough on your plate this summer, Jett. Don't worry, Darrien is a great help," she said.

"Speaking of help, I'm just going to finish up the girls' side before that new girl gets here," Darrien said and turned to the others. "Apparently, I have to stay away from her. Pearl's worried I'm going to fall in love and forget myself." He rolled his eyes.

"I think no such thing," Pearl said. "Get going."

"Nice meeting you," Darrien said to the others, then flicked a warning look my way. All eyes were on him as he turned and left the beach.

"You don't really trust him, do you?" I said to Pearl.

"I trust him, but he's about to meet someone very special and I can't have him losing sight of his job," she explained.

"What's wrong with a little summer love?" Laya asked as she took my hand in hers.

"Never knew you to be against your camp workers dating. What's going on?" I asked.

"This is different," Pearl said, her eyes on the place where Darrien disappeared.

"Okay…" I said and looked off to where she was staring. I was pretty sure that she wasn't seeing the trees anymore, but that her thoughts had taken her away from the beach and us.

"I like him," Jasper said.

"Of *course*, you do," I said and shook my head at him while pulling Laya in closer.

"No! There's something about him that…well, he's *hot*!" Jasper answered, giving up on a bogus explanation.

"Sure is," Rayna whispered. "Nephew, huh? How come you've never invited him here before?"

"I don't know," Pearl answered. "Hopefully, you will get to know him better some other time. He's a good guy, Jett. You have my word on that."

"Alright. I trust your word," I said, meaning it. "I suppose it's time we left. though."

"I suppose so," Pearl said and looked over the lake, her eyes losing focus.

"Thank you, Pearl. For everything," I said, trying to break the spell she was under.

"What? You don't have to thank me, Jett." She pinched up her nose and bit her lip. "Are you sure you want to do this?" Pearl asked, stepping forward, and placing a hand on my shoulder.

"We have to get some answers and The Fates are our only chance at getting them. I don't see another way around this. Do you?"

"I – uhh," she stuttered.

"Didn't think so."

"But-"

"We'll be *fine*, Pearl. Really. We'll be careful," I assured her.

"I feel like I'm failing Celia. She would be so upset to see you go."

"Its-"

"Oh!" Pearl shouted and ran for her cabin.

"What was that about?" Sam asked, as he watched Pearl disappear into her tiny log house.

"No idea," I answered. Pearl came out a moment later holding up two packages.

"I almost forgot about these!" she called.

"What are they?" Jasper asked.

"Gifts from your mother," she answered with a smile.

"Really?" I asked.

"Of course," she said with a beaming smile. "She left these for me in one of her last letters before she gave birth; with instructions to give them to you when the moment was right. I can't think of a better moment than this. You will need these," she said as she held forward two small packages wrapped in brown paper and twine.

"What are they?' I asked as she held out one for me.

"Open them," she said.

I moved the small package around in my hands. It was light and fit in the palm of my hand. I loosened the string and opened the paper slowly. I could feel the eyes of all in our group watching me as I unfolded the last flap to reveal my mother's gift.

"A ring," Laya whispered. "It's beautiful."

"It's *powerful*," Pearl answered. "Go on. Put it on, Jett."

"Alright," I said, slipping it on my finger. It was made of silver and was heavier than I thought. A large amber stone sat at the center of it, surrounded by a silver ring that was engraved with symbols I had never seen before. Shining in the light, the center of it glowed. It was truly a beautiful ring. The sun glinted off the cut surfaces of the stone and bounced around the deep center of it.

But, nothing happened.

I looked up at Pearl. She smiled, reached over, and turned the engraved ring that surrounded the honey coloured stone. It slid around smoothly and silently. The ring vibrated on my finger, but again nothing changed. That is, nothing changed for *me*.

"Jett?" Laya called, looking through me, even though I hadn't moved from where I was standing.

"I'm here," I said. Laya jumped. She reached out a hand gingerly, squinting her eyes.

"You can't see me?" I asked.

"No!" she answered with a laugh.

I turned the ring around the stone and Laya jumped back with a cry. "Sorry," I chuckled and steadied her before she fell over.

"It is the ring of Gyges and contains the power of invisibility," Pearl stated.

"Where did Celia find *that*?" Mazz asked, stepping forward looking at Jett. "It's been unaccounted for generations."

"She stole it from Midira," Pearl explained. "Don't ask me how Midira got it."

"It's…she wanted *me* to have this?" I asked Pearl. She nodded. I didn't know what to say. My eyes turned to Jasper, who held his package in his hands.

"My turn," he sighed. His hands pulled at the brown paper and twine. When the last bit of paper came away it revealed a vile of liquid. Silver in color, it seemed to move around the inside of the glass tube all on its own.

"Wow!" Jasper gasped. "What is it?" he asked after a moment.

"It's Water of Lethe. This water comes from the cave of Hypnos in the Underworld. It causes all who drink it to lose their memory. The more you drink the further back your memory is erased. From what I can figure, it's what was used to wipe Celia's memory. It can also heal any wound, no matter how fatal. Just a drop and it will heal without a mark."

"Wow. Thank you," Jasper said, putting the vial around his neck on the piece of twine it was tied to.

"Yes, thank you, Pearl. I can't believe you've kept these all this time," I said to her. Pearl's eyes lit in tears.

"Your mother was a friend that I desperately needed. She's the reason that I started saving the Sirens; why I risked so much and took my banishment without a fight. She is the strongest person that I have ever met. I'm happy that I am able to finally give you her gifts. She would be happy to know that you have them, though not happy that you need them. I imagine she would have been pretty protective of you two."

"Do you think that there's a chance that we would ever be able to meet her?" Jasper asked. I looked at Pearl with more hope in my heart than I wanted to admit. Suddenly, a mother I never cared existed pulled at my heart more than I ever thought possible of a Siren.

"I don't know," Pearl replied. "I hope so, Jasper. I really do. I would love to see you reunited with her. She would love that, but only if that meant that you weren't in any danger. The way that things are looking, I just don't know."

"I suppose I should have guessed that," Jasper answered. Sam took his hand. Jasper smiled a small smile at his husband. Sam kissed him on the forehead.

"You know; those gifts are quite valuable," Eros interrupted. "I know a few gods that wouldn't mind them. This one included."

"Well, you can't have them," Laya said, stepping in front of me. It was really sweet how she defended me.

"Relax, KyLaya," Eros said. "I'm not about to steal from my brothers, well not these ones at least. Take care of those. They are rare and you never know when they will come in handy."

I nodded.

"I hate to be the one to say it, but we really should be going," Rayna said.

"She's right." I looked at Pearl. "Thank you for…everything."

"I've been watching over you since you were babies. You are like my own boys. Keep each other safe. My love goes with you." Pearl pulled us both in for a warm hug.

"You, young lady," Pearl said looking at Laya as she moved away from Jasper and me.

"Yes?" Laya's eyes were wide as she looked at Pearl.

"You break my Jett's heart and I will *end you*," Pearl smiled.

Whoa!

My jaw dropped open, as did everyone else's; everyone's except Laya's. Instead, she walked up to Pearl and hugged her tightly.

"Never," she whispered. My heart thudded hard in my chest. Pearl grasped Laya's face and smiled.

"I know. I just had to say it," Pearl said with a sincere smile.

We all said our goodbyes, which had turned more bittersweet than I had anticipated. Leaving Pearl was like leaving the last remnants of our mother. My mind was flooded with questions about the woman who gave birth to us as we stepped into the water and swam to the bottom of the deep clear lake.

KYLAYA

IT HAD BEEN AWHILE since I transitioned between water and air. The feel of it never sat right with me. I had always hated the first breaths of water. It felt like I was drowning every time. The more that I worked with the Guard, the better it got, but it still hurt.

We dove under the waves and swam for the bottom of the lake, where the portal to Mer lay. When I hit the end of the air in my lungs, my mouth flew open of its own accord and water flooded my lungs. Three coughs later, forcing the water into my lungs, I had transitioned. My body would now breathe water…like a fish. Turned out that I wasn't the only one that had trouble transitioning between air and water.

Jasper. His air lasted a bit longer than mine but he full-out panicked when it ran out, trying to head to the surface. Jett and Sam grabbed him and held him under the water. It might have seemed barbaric to anyone that saw it, but it really was the only way to get him to breathe the water. You just had to do it, no matter the pain and panic. I felt for Jasper, remembering my first time breathing the water, as he tried to fight off Sam and Jett. Soon, his mouth opened and water flooded his lungs as mine did.

When he was able to catch his breath and calm down, he punched both Jett and Sam.

"Ow! What was that for?" Jett yelled at him.

"You *drowned* me!" he said.

"What? Did you expect to hold your breath for the entire trip?" Jett shot back at him. Jasper just glared at him.

"I'm sure there was a nicer way of helping me breathe than that," he said.

"There really isn't," Sam said. "Sorry, sweetheart. If it is any consolation, we hated doing it."

"Speak for yourself," Jett joked.

Jasper glared at him, but placed a kiss on Sam's cheek.

"Can we just not do that again?" Jasper asked.

"It does get easier the more you do it," I said to him. "It sucks, though, while you are training your body," I admitted to him.

"Yeah. That's an understatement," Jasper scoffed. Sam took his hand and we continued to the portal.

The lake was spring fed. No salt at all. It was sweet and fresh and unlike anything that I had swum in before. Suddenly, my skin felt rejuvenated and my blood raced strong and wild in my veins. It was amazing. Freeing. How did the Sirenites stand being in this water and not ache to live in it like Mer did? I looked at Jett and he turned to me, reaching across and taking my hand.

Strong and steady, he swam at my side down into the depths of the lake. I would never have guessed its depth from what it looked like on shore. The small little jewel of a lake was deceptively deep. From light and warm, to dark and cold, we swam. Our Mer and Sirenite powers propelling us forward as the water around our bodies pushed us through the smooth and silky water.

A pull in my core told me that we were near the portal. I felt drawn to it. An instinct that all Mer had, drove me toward it. I wondered if Jett felt it like I did. Did Sirenites feel drawn to Mer? Portals called to the Mer so that we could always find one. This portal was no different. The call of Mer was there, just as strong as it was in the sea.

"Wait," Jett said to us and stopped mid-water.

"What is it?" I asked.

"We're exiting right outside of Titus Prime. What's our plan if we run into the Mer?"

"Let us handle that," Mazz said swimming forward. "Ky and I have a lot of influence in Mer. Don't talk and don't make eye contact. Let us take care of it."

I could feel Jett stiffen at my side, and knew that placing his life in Mazz's hands was not making him feel good. I turned to him and snagged his gaze.

"You trust me, right?"

"You know I do," he answered.

"Good. Let's go," I said and swam through the portal.

Like the last time, the sensation of entering the portal was like being stretched out to my very limit and then snapped back into place; and, cold - very cold.

Saltwater filled my lungs as we moved from the fresh water of Crystal Lake to that of the deep. Darkness gave way to light as the grand city of Titus Prime appeared before us.

Emerging out of an invisible crack in the seafloor, behind an outcropping of rock, we filed out. The city looked spectacular under its dome of light on the seafloor. The ancient buildings from the first Mer were still in pristine condition, a constant reminder of the gift that Poseidon bestowed on our people so long ago. It was an ancient city that prided itself on tradition. To me - though it was beautiful - it was also just…old; lacking the innovations of Triton - something *we* prided *ourselves* on.

"Wow," Rayna uttered. Her eyes were wide as the lights of the city reflected in them.

"It is quite the sight," Mazz agreed with a smile, standing next to her.

"What now?" Jasper asked, looking at Jett and me.

"I think we should send a message to my father that you're safe and where we are," Mazz said.

"He's going to lose his ever-loving mind," I answered. Mazz nodded.

"Yup, but there's nothing that we can do about that. He's worried sick about you. Knowing that we're at least together would help him settle down. You know he thinks of you as his daughter," Mazz said, looking at me.

"Very well, you're right. We should tell him." I turned to Jett and the others. "Mazz and I will go to the city and send a message to his father. Stay here where it's safe. If someone comes you can always go back through the portal to the lake. We can go quickly and be back without drawing attention. We know where to go and people are used to seeing us in the city."

"No," Jett said immediately.

"This is the safest option. For everyone," I told him. His jaw tightened as he looked at me through narrow, thoughtful eyes.

"We shouldn't split up. What if one of Ares' people sees you? It would draw Ares right to you. I don't like it," he stated.

"Look, it's a risk, I know that - but I have to. Hasp is like another father to me. He needs to know I'm okay. He's also the only one that I trust to look after my father," I explained. Jett took a step back and shook his head. I knew he was fighting against it, but I also knew that he would never stand in the way of me protecting my father. When he stopped pacing, his eyes found mine.

"Thanks for understanding," I said. A half-smile pulled at the corner of his lips. He reached for me, pulling me into a tight embrace.

"You be careful," he said into my hair as he placed a kiss on the top of my head.

"I can handle myself," I answered, leaning back and looking up at him.

"Don't I know it." He laid a kiss on my lips. It was warm and sweet and jolted my heart.

Mazz cleared his throat. "The sooner we leave, the quicker we're back," he said.

"See you soon," I said and pulled away from Jett. He crossed his arms and chewed his lip as he watched us swim off toward the city.

JETT

"CALM DOWN, JETT. KyLaya is a fighter, she'll be fine," Jasper said. I was pacing the seafloor, cursing myself for letting her go. Splitting up was a terrible idea.

"Seriously, Jett. You're making me nervous, sit down before I plant you on your ass," Rayna threatened.

"Ha! I'd like to see you try," I said back. Rayna might have been a skilled fighter on the Watch, but that didn't mean that-

My feet were unearthed as the water around me swirled, pushing me to the ground. A shadow formed over me as my head hit the sand.

"You were saying?" Rayna said, looking all too satisfied with herself.

"Oh, sure, just 'cause you caught me off guard doesn't mean that you would win in a fight," I said, even though I was starting to wonder.

She had never been able to put me down before. Her new powers were bringing out a side of her that I had never seen. She was just starting to discover all of what being a guardian was about, and obviously putting me in my place was a perk she was enjoying.

"You wanna go?" she asked stepping back. The water swirled and pushed me back to my feet. Pink lit in my hands and ran up my arms.

"*You* wanna go?" I said and tilted my head.

"Okay, you two that's enough. Your light show is going to draw attention. Put that away," Sam said waving at my power as the flames grew higher. I squeezed my hands and they extinguished. Even in water, my powers ignited.

"He's right," I said to Rayna.

"Chicken," she uttered. I turned and zapped her with a shot of electric pink as she turned from me. She squealed and I was slammed with water that whipped me into the open ocean.

"Damn it!" I yelled, trying to right myself enough to get a shot off at her again.

"That's enough!" I heard Sam yell. The water dissolved. "Oh. I didn't think you'd actually listen to me…but good!" Sam added, nodding.

"Shh!" Rayna said, waving a hand for him to stop.

"That was really powerful. Where did you learn water control like that?" I asked her.

"Shut up!" she yelled at me.

"Sorry, I was ju-" Ryna clamped her hand over my mouth as her eyes searched the water.

"What is it?" I asked as he released my face.

"We're not alone," she whispered. Pink rose from my skin at her words. All eyes were on the water around us.

"I don't hear anything other than the sound of Jett's defeat," Jasper said. I shot him a glare, he smiled back at me.

"I *feel* it. My mark is hot, someone is out there. But…" her eyes clouded as she searched the water.

"What are you *doing* here?"

The voice came from behind us and we all turned in a flash at the sound of it.

"Who are you?" I demanded, stepping in front of Rayna and the others. A young woman stood before us. She was dressed in a flowing white gown with copper hair that billowed out behind her. With a round face and large eyes, she looked more like a cherub than a woman. It was her eyes that gave me pause. The startling blue of them hinted at a power that we weren't yet seeing, so I wasn't taking any chances.

"Never mind who I am. *You* aren't supposed to be here!" she shouted at me.

"Where? What are you talking about?" I asked.

"In *Mer!* She'll find you!"

"Okay, what is going on? Who are you?" Jasper asked stepping forward from behind Sam.

"You're here, too! Oh, this is so bad!" she said throwing her hands over her face.

Suddenly, from the open sea came a pulse of water. It broke against us, shaking the earth and pushing us over.

"What was that?" Rayna shouted.

"She found you! We've gotta get out of here!" the girl yelled.

She reached over and grabbed my and Jasper's hands. There was a *pop* and Titus Prime disappeared.

KYLAYA

I HATED LEAVING Jett, but I knew that they were safer outside the city than in it, even with Mazz and me there to protect them from arrest.

"We're in and out, you hear me? No visiting, no checking up on anything. We send the message and get back to the others," I said to him.

"I know. I can hear your teeth grinding from here," he said. I punched him and he laughed.

"It's weird being back here with everything that's happened," he said. I nodded as we entered Titus Prime through the main entrance, at the front of the city. Once you enter, you aren't in the water anymore. The bubble over the city protects it from the surrounding sea, just as Triton's does. The entrance is the transition from water to air.

It took me a minute to get my breathing in check from the transition.

"Yeah, seems like something out of a dream. But then, nothing seems real anymore to me. Things are so far from the life that I once knew I can't even recognize my old life anymore."

"You said it," he said.

We made our way quickly down the main road to Court, the government building at the center of the city. In it lived all the highest officials of Mer, including our king, Zale Reed. The Reeds had been on the throne for generations, being the offspring of the original Mer in Titus Prime. He was a good man that had always got along very well with my father. The two rulers, though different in many ways, always had aligned in their quest to bring the people of Mer forward. In Triton, it was easier, as it was a city of innovation. Titus Prime was a city of tradition, which made the minds of its people harder to change. I might have been able to save Jett and the rest from arrest in Triton, but I wasn't so sure if I would have had that kind of luck in Titus Prime.

The road to Court led over a bridge at the foot of the grand castle building. Mazz was one step ahead of me when he stopped dead in his tracks. I collided with his back.

"What the - what's wrong?" I asked, coming around to the front of him.

"It's my mark," he whispered as his hand rested on the guardian mark under his collar bone.

"You think-"

But, I didn't get a chance to finish my thought as a siren sounded. Everyone froze, including Mazz and me.

"Sirens!" someone shouted and all eyes flew up to the top of the dome. Circling the water above the city was a swarm of Sirens.

I looked at Mazz and he looked back at me. Without saying anything the two of us ran for the back exit out of Titus Prime. Anyone could leave through it, but no one was allowed in. Around the stone castle we ran as fast as we could.

"You think they found them?" Mazz shouted to me over the sound of the alarm.

"I hope not, but the timing is too good. They know we're here," I shouted and poured on more speed. I felt for the daggers at my side and flipped them into my hands.

Mazz hissed and grabbed his chest again. "You okay?"

"Someone else is coming," he said looking up at me.

"Damn it!" I cursed and ran. What fresh hell was coming for us now? I just hoped that we would be able to get back to the group before they were found. Whoever it was, wasn't there for a social call.

"Hurry," Mazz shouted as he rounded the back of the castle. "It's a swarm. They'll find them in no time."

"I know! Go! Go!" I yelled as we ran through the exit and out into the open water. Jetting around the city to where we had left everyone, we saw a group of Sirens descend on the hiding place we had left our friends in.

I grasped the dagger in my hand and charged forward. Mazz was at my side. Water was swirling like a vortex right where we had left everyone. The Sirens were staying a safe distance off.

"What *is* that?" I called to Mazz.

"It's Rayna!" he shouted back. *Rayna?*

Sure enough, I could see Rayna standing on the dry seafloor as a cyclone of water whipped around her, cutting into the Sirens and sending them flying through the water. Her raven hair whipped at her face as her piercing violet eyes scanned the water for Sirens. She looked *fierce*.

Mazz landed next to her. The water shook as his hands pushed out from his body. A wall of water thickened in front of him and shot away from him. It collided with a couple of Sirens that were on their way back from being thrown by Rayna. It hit them hard, breaking bones and bringing blood.

"Whoa," I uttered, never having seen a power like that before. Together, Rayna and Mazz were one hell of a deadly pair. My focus was pulled away from them as I scanned the water for Jett. My heart thudded hard in my chest the longer I went without seeing him.

"Where's Jett?" I yelled at Rayna. That's when I saw Sam…with no Jasper.

"What happened?" I asked. I threw a dagger through the water and landed close to where Mazz and Rayna stood. The dagger found flesh with a satisfying thud between the ribs of a Siren who was flying straight for us.

"They were taken!" she answered.

"The Mer?" I asked.

"No! Some girl showed up and poof they were gone!' she said. The cyclone changed course, pulling three Sirens into its vortex and spinning them so fast they were almost shredded. The water cut into their skin, as blood leaked out of them tinting the water red.

"Geez!" I hissed seeing the damage that she could make.

"Eros! Where are you?" I called to the open water, hoping that the god could somehow hear m-

"Hello, KyLaya. How are – whoa! What's going on here?" he yelled, looking at the Sirens screaming in our direction.

"Help us!" I yelled at him.

"What do you want *me* to do? I'm the god of passion, not super cool ninja moves!"

"What's a ninja?" I asked.

"Never mind," he said, ducking the blade of a Siren as she descended on us.

"Man, these ladies are *mean*," he pouted. I growled and plunged my knife into the base of the Siren's neck, letting her fall to the seafloor.

"If we don't get out of here, we are going to have to deal with a Mer army that is going to be coming out of the city any second," I said to him.

"Oh, well I might be able to help with that one," he said and snapped his fingers.

I looked at him and waited. Nothing happened.

"Any time now!" I shouted, blocking a Siren attack. I spun in the water, and plunged a dagger into her side. She screamed and it felt like someone was driving nails into my skull. I held on tight and twisted the knife. Her scream cut off and she went limp, falling to the sea floor.

"I don't understand!" Eros said, looking at his hands. He snapped again, but nothing happened. "What's wrong with me?" he shouted. The look in his eyes was sheer fear as he stared in horror at his hands.

"You didn't really think that you could hide from me, did you?" A deep voice rang out around us. Mazz and Rayan both cried out in pain and their water powers dissolved.

"KyLaya?" Eros called.

"Yeah?"

"Run," he uttered. I looked at him, but his eyes were on the open sea. "Get to the Fates. The gods have no power there. You'll be safe. Hurry," he said and stepped out from beside me.

"What about you?" I asked.

"It's time I joined my mother."

"What?"

"Don't worry, I won't be going without a fight. Now…go," he said.

There was a pulse in the sea and out of nowhere a man popped into existence.

"Finally, I get to meet the girl that can steal a god's powers." His hair was black as night. He wore all black leather, from his pants to his jacket. With no shirt underneath, you could see the immaculate array of muscle he was sporting. The man's eyes turned to me and I gasped. They were ice-blue.

"Ares," I whispered, more to myself than anyone else. My heart was in my throat and I was convinced that I would choke on it any second.

"Where is my family?" Rayna shouted as a wall of water formed and headed straight for him.

Ares flicked his hand and the wall disappeared.

"Why? Did you lose them?" Ares laughed.

"Your sons took them," Rayna bit back.

"Well, I can't control everything that they do, I have a life you know. You'd have to ask them where they put them," he said. My stomach flipped on its back.

"Deimos and Phobos don't take a piss without you knowing about it," Eros said.

Ares chuckled as he turned his eyes to Eros, "Well, unlike some, at least *they* follow orders."

Eros crossed his arms and shook his head. "If you think that's an insult, you'll need to do better."

"Always the disappointment," Ares groaned.

"Oh, ouch, *Dad*. You've wounded me to the core," Eros said dramatically.

"You said he would be here," Ares said to a Siren that descended beside him.

"He *was*," she said, scanning us with eyes as black as ebony. *Midira*. This time her body was a stronger Siren, one that looked like she'd seen many battles and held the scars to prove it.

"Where is he?" Midira demanded, looking at us.

None of us answered. We knew she was talking about Jett, and even though we didn't know where he was taken, there was no way we were going to tell them that. Rayna crossed her arms. I clenched my jaw and stuck out my chin.

"If you think that any of us are going to tell you anything, you're crazier than I thought," Eros said, crossing his arms and looking at Ares in the eye.

"I don't have patience for you today," Ares said and waved a hand. A long spear appeared in it, with a silver spearhead that looked sharp enough to kill a whale. In a blink, he sent it flying at Eros. Before I could shout out a warning, the spear pierced right through Eros's chest and out his back. His eyes flew wide.

"No!" I screamed.

Eros looked at me and opened his mouth, but no sound came out. There was a pop and he was gone.

"No!" I shouted again. I swam over to where he had stood. *He can't be gone! He just can't!*

"Nice shot," Midira said to Ares.

"You monster!" I yelled, fueled by anger and sadness. "He's your *son*!"

"We've never had the strongest relationship," Ares said with a shrug.

A snap in my core jarred me as rage filled my veins. I wanted to hurt Ares. Actually, I wanted to kill him. I could feel a hum in my veins and knew, deep down, that something was waking up. I just didn't know what.

Without stopping to think, I flew at Ares. A scream cut out of my throat, as the pain of seeing Eros killed came blasting out. Ares was not expecting me to attack him, his eyes widened as I came close.

I was going to grab him and pull until he was an oozy mess on the seafloor. When I brought my hand up a ball of white light ignited within it.

"How?" Ares whispered.

"Is that..." Midira began.

"Yes," Ares said and swallowed hard. I looked into his eyes and saw something that chilled me to the core...*fear*. Ares was afraid of me. *Me*.

Listening to the call of the power, that now flowed through my veins, I pushed my hand out toward Ares. The white ball of light shot at him. Colliding with the center of his chest, an explosion of light burst from his skin.

He clawed at his skin with a scream. His eyes were wide and wild as he struggled to pull the light from his wound.

Midira reached for the white light to try to help, but when she touched it, it burnt her hands. She screamed and recoiled.

"Yes, Ky!" Mazz exclaimed.

"This isn't over you little bitch! You think you've won? You've seen *nothing*!" Midira yelled. A pop sounded and she was gone. So was Ares.

I wilted. The power sank back into my skin and the glow retreated back within me. Suddenly, I was more exhausted than I had ever been before. The world was turning black and I knew that I was about to faint. I didn't know if it was the power, or the fight, or what; but it had taken just about everything out of me.

"Mazz," I uttered. I felt his arms catch me before I hit the seafloor. There was a *pop*.

"Who are *you?*" Mazz yelled. A voice I didn't know answered, but the world was darkening quickly and I couldn't make sense of it. Strong arms took me as everything went black…

JETT

THE WORLD SPUN and, before I could stop it, we were taken away from Titus Prime. When it came back into order Jasper and I stood on the stoop of an underwater castle. The giant grand building was made entirely of stone but didn't have a dome over it, as with Titus and Triton. I looked at Jasper, but his eyes were wandering the stone and the massive arched gate at the entrance. It reminded me of Court at Titus Prime, but this place was…older. Much older.

"Where are we?" Jasper asked as he looked around.

"No idea. Do I look like a G.P.S?" I snapped. Jasper frowned at me. "Sorry," I apologized.

"Who was that woman?" Jasper asked, turning around and surveying the open ocean around us.

There was something about the water that was different. Ancient. I couldn't put my finger on it, but it felt like it had been left alone for a very long time. The smell reminded me of walking into a house that had been left empty for years - stale.

"I'm going to guess the girl that took us lives here," I said and started to walk up to the large door. A small knocker hung at eye level to me on the door. I reached for it and paused. The knocker was a mermaid tale, the kind that you see in the movies. I grinned, hoping that it was a good sign that our captor had a sense of humor. I reached up and grabbed it.

"Is that really a good idea?" Jasper asked, taking a quick step to catch up.

"You got a better one?" I asked, turning to him. He looked back at me and opened his mouth, but nothing came out.

"Didn't think so," I uttered.

Grasping the brass tail, I knocked on the door three times. The sound of the knocks echoed around the inside of the building, as if it were completely empty. Jasper sighed.

"I don't think anyone is home."

"It doesn't sound like it," I replied. But just as I let go of the knocker, the door opened silently.

"Yeah, I don't like that," Jasper said, shaking his head and stepping back.

"Not a fan myself," I added, "but this seems to be the only option at the moment." I pulled my power, and let it lick across my forearms and swirl around my fingers as we entered. I didn't want to be caught off guard. We still didn't know who we were dealing with.

The inside of the castle could not have been more different from the outside. Where the exterior of the castle seemed neglected and cold, the interior was fully furnished and warm. As we entered, the water was pulled from us and we walked in completely dry. We stood on the floor of the main entrance without a drop of water on us.

A massive room, with large beige couches forming a square in front of the fireplace, welcomed us in. Heat was thrown from the blazing fire, warming us against the chill of the sea. Gold gilded mirrors adorned the walls; each of them a different shape, but just as beautiful as the last. A stunning bouquet of intricately arranged white flowers was under each mirror and on the tables beside the couches. It looked like a modern residence, not something that you would see in a castle. Especially one in the most ancient part of the ocean.

"Wow, this place is incredible," Jasper uttered in awe.

"Thanks!"

Jasper and I turned at the spritely voice coming from a door at the back of the room. Pink light shot down my arms and balled in my hands.

"Whoa!" the young girl said holding her hands up. "Friend," she said pointing to herself.

"How do we know that?" I asked.

"Well, for starters, I saved your lives back there. They were coming for you, you know," she said.

"No, we *don't* know. We know *nothing*! Want to fill us in?" Jasper said, placing his hands on his hips and staring at the girl. She was younger than us, but something told me that was only a façade.

"Who are you?" I asked.

"Oh! I'm so sorry, of course you don't know me! I'm Eurybia," she said and curtsied with her white dress. Her flawless tanned skin stood out in stark contrast to her white dress and her long wavy copper hair.

"Okay, Eurybia, why did you bring us here and just where *is* here?" I asked, watching her closely. She might have looked all innocent and sweet, but that didn't mean that she really was.

"This is my home," she began, "and I brought you here to save you."

"You keep saying that but save us from who?" I asked.

"Queen Midira and Ares," she answered.

"What?" Jasper and I yelled.

"You mean that you left our friends to face off against them without us?" I yelled.

"I – I…well I guess," she said. "Is that bad?"

"Yes, it's *bad*!" Jasper yelled. I planted my face in my hands.

"You have to take us back there! Now!" I shouted.

"No! I can't!"

"Why in Hades not?" I said stepping closer to her and forcing her back a step.

"I promised," she uttered, locking eyes with me. It was then that I saw it, something familiar that I was not prepared for at all. I staggered back.

"What? What is it?" Jasper asked me.

"Who asked you to protect us?" I asked, unable to break my gaze from Eurybia.

"My mother," she answered.

"And who is your mother?" Jasper asked.

"Gaia," she answered.

JETT

EURYBIA raised her chin and looked at us with new eyes. Eyes that didn't say innocent girl, but eyes that said goddess. Not just any goddess, a primordial one.

An original one.

A *powerful* one.

"Gaia?" Jasper blurted. "Like, as in, *the* Gaia," he asked.

"Yes," Eurybia answered.

"Like, the original goddess. Mother earth? The one that created all other gods? That Gaia?" Jasper asked.

"That Gaia," she replied with a giggle.

"This is insane," Jasper uttered and turned from us. His hands were on his head and I could tell that he was about to have a breakdown.

"Just why is Gaia interest in us? Isn't she…dead?" I asked, trying to be nice about it, I mean it was the girl's mother we were talking about.

"No, she's just…sleeping," Eurybia answered. She walked further into the room and sat on a couch. Where the young girl was, now sat a woman. The way that she held herself changed, she sat taller and more confident.

"Why the charade? I can clearly tell that you aren't some innocent, naïve girl," I asked taking a seat at a couch across from her. The fire snapped happily in the fireplace while Jasper paced the floor. He needed to get out energy, it helped him focus.

"Men, human or god, are much friendlier to innocent little girls," she smiled. "It's a trick I picked up eons ago. When they see me as a woman, they don't know if they want to fight me or fuck me. I'd rather take both options off the table at the very start," she explained crossing her legs.

I cringed. What kind of a life had she lived that she had to worry about that? But then I remembered that she was primordial, meaning that she had been around before the Titans existed, before Zeus was even a thought. I'm sure she had seen her share of tragedy and horror having lived through Kronus' rule.

"Okay, sit down, Jasp. You're making me dizzy," I said. Jasper glared at me, but listened.

"Sorry, it's just…a lot, you know," he answered.

"I know."

"I'm sorry for pulling you away from your friends, truly. I was just focused on you two," Eurybia commented.

"Why us?" I asked her.

She pulled her feet up onto the couch beside her and pulled her skirt over them. "I can't tell you."

"What? Why?" I demanded.

"The other isn't here. You must find out together. That is how it is to be," she said.

"Who's the 'other'," Jasper asked.

"She's a relative of mine…extremely distant, of course. She was supposed to be there too, but she wasn't," she answered.

"Laya," I said.

"What? No. What?" Jasper asked, looking from me to Eurybia.

"She's looking for Laya," I answered.

"How do you know that?" Jasper asked me.

"Because, I'd recognize Laya's eyes anywhere," I said and looked at Eurybia.

She looked back at me and tilted her head. "You said that the girl you were looking for was a relative," I explained.

"Yes. You know her?" she asked perking up. Her feet hit the floor and she scooted to the edge of the couch, looking intently at me. My heart thundered, thinking about Laya.

"Yes. She went into the city when you pulled us away," I answered.

"Well! I'll go get her!" Eurybia said standing. She was just about to wave a hand when Jasper jumped to his feet.

"Wait!" he shouted. Eurybia froze and looked at him.

"What's wrong?" she asked.

"There are people with Laya. Our loved ones. If you're going to bring her back here, bring them too. Please. We…I need to see that they are okay," he said, his voice getting quiet.

"Jasper's husband was left there as the Sirens attacked," I said to Eurybia.

"Oh. Oh! Yes. Yes, of course I will bring them all. You have my word," she said and with a wave of her hand she was gone.

"You really think she'll bring them here, all of them?" Jasper asked.

"I hope so, I really do. I don't want anyone getting hurt," I said.

"What the hell is going on with us, Jett? It's like our whole world has been flipped on its head."

"Yeah, it sure seems that way."

"You okay?" he asked me.

"Yeah, I think so. I mean, this is all *insane*, but other than that I'm good," I smiled. Jasper chuckled lightly.

"Yeah. I'm not as good, but I'll get there. You've always been better at dealing with shit than me. I really envy that right now. I could use some shit dealing skills at the moment," he sighed.

"Hey, no matter what, we're going to get through this," I said to him.

"I know."

There was pop and the room filled with people. Mazz and Rayna stood back to back and their eyes were about as wide as could be. In Mazz's arms was a lifeless body. My heart leapt out of my chest. *Laya*.

"Sam!" Jasper cried and launched off the couch, throwing himself in Sam's arms and kissing him good.

"What happened? Is she hurt?" I asked Mazz, running to Laya. Mazz walked over to the couch and gently placed her on it.

"She passed out after taking on Ares," he said.

"She what!" I shouted. "How could you let her do that? She could have been killed!" I two-hand shoved Mazz. He took a step back, but no more than that. His eyes narrowed at me.

"Last time I checked I wasn't the boss of her! Ky has a damned mind of her own!" he yelled at me.

"You should have stopped her!" I said, poking him in the chest.

"Because she's so helpless right? She kicked his ass, by the way," Mazz said, smacking my hand away.

My brows flew up. I wasn't saying that I didn't think that she could handle herself. I knew she was a deadly fighter. Her powers made her even more dangerous; but, taking on Ares…that was different. She could have been killed and that just didn't sit well with me.

"Why did she pass out?" I asked, focusing my attention on Laya and not Mazz.

"I don't know. Best guess - she exerted herself too much. There was a…new power," he added.

"New power? What new power?" I asked.

"White light. Scared the hell out of Ares," Mazz answered.

"Let me see her," Sam said, stepping to the couch and kneeling beside her.

He ran his hands over her body, sensing for any damage. His brows furrowed as he concentrated.

"I…don't feel any damage," he uttered, but he didn't stop.

"What is it?" I asked.

"There's — it's hard to explain. She's *different*," he answered.

"Different? Like how?" I asked.

"I don't know. She's not the same as she was the first time I healed her. It's like there's something protecting her," he answered.

At that moment, Laya moaned and her eyes opened. I heaved a heavy sigh and grabbed her hand.

"Hey, you. You had us worried." I ran a finger across her cheek. Her eyes turned to me. She grabbed me, hugging me fiercely, and sighing heavily into my shoulder.

"Jett! Thank the gods, you're okay!"

"I'm fine! But, how are you?" I asked, pulling her back from me and looking her over. "Mazz tells me that you fainted."

"I did?" she asked, looking at Mazz. He nodded.

"Right after kicking Ares ass," he added.

"What?" she asked.

"You don't remember?" Mazz asked. Laya shook her head and flopped back down on the couch.

"The last thing I remember is Ares and Midira showing up, but that's it," she said.

"Damn. You were amazing," Mazz said.

"True," Sam added.

"More importantly, how are you feeling?" I asked.

"Fine. A little tired, but other than that I'm okay," she answered. Relief flooded me. I couldn't imagine what she had done to knock herself out like that - or to scare Ares, if that is what she really did. I looked at Mazz.

"Exactly, what happened?" I asked, sitting next to her.

"Yes, please, Mazz. I need to know what I did," Laya plead, sitting up on the couch and watching Mazz closely.

"Alright-"

"Who's for tea?"

Everyone's eyes turned to Eurybia, who was coming from the kitchen with a tray. A tea pot and cups were on it and she was smiling like a good hostess. One of the other tricks that she picked up, would have been my guess.

"You!" Laya shouted, pointing at her.

"Me!" Eurybia shouted back and laughed. "What about me?" she asked.

"Drop the act, Eurybia," I scolded. The sweet innocent smile faded instantly, replaced by the powerful goddess beneath.

"Fine," she said with a roll of her eyes. "Some habits are hard to break. I *was* offering the tea genuinely."

"Why did you take Jett and Jasper?" Sam asked stepping away from Laya and toward Eurybia.

"She's a friend…of sorts," I answered for her.

"My name is Eurybia. I took Jett and Jasper to protect them. I didn't realize that they were with friends. I didn't mean to take them from you," she explained.

"Are you okay?" Laya asked me and Jasper, looking at us in turn.

"We're fine. Turns out that she was looking for you too," I said.

"Me?"

"Yup, apparently we are a hot commodity," I said. Laya looked from me back to Eurybia.

"What do you want from me?"

"I am to escort you to the Moirai," she said.

"What are the Moirai?" Jasper asked.

"The Fates," Mazz said. "That's their real name, the name they got before Zeus's time."

"They've been around that long?" Laya asked.

"Eurybia?" I said, looking at her.

"They've been around as long as I have," she said with a shrug.

"And how long is that exactly?" Sam asked.

"Oh gosh, I've lost track. How long have the seas been around for?" she asked, looking around at the group. "Well, that long."

"I see," Sam replied. "That would make you…"

"The primordial goddess of the sea; in other-words, one of the first," she explained.

"Wow," Laya uttered. "And this is your place? You brought us to your home?"

"Yes," Eurybia answered.

"Thank you," Laya said.

Eurybia's eyes widened and pink bloomed on her cheeks. A smile flashed to her face that was eerily similar to Laya's.

"It's been a very long time since I have had guests, I'm only too happy to help," she replied and I believed she was genuine about that.

"Umm, not to be rude, but why *are* we here, exactly?" Laya asked.

"Oh, I'm sorry. We should get down to business," she said, taking a seat on an adjacent couch to Laya. Sam and Jasper sat together on the last couch, with Mazz and Rayna perched on the arms. I looked at Laya, whose eyes were glued to Eurybia. I wondered if she had figured out that she was related to her yet.

"Okay, well, I told Jasper and Jett that I wouldn't tell them what was going on until you were here. So, let's get to it," she began. "As I said, I am to escort you to the Moirai. After that, I just don't know. I guess we will find out together," she said.

"That's it? We were already going to the Fates with Eros," Jasper said. "Where is he, by the way?"

Sam looked at Mazz and I knew immediately that something had happened.

"Ares…" Mazz started and then shook his head.

"What?" Laya said, sitting up.

"Ares killed him. I'm sorry," Sam answered.

"No," she whispered, bringing her hand to her lips. Tears sprang to her eyes. "But, he's a god…how?"

"He told us to run, but we never got the chance. Ares threw a spear…right through him," Mazz explained. I winced just thinking about that and was grateful that Laya didn't remember any of it.

"That's when you went all crazy powerful on Ares' ass," Sam said.

"What? What did I do?" Laya asked.

"This white power came from you-"

"I'm sorry…white?" Eurybia cut in, leaning forward.

"Yes," Mazz said.

"Are you sure it was *white*?" she asked standing up and staring hard at him. "This is very important, think hard."

"I'm positive," Mazz said and looked at Sam. "You saw white right?"

"No doubt," Sam nodded.

"Interesting," Eurybia said and started to pace the room.

"What is it?" Laya asked. "Is something wrong with me?"

Gods, I hope not.

I watched Eurybia closely. When you surprise someone who had been around as long as the seas, it couldn't be a good thing. By now, she would have seen everything - literally, everything.

"Nothing is wrong with you, but it is interesting that your power would be white," she said.

"Why?" I asked.

"All gods and goddesses have colour to their power. All do. The more brilliant the colour the further the generation away from the first gods. The paler their energy the closer," she said. Holding up her hand, she flicked her fingers open and a pale grey-blue power ignited in her palm. It was so pale that you could barely tell that there was colour to it at all.

"My powers are almost colourless, because I am the daughter of the first goddess." She closed her hand and walked to Laya. "Please, would you show me?"

"I don't know how. I don't remember even having that power!" Laya said.

"It is simple. I will teach you," Eurybia said and pulled Laya from the couch to a standing position.

"Clear your mind. Empty it of all thought. It is difficult, but you must focus," she said. I watched Laya and didn't dare to take a breath.

White power. What did that mean?

What was she?

Who was she?

KYLAYA

EURYBIA stood in front of me. Her hands were on my shoulders as she spoke in a calm, even tone. I closed my eyes and cleared my mind. At least I tried. There was a lot of chaos knocking around in there.

Okay, focus.
White light.
A power I can't remember.
Midiria and Ares together.
Eros dead.
Jett taken.

"You need to try harder than that," Eurybia said. I sighed.

"It's not easy with all these guys staring at me. No pressure or anything," I said and pointed to five sets of eyes staring at me.

"I suppose you're right. How about this," Eurybia said, backing away from me and turning to the others. "I have rooms made up for you all. You are safe here, I assure you. This is the last place on Earth, and beyond, that anyone would think to look for you. You are free to stay as long as you like. You all look like you could use some rest," she said. "No offense."

"None taken, I'm exhausted," Sam said with a yawn.

"Me too," Rayna added. "Got burnt by my mark a few too many times today, really zaps my energy. How about you?" she asked looking at Mazz.

"Uh, yeah. I suppose I could use a rest," he said to her and then looked back at me. "You okay?"

"Yeah. I promise. I'm fine," I replied.

"Okay," he said with a nod. "Thank you, Eurybia, for a safe place to rest. We appreciate it more than you know."

"Oh! You flatter me. You are welcome, of course. Please, follow me."

Eurybia lead us through a door in the back of the room and down a long hall. A large set of stairs wound their way up through a doorway at the end of the hallway. There were no other doors or landings along the stone steps as we climbed and climbed. I could feel the power and magic that held the place together, the very walls vibrated with it.

Reaching the top, Eurybia opened a large wooden door and walked through. Light poured into the darkened stairway, illuminating it in a natural light.

I could barely believe my eyes when I crossed the doorway and into the room beyond. Brightly lit, with high ceilings and windows, it opened before us.

All eyes were taking in the grandeur of Eurybia's home. Bright light shone in through the floor to ceiling windows. Where the sun was coming from, I had no clue. I was sure we were underwater. I could feel it outside the walls. The room was a beautiful pale shade of blue grey with white trim around each door. Crown mouldings on the ceiling. It was modern, clean, and yet looked like it was from another time. It was stunning. The space was big enough to hold a banquet in. Doors lined either side of the sitting room, which had three large couches arranged before a fireplace, leading to rooms beyond.

Huge flower arrangements of white flowers adorned every table along the outside of the room. The doors were much larger than any door I had at home in Triton. All white, they matched the trim around the room.

"You will find your rooms here," Eurybia said, pointing to the doors around the room. "I thought that you would be most comfortable being all together."

"Thank goodness for that," Jett said, looking around.

"Whoa," Jasper uttered, with an approving whistle.

"My gods. It's gorgeous," I said to Eurybia.

"Thank you!" she gushed. "I like it a lot. I do hope that you will be comfortable here. Each room has its own amenities. There will be food and drink here around the clock, in case you are hungry or thirsty."

"You don't-"

"Nonsense!" she interrupted as I argued. I smiled and shook my head.

"You are very thoughtful for someone that hasn't had guests in so long. Thank you," I said.

"My pleasure," she smiled. "Your rooms are simply ladies on this side and gentlemen on this side. Sam and Jasper, I assumed that the married couple would like a suite together, so I gave you this room with a larger bed."

"Very thoughtful," Sam said and opened the door, ushering in Jasper.

"Holy Hades!" Jasper yelled as he entered the room.

"What is it?" I shouted, worry flashing as I ran into Sam and Jasper's room ready for a fight.

"I could fit a baseball team in bed with me here!" Jasper said as he hopped up onto the bed.

"Whoa," Sam shouted, as he came in the room.

"Yes, I get it, your bed is huge," I answered him, shaking my head.

"No. Look at your *hands*," he said, staring intently at me.

I looked down at my palms. White light glowed from my skin, circling and winding around my fingers and wrists.

"Wow," I whispered, bringing my hands up to get a better look at them. "It's so…pretty."

"So, it is true," Eurybia said, looking at me closer. "White light. I can't believe it."

"What does it mean?" I asked her.

"I don't know, but I have a feeling it's one of the reasons I am to take you to the Moirai. There hasn't been a white power since my mother, KyLaya. This is…unheard of," she said.

I swallowed hard. *What does that even mean?*

"What kind of power did your mother have?" Jett asked.

"What didn't she have?" Eurybia answered. "She's *the* primordial. The mother of all gods. All power comes from her."

"Are saying that Laya has *all* the powers of the gods?" Jett asked. My heart slammed against my chest and jumped into my throat.

"No, I'm not saying that," Eurybia said as he watched the white light dance across my skin. "But it has to be considered. There's a reason her power is *white*. I just don't know what it is. The Moirai will though," she nodded.

Jett wrapped an arm around me and my heart settled slightly. Even my new powers didn't scare him off. I leaned into him and allowed myself to relax. I couldn't handle him freaking out. It was taking everything in me not to go down that road myself. The white light faded away back under my skin. I looked down at my hands, still unable to believe I had seen it.

The power of Gaia?

No. I can't have that. I can't.

How did I get it? Why did I have it? What was I supposed to do with it?

From the corner of my mind a memory surfaced. From a time I didn't remember, a whisper came.

"In a time of terrible darkness, a great light will be born. Together with the colors of heaven, a battle with the evils of old will begin."

With the last word a pressure in my core mounted. Swirling through my veins and around my bones, it consumed me.

Every pore.

Every hair.

It flowed through me.

It *was* me.

I screamed as the pressure overwhelmed every fiber of my being. The need to let go - to release - pushed against me with a ferocity that left me breathless. My mouth opened, but a scream didn't leave my lips. Instead the words that had been whispered to me poured out in a ragged voice that wasn't my own.

I couldn't see. I couldn't breathe. Every part of me had resigned itself to this new sensation. All I could do was wait for the agony to end.

JETT

"WHAT'S WRONG WITH HER?" I shouted.

"I don't know!" Sam shouted back.

Laya had just been standing there; then, out of nowhere, the air in the room felt like it was being sucked out.

Her eyes turned white - glowing light headlights.

Her hair moved around her, in a beautiful blonde mass - as if she were in water.

But nothing, *nothing*, scared me more than when she levitated off the floor.

Floating a few feet off the ground, she was the epicenter of her own storm. Wind whipped at us, pushing furniture around the room and forcing us to brace ourselves.

Laya looked stunning, ethereal, and…*powerful.*

"Laya!" I shouted, trying to get her attention. But, it was clear that whatever was going on with her had pulled her right out of that room. Wherever her mind was, it wasn't with us anymore. It wasn't with me.

"Laya, *please*," I called. But there was no response. "Options? Anyone?" I asked looking around.

Everyone was standing there and just staring at her. Even Eurybia.

"Great, thanks, guys," I barked.

Laya's eyes shifted and her head dropped to us. My damned heart stopped. Her eyes were shining the same white light that was in her hands as she looked at me through unseeing eyes. Then, in a voice that was not her own, she spoke.

"In a time of terrible darkness, a great light will be born. Together with the colors of heaven, a battle with the evils of old will begin."

When she was done, she looked up. The light in her eyes died, casting the room into shadow, and she fell. I caught her, heaving a sigh of relief as she rested safely in my arms. I rubbed a hand over her cheek.

"Laya? Laya?" I whispered, trying to gently wake her. She wouldn't respond.

"What happened?" I asked.

"She had a premonition," Mazz answered before anyone else.

"What? Now she can tell the future?" I said, not breaking my gaze away from her.

"It seems that way," Rayna said.

"If she has the same white power as my mother, she would be able to have premonitions and prophesies, just as my mother did. It takes a lot out of the person that has those gifts. The Claires are the ones who know the most about that," Eurybia said.

"What are Claires?" I asked.

"They are Mer with the ability to have prophesies. They are born with the gift, but it comes with a price. Each prophesy takes years off their life. Most Claires don't reach old age. You can see what the prophesies do to the body," Mazz answered.

"Years? You mean…" I looked at Laya again. No, that couldn't be right. She can't die young. She can't. I wouldn't let her.

"There must be something that we can do. What if she doesn't want the ability to see the future? Can't she just…I don't know, not do that?" I asked Eurybia.

"It's not that simple. It's in her blood. Bound to her, like her soul. I have never heard of a god saying 'no thanks' to the powers that they were blessed with," she answered.

"There's still the Fates, Jett," Rayna said. "We don't know what information they have for us. Maybe, they can tell us more about what's happening to KyLaya and why."

"We need to go," I said, looking at Eurybia.

"You need to *rest*," she said.

"No, we-"

"I understand your need to find answers, really I do, but your friends are exhausted and KyLaya won't be moving for a day at least. That was her first prophesy. Prophesies can kill, she's been through a lot in a short time. Let her rest," Eurybia said in a kind and gentle voice.

I didn't want to listen. I wanted to be on the way. I wanted, no, I *needed* answers. Laya's powers were amplifying at a rate that was dangerous. The next time they came out, I was scared it would kill her. We needed to know how to deal with them. The look on Laya's face during the prophesy haunted me. She was in agony. Thinking about it, my heart broke all over again.

So much pain.

So much power.

"Fine," I conceded. "Where's her room?"

"This one," Eurybia said, leading me into the room across from where Laya fell.

The sitting room was torn apart. Flowers had been thrown from their vases - which were toppled over, some smashed on the floor. It looked like a storm had blown through.

I suppose a storm has.

Laya's storm.

Her prophesy.

I picked Laya up in my arms, cradling her against my chest. Her face was pale and she didn't flinch in the slightest at being picked up. My chest squeezed looking at her. She seemed so innocent, but I knew, under those long lashes and flawless skin was the heart of a fighter. She would bounce back from this and come back stronger. I just feared how much it had taken out of her in the process and what that meant for our future. I honestly couldn't see my life without her in it. That was a damned scary thought.

Eurybia opened the door for me and I carried Laya to the bed, resting her gently on it. The room was massive, at least twice the size of my entire house. The bed was bigger than my entire room.

"Thank you," I said to Eurybia, as I pulled a blanket up from the bottom of the bed and over Laya.

"Your room is across the hall," she said.

"I'm not leaving her." I levelled a look at her, challenging her to argue. She didn't.

"I figured as much," she said and waved a hand. Another large bed appeared in the room beside Laya's.

"Now, that's a handy power," I commented. Eurybia chuckled lightly.

"It does have its benefits," she agreed. "There are fresh towels in the bathroom and food will be arriving soon."

"Thanks, I'm just going to sit with her," I said, taking a chair and pulling it up to the bed.

"I know you want to be by her, Jett, but you need your rest as well. You are no good to her if you are exhausted and starving. You must take care of yourself too, you know," she said.

"I'm not concerned with myself at the moment, thanks," I said, dismissing her comments. My stomach rumbled just to contradict me and made me grimace.

"Very well," she said and started for the door. "We will get to the Moirai and figure this out, Jett."

"I hope so," I answered. Eurybia left, closing the door silently behind her. My eyes went back to Laya as she rested peacefully. I grabbed the blanket and gently brought it up under her chin. Brushing her hair off of her face, I placed a kiss on her forehead.

"I love you," I whispered, only for her to hear, and settled into the chair. The bed Eurybia made for me looked enticing, but it was too far from. I would sleep in the chair, if I slept at all.

I'm here, Laya. Come back to me.

KYLAYA

DARKNESS wasn't as cold as I thought it would be. The world around me had disappeared the moment I released the energy within me. I only had the vaguest idea of what happened, but I was pretty sure that I said some stuff I had no control over.

I didn't like that - at all.

Control.

I liked control.

The black ink of the world around me was wearing thin on me the more time passed.

Is this a dream?

"Jett?" I called out, hoping that he would be there with me, somewhere. We'd figure it out. I knew we would. But, no response came.

"Damn," I uttered.

"Hello?" I shouted. "Anyone? Where am I?"

Nothing.

The soundlessness of the space was deafening. I found myself humming, just to hear my voice.

To hear a sound.

Any sound.

I didn't like my voice - I was a terrible singer - especially for a Mer. We were supposed to have been blessed with angelic voices. I was not.

My sister always made fun of me. KyLena would start singing for our parents and I, being the younger sister, would always want to join in. I inevitably would ruin her beautiful song with my crowing. She'd chase me around after and eventually we would tumble into a fit of giggles. My heart thudded in my chest with a sadness that had never really gone away since her disappearance.

"You miss your sister. I never had a sister," a woman's voice echoed in the darkness.

"Who's there?" I called. Instinctively my hands went for my daggers. They came up empty.

"Do not fear me," she said.

Her voice was velvet and honey in one. A spike of fear, lit my powers in my hands. The light filled the space, but I couldn't see anything. Even the floor beneath my feet seemed to melt into nothingness.

"I'm not here to hurt you, KyLaya. I'm here to help you," she said.

"Help me? How?" I asked.

"You're lost," she said.

"Ha! Tell me something I don't know," I laughed. "Where am I?"

"You are in an in-between. A place between living and death," she said.

"Like a coma?"

"Not really. Your mind has left your body and travelled a great distance, but it has lost its way."

"My mind can do that? Where was it trying to go?"

"Only you know that," she answered.

"Great. I know next to nothing about my body, lately," I said, placing my hands on my hips, extinguishing the light and plunging myself into pure darkness again. I focused and tried to pull the power out again, even if it only meant that I could see my feet - at least I could see something.

Nothing came.

"You must *focus*," she said.

"Really? I hadn't thought of that," I barked at the voice.

"You *are* a brave one. I'm glad of it. You'll need it," she said. I didn't like the way she said that.

"Who are you? Are you lost too?" I asked.

"No, child, I am not lost. I live here," she said.

"You live in this? No offense, but this place kinda sucks," I said. A beautiful laugh cascaded around me. I felt a warm breeze and, for the first time since I got there, my fears melted away.

"That is the first laugh I have had in longer than I can remember. Thank you," she said. "And you are right. This place *sucks*, but it was my choice and I wouldn't take it back."

"Why would you choose *this*?" I asked, genuinely wanting to know why someone would choose a dark abyss to live in.

"Oh, the same reason everyone does insane, crazy, and dangerous things," she answered. "For love, of course."

"Love? You agreed to stay here for love? That doesn't really sound like a good trade, no offense," I commented.

"What would you do for Jett if his life were at risk? If there was no other way to save him - and to guarantee that one day you would be back together?" she asked.

I thought about it.

What *wouldn't* I do to save Jett?

That was a scary thought. I knew I loved him, but until that moment I didn't realize just how much. I would sacrifice my life for his. No question.

"Yeah, I guess I do understand," I said.

"I knew you would," she replied.

"Why did you have to? How long have you been here? And you still haven't told me who you are," I said.

"Wow! You are not short on questions, are you?"

"No, I guess not," I laughed and sat down. I felt like I was having a conversation with the whole world around me. Something familiar and comforting about the woman's voice made me feel at ease. It was like talking with a long-lost friend. There was a connection there that I couldn't explain.

"I will explain all in due time. Right now, you must return to *your* loved one," she said.

"Wait! Who are you?"

"It was good to finally meet you KyLaya," she said and the darkness started to fade away. I could see light a great distance away and knew that was where I was supposed to go. I didn't have to walk.

I thought it - and was through the light and out the other side.

. . .

A GROAN MOUNTED in my throat and stuck there. The room was so incredibly light that I didn't dare open my eyes. I turned my head and planted it into something hard.

"Ow," I grumbled, again my voice sticking in my throat.

"Laya?" a deep voice said.

It took me longer than it should have to realize that I was not laying on a pillow, but in fact a body. Not just any body either - Jett's.

"Hey," I said, my voice ragged and raspy at the same time.

"Thank the gods," he whispered and pulled me into a hug. I managed to open my eyes, only to realize that the room wasn't as bright as I thought it was. It was like my eyes were still adjusting to coming through the bright light I saw in my dream.

But that was only a dream. Wasn't it?

"How are you feeling?" Jett asked as he tipped my chin up to him. My eyes looked into his and a smile pulled at the corner of his lips.

"Tired," I said. "I don't feel like I've been sleeping."

"Well, you were having a nightmare. You kept moaning and moving. I crawled in here when you started calling my name," Jett said.

I looked up at him and I could see the stress of the night in the dark circles under his eyes and the tightness in his jaw. His eyes worked over me tirelessly, like he wasn't completely sure that I was really there. I reached up and placed my hand on his cheek.

"I'm here. I'm okay," I said to him. He pulled my hand from his cheek and kissed the center of my palm. Immediately, warmth shot up my veins. My heart slammed against my chest, and demanded to be released. I drew in a quick breath at the touch of his soft warm lips. His eyes flicked to mine and I could see the worry disappear - replaced by something else. Something far better...and way more fun.

Desire.

"Jett," I whispered as he lowered his head. He stopped just as his lips were about to touch mine. Sweet agony ripped through me as I waited for him to close the gap between us. It was torture to feel him so close and yet keep so far.

"You scared me," he whispered.

"I'm sorry."

"Don't do that again."

"I will try not to," I responded. My heart fluttered tirelessly in my ribs and heat pooled in my belly, spreading toward my legs.

"You-"

"Stop talking," I demanded, and kissed him. He didn't wait. He flashed, his weight was on me and his hands on my waist. His lips worked against mine.

Hungry.

Starving.

I *loved* it.

When he broke away from me there was a flash of disappointment in me until his lips found my neck.

My. Gods.

With every kiss and flick of his tongue, heat pulsed within me. I gasped and moaned as my hands gripped his back tight. My body jerked with pleasure when he sucked on the base of my neck. I cried out. He flashed again and his lips were on mine.

"Do you know what you do to me?" he asked as he pulled back.

"I-I…no," I said honestly…breathlessly.

"Your every move. Your every sound, calls to me. Breaks almost every bit of self-control I have. You undo me, Laya. And, gods if I don't enjoy every last bit of it," he said and pressed another kiss to my lips.

Different than anything that had come before, we moved against each other. Desire matched with desperation as our limbs tangled around each other, mixed with the bedsheets. My shirt disappeared, as did his. I got an eye full of the gloriousness that was his perfectly sculpted chest and back. My gods, the man had all the muscles. I trailed a finger down his chest slowly, watching his eyes. He bit his lips as I got to the band of his pants.

"Laya," he warned, low and long.

"I don't want to wait with you," I admitted and realized that in that moment it was true. I was ready. At least I thought I was.

A low rumbling came from him and I could see the color in his eyes change from a subdued purple to a brilliant violet.

"I said, I wanted to go slow," he said as he leaned forward. I could feel the brush of his fingers as they trailed a delicate line over my bare shoulder and down along my bra strap. My breath hitched as his finger laced under it. Soft, warm kisses played on my neck and down my shoulder.

Oh, my gods. Oh, my gods!

I had never been touched like that. My heart was beating completely out of control. I was lost in the sensation of Jett's hands and lips.

His finger slipped up my strap to my shoulder as his kisses made their way to meet. When he got there, he slowly pulled the strap down my arm. My skin was on fire. I could feel my pulse everywhere.

Everywhere.

If this was his definition of going slow…yeah, I think I could get on board with that.

His hand caressed its way up my arm and around my neck. He pulled me to him, placing a hot hard kiss on my neck. I closed my eyes and bit my lip, but I couldn't stop the moan that came from deep within me. I could feel his smile against my skin. His tongue flicked against my skin and I pressed harder against him, wanting more. Needing more.

I had lost all control, but it wasn't scary. This time I trusted it. I trusted him. Pain and pleasure dancing through me, and I found myself at the mercy of his touch as his fingers trailed across my collarbone to my other shoulder. His lips came back to mine and it was like coming home again. Hot and sweet, his kiss deepened. His hand was on my shoulder when I felt his finger slip under my bra strap. My eyes opened at once. So did his. He watched me closely as he gently glided the strap down.

Holy Hades.

I could feel my bra shift as it settled into a much lower position. Jett's eyes dipped down and he swallowed. I blushed and smiled. No one had ever looked at me the way he did.

"You're stunning," he whispered.

"Jett…" I uttered as he closed the space between us. His hands were flat against my back, the heat from them sinking into my skin. Then I felt it, the flick of the clasp. The material loosened and fell. A shudder ran through me as Jett brought his hands up my back. He trailed a hand across my collarbone and slowly down the center of my chest. An ache opened in my core and I held my breath. He pulled back just enough to put a small space between us as his fingers slipped down between my breasts and pulled the only material between our bare skin down and away from me.

His lips found mine as he pressed against me. The feel of his skin on mine was intoxicating. I knew there was no way I could surface from this. I was being pulled under by the most glorious wave of pleasure I had ever felt.

I opened my eyes and the room was bright. Like a star had suddenly appeared. Looking down, I saw where the light was coming from.

Us.

I jumped back from Jett with a shout. He flashed away from me as the door burst open.

"What is it?" Mazz shouted as he tumbled into the room and blinding light.

"Get out!" Jett shouted at him, as I clamoured for a sheet to cover myself. The light faded as the situation completely lost its sexiness.

"You okay, Laya?" Mazz said, ignoring Jett. When Mazz finally saw me, covering my bare chest with a flimsy sheet he blushed hard.

"Oh," he said with a groan, glaring at Jett. No one said anything as he left the room.

"Well, that's definitely one way to kill the mood," Jett said as he sat on the bed in front of me. "Are you okay?" he asked.

"Yes, I'm fine. Did you see it? The light?" I asked him.

"How could I miss it?"

"What was that?" I asked.

"I have no idea," he said and reached out for me. When his hand touched my skin, light ignited between his skin and mine. I had this sudden urge to jump him and continue where we left off. It was so intense that I almost did it. He gasped and drew back is hand.

"Whoa," he said.

"Did you feel it too?" I asked him.

"Yes. This *desire*. I've always desired you, but this was next level stuff," he looked up at me and his eyes were white light. My heart jumped in my throat.

"What is it?" he said, placing his hands on my arms.

"I – your eyes, Jett," I uttered, unable to break away from his stare.

He grabbed a mirror off of the dresser and looked at himself.

"Holy shit!" he shouted, clearly just as surprised as I was.

"What's going on with us," I asked.

"I think I can answer that," Eurybia said from the open door.

"How long have you been standing there?" I asked.

"Long enough," she answered. "Get dressed. We have some Fates to see." With that, she closed the door. I looked at Jett. His eyes were dimming.

"I…"

"It'll be fine, Laya," Jett said, trying to comfort me.

How can he be so freaking calm? His eyes were just glowing!

"Try not to freak out. One step at a time, remember? Let's just get dressed and see what Eurybia is thinking," he said.

"Okay. Get dressed. I can do that," I said. Jett leaned over and placed a kiss on my lips. That same ache opened up inside me and I reached for him. I grabbed the back of his neck and pulled him in for a deeper, longer kiss.

"Whoa," I said, pulling back - finding a remnant of self-control.

"Yeah," Jett said with a tipped-up grin that made me want to grab him all over again.

Ugh, he was so crazy hot.

JETT

LAYA and I pulled apart from each other long enough for me to get dressed. If I stayed in that room with her, there was no way we would get more clothes on, so I decided it was better if I just left. When she went for a quick shower, I snuck from the room. With my hand on the door knob I paused, not wanting to face what laid past her door. She had destroyed the room with her prophesy. The power within her was staggering, and I had a sick feeling that we were only getting a taste of what she was truly capable of. When the shower started, I opened the door.

The room was…perfect.

Cleaned from top to bottom and put back exactly as it was before, it shone with a polish that wasn't dimmed by Laya's storm. I couldn't believe it. Eurybia was sipping tea, sitting on the couch, and staring hard at the wall.

"I'm really sorry about the mess, Eurybia," I said as I settled in across from her on the couch. She smiled kindly and handed me a cup and saucer. I accepted them, needing a taste of home more than I realized. Tea always calmed me.

"Please, don't apologize Jett," Eurybia said. "KyLaya has no control over her powers. She is just starting to wake them. There will be accidents, it's natural. As you can see, there is no harm done."

The room looked like nothing had occurred in it at all. Everything sparkled and shone as before.

"You have quite the talent for cleaning up," I said. "Or some really amazing housekeepers."

Eurybia chuckled. "I have my ways, I suppose."

I nodded and sipped from my cup of tea. The hot sweet liquid ran down my throat, warming me. I could feel it traveling along, all the way to my stomach. It was a sensation that I enjoyed immensely and one that I always looked forward to. I must have closed my eyes, because when I opened them Eurybia was staring at me.

"Sorry," I said and cleared my throat.

"No, it's fine. You clearly are enjoying it," she smiled.

"That obvious, huh?"

"A little."

I could feel my cheeks burn and knew that a change of topic was needed.

"What's going on with Laya and me? Why do we create light? How do we do that? What is it?"

"So many questions!" Eurybia said with a giggle. She leaned forward and placed her cup and saucer on the coffee table without a sound.

"I can't say for sure," she began, "but I *have* heard of a connection such as yours. It is very rare even among…people like you."

"People like us? What's that supposed to mean?" I asked.

"I've only heard of a connection like that being between *gods*," she said hesitantly. I sat back in the chair heavily. My hands dangling between my legs.

"I don't understand," I said. I mean, I knew what she was getting at, but that just couldn't be possible. It couldn't.

"Like I said, I don't know for sure. I *do*, however, know that we need to get to the Moirai. There are things at play here that are beyond even my knowledge," she stood. "Is KyLaya ready?"

"I'm ready," Laya said from the door.

"Let's go," Eurybia said.

"What about the others?" Laya asked, looking at the other doors around the sitting room.

"I'm sorry, this trip is just for you two," she said and grasped our hands. There was a *pop* and Eurybia's home disappeared in front of us.

. . .

At the sound of the *pop*, the air was knocked right out of me. I doubled over, drawing in a ragged breath that burned my lungs. My chest hurt like someone had run me over with a tractor.

I couldn't talk.

When coughing finally came, and I knew I was going to be okay - then I saw Laya.

"Laya!" I shouted and dove for her. She was spread out on the ground, at an unnatural angle. Her skin was white and blood was oozing from her nose and eyes.

"Laya! Come on," I coaxed, as I grabbed her up into my arms. "Eurybia! Where are you?" I shouted. No answer came. There was only silence.

"Wake up, Laya. Please," I begged, brushing my hand over her face. *Gods what happened? What did she do to you?*

"Help!" I called. "Someone, *please!*" I kissed her forehead and it was cold. I placed a hand on her neck and felt for a pulse.

Nothing.

No...

"No!"

There was a snap.

A rip.

The feeling of having my heart torn out of me, raw and ragged, rang through my body. Tearing and cutting deep in to my chest, the pain consumed me in a fire of rage and sadness.

I bellowed like a mad man. Grasping a lifeless Laya tightly against my chest, I yelled until I went hoarse. Until the sound of my voice was an echo in the back of my mind.

Pain. Agony. They tore through me like a ravenous beast; their talons carving into my heart and slashing apart my soul.

Hugging her fiercely, I succumbed to the pain.

Angry tears fell from my eyes as I lowered my head to hers.

"Laya, *please.* Don't do this," I whispered through my heavy sobs.

She laid there.

Still.

Silent.

Cold.

I rocked her gently. The feel of her cool skin against mine broke a new part of me every second. I closed my eyes and hugged Laya closer.

Take me, please. Not her.

Never her.

Her cheek rested against mine as scorching tears burnt down my skin.

"I love you," I whispered and kissed her forehead.

I let go.

Pain and sadness rushed out of me in a torrent of anguish.

Warm light lit under my skin and seeped out. Long tendrils of it lifted from me as I sat there with Laya in my arms. My heart broke all over again thinking about the light that the two of us had created.

Our connection.

Our love.

The light reached higher and higher. It lit my entire body, coming through my clothes and stretching for the sky. I looked up and eased a breath out.

Our light.

Waving in the air above us, it spread out in a stunning cloud of light.

Then it stopped.

I watched as the waves stilled. Breathless I stared and waited. With a turn, the tendrils plunged back down toward me and Laya. Instinct jumped to action. Throwing myself over Laya, I tried to protect her from the power of the light - but it was no good. The light went right through me and into her.

Her chest bucked off the floor, and her back arched against the energy that filled her. When her body couldn't take anymore, her eyes opened and light exploded from them. In a silent scream, her mouth opened and rays streamed out. It was terrifying. Her body, animated only by the power that we created, gave the appearance of life once again. I was still holding her when the last glow died away. She fell back into my arms again. Resting lifelessly against me.

An ache opened all over again, as my heart clenched tight.

I closed my eyes against the pain, unable to take it anymore. Scorching tears burned a trail down my face.

A hand pressed against my cheek and I flinched, opening my eyes.

Icy blue eyes stared up at me.

"Laya?"

"I'm here," she whispered back. Her hand moved on my cheek, warm and soft.

"It can't be," I uttered, staring at her. *I must be seeing things.*

"I'm here," she said again. "I'm here." She sat up and looked at me. *And hearing things.*

I reached out and placed a hand on her cheek. She closed her eyes and leaned against my hand with a wistful smile.

It can't be. It's too good to be true.

"Is it…really you?" I asked, the words barely able to form on my lips.

"Dreamstop?" she said with a smile.

My jaw opened, but no sound came from me. She looked at me, and I was lost in her eyes. A sob balled in my throat, choking and burning me. I pulled her into my arms - hard and hungry - as if she would slip through my grasp at any second. It was her. She was okay. I ran a hand down her soft hair. Sitting back, I looked at her. Really looked. My heart nearly exploded.

I was consumed with love for her.

I kissed her.

I mean I *really* kissed her.

"Yup, it's them alright," a crackly voice said.

Laya and I pulled away from each other and looked for the source. My eyes nearly popped out of my head. We weren't alone.

Eurybia and three ancient women stood off to a corner of the now lit room - the darkened space Laya and I had arrived at was gone. I stood slowly, placing Laya behind me. Pink lit across my skin as I looked at Eurybia.

"What did you do to Laya?" I shouted at her. It took everything in me not to blast her two faces right of her shoulders.

"I didn't have a choice," she said, holding out her hands.

I didn't care. Power lit over my entire body as the gravity of the situation took me. I was still hurting. Rage ignited within me once again, fueled by the pain of losing Laya.

She was dead.

She was *dead!*

There was a snap in my core. Vibration buzzed up my spine, radiating through my bones. A pulse exploded from me, like a plough wind. Something within my was opening - from it…power.

So much *power.*

I couldn't stop the release. With a holler that came from my soul, light shot out of me straight for the women and Eurybia.

Not just any light.

White light.

The impact of the energy shook the room, sending rock crashing down on us all. When the dust settled, I fell to the floor utterly spent.

"Jett?" A hand rested gently on my shoulder. I turned to Laya. The air was full of dust.

"Is she?" I asked.

"No, I'm not."

Laya and I looked up. Through the dust we could see the outline of an electric ball. Its light, blue in hue, lit the inside of the cave through the dust and debris of the explosion. Within it was Eurybia and the three ancient women. Alive and unharmed.

"How?" I uttered looking at them in astonishment. I had aimed to kill. I glared at Eurybia and the women behind her. Their hands lowered and the shield dropped. That's when I realized the women were the reason that Eurybia was alive.

"They took you both the moment we got here. I'm sorry. Truly, I am. I didn't know there was a test," Eurybia said, looking back at the women with anger.

"Test? What *test*?" Laya asked, coming out from behind me. Her eyes glowed and white power was lit in her palms. She narrowed a glare on Eurybia and the three women. "And who are you?"

"They are the Moirai," Eurybia said, answering Laya. Laya didn't say anything as she stepped toward them.

The three women stood tall and slim; their white robes draped to the floor in a delicate fabric like nothing I had ever seen before. They looked ancient, their eyes shaded by wrinkled skin, and their hair long and white. There was a great power in them - I could feel it in the air. The shield that they had created was no small feat of strength. Though, they may have looked old and fragile, I was no fool; their powers were as old as time itself.

"I don't give a shit who you are!" I yelled. "Why did you kill Laya? What the hell is going on here?" I yelled, glaring at all of them and pulling Laya behind me again. There was no way I was chancing her getting injured. I saved her once and I had no idea how I did it. I didn't know if I would be able to do it again - I certainly didn't want to have to try.

"We had to know if what Eurybia said was true."

Their voices echoed around us, but not one of the women opened her mouth to speak. The sound of them seemed to come from the air itself.

"The Moirai have a different way of speaking. Don't be alarmed. They don't mean you harm," Eurybia said.

"Bullshit," I bit back.

"They are the ones. There is no doubt. He brought her back. They are who you say they are."

"Just what the hell is going on here?" I shouted. As frustration mounted in me, my powers leaked through my skin seeping out in hair-like light. Laya placed her hand on my arm and the light retreated at her touch. I looked down into her eyes and relief flooded me again.

She was alive.

I grabbed her hand from my arm and pulled it to my chest, needing to feel her closer to me. Needing to feel the life in her veins, her warmth. Her hand tightened in mine, as if she knew my need. My fear. My pain. The absolute devastation of losing her. It would never leave me.

Ever.

"You have come here for answers. We will give you that."

"Yes. Answers," Laya said, squeezing my hand. "What's happening to us? What are we?"

I looked at the women, knowing they were the only source of the answers we needed, and yet not able to shake the urge to zap them out of existence. Grasping Laya's hand harder I reined in my anger. We had to have some answers to what was happening to us, no matter how much I wanted to blast the crap out of the three old crones.

"To answer the questions you have, we must go back to the beginning. To a time where Gaia ruled the world and Uranus, her love, reigned at her side."

"That's my mother," Eurybia said with a sweet smile.

"Gaia and Uranus had a love unlike all others. True. Selfless. Pure. It was this love that gave them the ability to set forth a plan that will protect the earth from the reign of the Titans."

"They helped the Olympians defeat the Titans, right?" I asked.

"No, they didn't."

"But I thought that you said-"

"We said that they will *protect the world, not that they already did."*

"Like, you mean in the future?" Laya asked.

"The Titans will rise again and bring with them the chaos and terror that they did long ago. Gaia and Uranus knew this. They also knew that the power the Olympians had the first time wouldn't be enough. Kronus was very strong, almost too strong back then. The Olympians wouldn't be able to do it again. There was, and still is, only one power that can take out Kronus."

"What power?"

"Kronus' power was close to pure power. Only power that is closer to the first power can defeat it."

Laya and I looked at Eurybia.

"Nope, not me," she said, waving her hands. "Kronus' power far exceeds mine. My father wasn't Uranus. I don't have the blood of both primordial gods in me, but Kronus does."

"So, you're saying that the only powers that can challenge Kronus are Gaia and Uranus," I said.

"They are the first. They are the white power, the purest of the gods. Only their power can stop him this time."

"But, aren't they dead?" Laya asked.

"Not dead. Sleeping," Eurybia explained.

"Okay, so how do we wake them up and, you know, tell them to stop Kronus," I asked. "Wait, is Kronus even…isn't he in Tartarus?"

"The rest of the Titans are locked in Tartarus, but Kronus is not."

"Wait, I thought *all* the Titans were locked in Tartarus," Laya said.

"That is what the gods wanted everyone to think - but it is not true. A special chamber was made just for Kronus. After all, he was the one who led the Titans against Uranus, and he was the leader when Zeus fought against him. Without his leadership the rest of the Titans wouldn't have fought in either war."

"Okay, so wouldn't that mean that he's in like a highly secured cell?" I asked, placing my hands on my hips.

"Yes, but that hasn't stopped him from collecting allies."

"Who would want to work with a guy like that?" Laya asked.

"Not all Titans were locked up. There are some that didn't fight on either side during the war. When the Olympians took over, the remaining Titans were cast aside, their powers reduced and their domains taken away."

"It wasn't a great time for us," Eurybia said. "Some of us took it harder than others."

"So, you're saying that someone is so mad that they are willing to unleash the Titans to teach the Olympians a lesson?" I asked. That seemed like a slight overreaction to me.

The Titans were true chaos. Fear. Violence. They reigned with supreme terror during their time. I couldn't imagine who would want to go back to that. Except for one…

"Ares. He's one of the supporters, isn't he?" I asked.

"It's got to be," Laya confirmed.

"With a child so violent and cruel, Gaia and Uranus sought out help and guidance. They came to us," they continued.

"Did they create you?" Laya asked.

"No. We came into existence as they did. You might say that the universe gave birth to us."

"Then your power must be light too. You are primordial."

"We are not gods. We are 'other'. We do not fight. We exist outside all."

"In other words, you're not helping us," I uttered. Laya nudged me and I shrugged. "What? It's true."

She shook her head.

"When Gaia and Uranus came to us, we told them that Kronus would one day rise against Uranus and kill him. Gaia was beside herself. She couldn't face living out the rest of her existence without her love. To save Uranus, she made a deal with Kronus. She wouldn't fight against him in the battle with the Olympians if he would let Uranus live. Kronus refused the deal. He knew that his parents' powers together could destroy him, and he wasn't about to let them wander together for eternity and plot against him. He planned to kill Uranus, thus solidifying his place as the most powerful being in the world. Unstoppable. So, with our help, Gaia put Uranus into a deep sleep. One that would last until Kronus was completely destroyed, and therefore keep Kronus from fulfilling his murderous plan. Once Kronus dies, Uranus will waken to join Gaia and they will live out their existence together once again."

"Once Kronus dies? Like, as in *we* kill him?" Laya asked.

"Yes."

"How? How do you kill a Titan when the powers you need to destroy him are *sleeping?*" Laya asked.

"You give your powers away to someone else."

"What?" Laya and I said at the same time.

"After Kronus was defeated by Zeus and the Olympians, Gaia came to us. The world was safe from her terrible son, and no longer needed her protection. She requested to be put in the same sleep as Uranus, as she refused to live in a world without her beloved. Knowing that the only thing that could open Kronus' chamber

was her power, she bestowed her power on another; so that one day, the chamber would be opened and Kronus would be released."

"Why in the world would she want Kronus released?" I shouted.

"Because, the only way for Uranus to awaken is Kronus' death. For him to die, he needs to be released and destroyed," Laya answered, looking at the Moirai.

"You are bright, KyLaya of Triton."

"She would risk the world for love?" I asked.

"Wouldn't you?"

I looked at Laya. Her hand tightened in mine and I knew in an instant that, yes, I would. I would release all the Titans myself if that meant that she would live. I hung my head and nodded. Laya tightened her grip on my hand and pulled me into a hug. I pulled her hard against me. My heart swelled having her against me.

"What is our part in all this?" I asked, as Laya drew back from me.

"You know what your part is."

I looked at Laya and she looked at me. I knew - I just *really* wanted to be wrong.

"It's been our job to steer you together since the moment you were born. Only together can the prophesy come true. Only together can Kronus be defeated, and Gaia and Uranus reunited," Eurybia said.

"But…"

"It's *us,*" Laya whispered, placing her hand on my cheek. "You know it is. We've always known there was something about us that was…*more*. Don't you *feel* it?"

"Feel it? Yes, I feel it." I answered, dreading that sensation more now than ever. The power. The knowledge. It all came to me when I snapped on Eurybia and the Moirai. An echo at the back of my mind fed me information that wasn't there before. I could feel a hum in my veins. My very skin felt different, new…invincible.

"You are the reincarnations of Gaia and Uranus. You have been blessed with their powers and knowledge."

"How is this…why us?" I asked.

"We saw you two long ago. Strong. Smart. It is your love for one another that created the bond. Even without the reincarnation, you would have found one another; you were destined to. There are very few pure loves in the world and yours is one of them. Just like Gaia and Uranus"

Laya looked up at me and I couldn't help but smile back at her.

"So, we're supposed to release Kronus and then kill him," I said, looking at the women unconvinced. "Did I get that right or am I missing something?"

"Why can't we just leave him in there? I mean, I know that Gaia and Uranus have been waiting to be reunited; but we aren't exactly equipped to take on a Titan - let alone the leader of them," Laya suggested.

Damn good idea.

"The gate to his prison was designed by Gaia. She knew Kronus better than anyone. She was his mother after all. The prison will open as soon as it senses her power. There's a chance that it is open already," Eurybia explained.

"Wouldn't we know if a Titan was walking around?" Laya asked.

"We don't know what condition he is in. There were other precautions made that would keep him incapacitated even if the door was opened. He needs a few…things before he can recharge," Eurybia explained.

"Things? What *things*?" I asked.

"His essence was pulled from him and split up. What's left in Tartarus is a shell. He needs his essences back to become the Titan he once was," Eurybia answered.

"Where are they?" I asked.

"Not *where*. *Who*."

"What do you mean *who*?" Laya asked, her eyes narrowing.

Please say it's not us.

"When Kronus' essences were pulled from him they were divided into three pieces: head, heart, and soul. Since his entombment, generation after generation, his essences are born into a being. When they die, the essence moves on to another."

"So, some poor schmuck is walking around sporting Kronus' darling personality?" I asked.

"In a way, yes," Eurybia answered. "His *head* is his personality and intellect. His *heart* is his aspiration and desire. His *soul* is the base form of him…and it's dark and dangerous."

"So, he can't become fully formed unless he has all of his essences?" I asked.

"Correct. He needs all of his essences to become full, but he can rise with just one."

"Great," I uttered.

"How do we stop him?" Laya asked.

"You must find the essences and destroy them."

"How on earth do we do *that*?" I asked.

"Your powers are more than just a gift; they have a purpose. Gaia's power can absorb the essence, power, and knowledge of a god. KyLaya has this power. She will be able to absorb the essences of Kronus. Once they are all captured, they can be destroyed."

"You want her to keep all of Kronus' essences inside her? Are you insane?" I yelled.

"Jett," Laya muttered.

"No! This is crazy! It's too dangerous!" I said. There was *no way* I was going to agree to Laya taking Kronus' soul into her. That kind of power was unlike anything that the world has seen in a millennium. He was the most violent, malicious, and deadly of the Titans. No way in Hades was I letting Laya absorb a drop of that.

"Is there any other way?" I asked the Fates and Eurybia.

"I'm sorry. This was set in motion long ago."

"Let *me* do it then. I'll take his essence. Not Laya," I said.

"Jett," Laya said placing a hand on my arm. I turned to her as her eyes met mine.

"I can't lose you again, Laya. I can't," I whispered. She rose up on her toes and placed her forehead against mine.

"I'm not going anywhere," she whispered. "I'm sure that Gaia's powers will protect me from Kronus. She would have known that his essences are strong. I'll be fine."

"You don't know that," I said.

"Neither do you," she answered. I looked into her brilliant icy blue eyes and sighed. Everything in me screamed that this was a bad idea.

"Gaia knew what she was doing," Eurybia said. "KyLaya is strong enough. I assure you. My mother wouldn't have chosen her if she wasn't."

"I don't doubt her strength," I said. "But there is no accounting for the strength of Kronus' essences. No one has ever done this before. You don't know what you are asking."

"We do know. We have had a very long time to think about it, and what it would mean to you and the world. There is no use fighting it. Kronus is rising and

if you don't help, the world is doomed to fall to his evil reign. You must decide what you will do."

Laya looked at me. Her back straightened, her chin went up, as she nodded. Royal Laya appeared in front of me before I could argue again.

"I will stop Kronus. Whatever that means for me in the end…so be it," she said with a determined nod. My heart hit the floor and then bounced up my throat.

"Damn it," I uttered. "You know there's no way I'm letting you do any of this on your own. I'm with you, no matter what."

"I know," Laya said with a smile that set my heart on fire. *Damn, I love her.*

"There is one more thing," Eurybia said.

"What's that?" I asked.

"KyLaya's powers are wakening. She has the power of Gaia, as you have the power of Uranus. There is a chance that her powers will consume her if she doesn't find a way to focus and control them."

"What?" Laya stuttered.

"Why aren't mine an issue then?" I asked.

"You already have a damper on you. It focuses your power and keeps it in check for you," she answered. *What?*

"No, I don't," I said shaking my head. "I have no idea what you're talking about."

"Your ring," Eurybia said, stepping toward me and pulling my hand up.

"My ring?" I whispered. "It was a gift from my mother."

"It has the ability to focus your power. It's been keeping your powers in check, not allowing them to take full form," she explained.

"I have *more* power?" I asked. Eurybia nodded and slid the ring off my finger in one swift motion.

I felt the change immediately and knew that what I had experienced up until then, was barely a taste of what I was truly capable of. I also knew, I had no control over it.

When the energy mounted within me, I felt the ancient voice of Uranus surge forward and a knowledge that had been held from me formed in the back of my mind.

So much knowledge.

So much power.

KYLAYA

THE AIR PULSED as Eurybia took the ring off Jett's finger. White light lit in his core, shining through bone and muscle. He looked like he was made of light - pure light. His unseeing eyes, white orbs as bright as a star, opened and looked at me – no, *through* me.

I couldn't catch my breath as I stared at him. He was both stunning and terrifying at the same time. Whited knuckled, his hands balled tightly at his sides. His muscles flexed and strained, strung tight and hard over his body. I could see Jett trying to take on the power raging inside him; fighting to maintain control.

A guttural shout broke from him as the light intensified. My heart kicked at my chest and I started to panic. It was hurting him. He started yelling and the blood drained from me. I looked at Eurybia, but she did nothing.

"Help him!" I yelled at her. Her eyes were stuck to him, watching with a curiosity that was disturbing. She wanted to see what would happen. I looked to Jett. His muscles were taut and his face clenched in pain. If he didn't get Uranus's power under control, it was going to kill him.

I watched in horror as his skin split on his cheek, just a small crack, and light streamed out of it.

I stopped breathing. Jett was breaking apart.

"Stop! Give him back the ring!" I screamed. Running to Eurybia, I grabbed for the ring. She moved her hand high, out of my reach. I stopped and looked at her.

"Give me that ring," I uttered. My words were laced with poison. If she didn't hand me that ring, I would pull everything from her and leave her like a Kronus shell. "Now."

She didn't even flinch. Moving faster than I intended, I clamped a hand over her arm and pulled. Immediately, I could feel her power course through me. Eurybia's eyes flew open and she screamed.

"The ring!" I demanded, sparing a look back at Jett. There was almost nothing left of him but light. When she didn't give it to me, I pulled harder. Another scream cut from her lips and pierced my ears, but I wasn't giving up. I grabbed her hand and pried her fingers open, forcibly taking the ring from her. In that moment I pulled more and was struck by a vision…a memory.

I looked at Eurybia. Her eyes were still on Jett, transfixed. I looked back at Jett.

Through the memory, fresh behind my eyes, I could see the terrible power of Uranus. Where Gaia created, Uranus destroyed. He was her compliment, her match. They evened out the universe. But, in the vision Uranus was out of control. Evil.

"No," I said. "Jett wouldn't. He would never…"

I saw Gaia pull power from him, sending him into the great slumber he was still in. The destruction he had brought upon the world was devastating. Earthquakes. Volcanoes erupting. Tsunamis. The world shook under his power. His destructive and violent power.

And now it was alive within Jett.

I grabbed the ring from her and rushed to him. The light was so intense I could feel it through my skin. It was the power I saw in the memory from Eurybia. That same destructive energy danced along the current's edges, craving havoc. Demanding to be unleashed.

"Gods," I hissed as I grabbed Jett's hand and forced the ring on his rigid finger. The moment it slid home the light went out. Jett fell to the floor in a dead heap.

"Jett!" I yelled trying to catch him. His weight took me down with him. I managed to stop his head from hitting the floor.

Gods, Jett. I'm so sorry.

"Why did you let it go on so long?" I asked, glaring at Eurybia. She looked dazed as she shook her head, clearing it. When she looked up at me, there was clarity in her expression for the first time since she took the ring from Jett.

"He had to understand the power of the gifts of Uranus. Through pain comes knowledge. He will be able to control more next time."

"Next time? You've got to be kidding, he's not going to want to do that again and I'm not going to make him."

"He must practice until sliding the ring off produces no flare up. You both will have to learn to control your powers. Taking on the essence of Kronus will take you both. You need control over your powers before you can do that."

"Can't you just teach us?"

"These aren't just any gift, KyLaya. Only through pain will you find the clarity and knowledge that you need. You must understand that."

I didn't understand that. I didn't understand any of it. Being strong and facing all this with faith in the power that was gifted to me, seemed insane. I needed to know more about what was going on with me, and how to deal with it. Trial and error was *not* the way to go about this. I needed training.

The power of *Gaia* ran through *my* veins.

Just that alone was enough for me to lose it. Add on the part about taking on Kronus and I was dangerously close to rocking in the corner sucking my thumb.

Then…there was the vision I saw from Eurybia.

My heart gave one solid, painful, thump.

I saw what Uranus's powers were, what they could do. My heart ached, knowing what was waking within Jett. From what I saw, Uranus had gone power-mad at the end and Gaia stopped him from destroying the world. Whatever their love story had been before that, was gone. She took him out to save the world, not to save him from Kronus.

I glanced over at Eurybia and the Fates.

That wasn't the story that they had told us – not even close. What were they hiding?

I looked down at Jett. His eyes weren't pinched in pain anymore. Sleep had taken him. The experience had been too much. I hoped against everything that the vision was a mistake - that the story they told us was the truth. That Uranus didn't go off the deep end with power. But, no matter how much I tried to push it to the back of my mind, there was now this shadow that hung over me…and Jett.

I could make my peace with my own death. I could. I knew that taking on the essence of Kronus wasn't going to be easy and could, in reality, kill me. But, if that meant saving the world from the Titans, I could do that. However, if it was Jett…

Pain erupted in my chest traveling straight to my stomach, as panic settled in.

I can't lose him. I won't lose him.

Anything. I would do *anything* to save him. To keep him from being hurt. There had to be a way to contain his powers so that they didn't take him over. The way that everything came out of him was downright terrifying. There wasn't a moment where he looked like he wasn't in complete pain. He can't keep doing that in hopes that, at some point, he will be able to control his power. It would destroy him; and, there was no way that I was going to stand by and watch as he slowly killed himself trying to control whatever it was that raged inside him. There had to be another way.

I wasn't going to give up until I found out what that was.

JETT

I MOANED and rolled over. It felt like I had been hit by a grain truck and driven over a couple of times. Yet, I didn't feel like anything was broken. It was all my muscles. Like, every single one of them.

"Hey, you," a sweet voice whispered in my ear. I turned over and looked into the most beautiful set of eyes.

"Hey," I said. My words came out sounding like I had a throat full of gravel.

"Don't talk," Laya said. "You've been through a lot. Rest."

I didn't say anything, instead I wrapped an arm around her waist and pulled her close to me. Everything in my world felt better and made sense when she was safe in my arms.

"How long have I been out?" I asked.

"A day."

"A day!" I rolled and scrubbed my face with my hands. "My gods, Jasper! He's got to be going insane."

"We're back at Eurybia's. And, yes, he was going insane. Right along with Mazz. Be happy that you were unconscious for all that," she laughed lightly.

"I'm so sorry, Laya," I said, pulling her across my chest. Her hand fell delicately over my ribs as she snuggled against me. "You okay?"

"Well, my ears are still ringing from getting yelled at, but other than that I'm fine," she said.

"Is it weird that I'm happy to be here?" I asked.

She turned her face up to me and raised an eyebrow. "A little."

"Being here in bed with you is way better than the tomb of the Moirai," I shrugged.

"True," she said and ran her fingers through my hair. "Very true."

"How are you…dealing?" I asked. At the edge of my mind there was something bugging me. I couldn't put my finger on it. The slight down-turn to her mouth. The quick flit away from my eyes. Laya was keeping something from me.

"I'm dealing," she said, looking away from me. I sat up and turned her face towards me.

"What is it?" I asked, forcing her to look at me.

"Nothing," she said, shrugging.

"Liar," I said. "I know when you're hiding something from me. What is it?"

"I'm not hiding anything from you, Jett. It's all…just a lot to take in, you know? I don't know what I'm supposed to do with all this information…all this power."

I settled down a little. *Am I being paranoid?* We'd been through a lot in the last few days, she was bound to be off. It nagged at me, but I decided to let it go for the moment.

"Is there anything that I can do to help you?" I asked, placing my hand over hers.

"You could kiss me," she said sincerely. Her gaze fell to mine and I was lost in it. "You scared me. I thought…I thought I was going to lose you for a moment there."

"I'm sorry. I tried. I really did. Uranus's power is…extreme." Just to make sure I remembered how extreme, I shifted and my muscles in my back and stomach screamed at me in protest. I grunted against the pain, as I moved to get more comfortable. Letting out a sigh, I sank back into the bed.

"I saw the extremeness," she said. "I can also see how much you are paying for it today." She ran a hand down my chest, grasped the blanket and pulled it up my bare skin. "I'm sorry Eurybia did that to you. She should have warned you or something."

"I don't think it would have made a difference what she told me. It still would have shocked me. There was so much more than just what the power brought. I felt more of what Uranus felt. For a moment, I had his memories, his thoughts. It was incredible and completely overwhelming. Imagine a primordial's memories all of a sudden appearing in your mind. There wasn't enough room in there for them. It hurt…a lot."

"My gods, Jett," she whispered as her eyes softened.

"It wasn't all bad. Through the pain, I could feel his love for you…for Gaia. It fell into pace right along with my love for you. Like the two of them were one. You look like her," I said. In the back of my mind was a picture of a stunning woman. When I saw Laya out of the corner of my eye, that woman popped into my head. Every time her face came forward, I knew that she was someone special to Uranus. I knew it could only be Gaia.

I leaned in and placed a kiss on Laya's lips. She was soft and sweet and a rush lit across my skin, like a warm breeze. When I leaned back again, there was a warm glow between us.

"I wonder if that has something to do with Gaia and Uranus," Laya asked.

"Seem most things are related to them, so my guess would be yes," I answered.

"That bothers you?" Laya asked looking at me.

"Kind of," I said with a shrug. "I've never put too much stock in fate and now it seems that my life is ruled by it. It's frustrating to know that every move, every decision I make is preordained. Like nothing is really *my* choice. I don't like it."

"I get that," she said and leaned in toward me. "I look at it another way. We *were* meant to meet, but the fact that I fell in love with you was my own doing. I might be a reincarnation of Gaia's powers but I'm *not* her. You're *not* Uranus. We could have met and hated each other. I don't believe that everything that we do is out of our control. I believe things have been put in our path to help us get to the truth. I mean, if I were Gaia, and had to worry about my son eventually taking over the world and turning it into a mass war zone, I would have done everything I could have to help the ones that could stop that. But, in the end, *we* have to decide what we're going to do. *We* have to choose that for ourselves. No one can do that for us, Jett."

"Sometimes, I forget how stunningly smart you are," I uttered, a smile stretching across my face. Laya's intellect was only a fraction of what I loved about her, but damn it was a sexy part.

She was a born leader. It was a role that she took on with grace and dignity. I knew she would be all on board. She would face Kronus alone if that's what it would take to save the world. I loved that determination about her; but it also scared the hell out of me.

I grabbed her face and kissed her.

She squealed in surprise, but just as quickly melted into me. She sat up and draped her arms around me, pulling herself into my lap.

Damn.

The feel of her on me was intoxicating. Threading my fingers behind her head and into her hair, I tilted her head back and trailed a line of kisses down her neck.

"Jett…" she whispered. The sound of my name on her lips brought a smile to mine.

"Gods, your skin is so sweet and soft," I whispered and I kissed her gently at the base of her neck. She gasped and moaned at my touch, and it took everything in me not to flash her under me.

A knock sounded at the door.

"Ugh," I groaned. Laya's head fell back down as she slid me a sly smile.

"Don't look so disappointed," she teased.

"I liked where that was going," I said. She bit her lip and smiled.

"Hello?" a voice called from the door.

"Come in!" I shouted in frustration.

The door opened and Jasper walked in.

"Hey," I started, but Jasper closed the distance between us in two steps and launched at me. I scrunched up my face, ready to be punched in it. I knew Jasp was mad that we had disappeared, and was ready to hear about it.

My eyes flew open when his arms wrapped around me, pulling me in for a bear hug.

"Thank the gods you're okay," he uttered into my shoulder.

"Oh, Jasp," I said and hugged him back.

"You scared the shit out of me, you jerk," he scolded as he pulled back. "Don't ever do that again, you hear me?"

"I-"

Jasper narrowed his eyes and pointed at me.

"Okay! Sorry!" I apologized again.

"Ky explained what happened, well, some of what happened," Jasper said and took a seat on the bed with Laya and me. "I'd like to hear it from you."

"We all would," Sam said, stepping into the room. The door opened wider and Mazz and Rayna stood on the other side, their eyes on Laya and me.

"Who ordered the bedroom party?" I asked Laya. She laughed lightly and waved everyone in. Mazz and Rayna pulled chairs up to the bed for Sam and them.

Laya and I went through everything - from the moment we were taken to the Fates by Eurybia to returning there. We filled in the empty spaces for each other, where the other was missing information. It was the first time that Laya had heard what happened to her and me when we first arrived at the Moirai. Until then, she hadn't known about her death. Her eyes were full of tears as I explained what happened. My throat closed up thinking about it again and for a moment I couldn't speak. It was her hand wrapped around mine that got me focused again.

Laya took over telling the story after she woke up. She told them what happened when Eurybia took off my ring and it was the first time I heard what it was like for her to see me like that. I felt terrible and guilty that she had to go through that.

"So, we have to go look for Kronus' essences now. It's the only way to kill him," Laya explained to everyone.

"Sure, no problem," Jasper said with an eye-roll.

"We know it's not going to be easy, but it's our only real option here. Either we find those essences and destroy them, or Kronus finds them and comes back full power," Laya reminded them.

"I don't know about you, but I'd rather take on the shell of Kronus than the Titan in full power," I said to them.

"True," Sam said with a nod.

"Not exactly the good news I was hoping for," Jasper said.

"What did you think was going to happen?" Mazz asked him.

"Honestly? I was hoping for them to say…no worries, we got this," Jasper admitted.

"Yeah…it was nothing like that. It's all on us. They won't help at all. The Moirai like to keep firmly out of the drama," Laya said.

"And danger," Sam uttered with a huff.

"We don't know where the essences are located, but I'm sure-"

The ground started to rumble.

All our eyes flitted around the room as the furniture pulsated with the pounding in the ground.

"Get down!" I shouted. A snapping and cracking sounded, and a chuck of the ceiling, the size of the bed, fell.

"Watch out!" Mazz shouted as he tackled Rayna out of the way of the falling debris. The chairs were completely crushed under the weight of the fallen ceiling.

"What's going on?" Laya shouted over the noise.

"An earthquake!" Mazz hollered back. His arms were around Rayna, as they sat on the floor staring wide-eyed at the room while it rumbled with each shake.

"No, it's not an earthquake." Eurybia had appeared in the door to the room. A smile spread on her face that was so serene and happy I almost didn't recognize her. She turned from us. We all emptied from the bedroom following her into the sitting room, trying to steady ourselves across the rippling of the ground. A giant shadow filled the stairway as the rumbling mounted. I stepped in front of Laya.

"Hello, my love," Eurybia cooed.

Through the door a man stepped out. Standing at least nine feet tall, the giant had to stoop to fit through the door. His eyes were sharp and when they landed on me, I felt cut by them. Thick, dark brows pinched together over shadowed, deep-set eyes. His hair was long and hung past his shoulders in great black waves over his dark skin. Shirtless, the man looked like a bare-knuckle boxer combined with a bodybuilder and Tarzan. In one word - wild.

I could hear Laya draw in a quick breath. My powers licked up my arms as he took another step in the room.

The giant's demeanor changed completely when he wrapped a massive hand around Eurybia's waist, making her look almost childlike compared to him.

"Cottus, you scared my friends," she scolded, but the smile on her face didn't change at all.

"You know I can't resist letting off a little steam after being with my brother," he said in a voice so low it was almost below a register I could hear.

"How is Gyges managing without you? Any news?" she asked, placing her hands on his bare muscular chest.

"The gate is open, but no movement. It must have sensed the reincarnation," he answered.

"She isn't fully awakened, though," Eurybia said, looking back at Laya. I was getting a little annoyed that we were all standing there, obviously listening to their conversation, and we had no idea who the new party was in the room.

"Who is this?" Laya asked, as if reading my mind.

"Oh! I'm so sorry, KyLaya," Eurybia exclaimed. "This is Cottus. He is one of the guardians of Kronus' chamber."

"I didn't know there were guardians," I said, running my eyes over the giant. I didn't doubt the guy's abilities. He looked like he could literally eat me in two bites.

"Yes, Cottus and his brother, Gyges, are the guardians to the chamber. They have been coming in and letting me know if there are any changes. It seems that there is an update, after all," she said.

"The door has opened," Cottus boomed. "Nothing has emerged, but we know it will only be a matter of time. We will keep Kronus in there as long as we can, but he'll get out eventually."

"That means that he knows that I'm here," Laya said, starting to shift her weight from foot to foot, moving restlessly between the two. I wrapped a protective arm around her.

"This is her? Gaia's reincarnation?" Cottus asked, pointing at Laya.

"Yes, that's her," Eurybia said with a proud smile.

"I should have guessed. She looks a lot like her," Cottus said.

"I'm sorry. Like who?" Laya asked.

"Gaia," Cottus answered. "My mother."

"*You're* mother?" I echoed. Looking back and forth from Eurybia to Cottus…who had the same mother.

"Oh…you're both. I mean, you two are together and you have the same…" Laya trailed off, having let her verbal diarrhea go far enough.

Eurybia laughed.

"When it comes to the gods, our biology works different than you humans. Brother and sister doesn't work the same as you. We have different fathers, which is about as far, biologically, as we can get as gods from our age. We're not humans that way."

"Okay," Laya said and stepped back, clapping her hands in front of her with a crooked grin.

"Smooth," I uttered, looking at her with a half-smile. She pushed me as her cheeks reddened.

"Shut up, don't tell me you weren't wondering the same thing," she whispered. I smiled at her and rolled my eyes.

"It is good to meet you, KyLaya," Cottus said, in a deep voice, taking Laya's hand gently in his giant palm.

"Thank you, you too," she said with a kind smile.

"Cottus…where have I heard that name?" Mazz asked.

Cottus looked at Eurybia.

"He has a rather unfortunate story," she said. Her warm eyes looked up into his.

"It's not the nicest form of me," he answered.

"What form?" Jasper asked.

"Nothing crazy - just fifty heads and limbs. No sense of self. No control over my anger issues. Cast into Tartarus…twice," he said. "That kind of thing."

"You had fifty heads?" Jasper blurted. "For real?"

"Yeah, well, not all of us are born as pretty as you," he said to Jasper. Jasper smiled and blushed. Sam narrowed his eyes at Cottus and rolled them at Jasper.

"Cottus and his brothers had a terribly abusive and misunderstood life, at the start. But, they've worked really hard to become the men that they are today," Eurybia said, tenderly embracing Cottus.

"I think a certain Titaness had something to do with that," he said, placing a kiss on her cheek.

"Anything for you, my love," she answered.

"Wow. You guys are too cute," Rayna gushed.

"Agreed," Laya added as she looked at the giant of a man next to the dwarfed Eurybia.

"So, what's going on with Kronus' chamber?" Mazz asked.

Cottus' gaze slipped over Mazz. His brow lifted at the end of his assessment.

"A guardian? Haven't seen one of those in…well it's been awhile," Cottus said, looking between Euryibia and Mazz.

"How did you know?" Mazz asked, looking at Cottus sceptically.

"Let's just say that I have developed a sense for godly powers over the years. I can feel your blocking ability," he answered.

"Is that a bad thing? Can Ares sense them too?" Mazz asked.

We were under the impression that the guardians' powers would block ours, not lead the gods right to us.

"No, it's something just a few of us have. It's helped us survive throughout the ages," he answered.

"So, we're not going to put them at risk?" Rayna asked, walking forward.

"*Two* guardians?" he asked, looking at Eurybia. "That means…"

"Yes," she said, taking his hand and watching him carefully.

"Where?" he asked, his eyes narrowing. Dread filled my gut without reason.

"Remember, it's not really him, my love," Eurybia said.

"Which one?" he said turning his eyes on us. When they landed on me, they didn't leave.

"Him." He pointed and took a step toward me. With everything in me, I stood my ground and looked back at him. A spark of a memory flashed in my mind. The picture of a wild monstrous man, uncontrollable and violent, appeared to me. I knew that was Cottus.

"Yes. He's Uranus's reincarnation," Eurybia. "But he is *not* Uranus."

Two steps across the room and he was toe to toe with me. He towered over me, a sensation I was not accustomed to, being relatively tall myself. Can't say that I liked it.

"You're the new version of my father, huh?"

"Not sure I would put it that way," I answered, looking straight back at him. Laya pulled herself up next to me, and looked directly at Cottus.

"He's not Uranus, Cottus. Jett is his own person," she said.

"That doesn't mean I have to like him," Cottus boomed.

"What's your deal?" I asked, feeling the pull of my powers as a threat presented itself.

"My *deal?*" Cottus said. "My deal would be that my father was a vicious, manipulative, sadistic ass. That's my deal."

"What?" I blurted.

"Is…is that true?" Jasper asked Eurybia.

"It's not…untrue," she hesitated.

"Bia…" Cottus warned. "Tell them the truth."

Eurybia sighed, her shoulders dropped. "Very well. Uranus wasn't always bad. His love for my mother was true and strong. They ignited the connection that all other gods aspire to. The light connection was a power all on its own, one that fueled their love even more. But, when they had their first child, Uranus saw a connection between Gaia and her children. Gaia loved her children more than anything, but not more than Uranus. He didn't see it that way and he wasn't prepared to share his love. That's when the jealousy set in."

Cottus stepped back from me, but didn't take his eyes off mine. The soft teddy bear that hugged Eurybia was gone. Rayna and Mazz stepped up to us. I could feel their powers coming to the surface too. But it was Sam that stepped forward and up to Cottus.

There was a rippling under Cottus' skin as Eurybia told her story.

"He started to hate his own children and the love that Gaia had for them. The ones that had it the worst were the Hecatonchreires - Cottus and his brothers. They were born…deformed."

"Having fifty heads and limbs is a little more than deformed," Cottus barked. "We were monsters. And that was all that our father could see. Our mother loved us unconditionally, but not Uranus. He beat us, humiliated us, and hated us for the love that Mother gave us. But, eventually, that wasn't enough and he locked us in Tartarus to be tortured for all eternity."

"They were left there until Kronus came to power," Eurybia said. I looked at Cottus. That was a long time to be locked in Tartarus - to be tortured in the most excruciating and inventive ways. I was starting to understand why he hated Uranus so much.

"What happened? Did Kronus release you?" Laya asked.

"No, he didn't," Cottus thundered "We were left in Tartarus while all of our brothers and sisters, that Uranus had also sent there, were freed. Kronus, our own brother, abandoned us." There was a vibration in the air and the ground started to rumble.

"Careful, my love. Your temper," Eurybia said gently. But there was nothing to be done for it, Cottus' anger was intensifying and we all could see it. The ground shook with more violence. Rayna toppled over the couch as it slid around the floor. Mazz dove out and caught her before she hit the ground. Jasper and Sam shuffled around, just barely keeping to their feet as Laya and I stood as best as we could, hand in hand watching Cottus.

As Cottus' rage grew, so did he. His face reddened, and his skin stretched and rippled. Laya gasped. For the first time, I could see what that rippling really was.

Faces.

Hands.

They pushed from under his skin, like a baby in its mother's belly. Against his flesh they strained, as he fought to maintain control.

"Cottus! *Please!*" Eurybia begged and ran to him. He pushed her away.

"Stay away from me!" he bellowed. The ceiling began to crumble, as Cottus started to lose his last bit of self-control.

Eurybia grasped his arms and shook him.

"Cottus, my love. It's me. You have to stop. Please! Stop!" she called to him.

"I can't stop them. They sense him. The rage. Their rage. Too much," Cottus said as a guttural scream broke from his lips. Eurybia's eyes widened and tears fell from them.

"No," she whispered, placing a hand over her mouth and shaking her head.

"What do we do?" I yelled at her.

"There is nothing that can be done," she said, stepping back with horror and heart wrenching sadness in her eyes.

The faces and hands pushed harder, exerting against Cottus' skin and stretching it thin. It must have been excruciating for him. I stepped in front of Laya and let my power come forward. Cottus' attention snapped to me, along with all the faces writhing under his skin. It was a sight that I would never forget.

"Jett…" Laya uttered behind me. I placed a hand on her and started to guide her for the door. Something told me that this was the Cottus from Tartarus and not the one that Eurybia was in love with.

"Uranus," an ugly ragged voice boomed, as if a choir of snakes had uttered the name. That was when I realized that it was the heads talking to me, through Cottus' skin.

"Gods," I uttered, my powers flamed higher on my skin. I knew that it wasn't really helping the situation, but I couldn't help it. My powers ignited as if the presence of Cottus called to them. If Cottus was going to come at me, I was going to defend myself; and, moreover, I would protect Laya.

Unfortunately, she didn't have the same plan.

KYLAYA

MY HEART HURT seeing the pain on Cottus' face. He had been through so much and he was still being tortured. Eurybia was nearly beside herself trying to get him to calm down. There was nothing any of us could do to calm him. Except for one.

Sam.

I caught his eye and immediately he understood what I was thinking. Jett had placed himself in front of me and was herding me toward the door - but I wasn't going anywhere. Mazz and Rayna were stuck on the other side of Cottus with Jasper and Sam. We needed to help. Jett's powers flamed brighter when Cottus turned to him.

Every hair on my body stood up when the voices beneath his skin spoke. There was no getting that sound out of my head. It was angry...*so* angry.

I looked at Sam and he moved into position. I knew what I was about to do would really tick off Jett, but he was just going to have to get over it.

I maneuvered around from behind Jett quickly and shouted for Cottus.

"Cottus! You need to calm down. This is not what your mother would have wanted for you." He stopped writhing, the faces turning to me. My heart turned to ice. The outline of fifty faces under his skin was morbid in a way I could never describe.

"I can feel her love for you. I can feel the hope she had for you. Please, you have come so far. Don't let this stop all you have done," I begged.

Cottus looked, for a moment, as if what I had said was getting to him. Then Jett moved beside me; his powers still lit across his arms.

Seeing Jett beside me flipped a switch and that was it. The ground heaved as Cottus lost the last strand of control he had.

"Now!" I shouted at Sam.

Sam ran toward Cottus.

"No! Sam!" Jasper screamed, trying to stop him. Sam slid under his arm and across the floor at a surprising speed.

Cottus reared back and arms exploded from his skin. I stared in horror. A hundred hands extended from Cottus' body, ripping through his skin and eliciting a scream of pain that crumpled Eurybia to the ground in sobs.

Cottus turned, slicing through the air with massive arms at Sam.

"Sam!" Jett shouted, releasing a bolt of white light at Cottus' hands as they swung through the air at Sam. Jett didn't aim at Cottus' chest, which surprised me. Luckily, it was enough of a distraction to allow Sam to get close to the giant. He rose up and placed a hand on Cottus' chest.

Cottus shouted, expecting pain I was sure - but what came next was nothing like that. Sam's power slipped into Cottus. The great man's eyes widened and his muscles relaxed. All his arms dropped and the rippling of the faces under his skin stopped.

Cottus turned his eyes to Sam.

I held my breath. *Please just let him help you.*

Sam said nothing as his power seeped below the skin of Cottus and into his body. Eurybia stopped crying and watched. Cottus stared in open awe at Sam, who stood before him, dwarfed in size compared to Cottus.

"You are in pain," Sam said, slowly and softly. "So much pain." Sam shook his head and a tear ran down his cheek. He lifted his eyes to Cottus'. "Please let me help you."

Cottus said nothing, but leaned down toward Sam, bringing his eyes level to Sam. Sam reached out and placed his hands on either side of Cottus' head, slowly and gently, and closed his eyes.

Sam's calming, healing, powers sank below Cottus' skin, coaxing back the faces below. Carefully and gently, we watched as Sam brought Cottus back to his original form. His new form.

Eurybia sprang from the floor to Cottus when Sam stepped back from him.

"My darling, is it you?" she whispered.

"I'm here. Just me," he answered, reaching up and wiping away a tear from her cheek. He bent and kissed her. I couldn't help the tears that sprang to my eyes. A light sparked between the two of them and I knew in that moment that their love was pure and blessed, just like mine and Jett's. I placed my hand in Jett's.

If Uranus was all those things that Cottus said he was, Jett was nothing like him. Whatever reincarnation had given Jett, it was a beautiful gift and nothing like the god that Cottus has described.

"I'm sorry," Cottus said, looking at all of us. "I wasn't prepared for facing my father today."

"I'm *not* your father," Jett said, placing his hands on his hips.

"That is true, but your presence…it is difficult to take," he said. Eurybia wrapped her arms around his neck.

"I'm here for you, my love. You can do this. I know you can," she said.

"You know I would do anything for you, Bia - anything," he said, trailing the back of his fingers across her cheek.

"I know," she said with a smile. She turned to Sam and reached for his hand.

"Thank you," she said and took his hand. "How did you do that?"

"It's…a gift," Sam said with a shrug.

"It's more than that. It's a blessing," she said.

"I just wanted to help. I've seen a lot of pain, but this was…different," Sam replied with a shrug.

"You aren't a normal Sirenite," Cottus remarked.

"You know what Sirenites are?" Jett asked.

"We all do, my dear," Eurybia answered.

"Really?" Jett answered. "Here I thought that we have hidden well from the gods."

"You have from the Olympians - we aren't Olympians," Cottus replied. "We see more and farther than they do. After all, we've been around longer. We know a thing or two," he answered, his voice low and loud and calm now that Sam had intervened.

"Now back to you," Cottus said, turning to Sam.

"Me?" Sam squeaked, backing up.

"Yeah, you," Cottus said. "You're a Sirenite?"

"Yes," Sam said, watching Cottus carefully.

"I don't think so," Cottus said.

"What are you talking about?" Jasper said, looking at Cottus and Sam. "Sam's a Sirenite. He just has a special power, like Jett. Oh…wait." Jasper turned to Sam and looked at him again. "Jett's powers *aren't* Sirenite powers. Are yours?" he asked Sam.

My heart beat so fast I thought that it might jump clear out of my chest. I looked at Sam, whose eyes didn't leave Jasper's. Jett stood stiff at my side, his eyes constantly going between Sam and Jasper.

"Jasper, I…" Sam uttered.

"Oh, shit," Jasper whispered placing his hands over his mouth. "Who are you? Who are you *really?*"

Oh gods…no. I could almost feel Jasper's heart ripping.

"I love you, Jasper," Sam uttered.

This can't be happening…

"No matter where I come from, I love you. Please don't forget that," Sam begged as he walked to Jasper.

"*Who are you?*" Jasper yelled and backed away from him.

The blood rushed right out of my body. My heart was breaking for him. I looked at Jett, his eyes never left Jasper. I can't imagine what was going on in his head. He had known Sam as long as Jasper had.

"My birth name is Asclepius," Sam said. "I…I am a son of Apollo."

Silence.

Jasper's mouth hung open as he stared at his husband in shock. They had been together for years. I knew he loved Sam with every fiber of his being. I couldn't imagine what a secret of that calibre would do to a relationship.

The betrayal…*gods, Jasper.*

I looked at Jasper, who just stood there. I had no idea what I would do if I-

"Jett," Jasper uttered, his eyes never breaking from Sam's.

"Yeah, Jasp," Jett answered, stepping to his brother.

"Blast him," Jasper said, looking at Sam.

"What?" Jett asked, looking at Jasper as if he had lost it.

"Zap him with your power," Jasper said, looking back at Jett with all seriousness.

"I…Jasper, I don't think that's what you really want," Jett answered.

"Do it," Jasper said, glaring at Sam.

"It's *Sam*," he said.

"No, it's *not!*" Jasper yelled. He turned and threw out an arm, pointing at Sam. His anger slipping through as his emotions started to take over. "I don't know that man. *My* Sam would never keep a secret from me! Never!"

I placed a hand over my mouth. Sam reached for Jasper.

"No! You son of a bitch! How could you keep that from me? How? All these years! We told each other everything! *Everything!* Was any of it true? Anything?" Jasper shouted at Sam.

"Yes, Jazz," Sam said.

"Don't call me that! Don't *ever* call me that again! You hear me? I don't know you! I don't know who *you* are!"

"Jasper, *please!*" Sam shouted. I had never seen Sam look panicked. He always had this peace and calmness about him, I guess that came from being around for so long.

"No," Jasper said, turning from him. That didn't stop Sam. He ran around to the front of Jasper and placed his hands on Jasper's face, forcing him to look at him.

"I will tell you everything. Everything that I have been forced to keep from you. All of it," he said.

"It's too late," Jasper said. Tears flowed down his face. "You have broken my heart, Sam."

"No," Sam said, shaking his head. "Please, Jasper. Please. You can't turn me away. *Please.*"

Gods. Sam dropped to the floor and grabbed Jasper's hands in his. He placed his face on Jasper's hands.

"You have my heart. My very soul. I can't go on without you. You don't know what it has meant to me to have you. You don't know what you have done for me. What being with you has meant. You don't know. I can't live without you."

"Don't. Don't do that," Jasper said, trying to push his off.

"Jasper. I *chose* you. I chose you over my godhood. I chose you over Olympus. Over immortality. I chose *you.*"

"Sam…"

"Hear me out, please."

Jasper didn't say anything, so Sam went on.

"I stumbled upon Stenen when I was searching for the reincarnations. My father sent me to look for them and my search led me to your town. I didn't know about the Sirenites and I soon learned why. The more I got to know your people the more I grew to like them. Then I met you, Jasper. You were so young and innocent, so full of life. You were everything that I had been missing in my miserable life. Immediately, I fell in love with you. *Immediately.*

"But there was a problem. My father.

"He wanted to know where the reincarnations were. I told him that I couldn't find them. It wasn't until much later that I had an inkling that Jett may have been the person that Apollo was looking for - but I never told Apollo, or anyone else. I would never do anything to put your people in danger, and I knew if I revealed my thoughts about Jett, I would jeopardize everything that your people had built. I couldn't do that. I cared for you all too much.

"As punishment for turning my back on my father, he cast me out of Olympus. I was forced to face eternity on earth without the chance to go home to Olympus…ever again. I had lived a very long time with the gods and knew that was a sacrifice I was more than willing to make.

"A lifetime with you was worth losing an eternity on Olympus. You made me happier than all the time that I had spent on Olympus. You, Jasper, made me a better man than I could have ever thought possible. In all the life that I have lived, *never* have I loved another like you. The first moment I saw you - that was it for me. I knew I had been waiting for you; but, to protect you and your people, I had to hide who I was."

Jasper crossed his arms. His lips tightened as he looked away from Sam and back again. Sam didn't take that as a sign to stop, so he continued.

"I have always respected my father, but he isn't without his vengeful side. I knew that he would punish you for taking me from him. He would remove you from the equation, securing me back at his side - but, only if he could find you. I waited for him to descend on Stenen. I was on edge all the time, ready for him to come. Ready to protect you - but he didn't.

"I figured out that there was some kind of spell over the town to block the power of the Sirenites from Olympus. My father was blind to your people, and, as it happened, me. There was no finding me or my power while I remained with you. I could use my healing abilities to help your people and stay with you, without having to worry about Apollo finding you. It was perfect; the only problem was that I had to hide who I was from you."

"Why couldn't you tell *me*? I wouldn't have told anyone," Jasper said, finally speaking. Sam stood.

"I know that. It wasn't that I didn't trust you. I didn't trust *myself*. Once I told you, I was afraid that I would go back to what I was before. The arrogance and selfishness that comes with immortality infects the gods. You made me a better person, Jasper. To go back to what I was…I never want you to see that person. I was afraid that you knowing would change everything. I was…a coward."

Jasper crossed his arms, but his eyes remained on Sam. I held my breath and looked at Jett. His jaw was tight but there was no mistaking the pain on his face. Sam was like an older brother to him. This wasn't just a betrayal to Jasper, it was one for Jett too.

"I'm so sorry, Jasper," Sam uttered.

"I know. I know you're sorry. I just don't know if it is enough," Jasper answered.

"What can I do? Tell me and I will do it," Sam said, looking at Jasper and grasping his hands tighter. "Anything."

"Do you get that I am questioning everything about who we are as a couple? How much of our relationship was based on a lie? What was real? What wasn't? *Everything* about us. About *you*. I don't know what is real," he said. Tears were welling in his eyes. My heart slammed at my chest.

Tears slid down Sam's cheeks as he stood in front of Jasper and levelled his eyes to his.

"It was all real to me, Jasper. There hasn't been a moment that I haven't been completely honest with you about how I feel about you. Everything that you know about me is me, the *real* me. As far as the stories we shared, they were all true, I just may have changed small things to make them less…godlike."

"So your dad is really a control freak who you want nothing to do with?" Jasper asked.

"Yup, and more."

"What more?"

"My crazy uncle that rages and spouts off about just about everything. The one with the temper issues?"

"Yeah?"

"That's Ares," Sam explained.

"Ah. I see," Jasper uttered.

"I know this is a lot and that you are hurt. I can't tell you how I have dreaded this day. Jasper, I love you more than anything. I would do anything for you. That hasn't changed since the day that I met you. One look at you and you had me. Heart and soul, I was yours, and I always will be."

I couldn't help the swell in my heart at Sam's words. I looked at Jasper, with no clue how he would take this. I knew he loved Sam more than anything, but would he be able to get over the betrayal he felt? I just didn't know. I hoped so. They had a rare love and I wanted so much to see them back in each other's arms.

"I don't know, Sam," Jasper said, turning from him and shaking his head. Placing his arms across his chest. "There's just…this is such a *big thing*."

"I know. I know. I will never be able to apologize enough to you for the hurt I have caused, but I *swear* to you I will spend the rest of our lives making it up to you," Sam pledged.

Jasper froze and looked at Sam. I mean really looked at him.

"I can't…*damn it*, Sam, I love you. You know I do. You were my first love and you'll be my last. There could never be another after you. But I need time," Jasper said.

"Yes, of course," Sam said standing and backing away from Jasper.

Jasper left the room and went into his, closing the door behind him. Our eyes followed him and then turned to Sam as the door closed. A moment of silence passed as we all decided exactly what we were going to say.

A flash of pink light lit the room as a bolt struck out from Jett and hit Sam square in the chest. Sam was flung straight back; his feet flew over his head as he hit the couch and tumbled back over it. Jett stalked over to Sam as he lay sprawled on the floor.

"You make this right with Jasp; or, next time, I won't waste my power on you - I'll enjoy kicking your ass the good old fashioned way," Jett said to Sam as he leaned over him. Sam looked up at Jett with wide eyes and nodded once.

"Good," Jett said and reached down for Sam's hand. Sam hesitantly grabbed it as Jett pulled him to his feet again.

"I deserved that," Sam said to Jett.

"I took it easy on you - don't think otherwise," Jett answered.

"Understood," Sam said, placing his hands in his pockets and giving a weak smile.

"Son of Apollo, huh?" Mazz asked. "How did you ever manage to keep that a secret all this time?"

"It wasn't easy, but it was worth it to protect my loved ones," Sam answered. "If Apollo found me, he would have punished the community and left Jasper for a special treat. As much as the gods might like to dabble in human relations, they really don't approve of falling in love with them."

"You mean they would have hurt you?" I asked.

"Possibly, but gods are more in favor of eternities of torture than all out killing. It's not easy to kill a god. It's a lot easier to torture them for eternity," Sam said.

"Don't I know it," Cottus chimed in. We all stared at him. He shuffled his feet awkwardly, "I didn't mean to out you to everyone. I just figured that you had a charm of some kind, not that you were a god in hiding."

"What's done is done," Sam said.

"I suppose, it's best that it came out now and not at their twentieth wedding anniversary," Jett added.

"Jett, what do I do?" Sam asked, looking at Jett with the most hopeful look on his face. Jett flexed his jaw and tightened his lips.

"Look, Sam. Jasp is really hurt. *You* did that. There's nothing I can say that will take the guilt of that away. Give him time. He loves you. He'll come around to understanding. The best thing you can be is totally and *completely* honest with him. Tell him *everything*. Every little thing. He needs to know that you're still the man that he fell in love with. Right now, you feel like a stranger. The more you share with him, the more he will know and understand you. If I were you, I'd get in that room and start talking. Don't expect anything. Don't touch him. Just talk," Jett said.

My heart. Oh, my *heart*.

What Jett said was kind and sweet and hit all the right notes. I was so proud of his advice. I threaded my fingers into his. He looked down at me and gave a weak smile. I knew he was hurting for his brother. There was nothing that we could do for Jasper. It was all on him and Sam.

Sam thanked Jett. He went over to the room he shared with Jasper and lightly knocked on the door. We all waited with baited breath to see if the door would open for him. It was a painful few moments before the doorknob turned and Jasper let Sam in.

"That's a good sign," Jett said as the door closed behind Sam.

"I can't imagine what he's going through right now," I said to Jett.

"Me neither," Jett said. We settled down on a couch together.

"Well, I think that we've all had quite the day," Eurybia said. "I'm going to bed."

"And I will be joining you," Cottus said, winking at her. Eurybia laughed as Cottus wrapped a massive arm around her waist and lifted her off her feet. "You, my lady, are a stunning being."

"Flatterer," she said with a giggle.

"I could never see you as anything but my saviour and my heart," he said. Eurybia smiled sweetly and kissed him. They disappeared through the door and down the stairs, leaving Jett, me, Mazz, and Rayna alone in the hall.

"Holy Hades," Mazz sighed. "What a day."

"Yeah," Rayna agreed. "I would prefer not to have another one of those for a while."

"Agreed," Mazz said smiling at her.

"I'm exhausted," I mumbled, leaning into Jett as a yawn caught me.

"Bedtime?" he asked, looking down at me. I nodded.

"You guys heading to bed?" Jett asked Mazz and Rayna. They looked at each other for a second and then Mazz answered.

"I'm going to stay up and have some…tea," he answered.

"I might join you," Rayna added. I looked at Rayna. "Tea sounds good," she said with a shrug.

"Okay," I uttered and looked up at Jett. He was still looking at Mazz and Rayna. I squeezed his waist. He broke his look away from them and dropped it to me.

"Wanna come to my room?" I asked him, and then realized what that sounded like. A deep blush burned my cheeks. "To sleep! I mean. I just don't want to be alone," I explained, making myself look all the more guilty.

Jett chuckled deep and low, "You know I could never say no to you."

"Good," I said back and we walked to my room to a chorus of "good nights" from Mazz and Rayna. Who were staying up late for…tea.

Sure.

A smile pulled at my lips.

Mazz and Rayna…didn't see that one coming.

JETT

THE MORNING LIGHT hit me like a slap in the face. I groaned and rolled over. A warm body stirred next to me, momentarily startling me until I remembered where I was and who was in my bed.

Laya.

Last night we had gone back to her room. She changed into a long shirt and shorts and crawled into bed. I brought over my sweats and changed into them. She insisted that I stay with her. I would never have been presumptuous enough to assume that I could stay, no matter where we were in our relationship. An invitation was a must for me.

"I just don't want to be alone," she said, climbing into the bed and pulling the white covers over her legs to her waist. She looked at me with a fresh face that she just washed and eyes so blue they could have been gems.

"I'm not going anywhere. As long as you want me, I'm here," I said and crawled on top of the covers beside her.

She looked at me and laughed. "What?" I asked.

"You can come under the covers, you know," she said, looking at me like I was crazy.

"Laya," I began.

"Look, I'm not going to jump you, okay? I just want to lay next to you and..."

"And...what?" I asked.

"Snuggle?" she asked, as a blush took her cheeks.

"Snuggle?" I echoed, not sure I had heard her correctly.

"Yeah. It's been a hard day and I just want to feel you next to me as I go to sleep. Is that a bad thing?" she asked.

"No! No, of course it's not," I said, lifting the covers and inserting myself in them. Truth was, I was afraid of being alone with Laya in the bedroom again. We nearly had sex the last time. I knew that I wanted to - I mean, my gods, *really* wanted to. However, I also wanted to take it slow with her. She was worth it and I didn't want to rush any part of being with her.

Laya moved in close, running her hand across my abs as she fit in against me. Her head rested on my shoulder and neck. I could feel her bare leg next to my hip and I had a hard time keeping my mind out of the gutter. Her strong body next to mine always did things to me, but now we were alone and in bed and she was only in a shirt and…I really was not helping myself out.

"You okay?" she asked, leaning her head back and looking up at me.

"Fine. Yeah. All good," I answered, trying to focus on her question and not the dirty train my thoughts were on.

"Fine? All good? What's going on with you?" she asked. "You're acting all…awkward."

"I am?" I asked, knowing damned well I was.

"Okay, you're scaring me. What's wrong?" she asked sitting up and away from me. Her brows furrowed over her warm eyes. I felt like a complete ass.

"I'm fine, really I am. Just having a tough time keeping…control," I said to her.

"Of your power?" she asked.

"No."

"*What* then?" she asked.

"Don't make me say it," I begged. It took a second, but a smile slowly spread from the corners of her mouth across her face.

"*Oh*," she uttered.

"Yeah, so, if you wouldn't mind, can you just lie down so we can go to sleep?" I asked her.

"Sure. I can do that," she said and laid back down on me. Her hand was warm and soft as it slowly slid across my chest. But it didn't stay there. *Oh no.*

"Laya…" I warned as her hand made a slow, smooth, move lower and lower.

"Turns out, I'm not as tired as I thought," she whispered, sitting up and looking at me.

Gods, she was sexy as hell. Her blonde hair was swept over her head in a tossed and messy way that looked incredible on her. Her eyes were shining and icy blue. Her lips were just begging me to kiss them; especially when she slowly licked them, leaving them gleaming in the dim light.

"What are you saying, Laya?" I asked, my heart knocking against my ribs hard and fast as she sat up taller in the bed.

"I'm saying that it's been a long, hard day," she said leaning into me, placing her lips so close to mine I could just feel them.

"Yeah?" I asked, swallowing hard.

"And, I just want to spend a little time with you," she purred.

"What kind of time?" I asked.

"Quality," she said with a smile.

"Quality time, huh?" I asked, and she smiled and nodded. I leaned in and she tipped her head up to mine, but I bypassed her lips and skirted down along her jawline. I could hear her quick intake of breath, as I softly touched her skin with my lips, trailing a line down her neck to her shoulder.

"Unfortunately, we really need our sleep," I said, placing a light kiss on her shoulder.

"You sure about that?" she asked, turning her eyes on mine.

"Laya. You've been through a lot today. I don't want to take advantage of that. Let's let things sink in a little, okay?" I said to her, not knowing where the hell the restraint came from. I was rock hard and wanting to take full advantage of her welcoming mood, but I knew it wasn't the time.

I knew it, but *she* didn't seem to.

Damn it, why did *I* have to be the one to know it?

"I'm beginning to question my sex appeal to you, Jett," Laya said, looking at me seriously.

"*Never* doubt that," I said immediately pulling her close and planting a kiss on her lips that wouldn't have her questioning my feelings for her any time soon. But that was a mistake.

The feel of her skin against mine was intoxicating and I soon forgot what I was saying to her when she crawled into my lap. Her lips worked against mine, keeping my mind in a cloud of sensation and pleasure. Man alive, the girl was a good kisser. My mind went blank when she shifted and rocked her hips against me.

Gods…

An animal sound worked its way up from deep within me and I flashed. She was under me in an instant. With a small squeal of surprise, I pressed her into the bed.

"My gods, Laya. What you do to me," I uttered. In that instant, she sat up, moved her hands down to the bottom of her night shirt and slowly, painfully so, pulled it over her head.

Her skin glowed in the dim light. Perfection. Smooth and warm, I couldn't help but run my eyes all over her.

"You are *stunning*," I whispered not able to find my voice.

I pulled her close, kissing her gently - at first. Soon our kisses mixed pleasure and pain as they become urgent and deep. She sighed and moaned against my lips, as I flipped her over onto the bed again. The sounds that she made sent a pulse straight to my groin.

From somewhere in the back of my mind, a voice reminded me that I had just been telling her it was the wrong time…and it *was*.

I stopped, pulling back slightly…painfully.

"What's wrong?" she asked. Her eyes were clouded in pleasure and I so wanted to keep her in that state. To bring her to the edge and crash her over it. I had been thinking about it for a long freaking time.

I sighed heavily and kissed her again. "We have to stop."

"What? Why?" she asked. "When are you going to accept the fact that I know what I want, Jett? I'm not some little girl that you're taking advantage of for Poseidon's sake!"

"I don't think that you're a little girl. I certainly wouldn't be crawling into bed with you if I felt that way," I told her. She lifted a brow and looked at me with a tilt to her head. "Look, Laya. I told you, I want to take it slow."

"Glacial slow," she uttered.

"Wow," I chuckled.

"Well, honestly. You're making me feel like I'm begging for it here."

"I'm sorry, that's not my intention," I said and pulled her to me. She let me and rested her head on my chest, putting her bare skin against mine as she slid in next to me.

"What are you waiting for, Jett?" she asked.

"I don't think I'm waiting for anything. Is it so bad to want all of you and not just one part?"

"I guess not," she answered with a shrug. "Is it so bad that I want you? All of you?"

"No. And you have me, by the way," I added.

"You have me, too."

"I know," I said with a smile. "You're pretty much throwing yourself at me."

White lit in her palm and a zap of it whipped out, striking me in the chest.

"Ouch! Laya!" I yelled through the laugh. Laya sat up and pulled her shirt back over her head and…bare chest. *Damn…*

"You deserved it," she said.

I zapped her side and she screamed. "You're not the only one-"

I yelped as her power snapped out at me again, cutting me off.

"Oh, you're going *down*," I threatened, throwing off the covers and launching at her. Sliding off the bed smoothly, she faced me. The most mischievous look appeared on her face and I was all about it.

She giggled with a nervous energy as she got into a fighting stance. I knew she was fast, but I also knew her moves. She always faked left and went right; and she didn't disappoint this time. I flashed right and went to grab her. There was a flash of white and she was gone.

"What?" I looked at my empty arms in astonishment. "How?"

A light laugh sounded from behind me. I turned and there she stood with her arms crossed.

"I guess I have a couple of new tricks up my sleeves, *Jettstream*."

I bit my lip at the sound of my least favorite nickname and took off after her. She squealed as she raced away to the other side of the room. Around the chair and onto the bed. Whenever I thought I had her, she flashed away from me. It was really frustrating, and sexy at the same time, watching her conquer one of her new powers like that.

"You can't flash from me forever you know," I said and dodged a bolt of white light from her that crashed into the wall behind me and disappeared, not making a mark in the paint.

"Well, see," she teased and smiled. I flashed to her and, before she could flash from me, grabbed her and tossed her on the bed.

"Gotcha!" I yelled as she flew through the air. To my astonishment, she turned in the air, like a cat, and landed in a crouch.

"Damn," I uttered, standing dumbfounded staring at her. "Laya, that was-" another zap in the arm stopped my words.

She laughed lightly and tumbled off the bed like a ninja. *What the heck?* I knew Laya was smooth, but this was new. It wasn't just that. The last bolt had *hurt.*

"Okay, Laya. I think it's time-"

Zap.

This time it collided with my shoulder and sent me back a couple of steps. A burn opened up in my skin where her bolt landed. Red and angry, it stung.

"Hey!" I shouted, looking at the wound and then back to Laya. Her smile inched higher on her face.

"Can't take a little hit? Baby," she chided.

"What?"

"Come on, Jettstream. Bring it," she said, calling me on.

This wasn't like Laya. Not at all. She was confident in her fighting, but she wouldn't hurt me, not even a little.

"Hold on a second," I said, holding out my hand. She didn't say anything, instead a ball of white light formed in her hand. I could feel the power from it and it was nothing like the energy that she had been bringing before.

"Okay, game's over, Laya. Stop," I said, but she just smiled and held on to the ball.

"Laya," I warned. She turned her eyes to me, and I watched as they went from icy blue to pure white.

The door burst open as Cottus and Eurybia ran in.

"What the hell?" I said.

"You were right," Eurybia said to Cottus.

"What's going on?" I asked.

The room lit with the light of Laya's power and all eyes turned to her. Her hair started to lift off her shoulders, moving in a breeze of their own.

"You're not playing fair," she scolded and sent the ball straight at me. I leaped out of the way, falling to the floor and rolling into a crouch. The ball crashed into the wall, sending bits and pieces of it flying around the room.

"Her powers are waking! If they aren't brought under control, they will destroy her and everything around her," Eurybia answered.

"What do we do?" I hollered over the noise of Laya's storm. Laya pulled more power into her palm and the room shivered, as if it were afraid of her.

"Cottus has a bracelet that will dampen her powers until you can get a piece that will help her control the full force of them," she explained.

"This isn't the full force of them?" I asked as the room grew brighter with the energy of the new ball she lit in her palm.

"Not even close. You remember what yours was," Eurybia said.

I looked at Laya and panic set in. Letting Uranus's power take over was excruciating. It felt like I was burning from the inside out. I couldn't contain it. Laya was in more trouble than I had realized.

"What do you need me to do?" I asked.

"Get this bracelet around her wrist. It will help her control the power – but, it won't work for the full force. For that, she will need another," Cottus said.

"Let's just cross that bridge when we come to it," I said to him, taking the tiny golden bracelet in my hand.

"Get it around her wrist. Snap it shut and it will do the trick," he said. I nodded at him and turned to Laya.

"Gods," I uttered looking at her. Her eyes were glowing white. She stood – actually, floated - above the floor. Her powers were swirling around her and the air in the room seemed to move at her will.

"Laya," I said. Her eyes turned to me, but there was no hint that she recognized me. "It's me, Jett." I took a step closer to her and her powers sped up, whipping the air at me. I squinted my eyes against it as I tried to gain some ground toward her. I had made the mistake of thinking that it was really her that was teasing me into playing and chasing using our powers, but that wasn't her. I knew that now.

It was the power.

It was Gaia.

KYLAYA

THE LAST THING I had full control over was settling into bed and snuggling up to Jett.

The feel of his skin under my palm sent a shiver to my core, and a need opened up inside me. It started out as it always did, the need to be beside him, with him - but soon it was more. Way more than I was ready for. Taking things all the way with Jett was something I knew I wanted; but I also knew that it was important to him to go slow - and I understood why. In the end, he was right.

But something woke within me that *strongly* disagreed.

Sex-demon Laya came out in full force. My self-control flew from me in a great gush, as if my body released all inhibitions in a deep exhale. It was as liberating as it was terrifying. I could feel power running through me and suddenly I was seeing things clearer than I had ever before.

Without my inhibitions, without a filter for my mouth, without a conscience, it was so easy to see what I wanted.

And, I wanted Jett.

So, I was going to have him.

The seduction came from a place within me that I had never touched before. A place that only existed in the back of my mind where I had no fear and not a self-conscious thought in my head. All hesitation flew right out of me as I drew a line down his bare chest right to the edge of his pants. I was greeted with a heavy, breathy, voice who said my name.

There was treasure to be found past those perfect divots in his hips and I was going to find it.

What I wasn't anticipating was his restraint. When he drew away from me, I would have been mad - if I didn't take it as a challenge.

"I like a challenge."

It was only a matter of time before he would fall to me. He was only a man after all. He couldn't say "no" forever.

No, Jett. It's not really me. Stop!

Somewhere in the corner of my mind a little voice called to me to stop; but it was small and fleeting, so I ignored it.

My attention turned to his perfectly formed lips and sculpted chest - that I wanted to run my tongue across. A guilt trip was laid on him, just enough to get him to kiss me…kiss me good. It didn't take long before I was sitting in his lap.

His eyes met mine and I knew I had him. There was no way he was coming back from that. But, just to make sure, I took my shirt off. He got a good look at my goodies and I locked him in.

Everything was going perfectly until…he pulled back.

Damned if he didn't have a godlike ability to step away when things were just getting tasty. Good thing I wasn't easily deterred. I saw the look in his eyes. I knew I could get him there, readily wanting me in bed. I was going to really enjoy pulling it out of him.

Pulling power from my core, I gave him a taste of some new tricks that I could do. No fear sure helped bring out my powers. Nothing was blocking them, no reservation, no frustration. I just let them come and they obeyed every command I gave them. Just as they always did. It was like coming home again.

But something was off.

Jett wasn't playing along. In fact, his was mad.

"What's his problem? It wasn't that bad of a shot! He's being a baby."

My frustration mounted and I zapped him, releasing some tension. It felt good, really good to just let go — so, I did it again. If I wasn't going to be bedded, I was going to get something out of the deal. Each release was a high that I had longed to have again.

When the door opened and Cottus and Eurybia came in the game was over. *"Damn it."* Jett's eyes flashed as anger darkened them. Something within me snapped.

"How dare he challenge me? How dare he turn from me?

"I am Gaia! I am the mother goddess. I created all who came after me."

Gaia? What?

The voice snapped logic back into me. I wasn't acting like myself. There was something else going on. Gaia's voice was strong and pushed against me for more room in my mind. I was being shoved out of my own mind.

Gaia surged forward, mixing with my thoughts. I wasn't sure where *she* ended and *I* began anymore. The disconnect with who I was broadened. I was confused and scared. How had I let it go on so long without realizing that I wasn't myself? I *did* want Jett, but everything that we had done…was that really me? The power came from within *me*. It was *mine*. And yet…that voice, that force, was gaining control.

I was losing myself.

Energy was building in my core. It was absolute. Incredible and overwhelming, it pulsed through my veins; conquering them and commanding them in ways I had never experienced before.

My senses ignited. Suddenly, I could feel the very air around me, and knew how to command it. With the slightest thought, the air picked up and swirled around me. My hair tossed lightly in the breeze it created.

"It's so nice to play again," Gaia's charged forward.

My gaze turned to Jett. *He has to know it isn't me. He has to.*

"He will have to learn his place until my love returns. They all will."

There was a jerk in my core. A rush of power escaped from the center of my being, filling me to the point of pain. I wanted to let it go, but it moved through me like a tidal wave, finding every last place within me to hide. My veins expanded with the pressure of it. A scream built deep in my throat, but no sound came out. I felt stretched thin under the pressure mounting within me.

A ban of light sliced through my center and exploded out into the room. The walls cracked and the ceiling split.

It's too much.

Stop, please.

No matter how much I wished it, there was no stopping the power, the force, the voice behind it all.

In my mind and I could hear a laugh. Like an echo from the past it surged forward, riding on the wave of power and pain.

All I could do was hold on and hope.

My scream finally sliced out of me like a knife - sharp and shrill.

Jett, please, help me.

JETT

HER SCREAM cut right through me.

Gods, Laya.

The bracelet Cottus gave me vibrated in my hand, as if it knew that it was about to get a taste of the power it hungered for. With every step I took toward her, the gusts of wind picked up and blew harder. Each step got harder as I pushed closer.

Laya's eyes were like two beacons in the night. Their light shone brightly around the room, casting stark shadows around us. No matter how many times I called to her, she didn't look at me. There was no mistaking it - there was something in her that wanted out. Something was controlling her. The being that I saw in front of me wasn't the woman I loved.

It was something or someone else.

Whatever was coming out of Laya was ready for a fight, and so was I; but I didn't want to hurt Laya. She was nothing more than a container to her power. I needed to save her before whatever was coming out destroyed her.

A ball of white light ignited around me. Her powers beat against it the closer I got. Protected from her assault by a shield I had no idea how I made, I pushed onward.

"Laya," I called to her.

No response.

"Hurry, she's getting stronger!" Cottus shouted. Just then a surge of wind slammed into me, throwing me back and knocking me to the ground. My defensive shield died and the full force of her storm cut and scratched at my skin. I was bloodied and bruised from it by the time my powers lit again around me. I stood and glared over at Cottus.

"Thanks for the distraction!" I shouted back. "Why don't *you* put this thing on her?"

"It has to be you. You're the only one that her power will allow through. If I tried, I get cut to pieces."

"This is her power letting me through?" I shouted back, looking at the storm raging around the room and the cuts in my arms from the blast she gave me.

"Yup. If she really wanted you dead, you'd be a bloody puddle, my friend," Cottus answered.

"Great," I mumbled.

That wasn't comforting. Laya wouldn't do that to someone. She defended those she loved with deadly force; but, just to hurt someone was not in her. This woman in front of me was not *my* Laya.

That scared the hell out of me.

My power pulsed and flared as her storm swirled around me, beating against the bubble of protection that I had. I felt like I was walking through a muddy bog in a windstorm. It was slow going, and I only had to get across the room.

I didn't stop until I was close enough to touch her. Her eyes, white orbs of light, cast the room into a fury of wind and power. Unlocking the ring, I got ready to clasp it to her. As soon as she saw it, her eyes turned to me.

Deep down a pool of dread opened.

I *knew* that Laya would never hurt me, but this wasn't *my* Laya. I was about to learn that the hard way.

Summoning her powers, Laya threw out a hand and a shot of white light burst from her, hitting the protective bubble around me and bursting it. The wind hit me like a sandpaper baseball bat. I was thrown back, landing on my ass.

Frustration built in my core. I didn't want to hurt Laya, but if it meant saving her from herself and from hurting others, I would. Her storm was building and pulling in Eurybia's home. Jasper and Sam barged into the room, followed by Rayna and Mazz. It wasn't just Laya, it was everyone that she loved at risk.

I stood and summoned my power.

If Cottus was right and my powers would register with hers, I needed all the help I could. I did what I never thought I would do. I pulled off my ring.

The power hit me hard, but it was a little easier this time than it was last time. Uranus's power flowed from me in wild waves. It surrounded Laya, filling in with her power. They wound around each other, like long lost lovers. I supposed they were.

It took every last bit of concentration that I had to stop the voice at the back of my mind from coming forward. To keep control on the power that was now surging from me. Cottus was right, though. Laya's power bounced off of mine as I walked right up to her.

Laya's eyes were closed now as her power swirled around her in a hurricane of devastation.

"Laya," I whispered and placed a hand on her cheek. She opened her eyes and turned to me.

"Jett?" A single tear fell from her eye. Her voice was weak, but it was there. I smiled and knew she was still with me, weak, but she was fighting.

"Help me," she uttered as the power consumed her once again, taking my Laya from me.

Laya raised a hand and I knew I was about to feel a blast that my powers wouldn't protect me from. I took out the bracelet and snapped it onto her outstretched wrist.

There was a pulse in the room as the power of the bracelet encircling her wrist sank into Laya. It felt like the air was sucked from the room as her powers pulled inside her body with the same ferocity that they came from it. When the last bit plunged inside her, she fell.

I caught her in my arms before she hit the floor.

"I've got you, Laya. I'm here," I said gently to her.

She opened her eyes slowly and looked at me. The last of the light in her eyes faded back within her.

"Jett?"

"Yes, it's me," I said to her.

"Thank you," she whispered, then fell back into my arms, unconscious. I sighed in relief, lifting her into my arms further. I took her to the bed and placed her gently on it.

With a sigh that came from deep within me, I placed my mother's ring back on my finger and felt the power of it pull my power lower within me. Safely stowing it away for the next time I would need it. Turning to Eurybia and Cottus I waved them out of the door.

"What aren't you telling me?" I asked them as I shut the door behind me.

"I'm sorry, Jett. I didn't think that her powers would reach this level so fast. She was showing so little of them, I thought that we had more time," Eurybia said.

"What can I do? What does she need?" I asked her.

"The bracelet that Cottus gave you will help her maintain control over them for now. Her powers aren't fully unlocked, neither are yours. What you both will need are the bracelets that will stop your powers from coming out unless you call upon them."

"Where can I get them?" I asked. Eurybia and Cottus looked at each other. "What? What is it?"

"They are the rings that the gods placed on the necks of the Titans when they were banished to Tartaus," Cottus said.

"Okay, so do they have some extras or something?" I asked.

"They may, but they aren't exactly available for pick up," Cottus said. "They would be in the stores of Hades himself. After all, Tartarus is located in his realm."

"Can't you guys ask Hades for them? I mean, we're supposed to be the reincarnations of primordial gods here that are supposed to save the world. A little help would be nice," I said.

"It sure would," Cottus said. "But the gods aren't known for their generous spirits. If you want something, you are going to have to go and talk to Hades in person and convince him that you need it."

"You know; you guys have been around a lot longer. Don't you think that it will be better coming from you?"

"We aren't really on the best terms with the Olympians, at least I'm not," Eurybia said.

"Why not?" I asked.

"I didn't fight on any side during the Titanomachy, the war with the Titans," she explained. "They still hold a bit of a grudge."

"Cottus?"

"Well, oddly enough, we have a better relationship with Olympus than she does. If it weren't for my brothers and me, Zeus wouldn't have won the war. I guess you can say he owes me a favor...or more," Cottus laughed.

"My love, what about-"

"This is more important, my dear. I will find another way," he said. "I will send a message to Zeus for you. Let's hope that Zeus hasn't forgotten the things that my family has done for him."

"Thank you, Cottus. Truly, thank you," I said.

"It's about time that the gods started to take responsibility for the fight that is coming. Whether they want to or not. Kronus is coming, they need to get on board with that reality."

With that, Cottus left the room. Eurybia turned to me.

"Listen, I don't want you thinking that a favor from Cottus is a little thing. Cottus is using his only leverage with Zeus to get you those rings. With Kronus waking, there will be no use for him. He was saving his family favor to secure a place with the gods, taking him out of his hell-hole guard duty. Now, he will most likely have to endure another prison to guard for eternity."

"I am grateful," I said to her. "But, if we can't stop our powers from taking over us, he will have no world to guard. I have a feeling that there is more to our powers than what we are seeing. It's like they have a life of their own. I don't like that. I can feel this spirit running just under the surface of the power I have, waiting," I uttered.

"Really?" she asked. "I've never read or heard anything about that. It might just be the power. You have primordial power now. That is something so great, no living being has any idea how that feels."

"Sure, that must be it," I commented.

I disagreed. I knew there was something beyond just the power; I just hoped that I was wrong - very wrong.

Everything in me told me there was an essence attached to my powers. Only one god's essence made sense – Uranus. If that was true, it meant Gaia was within Laya. The way Laya had behaved was like another personality had taken over. If that was Gaia, my theory made complete sense.

If it was the essences of both primordial gods within us, there was only one reason that they would have attached their essence to their powers; and, that was so that they could come back to life again.

In order to do that they needed vessels for their essences.

I walked into the room and looked at Laya.

"Gaia, if you are in there, leave her alone. Find another vessel for your plan; but, please, leave Laya alone," I said, placing a hand over Laya's

She stirred, breathing deeply in her sleep. She said nothing. My heart kicked at me and I pulled myself into bed with her, under the covers. With the bracelet on her wrist, her powers were in check.

I hoped in the morning that Cottus would have an answer from Zeus and we would be well on our way to getting the rings that we needed to keep our powers under control.

I fell asleep with Laya in my arms and the hum of my power in my veins.

Just as I drifted off, I could have sworn I heard Laya whisper one word in a voice that wasn't all hers…

"Uranus…"

"You feel that too, don't you?" I asked him.

"The presence behind the power?" he asked.

"Yes," I said, swallowing hard, knowing what that meant.

"The powers aren't the only thing that we were given, it seems," Jett said.

"I agree," I answered.

"To fos mou? Agapi mou? They were what Gaia and Uranus used to call each other, weren't they?" I asked him.

"I think so," he said.

"Well, that sucks. I liked them," I answered with a laugh.

"Me too."

"Dreamstop," I said and smiled at him. His eyes turned to me and a smile lit his face.

"Perfect," he said and kissed me.

"And that's the perfect answer," I said back.

For so long, Jett and I were stuck in our dreams, not able to share any location information or even touch. Anything that could reveal where we were or who we really were, was taken from us. If we touched, we would wake from our dream. We started to identify what we could and couldn't do. 'Dreamstop' was our way of saying what we *wanted* to say, even though we couldn't. It was our way of communicating that we wanted more. That we *felt* more.

To say 'dreamstop' and answer with a kiss was to fulfill our dream of wanting to be with each other. It was something only we knew and it was the perfect way of making sure that we were really ourselves.

"Well, I'm glad that's settled," Jett said. "Not a fan of needing that, though."

"Me neither. We need to find out more about what these powers really are. I have a sick feeling that we have only been given half information."

"I agree," he answered, "but, don't forget we have to find Kronus' essences too. We can't have him finding them himself and coming to full power."

"Right," I said. I had completely forgotten about what the Fates had told us. We had to find the three people that held Kronus' head, heart, and soul essence. Then I had to absorb them and destroy them. Sounded like fun.

I looked at Jett and he squeezed my hand.

"How are we going to find these people?" I asked him.

"I'm thinking that the gods have been keeping an eye on the essences. I'm sure that they haven't just let people walk around unchecked with a slice of Kronus in them. We just need to find out who they are and get to them before Kronus or his friends do," Jett said.

"Right, sounds like a plan," I said nodding.

"It'll be okay, Laya," Jett said. "I can take Rayna with me and go get these people and bring them here."

"What? You're not serious. I'm not going to just sit here like some helpless little lady, Jett. Seriously?"

"What? No! That's not what I was saying! I just meant that you would be able to stay out of danger and wouldn't have to worry about facing Ares or any-...yeah, okay, I can see where this sounds bad," he admitted. I looked at him straight in the eye.

"I'm coming," I stated.

"Got it," he said with a nod.

"The Fates said that it would take us both to pull this off. You need me just as much as I need you," I pointed out.

"Just not a fan of walking into a situation where I'm pretty sure we will be tailed by Kronus' posse," Jett said.

"Me neither, but we have some tricks up our sleeves," I said to him, lifting a hand and pulling my power out igniting a white flame on the top of my finger.

"You planning on lighting some candles with that?" he teased.

I pulled harder and the flames shot up my arms and across my shoulders. I could feel the power race down my back, engulfing the rest of me in flames. A warm feeling seeped into me as the white power took over my skin. I had never done that before, but I could feel the band on my wrist doing its job. Keeping the full force of the power back, I was able to command exactly what I wished. Picturing what I wanted. I put my faith into my ability to make it happen.

Confidence. It was all about confidence.

Jett's eyes widened as he looked at me. I smiled triumphantly. It felt so good to have control – to know that I was ultimately the boss of what laid within me. I hadn't felt control until that moment and it felt really good.

KYLAYA

AN ARM pulled tightly around me. The feeling of it grounded me and kept me safe. My eyes opened to a dark room. Breathing deeply, I took in the fresh air. I turned in bed and slammed my head into my pillow.

"Ouch!" I whined.

It wasn't my pillow; it was Jett's arm.

"Getting violent in your sleep, I see," he said, as he turned to me. His eyes were a new blue I wasn't accustomed to seeing, yet. They suited him. There was a smile on his lips that I was all too happy to see.

"Hey," I uttered and kissed him lightly on the cheek. "Sorry to wake you."

"I wasn't sleeping. You've been tossing and moaning all night," he said and yawned.

"Oh, no! I'm so sorry," I apologized, feeling guilty for keeping him from the rest I knew he needed.

"Don't worry about it. I wouldn't have slept anyway," he said.

"Too much on your mind?" I asked.

"Do you remember anything from last night?" he asked me.

"Of course!" I said to him and then stopped. I remembered snuggling into bed with him. Things started to get a little fuzzy from there. "We crawled into bed and went to sleep. Right?"

"Not right," he said, looking straight at me.

"Why? What happened?"

He grabbed my hand and lifted it up. Wound tightly around my skin was a golden bracelet.

"Where did that come from?" I asked and tried to grab it. My finger sailed over it, as if it wasn't even there. I looked at Jett.

"Don't panic. It's a blocker for your powers. Like my ring is for me," he explained.

"It's in my *skin*, Jett," I said, trying to scratch at it. Bracelet my butt. I had been tattooed!

"It sinks below the skin and keeps your powers under control, but it's not as strong as it needs to be for your full power," he said.

"What happened last night? Why don't I remember getting this bracelet tattoo?" I asked scratching at the bracelet. I didn't like it.

"Your powers woke up last night, at least some of them did," he said.

"What? How? Oh, my gods…what did I do? Where's Jasper? Sam? Mazz? Rayna! Are they okay? Where did this bracelet come from? What did I *do*?" I was on my knees facing Jett and my voice was nothing less than a yell.

"Everyone is *fine*. We are fine. You are fine. Things just got a little out of control for a while."

"Out of control, like how?" I asked, sitting on my feet and watching Jett.

"Honestly? I think something woke with your powers and kind of…took over."

"Took over?"

"Yeah."

"But…when? How?"

"I'm not sure exactly. We were snuggled in bed when you started…umm," he mumbled. A blush appeared on his cheeks and I knew what he was going to say.

"Oh my gods," I said placing my hands over my face. "What did I do? How can I not remember any of this?"

"You were under the spell of your powers. As far as I could tell, it was like you had one or a dozen too many drinks," he said.

"Did we…I mean, did I…" I couldn't finish the thought. *Did we have sex and I didn't remember it?*

"Gods, no," Jett chuckled. "I told you, I want to take it slow. You were not in agreement last night, though."

"Well, that's just fabulous," I said as I slammed my face into my pillow. I must have shaken something loose because an image jumped to the front of my mind. I sat up and looked at Jett.

"Did I shoot you with my power?" I asked. Jett's brows arched high.

"You remember something!" he smiled.

"That is not something to smile about, Jett!" I yelled. "Did I hurt you?"

"I'm fine," he said with a wave of his hand, but I wasn't convinced. I reached out and pulled his hand, turning his shoulder toward me. There, at the top of his arm was a red mark on his skin. A mark from a wound that had healed thanks to his new powers.

My eyes flew to his. He looked back at me and sighed.

"I'm fine, really. It was just a scratch," he said. I drew my fingers along the line on his skin, my heart hurting and angry. I did that. My powers. Me. I hurt him.

"It's okay, Laya. You didn't have control."

"That's a major problem, Jett! Don't you see that?"

"Hey," he said, as he moved in front of me and grasping my arms in his hands. "We will work through this together. Okay? You have the bracelet now. That will help keep you in control for the time being."

"And then what?" I asked. "When my powers get stronger? When this thing doesn't work anymore? I'll be a danger to everyone I love. I can't-"

"That's not going to happen. I won't let it," he said, gripping me tighter. I sighed and dropped my head. If I hurt anyone, I wouldn't be able to live with myself. I knew that.

"I – I have a confession."

"What now?" I asked, looking at him. "Did I sprout bat wings and fly around the room too?"

"No," he chuckled. "But I admit that it took me longer than it should have to realize that it wasn't really you in the room with me."

"Oh," I uttered, not knowing how to take that. "How…how long did it take you? I mean, did we *do* stuff?" I looked at him.

"No, nothing like that. I just should have known that it wasn't you."

"Did you know that my powers could turn me into someone else?"

"Well, no but-"

"Was it an extreme change right away?"

"No, but-"

"Did I scream, '*I want to have your babies!*' and you were like, '*Sure, that sounds reasonable.*'?"

Jett chuckled and shook his head.

"Well," I went on. "I'm not sure I would have been able to figure out that you weren't *you* either; not until you did something out of character. I'm going to guess that throwing myself on your crotch might have peeked your suspicion. At least I hope it did."

"It did," he said.

"There you go," I said sitting up and looking at him hard. "You did nothing wrong, Jett."

He slowly nodded his head, but he dropped his eyes away from mine. I knew there was guilt in there still. I wasn't mad at him for not knowing immediately - I was scared. Obviously, whatever was inside me could fake being me long enough to trick Jett. That wasn't good. Not good at all.

"You know what? Considering the situation, maybe we need a security word; just to check in with each other."

"What do you mean?" Jett asked, perking up.

"Something that only we know. That we can say to each other so that we know that it's really us and not the power," I said. "Would you like that?"

"I would," he agreed.

"Great! What do you want to say?"

"To fos mou," he said.

"What?"

"It means 'my light', in Greek," he answered.

"How on earth do you know that?" I asked.

"I'm going to guess that there's a little ancient Greek wandering around these powers. Those words pop into my head whenever you enter the room."

"Aww," I gushed. "Say it again."

"To fos mou," he said, slowly while wrapping a hand around my cheek.

"To fos mou," I repeated. The words struck something in me and I felt a burst in my core.

"Agapi mou," I uttered.

"What?" Jett asked watching me.

"Agapi mou," I repeated. "It means-"

"My love," he said, finishing my thought for me. His eyes connected with mine and I felt held by them.

"You feel that too, don't you?" I asked him.

"The presence behind the power?" he asked.

"Yes," I said, swallowing hard, knowing what that meant.

"The powers aren't the only thing that we were given, it seems," Jett said.

"I agree," I answered.

"To fos mou? Agapi mou? They were what Gaia and Uranus used to call each other, weren't they?" I asked him.

"I think so," he said.

"Well, that sucks. I liked them," I answered with a laugh.

"Me too."

"Dreamstop," I said and smiled at him. His eyes turned to me and a smile lit his face.

"Perfect," he said and kissed me.

"And that's the perfect answer," I said back.

For so long, Jett and I were stuck in our dreams, not able to share any location information or even touch. Anything that could reveal where we were or who we really were, was taken from us. If we touched, we would wake from our dream. We started to identify what we could and couldn't do. 'Dreamstop' was our way of saying what we *wanted* to say, even though we couldn't. It was our way of communicating that we wanted more. That we *felt* more.

To say 'dreamstop' and answer with a kiss was to fulfill our dream of wanting to be with each other. It was something only we knew and it was the perfect way of making sure that we were really ourselves.

"Well, I'm glad that's settled," Jett said. "Not a fan of needing that, though."

"Me neither. We need to find out more about what these powers really are. I have a sick feeling that we have only been given half information."

"I agree," he answered, "but, don't forget we have to find Kronus' essences too. We can't have him finding them himself and coming to full power."

"Right," I said. I had completely forgotten about what the Fates had told us. We had to find the three people that held Kronus' head, heart, and soul essence. Then I had to absorb them and destroy them. Sounded like fun.

I looked at Jett and he squeezed my hand.

"How are we going to find these people?" I asked him.

"I'm thinking that the gods have been keeping an eye on the essences. I'm sure that they haven't just let people walk around unchecked with a slice of Kronus in them. We just need to find out who they are and get to them before Kronus or his friends do," Jett said.

"Right, sounds like a plan," I said nodding.

"It'll be okay, Laya," Jett said. "I can take Rayna with me and go get these people and bring them here."

"What? You're not serious. I'm not going to just sit here like some helpless little lady, Jett. Seriously?"

"What? No! That's not what I was saying! I just meant that you would be able to stay out of danger and wouldn't have to worry about facing Ares or any-...yeah, okay, I can see where this sounds bad," he admitted. I looked at him straight in the eye.

"I'm coming," I stated.

"Got it," he said with a nod.

"The Fates said that it would take us both to pull this off. You need me just as much as I need you," I pointed out.

"Just not a fan of walking into a situation where I'm pretty sure we will be tailed by Kronus' posse," Jett said.

"Me neither, but we have some tricks up our sleeves," I said to him, lifting a hand and pulling my power out igniting a white flame on the top of my finger.

"You planning on lighting some candles with that?" he teased.

I pulled harder and the flames shot up my arms and across my shoulders. I could feel the power race down my back, engulfing the rest of me in flames. A warm feeling seeped into me as the white power took over my skin. I had never done that before, but I could feel the band on my wrist doing its job. Keeping the full force of the power back, I was able to command exactly what I wished. Picturing what I wanted. I put my faith into my ability to make it happen.

Confidence. It was all about confidence.

Jett's eyes widened as he looked at me. I smiled triumphantly. It felt so good to have control – to know that I was ultimately the boss of what laid within me. I hadn't felt control until that moment and it felt really good.

Jett didn't say anything, instead he closed the distance between us in a flash and kissed me. The fire on my skin parted for him, recognizing him. He was untouched by my powers as his hands grasped the sides of my face.

"Gods, you are so sexy," he whispered against my lips.

"Glad you approve," I giggled, surprised at his reaction.

"Oh, I approve. Especially since you burned your clothes right off," he said and lifted his brows.

"What!" I shrieked, looking down. The flames extinguished revealing my skin…only my skin. I dove at the covers, pulling them around me. "Oh my gods!" I whined and pulled the sheets over my head. I wanted to die right there.

Confidence gone. All gone!

The bed vibrated from Jett's laughing.

"Shut up!" I yelled from under the covers.

"I'm sorry-"

"No, you're not!"

"Okay, you got me there. I'm not," he said, still chuckling.

"Can you, please, get me some clothes?" I asked him, pulling my head out of the covers and glaring at him.

"I want to say *get them yourself*, but I prefer not to get my ass zapped," he said and stood.

"Smart," I said back.

He reached into the dresser and pulled out a grey tank and a black pair of leggings.

"Thanks," I said, yanking them from his hands.

"My pleasure." His smile reached his eyes and beyond, as his eyes dipped toward my chest - which was still covered by the sheets.

"Hey, perv, my eyes are up here," I said, pointing to my face.

"I know," he said, still looking at my chest.

I picked up a pillow and hurled it at him. He laughed and caught it.

"I'll give you a minute," he said and walked to the door. "Laya?" he asked as he grabbed the doorknob.

"What?" I asked as I threaded my arms into the tank.

"I'm proud of you," he said.

"What?"

"The power…it was beautiful," he said and left the room. I smiled to myself.

It *was* pretty awesome…just needed to work on not turning my clothes to ash when I used them.

Confidence, Laya. Confidence.

JETT

"YOU'RE TELLING ME that you *willingly* put something on your body to stop your powers?" Sam asked.

"Yes. We really didn't have a choice. It was that or…explode," I explained.

"I see," he answered.

"Why, what's so bad about the bracelet Laya has?" Jasper asked, taking a seat at the small table in the corner of the sitting room by the window.

It has been a day since Sam had revealed that he was really Apollo's son, Asclepius. Jasper was taking it well, I supposed. He was speaking to Sam, but I wouldn't say that things were back to normal. I wondered if they ever would be.

Well, that's a depressing thought.

"The rings that Cottus is talking about were used to bind the Titans. They are powerful and they are controlled by the Olympians. Before you put anything on you, make sure that you know who is going to have control over your power. If it is anyone but you…well, I would start practicing your control all on your own."

"Are you saying that the Olympians are using us?" I asked.

"No, but I wouldn't trust them outright either. They have their own agenda where Kronus is concerned, you can bet on that. How you fit into it, we don't know. Just…be careful," Sam said.

"I will," I said. "This isn't a long-term solution. I don't want to depend on my ring for the rest of my life. Don't want to explode with power either."

Jasper chuckled and I looked at him with a raised brow.

"Oh, come on. That was funny" he said. I rolled my eyes.

Sam watched Jasper closely. The awkwardness was there in their every move. Normally, you could see their relationship in everything they did. A touch of a hand here. A look there. Their connection was always extending between the two of them. But, now, I didn't see it. There was a wall there and it was Jasper that had built it. I understood why. Sam had really hurt him. I couldn't imagine how it would feel to find out that Laya had been hiding something so big from me.

The door to her room opened and Laya stepped out, pulling her long blonde hair up into a pony. She looked serious and adorable all in one. Her big round blue eyes looked at me over her long lashes and I wanted to turn her around and march her back in that room.

"Hello?" she said, waving a hand in front of my eyes.

"What?" I said, coming out of my sex-filled daydream. A light laugh tumbled from her glossed lips. I pictured picking her up and carrying her back to the room right then and there. Tumbling into bed for the rest of the day was more than enticing.

"You okay?" she asked, sitting down next to me at the table. She rested a hand on my leg. Gods…*what is wrong with me?*

"Good. All good," I said and smiled. Laya's attention shifted to Jasper and Sam. I could see the concern in her furrowed brow. She reached over and squeezed Jasper's hand. He gave her a half smile. My stomach dropped. Jasper's typically sunny disposition had dimmed; it was just so sad to see. I was used to this bright and loud person around me all the time. Sam's news had taken all of that out of him.

"Any news from Cottus?" Laya asked as she filled a plate with the fresh fruit that Eurybia has laid out for us.

"Nothing, yet. However, Eurybia said that he would be back soon," I said.

"Good. I want to get going. We still have all of Kronus' essences to find. Any ideas where they might be?" she asked.

"Eurybia said that the Olympians have information on that. We should be able to find them without too much trouble," I said.

"Ha! Famous last words," Sam laughed.

"What's that supposed to mean?" Jasper bit, staring at Sam with cold eyes.

"Just that the gods have guards for these essences. They weren't going to let them waltz around unprotected, just in case one of the gods decided to go rogue," he explained.

"Why is this the first time we are hearing about *this*?" Laya asked, sitting up straighter and leaning toward Sam. "What kind of guards are we talking here? Gods? Monsters? Humans? What?"

"I don't know," Sam answered. "The Olympians weren't the ones that placed the guards. It was the Fates. They are impartial and no one would worry about them wanting to release Kronus. It would serve no purpose for them," Sam said.

"They neglected to tell us that when we were there," I said, grimacing. *Of course.*

"Well, there's nothing that we can really do, now can we? We have to get the essences. Whatever is guarding them we'll just have to get through," Laya said with more confidence than I had.

I wasn't feeling the same. Going into a fight that we weren't prepared for was a risk that I wasn't willing to make. I looked at Laya and knew that she was going to fight me on it. But, deep down, I knew that if we were going to succeed some reconnaissance work was going to have to be done.

"Sam, can I talk to you?" I asked and stood from the table. Sam looked up and I could see the uncertainty in his expression. I rolled my eyes. "I'm not going to punch you, I promise."

Sam looked at Jasper.

"You can punch him, that's fine with me," Jasper said loudly. Laya grimaced, wrinkling her nose up and looked at Sam. Sam looked like he had been slapped.

"I'll keep it in mind," I said and pulled Sam away from the table and into the stairway. Laya and Jasper's eyes followed us through the door and down the stairs.

"Okay, if you're just trying to take me out of ear shot to punch me, this is far enough. If you want to kick my ass, can we keep going so that Jasper doesn't have to hear it," Sam said.

"Would you even put up a fight if I said that I wanted to kick your ass?" I asked him.

"No," Sam admitted. "I deserve it."

"You don't really think that I am going to beat you up do you?" I asked him.

"No, but then I didn't think that Jasper would ask you to," he answered. I nodded.

"True. But, that's not what I wanted to talk to you about." Sam's brows went up.

"Really?"

"Really." I shifted my weight back and leaned against the wall on the stairs, crossing my hands over my chest. "I want to scout out the locations where the essences are. I want to know what we are facing before bringing Laya into it."

"You want to go without KyLaya?" Sam asked, looking at me with wide eyes.

"Yes."

"And she knows about this?"

"No."

"And, you think that's a good idea?" Sam asked, looking at me unconvinced.

"This way we'll be prepared," I said.

"She's going to be pissed," Sam said. "This is a bad idea, Jett."

"She'll understand," I said.

"Really? She'll understand that you kept something from her that could have led to you getting hurt? Even killed? Something that she would have helped you with?"

"You're one to talk here, *Asclepius*," I barked back. Sam crossed his arms and tightened his lips.

"Well, learn from my mistake then," he said.

"Just take me to the first one, damn it!" I yelled. Sam rolled his eyes and grabbed my hand.

"Don't say I didn't warn you," he sighed.

There was a pop and the stairway melted away as darkness took us from Eurybia's.

. . .

A DARK ROOM took form before me. When I heard the *pop,* we were solidly there. Close to the size of my kitchen back home, our location slowly came into focus.

The cement walls were grimy and stained. There was no different in colour from the floor to the walls, everything looked dark and dank. But nothing was as bad as the smell that hung in the air. I could barely breathe through the stench of…blood?

"Where are we?" I asked him.

"In Stronghold," he answered.

"What?" I shouted in a hushed voice. "Why in Hades have you brought us here?"

"Because, you wanted to see where the first essence was," he answered.

"It's *here*?"

"Yes."

"In Stronghold?"

"Yes."

"Great. That's great," I placed my hands on my hips and started to pace. My feet stuck to the caked mess that was on the floor. I didn't even want to guess what I was stepping in. Just thinking about it, my stomach churned.

"Who is the essence, or rather, who has it?" I asked.

"I don't know. Eurybia didn't tell me. The first is the head, or the mind of Kronus," he said.

"How are we supposed to figure out which Siren has it?"

"There is a marker, but it is only visible to primordials," he said.

"Well then, I should be able to see it, right? I have primordial power."

"I suppose so," Sam answered.

"What's the mark?"

"It's a white glow, or at least that I've heard."

"Okay, a white glow. So, I'm supposed to just walk around here and look for a Siren that is glowing?" I asked.

"Hey, *you're* the one that wanted to come here," Sam said, shrugging.

"Alright, fine. But, what about the guard they were talking about. The essences are guarded."

"I'm going to guess the whole host of Sirens is the guards," Sam answered. "It's not like you can just walk up to the door here and look through everyone."

"Well, you just popped us into the place without invitation. What's stopping Ares and his friends from doing the same thing?" I asked.

"They would need more information about the essence carrier. There's no test for this. The mark can only be seen by primordial blood. You," he said. "Ares would be wandering around here just looking at everyone like a creep."

"You think he hasn't been? I mean, he's mine and Jasper's father with Queen Midira's daughter. He wouldn't be a stranger here."

"That's true," Sam admitted.

I sighed and crossed my arms, trying to decide our next course of action.

"Ares aside, if you want to find this essence before he does, we need to find a better way of blending in," Sam said.

"And, how do you propose we do that in an all-female place like this?" I asked, looking at him and placing my hands on my hips.

"Come with Laya," he said and looked at me.

"What?"

"You heard me. I said that this was a stupid idea, but you wouldn't listen."

"You *really* are no help."

"Just 'cause you don't want to hear the truth, doesn't mean that I'm not helpful," Sam answered back.

"Well, if your definition of help is just to complain - I'm good without it," I barked back.

"You want me to go? I can go," Sam barked back.

I glared at him.

"Fine, if you are determined to find this essence, we're going to-"

Voices sounded outside the door. We both froze.

"Shit!" I hissed.

"We have to hide," Sam said. "Back there!"

Sam pointed to the back of the room. There was an observation booth built into the back wall. There was no mistaking that this was an interrogation room. Sam and I dove into the room and closed the door just as the handle turned on the main door. Breathlessly, we looked out the window.

In walked a Siren. She was tall and lean, wearing her battle gear. A fitted blood-red leather-like suit that allowed her to move in the water and protect her skin from attack. It also masked the blood that she brought out of her enemies. But when she turned around my heart came to a full stop.

"What?" I whispered. Sam's eyes were just about as big as mine.

"It's not," he uttered.

The Siren looked like Laya. Almost exactly the same. From her blonde hair to her big eyes, there was no mistaking the similarity. If it wasn't for the violet color of her eyes, I would have sworn that Laya had just walked in.

"They could be twins!" Sam whispered. All I could do was nod. How was that possible? I knew that a fight with a Siren was just about inevitable but there was no way that I was going to be able to throw a punch at her, let alone use my power. I looked at Sam and could tell he was thinking the same thing.

Walking to the wall, the Siren retrieved a set of chains and a chair from the floor. Being a host for a few interrogations myself, I knew what she was doing.

"A Siren interrogation. This can't be good," Sam said. I nodded in agreement. The Sirens were viscous, known for their innovative ways of torturing their victims. We *relaxed* those that we interrogated into telling us what we needed to know back home. The Sirens hurt their victims for the fun of it.

The Laya doppelganger walked to the door and pulled it open. She looked down the hallway and gave a nod. In walked another Siren, pulling someone behind her. The prisoner was thrown into the room, where they collapsed on the floor. A messy mop of filthy hair fell over their eyes. Long, lanky legs with knobby knees folded under a tattered tunic, as the prisoner sank to the ground. My stomach dropped. It was a boy.

"What would the Sirens be doing with a young male?" I asked Sam. He shook his head. The Sirens were only interested in females. When they took prisoners, they were female. They had no use for males - other than for procreation.

The Laya look-alike grabbed the boy and slammed him into the chair, tying his arms behind his back. His head hung forward as the binds were tightened around his tiny wrists.

"This isn't right, Sam," I uttered. "I can't just sit here and let them torture a child."

"You have to," he said. "You walk out that door and we're both dead."

"I think you're forgetting who we really are," I said to him.

"I am not," he answered. "The Siren blades are poisonous, which won't kill us, granted, but they will slow us down. Enough of them could cause us to lose consciousness. While we are unconscious, the Sirens could then dismember us. Sure, we would still be *technically* living, since our souls are tied to our eternal bodies. We would never decompose, just be disembodied parts for all eternity in some room here in Stronghold."

My jaw dropped open.

"Are you serious?" I uttered, staring at him.

"Why would I lie about having my body drawn and quartered," he whispered, shaking his head. "There are a few things that you need to learn about immortality, Jett. It's not all it's cracked up to be, and you *aren't* untouchable."

"Okay, okay," I grumbled. "I won't blast out of here."

"Good to know. I was hoping to return to Jasper with all my parts in tact."

I turned my eyes out the window and watched as the Laya doppelganger circled the young boy. My muscles clenched when she grabbed the back of his head and yanked it up. His dirty face lit up in the dim light.

"Rall?"

"What?" Sam said, moving closer. "No, it can't be."

I looked closer at the boy and knew instantly that it was Rall. Rayna's brother. He was one of the Sirenites that were taken the night that Deimos and Phobos came to Stenen. I couldn't believe it; they had been taken to Stronghold.

Rall's eyes were wide and frightened; and, no matter how much I wanted to remain cold and distant from the situation, there was no way I was going to be able to do that. My heart was thundering in my chest as rage and fear battled it out within me. Sensing a fight, my powers flamed to life across my arms and shoulders. I could feel the rush of them along my skin.

"What do we do?" Sam asked.

"Well, for one, if she hurts a hair on his head, I'm going to blast her through that wall. Siren blades be damned," I uttered, glaring at the woman through the glass. Laya look-alike or not. No one hurts my friends.

The Siren looked down at Rall, her eyes narrowed and she dropped his head. I sighed in relief. I didn't know how we were going to get him out of there, but I would be damned if we were leaving him. He was coming home with us.

"I don't want to hurt you, young one," the Siren said. "But, I will if you don't start talking."

"I don't know anything," Rall cried.

"Now, that just isn't true. You've been living with the Sirenites for many years. You know more than you think. You just have to remember," she said.

"Remember what? What do you *want?*" he asked.

"The location," she said.

"Location? What location? I don't know what you are talking about," he said. My stomach turned. What was she looking for?

"Where are the reincarnations?" she whispered.

"I don't know what that is!" he sobbed. His dirty face scrunching up as tears left clean lines on his dirty face. *Gods what have they done to him?*

A smile that I knew all too well slid across her face. She glided a finger over Rall's cheeks and under his chin, and a chill went down my spine. His lip wobbled when she bent to look him in the eye.

She was so cold, not an inch of emotion or sympathy. Laya was all warmth but this woman, this Siren, was ice.

"Geez," Sam uttered.

I didn't break my eyes away from Rall for a second. He was just a child. What were the Sirens doing with him? Obviously, Deimos and Phobos had gifted them with the Sirenites. But, why?

"I don't know anything," Rall said again.

Three knocks sounded at the door. The Siren stood and looked at the door.

"We'll, see. Seems you have caught the eye of my Mistress. She wants to ask you questions herself. You should feel honored," the Laya look-alike said, as she trailed a hand gently over Ralls shoulder while she circled him. He shrank away from her touch.

"Who's Mistress?" I asked, turning to Sam.

"What makes you think *I* know that?" Sam asked.

"Not like you haven't withheld any information from us," I whispered back.

"I don't keep up with the Siren hierarchy. Kind of been dedicating my time to my marriage," Sam said. I sighed.

It was then that the door opened and another Siren walked in. The light from the hallway was almost blinding. I held my hand over my eyes to shield them.

"What's your problem?" Sam asked, looking at me like I had lost my mind.

"What? The light isn't too much for your godly eyes?" I barked back.

"What light?" he asked.

"The light from the hallway, Sam. Geez, how blind are you?" I asked.

"The hall is dark, Jett. You're telling me that you're seeing a bright light?" he asked.

"You mean you *aren't*?" I asked.

"It's her," he said, pointing to the Siren that had just walked in.

"You mean?"

"The essence," he nodded.

I dropped my hand and willed my eyes to adjust to the brightness in the room. The new Siren stood just inside the room. Her hair was a mousy brown, long and wavy, tied back in a standard Siren's ponytail. Taller than the other Siren, with startling violet eyes, she moved with a grace that was otherworldly and undeniably deadly.

"You can go, Lena," she said, tipping her head to the door.

"Yes, Mistress Ana."

Lena, Laya's look-alike, bowed her head and left immediately. There was no denying that Mistress Ana was a higher-ranking Siren. From what I knew about Siren culture that would guarantee that she was more vicious and deadly than the others. That was pretty much the only way that you could rise in their ranks - unless, you were royalty. However, having kids wasn't in Midira's power anymore. Mistress Ana circled Rall as his eyes followed her.

"We have to do something. She's here to extract information from him. It's not going to be pretty," I said.

"Agreed, but she has the essence. We need KyLaya. She can take the essence and we can rescue Rall at the same time," Sam said.

"I can't leave the rest of the Sirenites here. This isn't a scouting mission anymore, it's a rescue," I said to him.

"I agree," Sam said and popped out of existence.

"What the hell?" I gasped as he disappeared. "That sneaky, son of a Siren!"

I cursed out Sam a few more times and turned my attention to the room. To Rall.

"There's something in that small, little, head of yours that I need. That the Queen needs," Mistress Ana said.

"I don't know anything. No one tells me anything," he said.

"Well, that's not true. Adults talk around kids all the time, because you are invisible. Insignificant. No one cares about you. You know something very valuable. We just have to pull it from you," she said.

"I don't. I really don't."

"I have my ways of pulling information, but you are young and I would prefer not to use them on you," she said. Rall's shoulders sank a little in relief. "That's not saying that I won't. But you have to give me something."

She turned and placed her hands on either side of his chair. Leaning down in from of him she met his eyes straight on and shouted. "Bring her in!"

The door opened and the Laya look-alike came back in with a woman. It was Rayna's mother, Dee. Her clothes were torn and filthy, just like Rall's.

"Rall!" she screamed and ran for him. The doppelganger reached out, grabbed her hair and yanked her away. Her body continued to move forward, as her head was snapped back. Dee's scream cut right through me.

Shit.

Should I blast them all? I didn't want to hurt Rall or Dee. The two Sirens were strapped with blades that were tipped with poison. After Sam told me about the danger of them, I knew I couldn't just crash in and stir up stuff. I would have to do this quietly, so I could get the two of them out without warning the other Sirens that we were there. But I was running out of time.

"Mom!" Rall shouted and tried to go to her. His sobs pierced my heart and allowed panic to set in.

Damn it, Sam. Where the hell did you go?

"Now," Mistress Ana said, standing between Rall and Dee. "Someone is going to tell me what I want to know, or one of you is going to die."

"We don't know anything!" Dee yelled at them. I had to give her credit, she was throwing some serious glares at the Sirens. She may have been at their mercy, but she wasn't begging for it.

The Laya look-alike left, leaving Mistress Ana alone with Rall and Dee.

There was a pop in the room and I got punched in the head.

"Ow!" I hissed and turned, ready to defend myself. Behind me, Laya stood. Her hands were on her hips as she levelled a grade 'A' glare at me.

"You have a hell of a lot of explaining to do," she hissed at me.

"Fair enough, but later," I said and pointed out of the room through the window.

"Oh, no. Dee," Sam whispered, coming forward.

"What's the plan?" Laya asked, crouching down.

I looked at Sam who was looking at Laya.

"Can't you see it?" Sam asked her.

"The Sirenites? Yeah, I'm not blind," she whispered back and shook her head.

"No, the light," I said.

"What light?" she asked.

"The essence. She can't see it," Sam said.

"But-"

"You're meant to *find* them and she's meant to *take* them. Without each other, Kronus can't be defeated," Sam explained.

It made sense. Another fail-safe Gaia and Uranus put into place, I supposed.

"As much as I want to know what you two old ladies are gossiping about, we have a rather urgent situation here," Laya whispered with a glare.

"Right. We can't do this loudly, the rest of the Sirens would be here in a flash and we'll never find out where the others are being held," Sam said.

"There's no way we're leaving them here to be tortured," I countered.

"Agreed. What are the Sirens looking for?" Laya asked.

"I think-"

That's when Mistress Ana cracked Rall across his face. Pink flashed in the room as my power lit up. Rage in my core poured forth stronger than ever before. I could feel the power of Uranus coming and there was little I could do to stop it.

"Jett?" Laya's voice cut through the anger and sank in. I looked to her. Her eyes were white. "You need to calm down. Whatever you're doing…it's happening to me too."

I swallowed and willed myself to cool off…but when Mistress Ana drew a dagger my self-control went out the window.

"Jett…" Laya uttered, but that was the last of her voice I heard.

My eyes were only for the innocents in the next room.

"Get down," I said, in a voice I didn't recognize. With the slightest flick on my hand, the window exploded. All heads in the interrogation room snapped to me. Mistress Ana eyes were wide as they circled the three of us in the room.

"What the hell?" she yelled. "Who are *you*?"

I didn't answer. Power coursed through me like an electrical storm.

"Kill her." A voice demanded from the corner of my mind.

No…I shouldn't…

"Do it!"

I clenched my hands so tight I thought my bones were going to break.

"Laya. She has the essence," I choked out. She didn't hesitate or ask. She jumped through the window and charged after Mistress Ana.

Mistress Ana didn't wait to see what Laya was going to do, she flashed a dagger into her hand and pressed it to Rall's throat.

"If you take one more step, you better believe, I will cut his neck clean through," the Mistress yelled.

"Laya…" I uttered. The power was beyond a hum. Like a raging river, it banked and crashed through me. With every pulse it came closer and closer to breaking through.

Rall's eyes were wild as he looked at us.

"Who are you?" Mistress Ana asked, looking between all of us.

"You have something that *we* want," Laya said, keeping her eyes steady on the Siren.

"If you think that coming here has done anything other than spell your swift death, you're sadly mistaken," she answered.

Something in me whispered…

"She's going to call for reinforcements. Stop her. Now."

There was surge from inside me. Without thinking, I threw out a hand - acting on an instinct I didn't know I had. A bolt of white light shot from me, slicing into Mistress Ana's arm. She was thrown back away from Rall. Her dagger clanged off the hard floor, skittering out of her reach. Blood dripped to the ground from her open wound, mixing with the blood of countless victims of interrogations held in that room.

"Laya!" I shouted.

Laya ran forward. The Siren lunged for the dagger, but Rall turned in his chair and kicked it out of her reach. Before the Siren could turn her anger on him, Laya swung out an arm, hitting away the Siren's attempt on Rall. Mistress Ana's attention, now safely on Laya and not Rall, she started to circle Laya, trying to find a weakness. She wouldn't find one. Laya was an excellent fighter. Neither one having a weapon, Laya was now in a hand to hand grappling match with Mistress Ana. It took every ounce of control to keep my powers from exploding out as Laya tried to get her hands on the Siren.

Mistress Ana swept her arm through the air at Laya, strong and true. She ducked out of the way easily, coming up under the Siren's outstretched arm. Mistress Ana opened her mouth to scream, but Laya flashed forward in a blur and placed her hands on the Siren's face.

The Siren's scream cut through the room like a knife as Laya pulled. White light streamed out of Laya's eyes. Tendrils of brilliant light, reached out for every corner of the room from Laya's hands. I could feel a pull to her power, and keeping mine under control became that much more difficult.

There was a pulse in the room, the way I imagined a goldfish felt when someone tapped their bowl. Then an explosion of air burst from the connection between Laya and Mistress Ana. With the strength of a hurricane, it bowled over Rall and Dee. Sam fought his way to the two of them and dragged them out of the way of Laya's power.

I couldn't pull my eyes away from Laya.

Her eyes white. Her hair lifting off her shoulders and moving around her as if she were in water. The Siren's screams died on her lips as Laya pulled.

It's taking too long.

I knew Laya's powers were a force to be reckoned with, so I eased myself across the room to her side. As they did before, her powers parted for me as I stepped up beside her.

"Do you have it?" I asked Laya.

"It's…so…strong," she said, her voice strained. "I…can't get it to let go of her."

"You have to, Laya. You can do it," I encouraged her. Her brows furrowed as her concentration mounted. The light from the connection flamed brighter, but I wouldn't look away.

The Siren's eyes were wide and blood ran down her nose, as Laya pulled and pulled.

"You got this, Laya," I encouraged.

"I can't Jett," she said. "I'm not strong enough."

"You are!" I said to her.

She pulled harder and started to yell out of strain. There was another pulse in the room, and a dark plume of smoky air started to seep from the Mistress's eyes and mouth.

"You're doing it, Laya," I said. "You're doing it!"

She didn't respond, but pulled again. The darkness billowed out of the Siren into the air above her. Laya's power released the essence, slowly and painfully from the Siren. When the last of it was out, Mistress Ana collapsed on the ground, leaving the essence floating in the air above her. Laya's connection from the Siren was broken, plunging the room back into the dim that it was before. We stood breathlessly as the essence moved restlessly in the air.

Laya reached a hand out toward the darkness.

"What are you doing?" I asked her, watching the essence make lazy circles.

"I don't know. It just felt-"

The essence stirred and we both froze. Its movements shifted from lazy to energetic. If I didn't know any better, it looked excited. That didn't sit well with me.

"Laya," I said, but never got to finish as the essence flipped in the air and plunged for her.

"Watch out!" I yelled and threw myself in front of her.

I was too late.

The essence, moving faster than me, drove into Laya.

Her head threw back as the essence pierced her eyes and reached down her throat.

"My gods," I uttered. The sight was terrifying. The black mass pushed into her body, filling her.

She screamed.

She shook - like an electrocution victim.

She stood. Her arms outstretched, head to the heavens, mouth gaping open, and eyes wide as the black mass of Kronus' essence plunged into her.

"What do we do?" I called to Sam.

"I don't know!" he said.

"Stop it! Get it out of her!" I yelled at him.

"I don't have that kind of power. Only a primordial can do that!" he said.

Laya's eyes stared wide, unseeing and terrified. She was being hurt - tortured by the essence of Kronus.

"Laya, what do I do? What do I do?" I asked placing my hands on her face, forcing her eyes to me as I moved her head. I watched in horror as the black from Kronus bled into the whites of her eyes. The essence dimmed the light coming from her - smothering it with its encompassing darkness.

"Shit," I whispered.

Laya stopped shaking. Her body stilled as she slowly brought her head down and met my eyes.

Immediately, I could feel something off. She glared at me as the corner of her mouth tipped up. I staggered back a step. Her eyes were as black as ebony.

Gods.

"Laya?"

"Oh, she's not home right now," she said and tilted her head at me. Her eyes roamed my length and then came back to my eyes. "Funny. I thought father would have picked someone…bigger."

"Kronus?" I uttered.

"In the flesh…well," Laya shrugged as she ran her hands down her body. "Not *my* flesh. Not yet."

"Where's Laya?"

"She's kicking around in here somewhere. Most likely hiding in a corner crying. I tend to have that effect on women," Kronus said, a cold smile spreading across her face.

"I know you're in there, Laya," I said.

"Oh stop. That's not going to work. I've been bounced around from person to person for eons. Every time…weak, so infernally *weak*!" Laya started to pace, throwing her hands in the air. "Finally! I have a body worthy of *me*! Now, all I have to do is find the rest of myself! This is a great start, better than I could have ever wished for!" Laya smiled, nodding satisfied.

"This is not your body, Kronus. You have no right to it," I said.

"Blah. Blah," Kronus said in a mocking tone as she flapped her hands at me. "I don't like you." I felt power swell in the room before I saw it and knew to dive out of the way. Laya's hands glowed white as Kronus pulled on her power. A bolt of white light shot from her and collided with the wall behind me.

"Get them out of here!" I yelled at Sam. Rall and Dee needed to go. That explosion was sure to attract the attention of the Sirens. If they came in, I would end up losing them.

My focus turned to Laya. She was grinning like a cat with a mouse in its claws.

"Ahh! It's been so *long*! That felt *damn* good!" she yelled and threw another bolt at me.

"Laya!" I shouted, but yet another bolt cut me off.

Laya laughed, deep and loud.

It was unnatural.

It was Kronus.

I wasn't giving up. I knew Laya was in there and there was no way in Hades I was going to let Kronus walk around in her body. Jumping to my feet, I dodged a bolt that crashed into the wall behind me and shook the room.

Damn, she's powerful.

I didn't want to hurt her, but I needed to get through to her. When she summoned another bolt, I ran for her. The voice in the back of my mind told me of an arrogance that blinded Kronus to the strength of others. I abandoned using my powers, the obvious attack, and went for an old fashioned full-body tackle.

My arms wrapped around Laya, as I soared through the air at her. We went crashing to the floor in a heap. The light in her palms faded on impact. Her head smacked against the floor and blood started to ooze from it. For a moment, I thought that would be it; but she lifted her head and screamed a guttural, feral scream in my face that congealed my blood.

Rage etched deep lines in her skin as she struggled against my grip. As much as Laya was a great fighter, I was still stronger than her and I was really grateful for that at that moment.

"Get off!" Laya bellowed at me. "You're going to regret this!" I pinned her arms down so that she couldn't summon her power against me – at least I hoped she couldn't. Her feet scraped against the sticky floor as she tried to get out from under me, but my weight was across her hips and I wasn't moving.

"Laya," I said gently. "I know you are in there."

She bucked, trying to throw me, but I rode the wave and stayed on her. Sam's powers of calm would have been really useful; but I had sent him off with Rall and Dee. I was on my own. I couldn't let Kronus have her. I wouldn't.

Warmth spread from my core, filling my insides in a sweet glow.

"Come back to me, my love," I whispered and lowered my head to hers. "Please."

A light shone from the spot where I touched her forehead with mine.

Our connection.

Our love.

I could feel a pull in my core and I watched as pink light seeped from my skin, rising out of me in a shimmering mist. Swirling in the air, it gently wound its way around her body.

My power.

Not Uranus'.

Mine.

Soon, she was wrapped in a blanket of misty pink. Laya bucked against my grip and struggled to get away as my power enveloped her. Her black eyes widened at seeing my power.

"What is this?" Kronus shrieked.

I didn't say anything as my power closed in, all I did was hope. Hope that she could hear me. Hope that she could feel me.

"I'm not giving her up!" Kronus' essence bellowed through Laya's lips.

"She's not yours to give up!" I said.

Laya glared back at me with stone-cold, black eyes. Her head threw back as a cardinal scream broke from her lips.

KYLAYA

IT TOOK nearly all my energy to break Kronus' essence from the Siren. I could feel where it was in her - wrapped around her soul, waiting and watching. It was sleeping, for the most part, up until I grabbed it and pulled.

The moment I touched it; it woke up. A jolt surged from it and along it came a voice.

His voice.

Kronus.

Like something out of a nightmare, his deep voice filled my body with icy coldness.

"Well, now. I wasn't expecting a wake-up call like this," he hissed. *"You are…different than the others."*

To the very tips of my fingers I could feel a change in my body as his essence entered me.

"Mmm. You, my dear, feel amazing," he purred.

I couldn't help the shiver that ran from the top of my head to the bottom of my feet at his words. A slithering sensation skated across my skin, winding tighter and tighter as his essence plunged in me.

"Power. You have so much power," he whispered. I could feel the joy in his words.

What have I done?

There was no stopping the process as Kronus took me. There was nothing outside the pain of him forcing himself in my body.

"Don't you worry, my dear. I won't destroy you. You are too valuable to me. Your power…wait. My goodness, you have my mother's power! Did you know you had my mother's power? How nice. Mommy never did let me play with her things."

His words vibrated down my spine.

I knew it was my duty to take him on, but there was no preparing for it. Kronus was not gentle, he didn't just enter me…he violated me. He filled every part of me with a wickedness I had never felt or seen in my life. Even Midira couldn't hold a candle to him.

Fighting to maintain my power over him - to keep control over my body and mind - I tried to push him back.

You can't have me.

"Oh, but I already do."

Like a thousand needles piercing my skin and every organ, he sank fully into me. I couldn't help the scream that cut out of me. There was no controlling it. Kronus crawled over me like an unwanted lover, I could feel the pressure of him across my chest. The swipe of a hand across my thigh as his powers ran through me.

No. This is my body. You are my prisoner.

"I am no one's prisoner; but I suppose if I am to be in any prison, a sweet body like this is the way to go."

I am not yours. You are mine.

A dark, deep laugh echoed right through me.

"You have no idea what you have done, my sweet."

I had to lock him away somewhere within my body, but I didn't know how to – or if I had the power to. All I knew was that I did it, I had taken him out of the Siren - just like I was supposed to. Beyond that…well, no one really told me anything beyond that. *I really should have asked more questions.*

Jett appeared before me and I reached for him. At least that was what I wanted to do, but my body didn't move.

What in Hades?

I tried again to reach him, but nothing happened.

"You didn't honestly think that you were still in control, did you?"

No matter how much I tried or how much strength I put into moving my hand, nothing happened. The laughing just got stronger and stronger.

Shut up! Just shut up! You are not *in control! I am! I am!* I shouted, but the laugh just kept going.

There was no shutting it out, no covering my ears. It was all in my head and I couldn't get away from it. Kronus' voice was everywhere. It was all I could hear; all I could think of. The more I struggled, the louder he got until I was the smallest part of my own mind. Only a fragment of what I had been.

"I would feel sorry for you, but your powers are going to make rising again so easy!" he laughed. His voice boomed, shaking me to my very core.

You can't have my powers. I won't let you.

Kronus smiled. I couldn't see it, but I could *feel* it. I knew my words were useless. I didn't truly believe what I was saying. He was just too strong and I was...*nothing.*

A swell of power built within me, and my heart chilled. I was locked in my body, and had lost all control of it.

Pushed further from control, I just about lost all connection with my power and body. Then, he pulled at my core – the very center of my power.

No matter what I did, I couldn't stop him. Gaia's abilities. Her power. Her knowledge. He now had access to it all.

There was nothing I could do as Kronus released my power. I saw Jett in front of my eyes and my heart jumped into my throat.

No! I screamed, throwing everything into my words.

"Oh, do you care for this one?" he asked.

Yes! Please! Don't...don't hurt him. I knew begging with him was useless, but I didn't know what else to do.

Another blast echoed around the room as my power struck out for Jett. Fear and anger raced through me as Kronus used *my* powers to try to kill Jett. That was when another voice joined the conversation.

A whisper from somewhere deep within me. Like a memory from another lifetime. It was nothing like Kronus – so, I knew that it wasn't coming from him. It came from somewhere...deeper. Warm and full of light, it embraced me and wrapped my soul in hope.

Kronus sensed a change and his attention was momentarily distracted from his attacks on Jett.

"What is that? What did you do?" he demanded.

In that moment, Jett made his move. We were thrown to the ground as he tackled us. My head cracked off the floor on impact. I could feel the blood seep from me, and an angry throb erupt from the wound.

But that didn't stop Kronus.

You are not taking me over, Kronus. These are my powers. My body. Mine! You will let go.

"Not a chance, sweetheart."

I focused on Jett. Fighting to see through my eyes once again. Shutting Kronus out of my mind and putting all my energy into my love for the man in front of my eyes.

I'm here, Jett. I'm here. Don't let me go.

Jett leaned down and rested his head on mine. In that moment the connection between us was formed. Like a lighthouse, guiding me to the surface again, I followed its warm, strong, glow.

"No! You are mine!" Kronus hollered as he fought against me. But I could feel my powers again. I reached for them. They wrapped around me, pulling me forward and pushing Kronus back.

Don't let go of me, Jett. Don't let go.

"I'm here, Laya."

My heart leapt. It was him. It was really him. Jett's voice was sweet and warm and wrapped me in a safe strong blanket of love.

Kronus let out a rage filled yell as the connection between Jett and I grew, encompassing me and him in a powerful light.

Jett's power was with me. As if he was holding my hand, guiding me gently back to reality; I was led out of the darkness of Kronus and into the light once again.

The moment I broke through the black suffocating inkiness, the room and Jett came into focus.

"Jett?" I uttered, looking at him.

"Laya? Is that you?" he asked.

"It's me," I said smiling despite myself as I reached up to him, grasping him around the back of his neck and pulling him harder against me. "Thank you."

"You did it, Laya. I knew you would," he said, dropping lower and placing a single kiss on my lips.

I sat up and looked around the room.

"Where's Sam and-"

The door burst open and three Sirens poured in.

"Jett!" I yelled as I sprang to my feet. Pink lifted from him and white appeared in my hands.

The Sirens were dressed in battle gear, blades in their hands and when their eyes saw an unconscious Siren on the floor beside me and Jett, they didn't hesitate. Jett grabbed my hand and there was a pop.

The room and the Sirens disappeared.

JETT

I WASN'T SURE it was going to work, but I had to try. The first place that came to mind was the farm. I went with it. Focusing on my room, I wished us there. A surge in my power grew and popped in my core - the room with the Sirens disappeared.

Soaring through nothingness was bone chillingly cold. I could feel Laya at my side and knew that she was still there with me. It didn't matter where we ended up, we were together. That was all that I cared about.

A moment passed that seemed to stretch on for an eternity, and with a *pop* we were in the farm house again.

"Whoa," Laya uttered as she bent over, resting her hands on her knees.

"You okay?" I asked, kneeling in front of her. I couldn't help the relief when she looked at me with her beautiful blue eyes. Not a hint of black in them.

"Yeah. I just need a minute to wait for my stomach to return from my butt," she said with a crooked smile. I chuckled and stood.

"Fair enough. Not too bad for my first time," I thought aloud. I didn't make the bedroom, but the kitchen wasn't too far off.

"I'm impressed. Didn't know you did the whole popping in and out thing."

"Wasn't sure it was going to work, but certainly better than facing off against a bunch of Sirens," I said.

I walked to the wall and turned on the light. Laya gasped and I turned around in a flash, expecting a fight. What I saw was more of a shock

"Jett…" she uttered in a thin whisper.

I was speechless. The house had been *trashed*. Not just gone through - destroyed. The walls were ripped into down to the studs. The cabinets in the kitchen were pulled from the walls. Dishes were all over the floor, along with cutlery and food.

"What the hell happened?" I said finally finding my voice.

"Who would do this?" Laya asked, stepping to me and grasping my hand. "I'm so sorry, Jett."

"I just don't understand. Who…why would someone do this?" I asked.

"'Cause it was *fun*," a low voice answered. Laya and I both twisted around to the voice.

Ares stood in the doorway to the kitchen, his hand resting on the doorframe.

"Ares. What do you want?" I asked, pulling Laya behind me. I could feel the glare on the back of my head, but I didn't care. She had just enough strength to keep Kronus from taking her over. I didn't want her using an ounce on Ares.

"Well, I was looking for you, my son," he said, reaching his hands out in front of him.

"I'm *not* your son," I said, before I could help myself. I wanted nothing to do with Ares. Not. One. Thing.

"Ouch," Ares groaned.

"You don't care about Jett. All you care about is his power and what you can use it for," Laya said stepping up next to me. I didn't look down at her, but kept my eyes on Ares. I didn't trust him. He was there for a reason - whatever it was could only spell trouble.

"I'm here to make you an offer," he said.

"No thanks," I answered.

"Really? That's it? Well, I guess the Sirens can keep the rest of the Sirenites then. You obviously don't want them back." My breath stilled.

He nodded, knowing he had me.

"Very well, what do you want?" I asked, trying not to crack my teeth clenching my jaw. Laya moved at my side and I knew she was just as anxious about the situation as I was, but she knew better than to ask me to leave my people in the hands of the Sirens.

"I want you to join me-"

"I already said 'no'," I said, cutting him off.

"Let me finish. I know you have refused, but I think that you need to know more about what we are hoping to accomplish. My offer is to come with me. Learn what we are working towards and why. I will release your people back to their home once you are with me. At the end of it all, you make your choice," he said.

I didn't answer. How could I trust him?

"Jett…" Laya whispered.

"This offer expires at dawn," Ares said. There was a pop and he was gone.

"Shit," I uttered.

"Yeah, my thoughts exactly," Laya added. I looked at her. Her brows were furrowed and her attention on the floor.

"What do you think?" I asked her, pulling a chair from the debris and setting it up for her. She took a seat and looked up at me as I grabbed another that was missing its back, for myself.

"I think that there's no way that we can trust that he will release the Sirenites. He could turn around and just put them back in Stronghold if you say no to him; and, let's face it, you're not going to join him," she said.

I agreed. There was no way that I was going to join his pro-Titan-rule clan.

"I can't just leave my people in the hands of the Sirens. I can't, Laya," I said to her.

"Well then, we have to get them out of there ourselves," she said.

"I like where your mind is going," I said to her, nodding.

"Sam was able to pop up into Stronghold and you were able to pop us out. It stands to reason that we would be able to pop back in if we wanted to. The only problem is that we don't know where your people are being held…and we have no place to put them once they are out. It's not like they can just go back to town. Ares can just find them again and take them back. We need to take away his leverage," she pointed out.

"Right," I said. There was no way that he was going to just let them come back to Stenen and stay there, not when he could use them to get me to do what he wants. But, even if I went with him, would I be able to trust that he wouldn't touch them if I didn't join him? That he wouldn't take it out on them just to punish me. I raked my hair with my hands and scrubbed my face with my palms. No matter what I did, the people that I cared for got hurt.

"I don't know, Laya. I just don't know," I said. She moved off her chair and crouched in front of me; placing her hands on my knees she looked up at me.

"We'll figure it out, Jett," she said gently. "I promise. We will figure out a way to save your people."

I knew she really did mean that. She knew what it meant to lead people and be responsible for them. The only problem was that all avenues seemed to lead to the destruction of my people. There was no place that was safe from a god, no matter how good you were at hiding, we had found that out the night that Deimos and Phobos had arrived in Stenen.

I sighed heavily. Everything had changed that night. Suddenly we were thrown into a world that we were not prepared for. So far, we had managed to keep if together, but I didn't know how much longer that was going to last. Laya rose up on her knees and put her arms around me. The feel of her against me was calming and exciting at the same time.

I couldn't help the swell of love that surged forward at her touch. I pulled her harder against me, reaching around the back of her neck and threading my fingers into her hair. Her embrace tightened and I knew that she needed our connection as much as I did. I could have stayed in that embrace for the rest of our lives.

An overwhelming urge to protect her flamed within me. Kronus' essence almost took her from me. I wouldn't let that happen again. We weren't looking for another essence until we figured out how to destroy the one that she already had. There was no way she was going to take on more of Kronus' charming personality. This was just the first essence, the weakest. Who knew what the others would have in store for us.

I squeezed Laya tighter and she responded. My heart thumped hard and an echo thumped back against my chest. I pulled slightly away and looked at Laya.

"Did your heart just…"

"Yeah," she said and blushed.

"It's like…"

"They are connected. The same," she nodded.

A glow of light lit between us, just soft. She lifted her eyes to mine and I closed the distance between us in a flash. Her lips pressed against mine with the same passion. Gods, I wanted her. When she moaned in my arms I was done holding back. I couldn't do it anymore. I lifted her right off the floor as she wrapped her legs around my waist. We tumbled through the door into my room and onto the bed.

Making sure I didn't land on top of her, I kept my weight light. Ares hadn't made it to my room to trash. It was just as I had left it.

She squealed as her back hit the mattress, but she never broke away from me.

"Laya," I uttered at her hands trailed down my chest to the bottom of my shirt. I grabbed the back of my shirt and pulled it off.

"Wow," she gasped with a smile. "That's a nice view."

I chuckled. "My view is pretty good, too," I said looking down at her. Her hair had tumbled down around her shoulders. Her cheeks flushed a pretty shade of pink. "You really are stunning, Laya."

She smiled sweetly, and sat up, facing me. Reaching out, she ran her fingers lightly over my chest. Immediately, my skin was on fire. A bolt of pressure mounted inside me and I closed my eyes.

"What you do to me..."

"I can see," Laya replied in a low, smooth tone. I smiled. There was no hiding how I felt about what we were doing. No point in being embarrassed about it.

When her hand reached the button on my pants, I looked down at her. Those blue eyes met mine and I was under their spell. I took her face in my hands and kissed her. What was gentle at first quickly became heated and breathy as I deepened the kiss, unable to get enough of her.

Pulling away, only moving an inch from me, Laya grasped the bottom of her shirt and pulled it off. My breath caught in my throat. I don't think that I would ever get used to seeing her like that. I ran my hand down her shoulder, feeling her soft skin.

"Gods, Laya." I had no words left. I was in awe of her beauty.

How - why did she pick me?

She pressed against my chest and kissed me – deep and desperate.

Shit. I was done.

The feel of her against me was just about enough to make me explode right there. Placing my hand on her back, I lowered her down to the bed. Unflinching, she ran her hands down my chest as her eyes wandered along with them. Up my arm and around my shoulder, they made their way to my back.

She leaned into me. I broke from her lips and trailed kisses down her neck. Her sweet gasps and moans made me want her all the more, if that was possible. Laya's nails bit into my back when I kissed the base of her neck, drawing her skin into my mouth. She rose to me as a moan left her lips.

"Gods, Jett," she uttered. The sound of my name on her lips was intoxicating. I ran my fingers along her arm up and around her bra straps. Her eyes met mine as I pulled the straps down. She lifted her arms out, wrapping her hands around my neck and planting a hot, deep kiss on me. I couldn't help the deep moan that sounded somewhere within me. There was something carnal about the way I reacted to her.

I couldn't have wanted her more in that moment.

I couldn't have loved her more.

I wanted to die on her lips as she moaned my name. Gods, she had me. She had all of me and always would.

KYLAYA

JETT KNEW what he was doing. Gods, did he know.

Every kiss, every touch, sent pleasure spikes through me. I had never felt that before. Every time that I thought it couldn't possibly get better, his next kiss proved me wrong.

Jett ran his fingers softly along my bare shoulder as he kissed me. I could feel a pool of warmth settling low in me and knew that it was all for him. Every sense was heightened and on edge, raw and ready to take on the next part of this journey. Our journey.

My breath stilled in my chest as Jett's hand delicately ran a line from my collarbone straight down my chest. My heart thundered as his hand made its way over the swell of my breast to the top of my bra. I could see the lust in his eyes as he watched his hands move over me. A quick breath broke from me when his fingers slid behind the fabric, touching my skin where no one had ever touched. No one but him.

Oh. My. Gods.

I thought I was going to explode. How does someone survive a feeling like that? My body was a mess of sensation…all good. All I could do was watch as he ran his fingers along the tops of both cups, trailing a light touch on my skin underneath. When his hands got to the edge, they slowly, carefully made their way around my back. His eyes lifted to mine, as if he was waiting for permission to do what I wanted him to do so badly.

I leaned forward and kissed him.

"Yes," I whispered.

He kissed me again as the clasp on my back was undone and the fabric around me was pulled away and discarded. Jett pulled me to him. Gods, the feel of his skin on me was everything. Everything I never had the imagination to come up with. When his hand moved from my back and gently, tenderly, formed around me, I gasped. To be touched like that by him was…amazing. I kissed him harder.

I wanted him to know it. I wanted him to know that I was his. All of me, was his.

His grasp tightened and I moaned loudly against his lips. I moved into his lap, wrapping my legs around him and sitting on him. I could feel him under me and it drove me to move over him. I needed him to feel what he was doing for me. I wanted him to feel the same kind of pleasure. Gods, I wanted him.

With his hardness pressed against me, I rocked across him. A low sound came from him and I knew I was doing something right. When he grabbed both my breasts in his hands the ball of tightness in my core nearly gave way. But it was when he brought his lips down to my delicate, hard tip I nearly lost myself.

"Jett," I moaned, but I couldn't form any other words. My brain was lost to the sensation of his hands on me. His lips kissing. His tongue flicking. *Gods…*

I slid myself over the thickness rising from his jeans, aching to have the barriers removed. His hands ran up my back and into my hair. I arched against him and his fingers ran down my chest and abdomen, stopping at the button of my jeans.

Our eyes met.

But he didn't stop. His hand slowly crept down my body and between my legs. I gasped and moaned as his hand found the button of nerves. If I thought that I had experienced pleasure before…I now knew I hadn't.

"I know we could take this all the way tonight, and, gods, I would be lying if I said I didn't want to; but I can't help wanting my hands on you. All of you first," Jett whispered as his hand worked over me. I moaned again.

"Is that okay with you?" he asked. I would have agreed to just about anything in that moment. So, I nodded, and buckled in for the most amazing night of my life.

JETT

LAYA LAID BESIDE me in bed fast asleep. I smiled looking at her serene face. The pink in her cheeks was still there. Her bare shoulder was exposed with her arm as she peacefully slept. I knew under those covers laid the most stunning and sensual woman I would ever meet…naked. While we didn't have sex, I had spent the night getting to know Laya in a way I had only dreamed of and like everything about her, she was more amazing in real life than in my dreams.

Everything was a first for her and that made it extremely exciting for me and a damned turn on that I was still trying to calm. Just looking at her was enough to get me to rise to the occasion. She sighed in her sleep and I wanted to wrap her in my arms and stay there forever…but I couldn't.

Looking out the window, I could see it. The sunrise. Dawn was coming and I had to let Ares know what I was going to do. My jaw clenched.

I knew my answer, I just wished it was a different one. Even though it was the right move, there was no way Laya was going to see it that way. I looked down at her. There was nothing that I wouldn't do for her, but this wasn't about us. This was about saving my people.

They needed me and the only way I would be able to help them was if I could get Ares to swear not to touch them again. It wasn't a promise I could completely trust, but it was better than nothing. I leaned down and kissed Laya on the forehead. She was going to be *so pissed*.

Wrapping an arm around her, I focused on her bed at Eurybia's home. With a pop and a rush of cold air, that I sheltered Laya from, we were back. Laya moaned in her sleep as she settled into the new bed. My heart spiked. I knew that if she woke, and I had to tell her what I was doing, there was a good chance I would lose my nerve.

When she settled back down and the furrow of her brow softened, I sighed in relief.

"I'm sorry," I said and kissed her again. I focused on the farm house and was back in a moment. The sun peeked over the grain fields just as I popped back. I was outside of the house, facing the sun rise and I wasn't alone.

"So, what's your decision?" Ares asked.

"You know what it is," I answered.

He nodded with a smile, "Good. Let's go."

"Just one thing," I said, turning to him.

"What?"

"I will go with you under one condition," I said.

"What condition? I'm not a fan of conditions. They are so…limiting," he said with a frown.

"Once I go with you, you will return the Sirenites to Stenen," I began.

"That *was* the deal."

"And never harm, touch, talk, or interfere with them again. Ever," I finished.

"Ever?"

"Ever. No one you are involved with in this Titan plan of yours will hurt or harm them in any way. You are to leave them alone, forever," I said, crossing my arms. I didn't know how much he really wanted me to see his grand plan, but I had a feeling that it was enough to make him swear to leave the Sirenites alone for all time.

I stood there for a moment while he contemplated my offer. I was starting to wonder if I had pushed too far when he finally spoke.

"Done," he said.

"Done? You agree to my terms?"

"Yes, I do," he said.

"Okay. Let's go," I said frowning.

"Why so grim? This is going to be fun, son."

"Don't call me that."

"Before this is over, you're going to be calling me Dad, just wait and see," Ares said.

"Don't hold your breath," I said. My plan was to hear him out, get the heck out of there, and back to Laya as fast as I could.

My heart sank as I stood next to Ares knowing I had betrayed Laya going with him. She was going to be upset.

Livid was probably a better word.

Yeah, she's definitely going to punch me.

KYLAYA

THE LIGHT STREAMED in the room and pierced my eyes. I groaned and turned over in bed. Reaching out, I felt for Jett. When my hand came up empty, I opened my eyes. The room was empty.

Wait…what the crap?

I was back at Eurybia's place. I threw the covers aside and charged to door before I realized that I was naked. Turning on my heel, I raced to the closet and pulled out a pair of leggings and a shirt, getting dressed faster than I had ever before. I threw open my door and charged across the hall to Jett's room.

I didn't knock, I opened the door and my suspicion was confirmed. His bed was made perfectly. No one had slept in it.

"Damn it, Jett!" I shouted. I slammed the door and stalked across back to my room. Pacing the floor, I ran over everything that had happened during the night. At no point had he said that he was planning to go with Ares. He must have made up his mind…after. I blushed just thinking about what went on between us.

It had been the best night of my life, by far. Which only made Jett's disappearance all the more aggravating. *Why didn't he tell me?* We were a team. At least I thought we were. Why would he go without telling me?

I was rage-pacing in the room mumbling to myself when Mazz walked in with Rayna beside him.

"You think you could turn down the hate speech a little Ky?" he asked as a yawn pulled his mouth open. He stretched and when he brought his arms down, one of them fell over Rayna's shoulders. Immediately, he lifted it off her.

"Sorry," he said.

"It's okay," she said as a blush lit her cheeks.

I shook my head. I *couldn't even* at the moment. Where the hell was Jett?

"What's going on?" Rayna asked, stepping further into the room.

"Jett freaking left!" I said and started to pace again.

"He did *what?*" Rayna shrieked.

"It's okay," Mazz uttered with a shrug. "He's a grown-up boy, he can do what he wants, Ky."

"No, he can't! Damn it!" Rayna shouted. "How in Hades are we supposed to protect you two when you keep running off on us?"

"He'll be fine. I'm sure he'll be back soon," Mazz said.

"Would you stop being so calm about this?" Rayna cut in. "It's a big deal! You know what we've seen-"

"Yes! Fine!" Mazz interrupted her, staring hard at her as she glared back.

"You don't understand. We saw Ares last night and he gave Jett an offer," I explained.

"What offer?" Rayna asked.

"That he would release the Sirenties from the Sirens if Jett would go with him. He's trying to convince Jett to join Team Destruction," I said. Rayna's eyes widened as Mazz placed a hand on his hip.

"He *went?*" Rayna asked.

"Yes! He went without so much as a word! I can't believe that he would do that! *Again!*" I was shouting and I knew it, just didn't care.

"Jett isn't going to join Ares, Ky," Mazz said. "We all know that. What are you afraid of?"

"That he's going to get hurt? Captured? Brainwashed," I admitted.

"I think that you need to give him more credit than that," Mazz said. I looked at him and my mouth dropped open.

"Yeah, yeah, I know," he said, waving a hand at me. "I'm not exactly Team Jett, but the guy is a stand-up guy and bullheaded with the best of them. He loves you too much to do anything that could hurt you, or disappoint you. He'll be back…then you can zap his ass into next year," he said as another yawn stretched his face.

"Did I wake you?" I asked, starting to calm down as Mazz's words sank in.

"Sam got back late with Rall and Dee. We've been up most of the night talking with them and getting them settled in. Rall is having nightmares. He's terrified that the Sirens are going to come for him again," Mazz explained.

"I laid with him until he fell asleep while Mom slept. They've been through hell. Literal hell. I…" Rayna choked up as her words caught in her throat. Mazz looked down at Rayna, concern furrowing his brow.

"I'm sorry, Rayna. Are they family of yours?" I asked. When Jett brought me to the farm, I didn't get to meet the Sirenites other than the ones that had beat me up and tried to rape me. I saw the little boy and the woman at Stronghold. I didn't know who they were.

"Yes. My mother and brother," Rayan explained.

"Oh my gods, Rayna. I'm so sorry," I said, going to her and pulling her into my arms. "Is there anything I can do?" I pulled back and held on to her hand.

"Thanks, KyLaya. Not right now; but I will let you know if there is," she replied and squeezed my hand.

I didn't know what I would do if I had found my family in the state that she had seen her own mother. I would be torn to pieces by that. If there was anything I could do to help, I would.

"Back to Jett and Ares," she said with a shake of her head. Mazz placed a hand on her shoulder. She looked up at him and smiled.

"Right, Jett," I uttered. "Ares gave him until dawn to decide. He didn't say anything to me about his answer last night. When we talked about it, it seemed that no matter what we did we lost. I don't know what Jett's doing. I don't get why he didn't *tell* me," I said sitting on the edge of the bed, my rage-pacing at an end.

Rayna looked at Mazz.

"What would you have said to him if he would have told you he was going?" Mazz asked me.

"That there was no way in Hades I was going to let him go into Ares' realm," I snapped.

"What if he came up with a good plan for keeping the Sirenites safe from the gods?" Rayna asked.

"There is *no way* that we can trust anything that Ares says," I pointed out.

"That's true, but if a god enters into an agreement, it is pretty binding. They are old souls that way. They don't tend to break promises," Sam said as he came in the door.

"Really?" I asked, hopeful that Jett had come up with something that would free his people and keep them safe going forward.

"Yes," Sam affirmed nodding. "When I first ended up in Stenen, it wasn't always that easy to hide my powers. I was found out by a god and, even knowing that the amount of time that I was spending with humans was against Zeus's rules, he promised to keep it to himself. He never betrayed me. Even to this day," Sam said.

"Really? 'Cause Ares found the Sirenites," Mazz said.

"That was a coincidence. I did my part to keep the community from the eyes of the gods as much as I could, but hiding a primordial power? That was beyond anything that I was aiming for. Jett's and Laya's powers got past my blocks and the original guardians combined."

"Okay," Mazz said, unconvinced.

"Anyway, the truth is, gods aren't completely terrible beings. We do have a kind of code of ethics that we listen to," Sam said.

"Didn't you say that you went against Zeus's rules to be with Jasper?" Mazz asked.

"That was love. All rules are null and void when it comes to love. Everyone knows that," Sam reasoned. I laughed to myself. Truer words were never spoken.

"All I'm saying is that, if somehow Jett figured out a way to keep Ares away from his people, his plan just might work," Sam repeated.

"Great, well what are we supposed to do in the meantime then?" Mazz asked.

"Look for the other essences," I said. Sam looked at me like I had lost my mind.

"You're not serious," he said.

"I don't plan on just sitting here! We have a job to do! Kronus is still trying to rise and the only thing stopping him is us. Destroying those essences is our next step and I don't intend on stopping just because Jett's off with Ares," I explained.

"You were barely able to contain the first essence, KyLaya. That one was the head. The next is the heart…the heart is *strong*. I don't think you fully realize what you are putting yourself into when you say that you want to take on the next part of Kronus. Not to mention that you can't even *see* the essence!" Sam said. Mazz looked at me.

"What happened when you left? Still not impressed that you went without me, by the way, but we'll deal with that later," he added.

"The essences are pretty attached to the person that they were born into. The one that I got had been sleeping since it placed itself in the Siren. Me pulling on it woke it…and woke that part of Kronus," I explained.

"Gods. How did you ever manage to keep yourself in control? You took a part of a Titan's soul within you! Do you have any idea what that can do to a person?" Rayna asked.

"She does now," Sam said, looking at me.

"Straight up? It was torture. Pure torture. But the pain wasn't the worst part, it was losing control of myself that was. He took over my body. I had no control over what I was doing…and he was attacking Jett," I said, realizing that I *so* wasn't selling them on the idea that I should be going out and doing this all again.

"You lost control of your body to Kronus? Are you kidding me, Ky? And you want to do this *again*? Have you lost your mind?" Mazz yelled.

"I have not. I got control back," I said waving at myself to answer the obvious. "I figured out how to regain control."

"And how do you do that exactly?" Sam asked.

"My connection with Jett. It showed me the way back. I can tap into that if I get lost again. I know it will work," I said with a nod.

"No. This is insane," Mazz spat.

"I know what it sounds like; but, the first time I didn't know what I was doing or how strong the bond between the essence and the person would be. The essence is so strong; I didn't know how to block myself off from it. I know all that now. I'm better prepared to take on the next one," I explained.

I knew that Mazz was going to say no, no matter how much I knew what I was doing. He simply didn't want me doing any of it…at all. I couldn't blame him. If I had a choice, I wouldn't be doing this either.

"This time we will all be there with her," Rayna said. "No more, jetting off on our own. Got it? We're a team, damn it. Mazz and I are supposed to be protecting you and Jett. You two don't make that an easy job when you wander away all the time. That needs to stop now."

"Hey, I'm not the one that took off to Stronghold on my own," I pointed out. "You're preaching to the choir here. I don't *want* to take anyone on myself. However, the truth is, I *have* to do it on my own.

There is nothing that you *can* do. It has to be me that takes the essence. I don't want to put you in any danger. I have to go."

"True, but you don't know what you will have to do to get close to the essence. We can help with that," Rayna said.

"That's right! There may be monsters! Or…or stuff!" Mazz interjected. Rayna looked at him with a crooked frown. He didn't care, but looked at me straight on, owning what he had said.

"Alright. I won't leave you behind. I promise," I said reassuring them. They both nodded.

"Just one more thing," I said. "Jett's the only one that can see the marker on the essence." I looked at the two of them.

"Um, okay," Rayna uttered.

"I think I might be able to help with that," Mazz said.

"What?" Rayna said. "How?"

"I had a dream, more of a vision. I've had them before," he began.

"What kind of vision?" I asked. His eyes went immediately to Rayna. She watched him carefully.

"A glimpse into the future. All of the ones that I have had have come true. I just didn't realize what I was seeing was a vision and not just a dream."

"What did you see?" Rayna asked.

"I, uh, saw Laya drawing from a woman. Her skin was deathly pale. Eyes black. It must be the next essence."

"I was drawing from her?"

"Yes," he nodded, looking at the floor. There was something that he wasn't telling me.

"What is it?" I asked. Mazz shook his head.

"Tell her. Whatever it is, we need to know. We have to be prepared," Rayna said.

"I – damn it. I think you kill her," he said, looking up at me.

"I kill her?" I whispered.

"Yes," he said. "I see her on the floor. Dead."

I placed a hand on my mouth and stared at him.

"Laya-"

"It's fine," I said, cutting him off. "I…"

"KyLaya," Rayna stepped forward, "whatever situation we face, we are there with you. If Mazz has seen you taking the essence and it kills the vessel…that is the gods' doing. Not yours."

"She's right, Laya," Mazz agreed, taking my hand in his. "We need the essences. The gods are the ones that can put a stop to all this, but they aren't. If dealing death is the only way we can do this...so be it."

"We are with you," Rayna said. "Whatever comes. We will be there."

"Thank you," I uttered, still aching inside. I didn't want to kill anyone; but if it came down to defeating Kronus or letting him come back to power, I would do it. I couldn't afford to hesitate. Killing an enemy wasn't something new to me, but the people that housed the essences were innocent. They didn't even know what they help within themselves. Killing an innocent wasn't something that I wanted to do.

I straightened up and nodded. Mazz and Rayna straightened and nodded back as well.

"Now, who's going to tell Jasper that Jett has gone with Ares and you plan on taking on Kronus without him?" Rayna asked, looking between us.

"Oh crap," I uttered.

JETT

UNLIKE WHEN I popped in and out of space, Ares' journey was smooth and gentle. I didn't feel any different than when we were standing at the farm. Normally, it took a few moments for the chills to subside, but not with Ares.

"Where are we?" I asked, looking around the room that he had brought us to. We were in a house, a big one, but more than that I couldn't tell.

"I can't tell you," he answered.

"Why the hell not?" I asked.

"Because, I'm no fool. I'm not going to reveal where we are and risk you letting that out."

"Whatever," I muttered and looked around. The room was dark and dim, though I could see a light down a narrow hall to the left. Looking up I was stunned to see the ceiling went up a good hundred feet. My neck craned looking up at it. Stone walls ran around us and up to the roof of the room, which I couldn't see. There were two chairs against the wall, which gave the appearance of a waiting room of some kind.

"Okay, don't tell me where on earth we are, but what *is* this place?" I asked.

"It's my palace," he said, waving a proud hand around.

"Uh huh. It's a little small," I commented looking around the room. "Nothing much to look at."

"Out here? No. Follow me," he said, and walked toward the lighted hallway.

My nerves were up. I really had no idea what Ares wanted me to see or how he thought he was going to convince me to join him. It put me on edge.

At the end of the hall a giant room opened up in front of me. Unlike the waiting room, this room was lit with lamps and candle light. The walls were dark red-brown with gold trim running around them. It looked like a smoking room from long ago. Deep browns and reds, mixed with mustard and gold trimmings. Leather couches the color of blood stood around a huge fireplace, built with dark stone. The room was dimly lit, but yet bright enough that I could see everything clearly. It was stylish, not at all what I would have thought Ares to live in. I was leaning closer to a medieval torture chamber. Lots of chains. Spikes and such.

"Not what you were expecting?" Ares asked as he watched me.

"No. It isn't," I admitted. "It's…lighter."

"I may be the god of war, but that doesn't mean that I want to live in blood and bodies."

"Are we on Olympus?" I asked.

"No. All of us have homes all over the world. Our homes on Olympus are left empty most of the time. Only Zeus remains in his all the time," Ares explained.

"I see. What are we doing here?" I asked, looking around the room.

"There's a few people I would like you to meet," he said.

"Why?"

"I know nothing that I say will change your mind, but there are others who feel the same as I do. Maybe if you hear what they have to say, you'll be more open to hearing me out," he said.

"Doubtful," I said.

"We'll see," Ares said and lead me through the large room. On the back wall was another door. He grabbed the knob and turned, ushering me into the adjoining room. I prepared myself for the worst. I had no idea who would be in that room. Deimos and Phobos came to mind…waiting with some kind of terrible torture devices. But there was no preparing me for what I saw.

The sitting room was furnished with a lighter set of colors than the one we had just left. A smaller fire place was the centerpiece of the room and everything faced it. Four wine colored wing-backed chairs were arranged before the fireplace with a matching couch between the sets of two. In the chairs sat two people. When they turned their heads, all sense left me; because I couldn't grasp what I was seeing.

"Hello, Jett."

"Eros?" I blurted. "But…but I thought…"

"That I was dead?" he asked smiling and standing.

"Well, yeah. The others said that Ares killed you," I said.

"It's not *that* easy to kill me," Eros said. "But he did put me out of commission long enough to bring me here. It took a while, but I have finally seen the light. Plus, I got my mom back."

My eyes turned to the other person on the chair. The woman stood and I was struck dumb by her beauty. Long blonde hair draped down her back, almost to the floor. Her eyes were a stunning blue green with thick lashes. An elegant light purple gown clung to every curve of her body and billowed to the floor in a pool of delicate fabric. She was truly the epitome of beauty, ethereal beauty.

"Aphrodite?" I managed to squeak out, wanting to make sure that I wasn't seeing things.

"Pleased to meet you, Jett," she said. "My son has had many good things to say about you."

I looked at Eros and he smiled back.

"It's not too hard to say nice things about the only brother that I like," Eros admitted.

"I don't understand. I thought you said Ares had taken your mother," I asked.

"He did take me. Just as he took Eros. I wasn't about to go willingly," she explained.

"No one really trusts Ares, so his methods of getting heard are…imaginative," Eros explained.

"That's an understatement," I said. "He said that you would be able to convince me what's going on with Kronus is a good thing. My ears are open," I said and took a seat.

"I know exactly how you're thinking; but you, like us, just may change your mind," Eros said.

"Ares savagely raped my mother and took my people. There's nothing you can say to me that will make me believe that he is the misunderstood good guy in all this," I said to them.

Eros looked at his mother and she nodded.

"Ares didn't rape your mother," Eros said.

"You know that's not true. You know that she was forced to be with him so she could carry a child," I said to them.

"Ares did lay with your mother," Aphrodite said. "But he didn't rape her. He loved her and…she loved him."

"That's…what?" I asked, not sure that I had actually hear her right.

"They loved each other," Aphrodite repeated. "I made sure of it."

"How? How did…what?" I was still trying to process that information. "Aren't you married to Ares? Why would you want to make him fall in love with a Siren?"

"He had gone and made this horrible plan to impregnate an innocent Siren with a child that would serve him. It was cruel even for him. So, to punish him, I made him fall helplessly, hopelessly in love with her. The only way for her not to get hurt in all this was to make her fall in love with him, too. They *were* happy for the time that they were together, while she was pregnant. I knew, this way, she wouldn't be harmed in the transaction."

"But she wrote to Pearl about the rape and the pregnancy! She was a victim!" I argued.

"The letters to Pearl weren't written by Celia, they were written by me."

"You gods just have no problem destroying lives do you?" I said to Aphrodite.

"I did what I needed to do to secure your safety and hers as well," Aphrodite said. "I have no regrets and no amount of badgering from you will change that."

I threw up my hands.

"I think what my mother is trying to say is, it was the only way to keep the secret of their love. She took Celia's memories to punish Ares and to let Celia move on with her life and find real, true, love. The love with Ares was fashioned by Mother, it wasn't real. Pearl's deception was necessary as it locked in her passion to help Celia. That need to protect and help her directly affected you and Jasper. Pearl felt strongly that she needed to protect you two as well. No harm was done. No one was hurt," Eros explained.

"Oh, *sure*! You gods seem to think that making up life altering secrets and lies is no big deal as long as it doesn't hurt anyone. The truth is that any lie hurts. Pearl built a relationship with Jasp and me based on a *lie*! She started rescuing Sirens because she felt driven to do something after all that my mother had been through…and that was a lie! You have altered people's life paths with your lies!" I shouted.

"Yes, we have. But what harm is there in giving someone a push to do good?" Aphrodite asked.

"Good?"

"Yes. Pearl has saved many lives with the push we gave her," Aphrodite said, sitting down and gracefully crossing her legs as she looked at me. "Your mother left the Sirens and found true love. She got to experience happiness. You grew up under the protection of Pearl and in a community that loved and respected you, becoming the strong person that you are today. You might not agree with our methods, but we are not new at this. Life altering as we may be, this is what we do. As a god, we see a path and we see potential, and we do all we can to lead the lost to the path that they should be on. I will not apologize for that."

I sighed. There was no point in lecturing them. They were gods for goodness, sake. They had been around for too long, and were clearly stuck in their ways.

"What about Ares? How exactly was he punished in all this?" I asked.

"Ares has never really loved another being. Ever," Aphrodite explained. "But, this time, he did. Truly and deeply. To my surprise, his love was not completely a product of my spell. I gave him a strong push, a very strong one, but he threw himself in on his own. He cared only for her. He treated her like a goddess, Jett. Make no mistake about that. They were very happy."

"I just…" I didn't know what to say.

"I know this is difficult for you. Once you and your brother arrived, I took Celia's memories. Do you know the pain of having your love taken from you? Celia didn't remember Ares; but I planted an intuition in her that came forward whenever he was around her. She would become deeply terrified. He couldn't get close to her without her panicking and running. He tried to get her back many times; but, every time she ran, breaking his heart open again. Again, and again." She smiled. It was a cold smile. A proud one.

I had never considered Aphrodite a dangerous goddess, but there was no mistaking that she took pleasure from the pain she had inflicted on Ares. I don't know of a pain that can compare to losing the one you truly love. It was possible that Aphrodite had put Ares through the most excruciating torture that ever existed. And she was damned proud of it.

"But, why didn't he just undo the memory thing? Couldn't he have restored her memories so they would be together?" I asked.

"Oh, he tried," Eros said.

"Memory alterations are a specialty of mine. Plus, there's this limitation that we have. We can't undo the work of another god," Aphrodite explained.

"When Ares tried to restore her memories, she was only left with the terror of what was put there. She wanted nothing to do with him. She was scared of him, something she had never been before," Eros explained.

Suddenly, I was feeling something I really didn't want to feel for Ares. Sympathy.

"It may seem cruel, but think of the alternative," Aphrodite explained. "Celia was fated to find her true love. Ares was messing with that. Because I erased her memory, she went on to find Zale; the man that she was supposed to fall in love with. Real. True. Pure love, Jett. She didn't have that with Ares. If I didn't step in, he would have savagely raped her and bore you and your brother anyway. Celia would have been locked up in a Siren prison for her entire pregnancy. Instead she was loved, waited on hand and foot, and cherished. Which would you have preferred for your mother?" Aphrodite asked.

"Okay, fine, I get it. I still hate Ares. He took my people and gave them to the Sirens," I said, not knowing what else to say. "Putting all that aside - how is what Ares is doing *now* good? I still don't understand why I'm here," I asked.

"Ares is still in love with your mother. When he started this journey, he wanted to destroy the world and use the Titans to do just that. But, after Celia, unbeknownst to me, his plans changed," Aphrodite said.

"He wants to *stop* the waking of Kronus," Eros said.

"The waking has already begun," I pointed out.

"Not really," Aphrodite explained. "For Kronus to wake his essences need to rejoin with his body."

"We know that. Laya already has the first essence," I said. Eros and Aphroidte looked at each other.

"When did that happen?" Eros asked rising from the couch.

"Just the other day. We found the essence of the mind in Stronghold, in a higher Siren."

"So, we're too late," Aphrodite said with a sigh and sank back in her chair.

"What's going on?" I asked. I thought they would have been happy.

"The essences were locked into certain people at birth for a reason. Those people were born with the ability to block him. They were perfect tombs for his power. KyLaya was not born with that ability," Aphrodite said.

"But she's got it under control. I mean, I had to help and it was…well, it was terrifying, but I just assumed that anything to do with Kronus would be terrifying," I said.

"She may be holding it together now, but eventually whatever defense that she has against the power of Kronus will fail. A moment of weakness. An injury. Anything that brings her guard down. She will be lost to him. Once he takes over, having her power to wield, there will be no stopping him," Aphrodite said.

"What? Why the hell did the Fates tell us to collect these damn essences then?"

"We don't know. The Fates have always been a neutral party," Eros said.

"They've had a heavy hand in waking Kronus - that doesn't sound neutral to me," I said.

"I agree," Aphrodite answered. "They started a war that the gods are not prepared to fight. We don't have the strength we did the in old days. Those days, those powers, are gone for us. If Kronus rises, he will break the Titans free. Even if he goes it alone, he will destroy this world."

"And you're telling me that Laya is walking around with him inside her, just biding his time before he takes her over?" I asked.

Running my hands into my hair I grasped tight. *How did we get in this mess so deep?*

"I'm sorry, Jett," Eros said. "I honestly didn't know all this when I came to Stenen to see you. I was just following my brothers."

"Brothers! Right! Deimos and Phobos. They're Ares' sons too! You said that they wouldn't do anything without his approval. They came to take us out, Eros. They came on his orders," I said to him.

"They've gone rogue, at least according to Ares. I don't know what happened, but they are not part of Ares' plan anymore," Eros said.

"I'm sorry but I don't believe that," I said.

"It is true," Aphrodite said. "They haven't been around Ares for a long time now. The two of them have always needed an alpha dog to follow. The only way that they would leave Ares is if they had found a bigger alpha dog to follow. Someone more powerful."

"Kronus?" I asked.

"That's my guess, but there are others that have started to stir too," she said.

"Others? What others?" I asked.

"Oceanus for one," she answered. "Though a Titan himself, he never fought in the Titan War. He didn't help either side. As punishment, Zeus stripped Oceanus of his realm and gave it to Poseidon. He's had a hate for Zeus and the Olympians ever since then. He's formidable, with more power than he lets on. There's been movement in his realm as of late, Zeus has been watching him closely," Aphrodite said.

"So, we're not just talking Kronus waking, we're talking a full-scale Titan invasion," I said.

Eros and Aprodite nodded.

"What can we do? I mean, what is going to stop this from happening? If Laya can't take on the essences, what are our options here?" I asked.

"There's more going on than just the Titans rising," Aphrodite said.

"It is our belief that after Uranus was put to sleep by Gaia, she set in motion all of this. This is *her* plan - a way to get her love back," Eros said.

"She planned world domination by the Titans?" I asked.

"Yes," Eros answered without hesitation. "We believe that the plan is for the Titans to destroy the Olympians. Then, with Gaia and Uranus at full power, they would be able to destroy the Titans. Once everyone is out of their way the two of them would be left to rule over the world once again," Eros said.

"You really think that Gaia wants to kill all her kids? That seems…extreme," I answered.

"You don't understand how the gods work," Eros said. "The primordials don't view their children like children. They are just other entities. Gaia may have loved her children, at one time, but we don't believe that she does anymore. Uranus was poisoned by his jealousy of their children. Gaia watched as their love created the very things that ended up destroying them. You don't know the darker side of a god's love. Obsession. Possession. Murder. Gods are not benevolent creatures," he said.

"Wow, way to talk yourself up," I uttered.

"There's no point in pulling punches. We are too far gone for that. You should know the truth. Love, real love, between gods is dangerous," Aphrodite said. "Why do you think there were so many demigods running around? For all the time that the gods have been in existence, there are *very* few offspring. The Olympians have done a good job understanding the problem with a god's love and putting it to a stop, for the most part. There are very few couples that remain within the Olympian realm. The rest find their conquests among humans."

"So, are you saying that Laya and I are dangerous?" I asked.

"Yes. And no. The direction your love goes will determine how dangerous you are," she replied.

"That's a convenient answer," I said, shaking my head.

"Gaia and Uranus had a pure love, to start, but with the birth of their children came a jealousy that destroyed what they had, instead of strengthen it," Aphrodite said. "You and KyLaya, like it or not, are their reincarnations. There is no doubt in my mind that you will be doomed to the same fate."

"I'm just going to push past the part where you are insinuating that I would hate my own child, and straight to the fact that Laya and I aren't exactly planning on popping out any kids any time soon," I said. "You know what? It doesn't matter what you say, I'm not leaving Laya. I don't care if you think that we will bring down the world. I'm not leaving her."

Aphrodite and Eros looked at each other.

"Wait, you think that we *are* going to bring down the world?" I asked, in shock that they would even think something that ridiculous.

"Not you - but the powers within you…yes, that is a possibility," Eros said.

"Why are you telling me this? What purpose does this serve?"

"You wanted to know what Ares was doing and why we were on his side now. He is trying to stop all this from happening!" Eros said.

"How?"

"He believes that the Golden Fleece has the ability to contain all the essences of Kronus. As long as the wearer has the Fleece on, they won't be taken over by him. It would be a safe way to stop him from rising again," Aphrodite said.

"In other words, Jett, it would keep KyLaya safe from Kronus' power," Eros said.

As much as I didn't trust the idea of Ares genuinely wanting to help Laya, it seemed that's what was going on. I would do anything to keep her safe – even if that meant listening to Ares.

"Where's the Fleece?" I asked.

"It's hidden in the Arctic," a deep voice answered. I turned to see Ares standing at the door. This time, I didn't want to kill him. I wasn't sure if that was a good thing or not.

"Why the Arctic? Not exactly your realm," I said.

"That's kind of the point don't you think?" Ares responded. I shrugged. I still didn't trust him.

"Why haven't you just gone to get it yourself?" I asked him.

"I have. I…there's a force that I can't get through," he said furrowing his brow.

"What kind of force?" I asked. If Ares couldn't get past it, what chance did I have?

"Creatures with a power that I have never seen before. I honestly don't know how the Fleece was even put there with them!" Ares said.

"Can't you just ask Zeus to go get it?" I asked him.

"Zeus…is busy with another issue," he answered.

"You know; it's no wonder the Titans are waking up with the kind of effort you guys put into stopping them," I said. What could Zeus possibly be involved in that was more important than the waking of the Titans.

"I can't force Zeus to turn his eyes to us. We are on our own," Ares said.

"But, you're not alone."

The new voice came from the door and we all turned to see who it was.

"Athena!" Aphrodite said, a beautiful smile stretched across her face as she stood from the couch and ran to the woman at the door.

"Franny!" Athena cried and hugged Aphrodite tightly.

"Franny?" I asked, looking at Eros.

"Athena and my mother have always been close," Eros said.

Athena was much taller than Aphrodite. Her dark brown hair was pulled sharply away from her head, threaded through the cap on her head. She was dressed in tight jeans, with hiking boots. A military green bomber jacket with a white tank under, showed off her muscular frame. She looked like she could kick some serious ass.

"I'm so happy to see you," Aphrodite gushed as she pulled back and held Athena's arms tightly.

"When Ares told me you were here, I had to drop in and see you. It's been too long."

"Fifty years, my friend," Aphrodite said.

"Like I said, too long," Athena said.

"What are you doing here?" Aphrodite said, guiding Athena to the couches we were sitting on. On her way by, Athena hugged Eros and nodded to Ares.

"I came to meet Ares' newest recruit," she said, looking at me.

"Recruit?" I asked, looking at them.

"It seems that we are Team Ragtag at the moment," Eros explained.

"What does that mean?"

"It means that it is taking more time than we anticipated gaining support," Ares said.

"Well, you can't really blame the others, can you? You haven't exactly had the best track record," Athena said to Ares.

"True," he admitted. "But, this is different. We are talking about the extermination of our kind. Why the hell can't they see that?"

"Who are you talking about?" I asked.

"The other gods," Athena answered. "They seem to think that this is an elaborate ruse to get them to fight in a war that isn't worth fighting. They don't believe that Kronus is rising again. If we don't start to build our strength and work to put a stop to him, it will be too late."

"Again, why isn't Zeus here?" I asked.

"He will be," Athena answered.

"What?" Ares, Aphrodite, and Eros blurted together. "I have just come from Olympus. Oceanus is on the move, gaining strength and allies in the seas. There's no doubt that he is teaming up with the Titans. It is absolutely essential that we stop Kronus from joining him," Athena reported.

"Why aren't the other gods hearing this?" I asked.

"They don't believe that the Titans will be able to get out. Their chamber takes the heart of a god willingly given to open it. No one is going to willingly give their heart to open the Titan's chamber," she said.

"What's the problem then?" I asked. "If the chamber can't be opened why are we worrying?"

"Because, Oceanus is no fool. He wouldn't start something that he can't finish. If the chamber takes the heart of a god willingly given, he will have a way to get that. The others just can't see that. They would prefer to live in ignorance until the Titans are knocking at our doors on Olympus," Ares said, his voice dripping with distain.

"You know; I would think, being the god of war and all, that this is right up your alley," I said.

"It is," he said with a shrug. "I'm loving the idea of a war; but, I want to win and at this point we won't," he said.

"I agree," Athena repeated. "If we don't take out Kronus before he is at his full power, we will lose this war. You don't know Kronus, Jett. He is the most violent, deranged Titan there ever was, and that's saying something," Athena explained.

"You won the first time, surely you could do it again," I said. "You know; as a last resort."

"There is no last resort, Jett. We can't have open war. It would destroy the world as we know it. We're talking every major natural disaster known to mankind. The world would end before the winner was proclaimed," Ares said.

"Well, that's not good," I mumbled. "What are we supposed to do?"

"Get The Fleece. After that, the essences can be collected, but we don't have a lot of time. If it's true and KyLaya has the first one, it's only a matter of time before Kronus breaks through her and seeks out the other essences himself. If that happens, she will turn into Kronus and he will have her primordial powers at his dispense," Ares said.

"Look, I don't trust you," I said, turning to him. "Quite honestly, this is all a little too convenient. I'm not convinced that you aren't a complete dick." I crossed my arms and glared at him.

"Fair enough, that seems to be the consensus around here. Why not my son too," Ares said.

"It took a love spell for you to change the way you are. That doesn't make you a better person, Ares. That makes you someone under a spell. What would you have done if Aphrodite didn't step in to save Celia?"

"I would have done anything to stop Kronus from coming back. I just might have gone about it a little rougher," he admitted, lowering his eyes to his fingers.

"Sure," I muttered and turned from him. "I need time to…think."

"Of course," Aphrodite said. Athena opened her mouth but Aphrodite placed a gentle hand on her shoulder and shook her head. Athena closed her mouth and nodded.

"Take your time. We will be here when you have decided what to do," Aphrodite said and led Athena from the room after taking her hand.

Ares stood at the doorway as the goddesses exited. His eyes were on me.

"You look like her," he said softly. His expression softened, as he spoke. I was so shocked I dropped my jaw. Ares cleared his throat and his expression hardened once again.

"Don't take too long. Time is short," he grunted and left. I watched until he was completely gone before I turned back to the seats around the fire and sat in one.

Eros took a seat on the couch. I stared at him, hoping he would get the message to leave. A moment to myself was what I really needed; time to think of the implications of everything they just told me.

Saving the world from the rise of the Titans? Defeating Kronus? Who did they think we were? Laya and I might have been the reincarnations of Gaia and Uranus, but that didn't mean that we *were* them. We didn't have their skills or their control over their power. I wasn't naïve. I knew the powers I had weren't anything compared to what Uranus once had. He built the world and gave birth to the Titans with them.

I sank into my chair and placed my head in my hands

"It's a lot, isn't it?" Eros said. I slid my hands down my face and placed them under my chin, looking at him.

"Yes. It is a lot," I said, repeating the obvious.

"I find, if you simplify it down the core of it all, it makes things easier to deal with," Eros said, putting his feet up on the couch.

"Really? It's just that easy, huh?" I said, not believing him for a moment.

"It is."

"Whatever," I uttered.

"At the heart of all of this is a choice. What would you do to keep KyLaya safe?" Eros asked. I lifted my head and looked at him.

"Anything," I said immediately.

"Precisely," Eros said, pointing to me.

"You knew that," I said sitting forward.

"So, focus on it. Let it drive you. Don't think about Ares' plan; or, Gaia and Uranus, or the Titans. There's only one thing right now that you need to do and that is to protect KyLaya from Kronus taking her over. If you find the Golden Fleece, you have a way to protect KyLaya," Eros explained.

I was struck dumb. For once, he was helpful. There was nothing that I wouldn't risk for Laya.

"You're right," I said sitting up.

"See? Simple," he said, waving a hand at me.

"But, what about-"

"Don't think about it. All that other stuff will wait. Right now, you need something to aim your energy at," Eros said.

"Fine. But, why can't *you guys* go and get the Fleece?" I asked. "Why does it have to be me?"

"Ares didn't mention it, but it's the water. That's the real force he can't get past. He can't breathe in the water. Most of us can't," Eros explained.

"What?"

"I know it seems ridiculous, but we can't. We won't die, but we fall unconscious and are useless. Ares tried, but he couldn't make it. We all have tried, but we can't get there," he explained.

"Poseidon?"

"He has tried too, but has been unsuccessful," Eros said.

"Great. Feeling really confident about this, Eros," I said, dropping my clasped hands down onto my knees.

"There is no fighting with the creatures that guard it. Their magic is simply unfathomable. Equal to the gods and beyond," Eros said.

"Again, you're really instilling some serious confidence," I said smiling. The truth was, I didn't care if the other gods had failed. I wasn't going to. No matter what it took, I was getting that Fleece for Laya.

As long as she didn't take on any more of Kronus' personality, she would be fine until I got it.

KYLAYA

"YOU SAID it was right here!" I exclaimed as I looked around the library.

We had travelled from Eurybia's home to the location of the next essence. Jett was scoping things out in the enemy camp, the least I could do was go on collecting the essences before someone else found them.

"If he said that it's here, it will be here," Rayna said.

"I don't know, something seems off. This place doesn't…feel right," I said. We were in the library of the University of Lost Souls. I had never heard of a university named that before and I wasn't totally convinced that it was a real place, at least not for humans, which I assumed were the ones who went to it. "Where is this place exactly?"

"It's in Greece," Mazz said.

"Really? I've always wanted to see the birthplace of the gods," I said with a smile.

"I don't think that we will get the chance for much sight-seeing," Mazz said.

It was only Mazz, Rayna, and me for this trip. Jasper had asked Sam to stay behind with him so that they could talk. I knew Sam wanted to come, but he would do anything for Jasper, including missing out on the action of gaining another essence.

"Yeah, you're right," I said, not able to keep the disappointment out of my voice. One day I'll come back…with Jett. A smile spread across my face at the thought of sharing this place with him.

"Stop thinking about your man, we have a job to do," Mazz groaned, looking at me. I blushed, clearly caught daydreaming.

"Right," I said. "I know."

"Sure," he uttered and hip checked me. I laughed and shook my head.

"There's no one here," Rayna uttered.

"Hello?" Mazz called. His voice echoed off the walls of the empty room. I frowned.

"You sure that you saw *this* place?" Rayna said, turning to Mazz.

"Positive," he replied.

"I don't get it," I said and turned to Rayna and Mazz. "Where is everyone?"

The hairs on the back of my neck stood up.

I could sense something in the room, but I couldn't put my finger on it. Stopping in the center of the two story library I looked up into the domed ceiling. A beautiful mural was painted above us depicting the Titan War where the Olympians defeated the Titans. Zeus looked strong, young, and like the hero from the ancient texts that I read as a child. The painting was stunning, even in the dim light.

Then, out of the corner of my eye I saw movement. I could have sworn that a shadow in the corner of the painting moved. My gaze zeroed in on a far, darkened corner of the second floor.

I stepped back to get a better look at the upper chamber. The shadow had disappeared. Shelves extended from the floor to the ceiling in the low roofed top floor, creating deep shadows that disappeared into black. The top floor was a maze of bookshelves and would take a while to navigate. My gut told me that I didn't want to be the one to go snooping around in it. Just as I was about to turn back to the group, I saw movement again. This time I didn't miss where it was coming from.

Darkness had pooled in one corner of the upper floor, reaching up into the mural on the ceiling. It looked like it was a part of the painting, but when I looked closer I realized that it was far from it.

"Guys?" I shouted, not peeling my eyes from what I couldn't believe I was looking at.

"What?" Mazz asked as he stepped up next to me. I didn't say a thing, only pointed at the shadowed area.

"What *is* that?" he uttered.

"A web," I uttered.

"No spider could make a web that big," he said.

"That's not a normal spider," I answered.

"What are you-"

Before he could finish, a scream sounded from behind us.

"Rayna!" Mazz yelled and ran for her. I was hot on his heels.

"Rayna?" Mazz called again.

"Where are you?" I shouted.

Her scream had come from the main level, behind the librarian's desk, close to the front door.

My eyes made a careful loop of the room making sure to take extra time on the shadows, no longer trusting them. Mazz stayed at my back. Whatever was in that building with us was strong enough to take on Rayna, and that was no easy feat.

"Stay close," Mazz uttered, his eyes circling around us with an intensity I rarely had seen growing up.

"You too," I said.

"Any thoughts on what we're dealing with here?" he asked.

"Other than huge spider…no," I answered.

"Okay, so we're on the same page there," he said. In that moment a cold laughed echoed off the walls and around the library. A shiver ran down my back.

"I'm thinking it's not a spider," I said to Mazz.

"You would be half right."

Mazz and I turned around in a flash, facing the voice. From a shadow in the over-hang of the second floor, a set of glowing red eyes appeared. I took a step back and pulled at my power.

The red eyes narrowed as the being dropped to the floor of the main level and pulled itself up to full height. Towering above us was a creature unlike anything I had ever seen before. With the head and torso of a woman and the legs and abdomen of a spider, the creature was a frightening blend of the two. Her flesh was a sickly, pale grey across her chest blending into stark black at her fingertips. Long black oily hair hung across her face, as a sharp nose and eyes peered through her chunky locks. Her nails were needle sharp, extending from her fingers like talons. I didn't want to come anywhere near them; there was no doubt that they were made for slicing.

That voice in the back of my mind echoed and a name came to me.

"Arachne?" I whispered, more to myself than to anyone else.

"Very good, young one, you got it," she said. Her voice was breathy, like fast wind through a tree. I felt whipped by it.

"What are you doing here?" Mazz asked her, drawing a blade from his back.

"The same as you," she said with a smile that revealed pearly white sharp teeth, made for piercing flesh, with back gums that looked like she had rinsed with some black tar mouthwash.

"The essence?" I asked. She laughed.

"You're too late, Mer child," she said as she took another step toward us. "I have it."

"You only have the person, you don't have the essence," Mazz said.

"Perhaps," she replied. "Kronus will take what he needs and I will be rewarded for healing my master."

"Your *master*?" I blurted. "Are you kidding me? He's an evil creature that will destroy the earth! Is that what you want?" I asked her.

"You think I give one spider egg's width about this place? Once the world has been brought to its knees I will be able to roam free. Free! No longer forced to hide in the shadows, practically starving. Feeding on whatever wanders into my webs. Forced to live in this form for all eternity because I dared to challenge a goddess! I was young, prideful and stupid. I didn't deserve this," she hissed, waving a hand at her body. "Athena will pay for what she has done to me. They all will," Arachne spat, her anger surging forward.

"We can't let you take the essence to Kronus, Arachne," I said. "Surely, you know that."

"Know it? I was *hoping* for it," she smiled and ran forward. I dove to the left, out of the way of her long spider legs as one came down right where I was standing. The ground shook with the force of her strike.

Damn it.

I reached for the daggers at my hip and sighed in relief when I found them. I might have had some serious goddess powers, but a dagger would always be my go-to weapon in battle. I rolled to a crouch and swung my head in Arachne's direction.

"Mazz?" I called.

"Yeah!" he called back. "You okay?"

"Fine! You?"

"Good!" I shouted and ran for Arachne. She shot out a hand, sweeping it through the air at me as I arched toward her. I couldn't stop myself and was too late to stop mid-air. Her nails bit into my side, slicing clear to the ribs. I came down hard. My legs crumpling under me as I hit the hard marble floor.

Shit! Gods, my ribs!

"You think you're the first hero to come for me?" Arachne laughed. "I have survived them *all*. You will be no different." She charged. A web shot from her hand, wrapping around the columns on the main floor and cutting off the exit. I looked at Mazz, who turned his eyes to me.

I drew my hand from my side, and cringed seeing bright red blood drip from my fingertips. *Damn it.*

Mazz took the bow off his shoulder and strung an arrow.

"Get behind me, Ky," he commanded. I didn't argue. The ache in my side was burning. I had faith that my powers would help to heal the wound; but, how fast they would work, I had no idea. I hadn't exactly tested them out.

"Mazz, careful," I uttered. He didn't say anything as he drew back his arrow and turned to Arachne.

But she was gone.

The room was silent, except for Mazz's and my breathing. Our eyes circled it tirelessly, looking for her.

"Keep your eyes on the top floor," I said. "That's where I saw her the first time."

"She has Rayna, Ky," Mazz said, his jaw clenched tight.

"We'll find her," I said, trying to keep him focused. I needed his help. There was no way that I was taking on the giant spider lady on my own, especially injured.

There was a *clunk* and the building was plunged into darkness. Not even the light from outside could illuminate the room enough for Mazz and I to see.

"You really should just go. I have won, don't make me prove it," Arachne said from the din.

"You haven't won shit!" Mazz shouted.

My eyes were starting to adjust to the dark. Slowly the room was taking form again, but it wasn't fast enough. I was hit from behind and sent sailing through the air.

"Ky!" I heard Mazz shout just before my back smacked against a wooden shelf, knocking the air out of me and stunning me. Books toppled off the shelf, pelting my back as I laid on the floor, gasping for air.

A rage filled shout echoed around the room as Mazz strung an arrow. I could hear the tension on the bow from where I was. A loud thump echoed from where Mazz was. He shouted again and I could hear the arrow take flight. It cracked off the shelves on the other side of the library from me, not hitting its target, which was rare for Mazz. He was an expert bowman.

"Ky!" he shouted.

"I'm fine!" I yelled back, staggering to a stand.

Everything was still spinning a little as I stood on shaky legs. Breathing was painful, but I was pulling in air as required. That's when I heard Mazz get hit. He shouted as he was thrown off his feet and out of sight over the top of the railing on the second floor.

"No!" I shouted and ran for the stairs. "Please don't be dead. Please don't be dead!"

I launched up the stairs to the second floor, right to where he had landed; but, he wasn't there. I twisted around, scanning the room. Darkness dimmed every corner, making it hard to see. Was he hiding?

"Mazz?" I whispered.

Nothing.

"Mazz!" I whispered again.

Silence.

The room was so quiet it hurt. My heart squeezed tight.

Arachne has him.

I didn't know what her eating habits were, but I assumed since she used the word "feed" that she wasn't opposed to eating human flesh. My stomach churned just thinking about it.

No. Stop it.

It wasn't going to do any good to freak out. I needed to focus.

I closed my eyes and just let my ears plot out the room for me. The building was old, so there were creaks and snaps coming from everywhere - but that wasn't what I was looking for.

Then I heard it.

A *tap* and a *shuffle.*

The sound of a large spider leg on the hardwood floor as it dragged its prey away. I moved fast, following the sound.

As quickly and as quietly as I possibly could, I crept my way toward the back of the second floor. Taking care not to trip on anything littered on the floor, I was surprised to find that the floors were clean.

Did she just move in?

Nearing the darkened corner, where I first saw Arachne, the hairs on the back of my neck stood up. A shiver ran down my back, like ice sliding down my spine. Every cell in my body was screaming at me to get out; but, I couldn't.

I wouldn't leave Mazz and Rayna to whatever horror Arachne was spinning for them. I had to get them out, then I would look for the woman with the essence that Mazz saw in his vision.

Creeping past row after row of tall shelves, I took a moment before revealing myself around each one. My pulse was rapidly beating in my veins, fully expecting her to jump out at me at any moment. The upstairs was blanketed in inky darkness, which made seeing where I was going and any danger that much more difficult.

Through a door at the back of the library, a shuffle sounded. It was soft, almost indiscernible, but it was enough for me to zone in on and move toward. My powers vibrated in my veins as I made my way across the wooden floor to the door.

A scream bit at my throat as I peeked my head through the door. I choked it back as I stepped silently into the room. From floor to ceiling, the room was coated in a thick silky webbing.

I had entered Arachne's lair.

My every footfall crunched and grinded debris that was layered on the floor. I didn't have the stomach to look down and see what I was stepping on. My imagination was good enough to have me near gagging.

The further into the room I went the faster my heart beat. I could feel my pulse pounding in my fingertips, it was so hard.

"Mazz?" I whispered, hoping that he was close.

No answer.

The webbing thickened the further in I went; but, it wasn't the sight of it all that stole my breath – it was the smell. Like a rancid rag shoved down my throat, I gagged on the thick putrid stench. Breathing through my mouth helped to avoid only a fraction of the foulness that hung in the air. Only a few steps in, I found what I was smelling.

Plastered to the wall, tangled in the sticky yarn, were bodies. Many bodies. In various states of decay they looked out with dead eyes at me as I walked past. The corpses of innocent people that had been lured into Arachne's web.

A piercing chill pelted me, as I passed body after body. Milky eyes, wide in horror, stared at me from behind a thin layer of gauze. If I wasn't close to vomiting before, I was there now.

Walking through the room, with the softest steps I could muster, I pushed the horror of the bodies down. The corpses looked like they were on display more than waiting to be eaten. Their arms and legs were splayed out, open to the world around them. Head's pulled back, mouths gaping open, their whitened glassy eyes gaped open at endless nothingness. Black tar seeped from their mouths and eyes, as whatever venom she injected them with did its job. Their skin was as grey as hers and pulled tight against their bones.

I clasped a hand across my mouth as the body count mounted the further I walked into her lair. The room was showcasing more than twenty corpses, hanging from floor to ceiling. None of them were Mazz or Rayna.

There was a *shuffle* from the doorway at the back of the room - the access to the attic space. I reined in my failing courage and travelled through the open door. Looking up at a steep, narrow set of stairs ascending into the attic above the library, I swallowed hard.

"Of course," I sighed. "Spiders love attics."

I held my breath as I climbed the stairs, cringing at every tick and creak that the ancient steps gave. It didn't matter how light-footed I was, I might as well have announced myself - *Now, ascending the stairs to take on the world's biggest spider, KyLaya of Triton!*

There was no way she didn't know I was there. Pulling at my power, I prepared myself for an attack as I neared the top of the stairs.

My powers slid just under my skin; not wanting to give off light and therefore my location, but ready for whatever was up there. A humming in my core began aching for release. Arachne didn't know who she was picking a fight, and damned if I wasn't going to let her find out.

I pulled a dagger from my leg and flipped it into my hand. If there was one thing I was confident in, it was my aim with a knife. Stepping lightly, I entered the large arched roof of the attic.

The open beams were clouded in webs. A tunnel of webbing went straight down the center of the attic to the back. It was her nest and she had taken Mazz and Rayna straight to it.

A loud thud sounded above me. Before I could duck I was struck from behind. I staggered forward; but, not before turning and finding a target.

Arachne stood behind me. A smile slick across her face. I launched the dagger at her. True to form it landed, sinking into her shoulder. A loud ragged scream broke from her. I rolled to a crouch on the floor as she pulled the dagger from her shoulder. With a scoff, she threw it to the floor with such force it embedded itself in the solid wood up to the hilt.

Shit.

"Stupid. Little. Girl," she hissed. Webbing shot from her hand and wrapped around my wrist, as I threw it out to block her attack. She pulled back on the rope of web. I was shot off the floor and into the air, yanking my shoulder out of its socket. I screamed in pain and shock as I landed in a heap in front of her.

I tried to get my arm to move, but it wouldn't as I dragged myself to a sitting position.

"Arachne, you don't have to do this. The Titans are evil, surely you realize that you will be just as miserable if not more under their rule," I said.

"Oh, no. You see, I have been promised my human form back. Once the Titans rise, I will have my body back!" she said with a genuine smile.

"Who promised you that?" I asked, buying time.

"Wouldn't you like to know," she laughed.

"Unless it was Athena, you're going to be out of luck. Only Athena can give you your body back!" I said to her. From the back of my mind, the knowledge came. The gods couldn't undo a spell cast by another. It had to be the god who cast the spell, to undo what they had done. Someone was lying to Arachne. She was being manipulated and I had to make her see that.

"You don't know what you are talking about!" she yelled at me. "Kronus has the power to change me back. He *will* give me my body. Athena turned her back on me! All the gods have! She will pay! They all will!"

Her scream was like needles as her anger swelled. I could feel the pain in what she said. I couldn't imagine what she had gone through; and, for what? She bragged about being good at weaving? How fragile was Athena's pride to get so mad over something like that?

I looked at Arachne, really looked at her. There was a soul in there that was suffering. She was scared.

"I don't know why Athena turned you into a spider, but I know that the only one that can turn you back is her. Not Kronus. Whatever they are telling you is a lie! If you help us, though, Athena might be more willing to change you back. Please, Arachne. Help us!" I begged.

"She has *never* answered my prayers. In all the centuries I have been locked in this grotesque form, she has never heard me; or, if she did, she ignored me. What makes you think that would change now?" she scoffed.

"There is far more at risk now than her pride," I said. For a moment, I thought that I had Arachne's attention. For a moment, I thought that I was getting to her. Quickly, I looked around for Mazz and Rayna.

When I spotted them, my heart sank. Their bodies hung lifeless in webbing off to the side, along with two others. Black was starting to seep into their skin around their lips. I didn't know how much longer they could stand her poison. I had to get them out of there.

Turning to Arachne, I allowed my power to bloom across my skin. The room lit with the white light of Gaia's power as it came to life. Arachne's eyes widened.

"It's true, then," she uttered. "The Mother goddess has come again."

"Please, let my friends go. Give me the essence."

"I cannot," she answered softly. Her face looked, for a moment, remorseful. Quickly, her expression changed and I knew I was in for a fight. Her eyes narrowed as her hands shot out. Webbing streaked through the air at me. I leapt to the side, careful not to touch the webbing that surrounded the room. I knew that if it got on me, I would be pulled into it.

Light burst from my hand, flying straight for her. She skittered out of the way, up the wall to the roof. She was quick and graceful, and had me spinning around to keep my eyes on her. She had many more legs than I did, each one of them with a razor-sharp tip. One good slice from them and my guts would be meeting the floor. I wasn't naïve enough to think that wasn't a possibility.

Arachne shot a spray of webbing at me. It missed my arm, landing on the floor. I smiled at her.

"Guess your aim isn't what it used to be," I said.

"Think again," she hissed. I turned and nearly fell, my foot was stuck to the floor.

My heart stilled. *Uh oh.*

Arachne dropped from the ceiling in front of me. A smile broke out across her face. I lifted my empty hands, my dagger was still buried in the floor. I pulled at my foot again, but it didn't budge.

"You think that you can just walk in and *take* the essence? You didn't really think that you would win did you?" she laughed raggedly.

"Yes, I did," I said.

She leaned into me, placing her face so close I could feel the cold coming off of her flesh.

"Foolish girl," she said.

"We'll see," I said and grabbed her face in my hands.

I pulled.

Her eyes widened as the power within her, the thing that made her what she was, was cut away. A scream built in her throat and burst from it as a bloody red haze lifted from her skin.

I could feel the anger in her power, the hatred for those who had made her into what she was. But, I was not prepared for the sadness. It washed over me like a heavy wave, and I was pulled under and into a memory that wasn't mine.

A stunning beauty she was, but prideful to a fault - believing that she was superior to everyone, even the gods. Boasting that she was better than Athena was the last straw for the gods. Striping away her beauty, they stole everything from her that she had once coveted — leaving behind a hideous creature to roam the earth for all time.

But, that was centuries ago and she had learned her lesson. Her sadness at her naivety weighed heavily on her. She ached for forgiveness and a chance to be a better person than the selfish, prideful one she had been so long ago.

I felt the sadness. The anger. I saw the many, many, times that she tried to take her own life. Hating her very existence. She hated everything about herself.

Arachne was hurting in a way that I couldn't have ever fathomed. What a terribly tragic and sad life. How long would she be able to go on?

A swell of pity formed in my core. She made a mistake, a vain and stupid one, but it was just a *mistake*. The punishment didn't fit the crime. Athena should be ashamed of what she did to Arachne. It made no sense.

Light lit under my hands against her skin. Pure white light shone brightly, piercing the darkness and illuminating the room. Arachne screamed against my touch, but I held on. Her sorrow, her sadness, and her regret coursed through me.

I wanted to save her from it. I *needed* to.

A rush of power surged through me like nothing I had felt before and the room disappeared into light. Like a whirlwind of energy - it spread through me, igniting my blood. I could feel it pulling at the power within Arachne, bringing it into me, and making it a part of the power I had. Adding to mine.

The call to power lit in me once again, just as it did the first time I pulled from Deimos. I wanted more. All of it. All of the power, the curse, within her.

And I took it.

All of it.

JETT

IT WOULD HAVE taken me days to get there, but luckily, it only took me an hour thanks to my newly developed ability to pop in and out of places. I may have popped into the wrong place a few times. Scared some fishermen - and a sleeping polar bear.

I had lived in Saskatchewan all my life, so the cold was no stranger to me; but, there was no preparing myself for the mind numbing pain of the arctic waters. I had taken a dip in a frozen Crystal Lake when I fell through the ice one winter. That was like a warm bath compared to the waters by the Golden Fleece.

The cold wasn't the only thing unnatural about the sea. Magic, old as the ancients ran through those waters. I could feel it.

While the water was terribly cold, I did have a barrier around myself that helped. The sensation of my Siren blood taking over was completely familiar to me and a welcome change to the chaos that seemed to come with my new abilities.

No new powers, no calling to a long lost memory. It was all me.

Surprisingly, my Siren blood took to the water better than my god side. I could feel the battle between the two sides of me. The godly side wasn't able to keep my alive in these waters.

Maybe Ares was telling the truth and I really was the only one that could get the Fleece.

I flew through the water at a speed that I had never managed before. Blasting through it like a torpedo. The power of it was intoxicating and I had to remember that I was on a mission and not a joyride.

Freezing cold or not...I liked it.

Being back in the sea was like coming home. It rejuvenated me. I felt a freedom and peace that I hadn't had in a long time. The water over my skin was everything that I didn't know I had been aching for.

The Fleece was in a cove, under the water, in an ancient iceberg according to Ares. Sounded easy enough to get to, all I had to do was find the-

A blast of energy shot out of the open water and hit me square in the chest. A wound opened up, seeping blood into the water around me.

Damn, that hurts.

Looking around the water, I could see nothing.

Nothing that could have-

Another blast of energy tossed me head over heels. Flipping around, I narrowed my eyes and searched for the source.

A wound widened in my shoulder and throbbed terribly, but it would heal. I allowed the water to it, knowing that it would help heal it as it always had. As soon as the water hit the wound, though, the pain intensified. I cried out, grasping the meaty mess.

What's going on? I looked down at my shoulder. It wasn't healing. At all. I looked around the water.

Now I understood why the gods wouldn't come there. The water took your ability to heal!

Damn, cowards won't risk dying, but apparently it is just fine if I do!

My heart started to race.

No playing around, I needed to get the Fleece and get out of there. If I couldn't heal I could die, and I wasn't about to do that.

Surging forward in the water, I aimed at the largest iceberg in the area. All the other icebergs were smaller, bits breaking off as the air and water warmed around them. But, not the big one. There was no evidence of anything shedding off of it. It was like a floating ice mountain. Something was keeping it from being affected by the climate.

If I had my guess, it was the Fleece.

I poured on speed as I aimed for a hole in the surface of ice. The water around me bubbled and a barrier of water rushed up in front of me, cutting me off from the iceberg. It moved at such a speed that I drew instinctively back from it.

I didn't dare try to go through it. Water could cut and there was no doubting that wall would slice into me like a knife. Without being able to heal, I couldn't risk it.

I turned and aimed around the ice, jutting into the deep. Hoping to outrun its movement, I blasted through the water faster than I had before. Skating around the edge of the wall, I was hit from behind and thrown hard into the surface of the iceberg. My head cracked against the side of it, dazing and clouding my vision. In that moment, I thought that I saw a group of creatures in the water. A long, delicate, horn protruded from their heads, with strong tails propelling them forward.

"Is that-"

A ball of energy lit in the water, and my attention was drawn away. I watched as a torrent of energy roared toward me. Dodging just in time, I rolled away as the wall of the iceberg exploded behind me. Breaking into sharp pieces of frozen shrapnel, the jagged daggers burst from the surface and straight at me. Deep cuts sliced into me across my arms and chest.

My Sirenite powers were keeping my blood in the wound, acting as a supernatural bandage, but it wouldn't last forever.

"Where are you?" I whispered. Searching the water for the horned creatures that were attacking me.

The blue sea spread before me, filled with the shadows of icebergs floating in the deep water. But there was no movement, none that I could see. The wound in my shoulder was throbbing, but manageable. I knew that I would heal, but another one of those hits and I would be in trouble. That did nothing to ease the frustration building in me.

I swam to the side of a close iceberg, flattening myself against the surface of it. Where could they be hiding?

Looking around the edge of the ice, I gazed out at the water. It was strangely empty, not a fish in sight. There was nothing, not one other creature in the water with me - other than the ones bound on killing me.

A blast against the iceberg split the ice that I was clinging to. The blue-green tip broke from the base and fell, slowly gliding to the seafloor before it would eventually bob back up to the surface. I took off, away from the iceberg to another.

The water swirled around me. I could feel the presence of some kind of being close to me, but I could see nothing.

White power ignited across my skin, lighting the water around me and drawing more attention to my location than I should have. I couldn't help it. I couldn't see the cove anymore. Though I knew there was only one way into that cave, I was seriously debating blasting a hole in the side of the iceberg. I watched the particles in the water stir and swirl as the creature went by once again. With every lap it made, I tensed, readying myself for another blast.

None came.

It seemed that as long as I stayed away from the cave they would leave me alone. The moment that I released the wall of the iceberg, to head for the cove, there was another burst. It was clear they were protecting the Fleece. Every time I made a move for the cove they would attack, keeping me against the iceberg. Without being able to see them and defend myself, there was no way I could get to the Fleece.

I was running out of options and my patience was at its end.

"Gods! I need that Fleece!" I yelled. I didn't know who I was yelling at. The creatures? The sea? It didn't matter. No one was going to answer.

"No gods will come here to rescue you, boy."

"What?"

"You are all the same. Selfish. Proud. And, in the end, cowards."

"Whoa, who are you talking about?"

"The gods are not welcome here. Go home, baby god."

"I'm not leaving without the Fleece!"

A shot of energy slammed into me, ripping a wound open across my chest. I sank in the water as my blood leaked past the Siren barrier around me.

Gods. Shit.

"That was a warning shot, baby god. The next one won't be so kind."

"Kind?"

I grasped the wound and winced against the growing pain. *I could really use those nice healing powers right now!*

"Why do you hate the gods so much? What did they ever do to you? No one even comes here!"

"What did they do to us?" the creature shouted. *"What did they do to us?"* The sound was enough to make my ears bleed and that was when I realized that they were bleeding.

"They took us from our home. They tore our families apart. Stole our children and cursed us. All because we had a power that they couldn't control. They were jealous. *Now, we are stuck here guarding their precious Fleece! They don't even trust their own king to look after it!"*

"How can they keep you here if you are more powerful than they are?"

"Did you miss the part where I said that they have our children? If we leave, they will kill them!"

"What?" my mouth fell open.

"You should really learn your history, baby god. Yes! Our young's fate is tied to the Fleece. If it is removed from the cove, our babies die!"

"Who did this to you? *Who?*" I demanded.

"They all did!" the creature yelled. The sound of its voice came from all around me. The icebergs vibrated at the sound of it.

"For so long, we had lived in harmony. Then, one day, the skies darkened and everything changed. Our females were taken as they roosted with our young. The babies ripped from their mothers' embrace. Us males, were picked off one by one as we protected our lands and came to their aid. We were separated from our loved ones. They took our babies from us and cast us out. That was the first round."

"They kept your babies and set you free?" I asked. "Why would they do that?"

"So we would have more young, of course."

"Damn it," I cursed, shaking my head. Poaching was something that I was familiar with, being on land. I detested a poacher, now it seemed that I was being lumped in with the gods who had poached the children of these creatures. These creatures could speak. How could you take the young of something that can you can talk with? It was barbaric. It was closer to what the Titans were than I wanted to think about.

"The gods have a lot to answer for, but we will not risk the lives of our young to get revenge."

"Where are your children?" I asked.

"Olympus. They took them to the one place we can't get into - where their defenses are the strongest. Their powers repel us and we can't break through. We tried. For a long time, we fought against them in an effort to get back our children; but, our final assault on Olympus sealed our fate. Those of us that weren't killed were captured and brought here to serve for all time."

"Why – you know what? It doesn't matter why they did it." I ran my hand through my hair. There was no way that I was going to steal the Fleece after learning that. I wouldn't be responsible for the deaths of innocent young. I'm no monster.

For the moment, Laya had Kronus' essence under control and she was safe. The Fleece could wait for the time being.

"I want to help. Let me help you."

"There is nothing that you can do."

"We'll see about that."

I thought I had been sent to take on some horrible beast that guarded the Fleece because it wanted it for its own. Turned out that was not the case at all. It was one thing to take on a monster and destroy them, but to take on those who had been enslaved was another. I would have no part in harming a creature that was being held against its will. Not to mention there were innocent lives at stake if the Fleece were to be taken. Didn't Ares and Athena care about them?

I could see the water stirring around me and realized that it wasn't just one creature in the water with me, but many. They remained hidden to my sight, but they were no longer attacking me.

"I want to help you, but I need to know who you are. I can't find your youth if I don't know what you look like. I assure you, I'm not a danger to you or your children. I want to help," I said.

No answer came but the water stirred faster around me. If I wasn't mistaken, they were communicating. Deciding to trust me. Or not.

"If I bring back your children, will you be able to give me the Fleece?" I asked.

"If you bring our youth back, we will give you what you want, gladly."

A rush of water blew past me. I closed my eyes against the brush of it. When I opened them I was astonished to see what I had been in the water with.

In front of me swam the most magnificent creatures that I had ever seen. Made of water itself, shimmering in the light from above, a unicorn galloped toward me. Its eyes were made of light, white and intense as it looked at me.

I was breathless. Unicorns were extinct. At least that was what the world had thought. The gods had been keeping them under water for an age.

"Unicorn? You're unicorn?" I asked breathlessly.

"We are only a shadow of what we used to be," the unicorn before me answered, looking into my eyes.

They communicate telepathically. Amazing.

"I thought that you died out."

"Well, now you can see that is not the case."

There was more to this story than what I was seeing. The gods were gaining nothing by keeping the unicorn's young. Why take them at all? It made no sense.

Whatever the reason, I was going to find out.

I took one last look at the creatures and focused my thoughts. Zeus was about to get a drop-in visitor.

KYLAYA

ARACHNE'S POWER filled me. I could feel them running through my veins. Filling a need that I had kept under control. I knew I should stop - but I didn't. It was too good.

I drained her. There wasn't a touch of power left in her when I was done.

With an exhale, a burst of light exploded from me in a shockwave that shook the room. Everything around us went white as I threw out my arms and just let the high ride over me. I revelled in it. Loving every second of the seductive power as it glided gloriously through me.

When it subsided, I took a deep breath; a smile catching the corners of my mouth.

The sweet air was thrilling to my senses.

Wait…sweet air? It hit me…the stench in the air was gone. I opened my eyes, not even realizing that I had closed them.

Gods…

The webbing had disintegrated from ceiling to floor, falling from the walls and turning to dust. The death in the room had disappeared, leaving behind a startlingly clean floor and scent to the air. There was no sign that Arachne had ever been there.

"Ky?" Mazz's voice travelled over to me, but I wasn't really hearing it. I was stuck on the room. *How…*

"How did you do that?" he asked me.

I just shook my head.

The room was…empty.

The bodies…gone.

The webs…gone.

Everything except a woman at my feet.

"Who is she?" Mazz asked as he knelt down beside her.

"I – I don't know," I uttered.

"Mazz!"

Mazz turned and a smile lit his face. Rayna jumped into his arms and hugged him tight.

"Thank the gods," Mazz uttered.

"Are you okay?" Rayna asked, looking at me.

"I'm…fine," I said and knelt beside the woman. *Why was she left here?*

"Who is she?" Rayna asked.

"I don't kn-"

The woman moaned and turned.

"She's alive!" Mazz shouted and fell to the floor next to me.

The woman turned and opened her eyes.

"You're okay," I said gently. "Can you sit up?" She looked at me, her eyes wide. She didn't say anything as she sat up, but just stared at me.

"I'm KyLaya. What's your name? Do you remember how you got here?"

The woman was beautiful. Long black hair hung down to her waist. Her large brown almond shaped eyes looked around the room. Pink had started to grace her cheeks, a good sign that she would be okay. She turned to me and grabbed my hand.

"It's okay, we won't leave y-" I said, but stopped when she raised her hands up and started at them. Tears came to her eyes as she wiggled her fingers.

"Oh my gods," I uttered.

"What?" Mazz asked.

"Arachne?" I whispered, looking at that woman. She turned to me.

"Yes," she said as tears streamed down her cheeks.

"What?" Rayna and Mazz said at the same time.

"How?" I gasped, staring at the woman, who was definitely *not* a spider anymore.

"You broke the curse! You…you saved me, KyLaya," she said, grasping my hands and squeezing them tightly.

"I don't understand."

"I don't really understand either. I thought you said that only Athena could remove my curse," Arachne said.

"That's true!" Mazz said. "Only the god that placed the curse can remove it. I have no idea how Ky would have been able to do this." He looked at Rayna. Her brow was furrowed.

"It must have something to do with her primordial powers," Rayna said. "There isn't much known about them. Maybe, since they are the source, they can undo all that has come before them."

"That is…" Mazz shook his head.

"What?" I asked. "What is it?"

"That kind of power, Ky. It's limitless. If what Rayna said is true, you can undo everything that the gods have done…ever!"

I sank down to the floor. That can't be right.

"Well, I don't care about all that stuff! You saved me, KyLaya! You *saved* me!" Arachne pulled me into a hug. "I owe you my life! I owe you everything."

"No, you don't. I wanted to help you, but I…" I had no words. When I pulled from her, I wanted to end her pain. I wanted her to be safe from the curse that Athena gave her. I needed to do that for her. In that moment, I wanted to cure her. Is that what I had done?

I also wanted her power. I pulled to feed myself, not to help her. Which was it?

Did I pull from her to save her or to feed off of her?

My stomach sank thinking about it. What did that make me?

I was no saviour. I knew that much. I didn't deserve her thanks.

"Whatever you need, KyLaya. I will do it for you. Oh! You came for the essence didn't you?"

That snapped my attention away from myself.

"Yes. We need to destroy the essences," I said. "Do you know where it is? Our information lead us here."

"I know where it is."

"Where?" I asked standing and looking around. "Please don't tell me it was in one of those dead bodies. I have no idea where they went."

"No. It's in me," she said simply.

"What?"

"It's in me. What better place to put the heart of a Titan than in an immortal who can't be killed? There have been others through the years come and try to take it, but none have ever succeeded…obviously," she laughed. "You can have it. My gift to you."

"It's not that simple," Mazz said.

"I realize that. All I'm saying is that I'm not going to fight her for it. Not sure how much of a fighter I am anymore, but imagine I still have a couple of moves. Might be tougher to do without the rest of my legs, though," she said looking down at her two long legs and smiling wide.

"Okay, well…I guess there's no better time than the present," I said stepping up to her and raising my hands toward her face.

"Wait," Arachne said and stepped back.

"What?" I asked. "I won't hurt you. At least I will try really hard not to. I'm not an expert at this. I'm sorry."

"It's not that. Are you sure you want to do this? He's sleeping right now. I don't know what will happen if you try to pull him out."

"He will wake," I said to her. Arachne's eyes widened.

"Then no," she said stepping back from me.

"What do you mean 'no'?" Mazz asked.

"There was a time, at the very beginning, when he woke within me. It took me a long time to suppress him and put him to sleep. Even with my powers and all the time in the world to devote to keeping him from taking me over, it took a century," she explained.

"A *century*?" Rayna gasped.

"Yes. This isn't a small power, KyLaya. If you wake him, he will take you over. I know that without a doubt."

"Thank you for your concern, Arachne. But, this is my fate in all this. I must take in all the essences so that they can be kept safe and then destroyed," I explained.

"You're taking in them *all*? And they are *awake*?" she shouted. She looked at Mazz and Rayna, "You guys are all good with this?"

"Not in the slightest, but we haven't been given another option," Mazz said.

"That…no," Arachne said and looked back at me. "I can't let you do that. I can't. Not after you saved me."

"Arachne."

"No. I owe you this. I will keep the essence and come with you. That way you will have it with you, but you won't have to take it on."

I didn't know what to say.

"Why would you do that for her?" Rayna asked.

"Do you have any idea how long it has been since someone did something kind for me?" Arachne asked.

We were all struck silent. Arachne's eyes filled with tears.

"She could have killed me," Arachne said and took my hand. She turned and looked at me. "I know a part of you questions what happened when you pulled my powers from me."

I didn't say anything, I just nodded.

"You felt the hunger didn't you?"

"Yes," I nodded.

"That is a primordial urge. I have heard of it. Uranus had it, as did Gaia. It is why there is a myth that he ate his children. He didn't eat them; he drew from them. He pulled their powers from them, to feed his own. Something about the primordial power makes those that have it seek more power, even though they have ultimate power. It is greed in its most basic form. You can control it," she grasped my hands tightly. "You can. There isn't anything wrong with you. It is a hunger that you can control."

"I can't," I said. A sob bubbled up my throat as tears built in my eyes.

"You *can*. You could have killed me, KyLaya. But, you didn't. You *saved* me. You *cured* me. Your heart, your *love* for others…I felt that when we were connected. I could feel your hope for me. Your empathy. I felt it *all*."

Tears came hot and fast.

"You *saved* me. *You* did."

She drew me into her arms and I felt a release. I didn't know if it was guilt or relief. But it was peaceful.

In that moment I dropped my guard.

"Poor, poor little girl…"

JETT

WHEN I POPPED back into existence, I was in the middle of a street.

There were massive mansions lining the cobblestone street, reminiscent of the old plantation homes. Lights were lit in the streetlamps, giving a surreal glow to the path before me. It was unnaturally silent.

Ares and Aphrodite had said there was no one in Olympus except Zeus, but I didn't really believe them until that moment.

I could see why, though.

The place was stunning, but cold. The long road was lined with homes that were department store big. Each home was uniquely designed to match the god who owned it. I could tell immediately which gods belonged to which homes.

Aphrodite's home had flowers and pink…everywhere. Ares' home, with various statues dying in battle that littered his front lawn, had been a dead giveaway. Then there was Poseidon's home, which was behind a wall of water.

Every one of them was the stereotypical version of the god or goddess that it belonged to. Ares' home here looked nothing like the one that I had visited. I wondered if that was why he didn't come here. Maybe it wasn't a representation of him that he liked.

But, it was the unicorns' young that I was looking for. *Where would the gods hide them?* Immediately, I stopped and turned toward Poseidon's home. His underwater mansion would be the perfect place. Their parents were in the water, stood to reason that the gods would keep the young in water too.

Deciding that was my best shot, I walked up to the gate. *It must be some kind of portal.* I reached out a hand carefully. *Do the gods lock their doors on Olympus?* The water swirled before my hand. Even without touching it, it sensed me.

A grey whale swam by, it's large, long lashed eye on me as it moved gracefully by and out of view. That was when I realized that I was looking at a window to the ocean, not real water. There was no way a real whale was swimming around Poseidon's front yard. It was nothing more than an illusion.

Taking a breath, I stepped through the wall of projected water.

The instant that I touched it the water-wall fell, crashing down on top of me. I was thrown hard to the ground, my head cracking off of the stone road. Waves pummelled me, rattling my bones as they were scraped and slammed against the cobblestone. I was washed out onto the street, where the water receded back to the wall and the window to the ocean reappeared. The whale was there once again…watching me.

"Damn it," I cursed as I pulled the water from me with my Siren power and stood.

"Kids today," a booming voice rang. "Don't even bother knocking."

I turned around and came face to face with a man. I yelped and stumbled back, nearly tripping and landing on my ass all over again.

"Where did you…never mind. Who are you?" I asked.

"The real question is: who are *you* and what are *you* doing here?" the man said.

"My name is Jett," I said, looking hard at him.

My guard was up. I didn't trust gods. There were agendas with these beings that went as far back as time itself. Every last one of them had something that they wanted and were willing to kill for. Whoever this guy was, he was no different.

His bright blue eyes gazed at me from a young face. He didn't look much older than me.

"Jett. What are you here for?" he asked. He was the same height as me, and walked with an air of power and authority. His perfectly tanned shin shone in the light from the lamps. Round almond eyes looked at me from under a thick brow. A thin nose split his chiseled face. I assumed I was looking at the god of the sea. Poseidon.

"Why won't you tell me who you are?" I asked him.

"It's not a secret," he said with a shrug. "I look after this place," he said angling his head back towards Poseidon's mansion.

"You're not Poseidon?" I asked.

He smiled crookedly.

"No," he said quietly.

"Oh," I uttered, guess I was wrong.

"He doesn't come here much."

"Okay, well I think that he might have something that I'm looking for," I said to him.

"Is that so?" He placed his hands on his hips and tilted his head.

"Yes."

"What did he take this time?"

"Excuse me?"

"Oh please, the gods are not accustomed to asking for anything, they just take what they want and ask for forgiveness later…if ever," he said, crossing his muscular arms over his chest.

"I take it you aren't a big fan," I said.

"I was…a very long time ago. When I said 'yes' to this job," he answered.

"I'm sorry. Who are you exactly, if you aren't Poseidon?"

"I'm Nerites. Guardian of the palace of Poseidon," he answered with a small bow and a roll of his eyes.

"Well, Guardian Nerites, I think that Poseidon has some unicorns that don't belong to him," I said, watching Nerites closely.

"Is that so?" he smiled and shook his head.

"You know where they are?"

"I may," he said looking me up and down.

"Can you take me to them?" I asked.

"I could," he answered with a smile.

"Okay, what's your deal?" I asked, crossing my arms.

"Deal?"

"What do you want?"

"What do I want?" he asked, pointing to himself. "Are you really asking me what *I* want? Truthfully?"

I nodded. I had no money, so I had no idea what I was going to pay him with. It had to be something valuable. I was running out of time, so whatever it was I was going to pay it.

"Do you have any idea how long it's been since someone asked me what I want?" he asked.

"I'm guessing a long time," I answered.

"Yes. Longer than I care to think about," he said.

"What do you want then? Please. I…it's really important that I get those unicorns back to their families."

"You're returning them home?" he asked looking up with wide eyes.

"They were stolen from their families. Yes. I want to take them home," I said, placing my hands on my hips. "Now, are you going to take me to them or not, Nerites?"

He clenched his jaw and looked up at Poseidon's home.

"I will take you to them on one condition," Nerites said.

"What?"

"You take me with you when you leave."

"What?" I blurted. "You live on freaking Olympus! Why would you want to come with *me*?"

"I have been alone here for centuries! All I do is wait for Poseidon to come home. You know how often that is?"

I shook my head.

"Every fifty years or so," he answered. "It's always the same thing. He 'lost track of time'." Nerites shook his head. "He's just tired of me."

"Tired of you?"

"Yes! At first things were all hot and heavy, and we couldn't spend more than a day away from each other. He even brought me here to live with him and take care of his place while he was away. I was so honored! But…that was a very long time ago."

"You and Poseidon were-"

"Lovers? Yeah. Emphasis on the '*were*'. You know the last time we had sex?"

"Whoa, man. I just met y-"

"A hundred years ago!"

"Wow, okay, yup, you went there." I clasped my hands in from of me and fought the blush climbing up my neck to my cheeks. I really didn't want to know that much about Poseidon's love life.

"One. Hundred. Years. Jett. A century! That's not a dry spell, that's an apocalyptic drought."

"Sure seems that way."

"Anyway, it's time I moved on. Even if that means…"

"What? Means what?"

"You know what? It's not important. I want out of here and you want those unicorns. We can help each other. Deal?" he reached out a hand for mine and waited.

I looked at him and hesitated. All I had to do was take him out of here with me. I didn't have to babysit him. I took his hand in mine and shook it.

"Deal."

"Yes!" Nerites exclaimed, jumping in the air. He was so fast I didn't have time to react. He grabbed my shoulders and kissed me. I froze. My hands were glued to my sides and my eyes were wide in shock.

He stumbled back and smiled sheepishly.

"Sorry about that," he said as redness took over his skin. "It's been a long time since I have talked with anyone, let alone kissed anyone. You…well you're a sight for sore eyes in more than one way if you know what I mean."

"Okay, well, umm thank you, I guess. But, I'm not into guys. You have the wrong brother," I said.

"You have a brother?" he gasped.

"Yes. We're…well, we're twins, actually," I answered.

"Holy Hades! Can I meet him?"

"Yeah, well, he's married," I said.

Nerites shrugged. "So was Poseidon."

"Ah, okay," I uttered.

"Now, off to the unicorns!" Nerites turned and stepped through the wall of water without any trouble.

"Alright, let's get this over with," I uttered and stepped through behind him.

KYLAYA

THE VOICE was like an ice shower that slid down my back and ran into every part of me, chilling and prickling my skin as it went.

I pulled back from Arachne.

"What is it?" she asked, her human eyes still gleaming with tears that she had shed for me. *Me.*

"I thought I heard a voice," I said. I brought my hand to my forehead. *Am I sick?*

"I didn't hear anything," she said.

"You okay?" Mazz asked, and placed a hand on my shoulder.

There was a snap and a flash at his touch. He cried out in pain, pulling his hand away and grasping his Guardian mark.

"Mazz…" I uttered. A haze was clouding my vision. The room was fading from me as if a thick fog had surged forward. But, where did it come from?

"Do you really not know?"

Kronus.

"You didn't think that I was gone did you? That you had somehow defeated me?"

The chill came again, this time it ran down between my breasts, like a dead man's finger on me. Dread bubbled up from the pit of my stomach as panic choked at my nerves, strangling them raw.

You don't control me, Kronus. Crawl back into the corner I put you in.

"I don't think so."

"Ky?" Mazz's voice filtered through the fog. I raised my head, and looked up, but nothing came into focus. There was nothing but darkness…just like before.

My heart kicked at my ribs like the slap of a whale's tail. It wanted out of there, possibly more than I did. It was smart.

"Mazz?" I called, but I knew my mouth didn't open. I knew no sound came out. I knew I was standing there still and silent…and that was terrifying beyond belief.

"Your power…so strong. So, untapped. So ready for a real master. Ready for me. Mother always liked me best. Stands to reason that I would get to wield her power. Now-"

You aren't getting anything from me.

"On the contrary. You have brought another part of me together."

I have done no such thing. We don't have the next part of your soul.

"We will now."

My hands snapped up. The fog cleared and I was looking into Arachne's eyes. Her brow furrowed as she looked at me.

"KyLaya?" she asked, bringing her hands up to the backs of mine and trying to pull them from her cheeks. "What are you doing?"

"I – I can't…" I stammered, but nothing came from my lips.

Before I could stop it, I felt the pull in my core and knew that Kronus was trying to wield my power.

No. This is your body, Laya. You have control over it. Come on, Laya. Get it together. You can do this. Think of Jett. Focus on him. On your love.

"Nice try, young one, but that's not going to work this time. The longer I'm awake the stronger I get."

"Something's wrong," Arachne said, and looked back at Mazz.

"It's Kronus," he bit. Grabbing my hands in his, he yanked them from Arachne. "Look at me, Ky! You can do this! Fight the bastard! "

"I'm trying," I managed to choke out.

"What can we do?" he asked me.

"The essence…" I mumbled and looked to Arachne.

"It's me," she said. "He wants the essence."

I couldn't nod, but my silence answered the question for her.

"Say no more," she said. She turned and ran from the room.

"Arachne!" Mazz shouted.

"I'll go!" Rayna said and bolted after her.

Mazz turned his eyes to mine.

"Stay with me, Ky. Don't you give that asshole a finger nail's width. You hear me?"

I locked eyes with him.

"He's too strong," I choked.

Mazz grasped my face in his hands. "Not as strong as you, Ky. I believe in you."

A tear trickled down my cheek as his words cut through the fog of the room and into me.

"I believe in you."

It echoed through me as Kronus fought against my weak walls to gain control.

Jett...

"He can't help you now."

The fog rolled in thicker and darker than before and swallowed me whole.

JETT

THE WALL to Poseidon's palace was nothing like I thought it would be. It wasn't like stepping through water, more like jelly. Warm jelly.

I gritted my teeth and followed Nerites through. His tall, thin frame didn't flinch at all when we came through to the other side and into a garden. I was right, the wall was a projection of somewhere in the sea. The garden was bathed in sunlight and was stunning beyond anything I had ever seen. I had been to my share of pretty gardens back home, but nothing this…lush.

Nerites walked confidently around the side of the palace.

"You look after all this?" I asked as we rounded the side of the mansion. The massive garden stretched around the side of the building and out behind.

"All of it," Nerites answered with a nod.

"By yourself?"

"Well, I have nothing but time, so yeah."

The place was bigger than any home I had ever seen. It looked more like a university dorm. How someone could look after all that by themselves was beyond me. One thing was clear, though. All that space and no one to share it with would be really lonely.

On the other side of the palace was located a massive stable. In all my years and all the farms that I had been to, I had never seen a stable that big.

"What on earth do you have in there?" I asked.

"Well, we're not on earth are we?" he said with a sly smile as he led the way through the large stable doors.

"I suppose not," I answered and followed him in.

It was grander than anything I had ever seen at home. The sheer size was mind blowing to me; but it wasn't just that, it was the creatures that greeted us from their gated stalls. I stopped dead in my tracks the moment that they stuck their heads over their stall doors and looked at me.

"Those are-" I uttered, staring wide eyed at the creatures.

"Yup. Unicorns." Nerites walked up to one and dipped his head down. The stunning creature dipped its head until the two of their foreheads met.

"These can't be the ones that I am looking for," I stared at the full-sized unicorns and shook my head. "These are full grown."

"They might look like it, but they are uniborns."

"Uniborns?"

"Yes. Baby unicorns. Uniborns," he said with a shrug.

"But they're so big," I commented.

"Yeah, I suppose they would be to you. Even a full-grown horse is a mini version of a unicorn. Uni's are huge full grown," Nerites said and walked toward one, who bent down its head and placed it to Nerites' forehead.

"What is it doing?"

"Oh, it's our way of saying 'hi'. They have a unique way of communicating. It took us awhile, but we figured it out," he said smiling at the unicorn.

"You acted surprised that Poseidon had them here when I asked. Why?"

"I don't know," he shrugged. "I'm so used to lying when it comes to them that I just do it. Second nature and all."

"Uh huh," I said, not entirely believing him.

"Look. You want them or not?"

I stared at the dozen or more unicorns, who were sticking their heads out of their stalls looking at me and it occurred to me that I had no idea how to take them home. I placed my hands on my hips and clenched my jaw.

"Umm," Nerites said, shifting from foot to foot. "You *are* taking them, right? 'Cause, I kinda just told them that they were finally going home."

"Why have you taken care of them knowing that they were stolen?"

Nerites laughed and crossed his arms. "You don't get it, do you?"

"What?"

"I'm a prisoner here too. Sure, I willingly came at first, and this is a stunning place to be; but, that doesn't mean that a prison can't be pretty. If I could have returned them home, I would have done so long ago; but, I don't have the power to." A unicorn nudged Nerites and he smiled back at it. "We've become friends over the years. To see them with their families would be a great gift to me."

"Well, I – I'm not sure how to get them out of here. I haven't exactly mastered the popping-in-and-out thing myself."

"You came looking for unicorns and you didn't think about how you were going to get them home?"

"They are holding hostage the Golden Fleece! I need it to save Laya! That's all I was thinking about."

"Who's Laya?"

"My girlfriend - though that doesn't half cover the extent of our relationship."

"Oh, so you're taken," Nerites said and bit his lip.

"Yes," I answered slowly. "Sorry?"

"Oh, no. Don't do that." He laughed and shook his finger at me.

I sighed and put my hands in my pockets. Nerites was a nice enough guy, as far as I could tell - having only known him for a second. That didn't stop a spark of guilt from blooming at the look of regret that crossed his face when I said that I was taken. The guy was lonely and had been for a long time.

"Anyway, why don't you just try popping out with one and see how that goes," Nerites suggested.

"Yeah, okay, that just might work," I answered.

I walked up to a unicorn that was standing next to Nerites. It reared up and snarled at me.

"Uh, I don't think that it trusts me," I said.

Nerites reached up and placed a gentle hand between the unicorn's eyes, just under its horn. The unicorn settled down immediately, its long lashes closing as it communicated with Nerites.

"They're shy," Nerites said. "It takes them a while to trust. I mean, they *were* kidnapped from their families. Only stands to reason that they are a little jumpy."

"Of course," I said. "I'm no stranger to animals, but these guys are different than anything I have dealt with on the farm."

"Yeah. They are unicorns. Sentient. Smart. Powerful."

"I can see that," I said as I locked eyes with the unicorn in front of me. Without thinking about it, I did what instinct told me to.

Closing my eyes, I reached out with my mind.

I have met your family. I want to take you home to them. You can trust me.

Not knowing what would happen next, I left my mind open and hoped that it would be enough to speak to the unicorns. They were my only hope to save Laya. I needed them as much as they needed me.

A voice filtered from the back of my mind to the front. Like a trickle of warm honey, thick and sweet, down the back of my neck it crept. It echoed around my mind, like the sound of a choir, as deep and limitless as the sea itself.

"What makes you different from the last god that came to us?"

I nearly staggered back as the stunning creature spoke to me. It was not the voice of a young creature to my limited mind. It was strong and powerful. A leader. I got the impression that even though I was there to release them, they had every right not to want to come with me. This wasn't going to be a simple as I thought. They were intelligent creatures, and even a rescue would take convincing.

The last god that came to you was Poseidon. I am not him.

"And who are you?"

I'm…I'm no one, really. I'm just trying to save the one that I love.

"The one you love?"

Yes. She's in danger of being consumed by Kronus. If I don't get the Golden Fleece, I will lose her to his power.

"What does this have to do with our family?"

Your family guards the Fleece.

"You hope that by saving us, our family will give you the Fleece?"

Yes.

"That isn't a selfless act."

No it isn't. I won't lie to you. I need that Fleece to save her. I can't lose her. I can't.

"You faced our family?"

Yes.

"Seeing that you survived, there must have been something that my family saw in you. They don't leave any alive to who attempt to get the Fleece. It is our family curse."

Well, I can't say we didn't come to blows.

"If you lived through the blows my family gave you, you are unlike any other that has come against them."

Thanks, I think.

"What does Kronus have to do with your loved one?"

He is waking. He's searching for his essences. Laya has one of them within her. It's strong…too strong. If I don't help her, if I don't get the Fleece, I fear it will consume her.

"This Laya, she has one of the essences?"

Yes.

"Kronus needs only one body to waken the others. If she has taken one into her, she has woken them all."

What?

"They are connected. The other essences will know one has woken and be ready for the others to come for them. When the awakened essence gets close, the others will jump. Your Laya won't have to pull them from their host, the essences will simply force their way in once they are called to it."

I lost the connection in that moment. Slapping my hands to my face I ran my hands hard through my hair.

"Shit!"

"What happened?" Nerites asked.

"Laya. She's in more danger than I knew. We've been lied to! I have to get back to her. Now!"

"What about the unicorns?" Nerites called as I started to walk for the door.

Frustration mounted within me, I could feel my power pull at my core as fear raced through my mind. I had no time. No time to take these creatures one by one back home, get the Fleece, and get to Laya. Laya was my priority. I needed to get to her first.

"You can't just leave them here!" Nerites yelled. "They've been captive too long! They don't even remember what it is like to be a true creature of magic! They will die here!"

"I can't-"

"Yes, you can!" Nerites shouted at me.

My powers snapped with my anger, as panic flooded my senses. I was pulled in every which way and no way lead me to an answer that could save Laya. I grasped my head, willing my anger to check itself, but it raged on.

From the back of my mind an image crept forward, knowledge that was hidden within the powers awakening in me.

Calm washed over me as I understood what I needed to do, more like what I knew I *could* do.

White light lit in my palms.

"Whoa!" Nerites shouted and stumbled back from me. "That's-that's not possible!"

I lifted my hands up toward the unicorns. White tendrils of light burst from my palms, streaking toward the creatures. They bucked and whinnied, but as each tendril wrapped around the creature, they popped out of existence.

The room was flooded in light as the unicorns disappeared one by one, sent home to their family. As the last one popped out of the stable, I turned to Nerites.

"Sorry!" he yelled and held his hands up.

"What are you sorry for?" I asked him.

"I don't know. Seemed like the smart thing to say under the circumstances."

"You wanted to see them with their family right?"

He just nodded.

"Come on then." I grabbed his hand and we popped out of the stable.

. . .

"FOR THE LOVE of everything sacred in this world, stop screaming!"

Nerites clamped a hand over his mouth. He hadn't stopped screaming since I had grabbed him.

"Seriously? Didn't you get used to this when you were travelling with Poseidon?" I asked him.

"No offence; but, you lack a certain finesse in the 'popping' department, as you put it." Nerites doubled over, placed his hands on his knees, and breathed heavily.

It had occurred to me that Nerites probably couldn't breathe under water, so I took him to the closest landmass to the unicorns that I could. From there, I hoped that the connection that he had with them would be able to bring them to us.

"You could have brought a jacket for me, you know. Or at least warned me that we were somewhere that was going to freeze my balls off," he barked at me as he ran his hands up and down his arms.

"You know; I think you could complain a little more if you put some more effort into it. I don't think you're really giving it your all."

He turned a glare on me and I shrugged.

He opened his mouth to say something, but slammed it shut when the water in front of us began to bubble.

"I think we have company," I said. Sure, we were in the arctic and it was minus a million outside, but I couldn't spare a thought for that. All I wanted was to see that Fleece.

Through the bubbles came one long pointed horn.

"Oh! Yes!" Nerites shouted. "I've been dying to see them in their other form!"

A water unicorn breached the water, followed by a dozen and more. Their heads bobbed in the water up to their necks. Their brilliant eyes glowed in the misty morning light.

"Ah! They look incredible!" Nerites gushed.

"Agreed! Did everyone make it back?" I asked them.

"I hardly believe what I am seeing. You did it," the largest of the unicorns spoke. His voice was deep and seemed to come from all around us. No private connection this time, there was no doubt that Nerites could hear him too. The unicorn's voice penetrated every other sound around.

"We did it," I said pointing to Nerites as well. "Nerites has been looking after your young. I just popped them back to you."

The unicorn turned to Nerites. Nerites smiled sheepishly and gave a little awkward wave.

"It was my pleasure. Truly," Nerites said.

"You took care of our young?"

"Yes! We are…friends," Nerites said, sadly.

"And yet you didn't bond with them?"

"I…well, no," Nerites answered.

"Interesting."

"I'm sorry to interrupt, but I held up my side of the bargain. You have your children. Do you have the Fleece?" I asked.

The unicorn blasted out of the water in a geyser of sea spray. Jumping clear out of the sea, it sailed easily over our heads. When it landed it was no longer in its water form, but a full grown unicorn. Closer to the size of a giant moose than a horse, it shook the ground as it walked. The very air around it seems to vibrate with energy as it turned and walked slowly toward me.

"Wow," I uttered, truly stunned and awed at the ethereal beauty of it.

"You said it," Nerites echoed, staring wide eyed at the splendor of what now stood before us. Silver hair in colours unlike anything that I had ever seen, danced in the light of its silver horn. Its body looked like it was made of iridescent glass. The unicorn stood on strong legs, its coat a million colors that swam around in a pool of silver. Like oil on water, silver water.

I could barely catch my breath standing before its majesty. It took a lot to humble me; but, I was damned humble in the presence of that creature.

"I am Spyres, leader of the Herditim, the last of the unicorns," he said and bowed. Nerites and I staggered forward in a, less than fluid, bow. *"Our young have been restored to us. Something that not even our magic was able to do. How can we thank you?"*

"Oh, I don't really need anything," Nerites said shaking his head.

"The Fleece," I answered.

Spyres looked at me. His gaze went straight through me, scattering vibrations through my veins as his powers searched for something within me. I hadn't experienced anything like that before.

"You are an ancient, or at least you have ancient in you," he said moving toward me. I took an instinctive step backward and raised a hand, ready to defend myself.

"What's an ancient?" Nerites asked, inching forward.

"The first ones. Gaia. Uranus. Primordial blood." Spyres circled around me, his dark eyes studying me closely.

"Yes, supposedly," I answered hesitantly.

"You're - what?" Nerites shrieked. I angled a look at him.

"The – reincarnation of Uranus," I grumbled.

"Unbelievable! You didn't think to mention that to me?

"No offense, but we just met," I said. Nerites threw his hands in the air.

"You think you know a guy," he mumbled. I shook my head.

"You possess a power unparalleled by any god on earth; and yet, you didn't use that power to bond with the young. Why?"

"What is this *bond* you're talking about?" I asked.

"Bonding with a unicorn is a rare thing. As such, the bonded two are gifted with new abilities and power. An immortal blessed life. Nothing can destroy a bonded god. A bond is a sacred thing. Very few unicorns have offered themselves over to a bond with a god - they lose part of themselves to it. The god reaps the rewards for the most part."

Nerites leaned down and placed a hand on the forehead of one of the unicorn babies in the water. Several of them swam up to him, making noises that I could only interpret as affection. They were in their water forms, which were much smaller than their land forms. The adult unicorns stayed close by, watching restlessly as the youth swam about in the waters they had been taken from long ago. Nerites was all smiles and laughs. The cold no longer bothering him now that he saw the babies back home. He obviously adored the unicorns.

"Why didn't they bond with you?" I asked him.

"I'm not a god. They can't bond with me," he said.

"That doesn't seem fair," I said. Nerites shrugged.

"It's fine. I'm beginning to realize that immortality just isn't for me."

"What do you mean?" I asked.

"In Olympus I don't age, but the moment I left…"

"You…you mean that because *I* took you out of Olympus you'll *die?*"

"Well, not tomorrow, but yeah…eventually," Nerites said. He leaned down and rubbed the head of another baby who swam up to him.

"You might have mentioned that before I got you out of there," I said, not sure how I felt about giving Nerites a death sentence, no matter how far away it was.

"My choice to make, not yours, Jett," Nerites said. I sighed and looked back at Spyres.

"Our children are bonded to gods to increase their powers."

"The uni's are worth a lot to a race of gods that are dying," Nerites finished.

"Dying?" I uttered.

"Yup. Their powers are weakening and their time is coming to an end. The dawn of a new age is upon us. The gods are in a race against time. Some are ready for it, welcoming it actually; but, some…will fight against it with all they've got. A bond with a unicorn would guarantee a power boost to them and the ability to tie their lives to another immortal," Nerites explained.

"Why not an adult unicorn? Why does it have to be a uniborn?"

"Our young are easier to bond with. The older we get the more stubborn we become. You can't force a bond on an adult. It would kill you…but not the young ones."

"It takes a great amount of power to force a bond," Nerites added. "Young ones won't bond with someone that they don't trust or respect. They are smart little ones," Nerites said and looked adoringly at the young splashing in the water.

"Which poses the question, again, of why you didn't bond with them. Your powers are beyond that of a normal god. You could have…forced the bond."

"I would *never* do that," I said as a bitter taste rose in my throat. Forcing a bond would be like ripping the young unicorn's free will away from it. Any being that did that to such an innocent creature utterly disgusted me. I squeezed my hands into tight fists in an effort to quell the rising anger, and surge of power that was riding its coat tails.

"No matter what. I would never force another creature to do something like that. Besides, I didn't even know I could bond with them," I answered, spreading my fingers wide before my short nails cut into my skin.

"That's not true. You could feel it," Spyres said, his voice a low thundering rumble.

"No, I-" but then I stopped; and, really thought about it. There was *something* when I came upon the young unicorns. A pull to them. I could feel their power. It called to me. Was that the bond? I looked up at Spyres.

"Yes. You can sense it."

"I didn't realize that it was there, but I sense it now. I can almost feel your power. It's…like an energy boost. Wow," I smiled. "But, if I'm not bonded, how am I feeling that?"

"The young ones can't mask their power yet. Other magical beings can sense it and feed off of it."

"Feed?" Nerites uttered and glared at me, turning away from the young he was playing with. He stood, anger flashing in his eyes.

"No…I-"

"He is not feeding on them, Nerites. Rest assured I would not allow such an act in my presence. It is the Titans who feed on our magic. During their rule we were almost hunted to extinction to feed their power hungry nature," Spyres shook his great head and stomped at the ground. The earth shook with his movement.

"How does the Fleece play into all this? How did you get tied up with guard duty on that?" I asked.

"During the dark time of the Titans' rule, we went to the Olympians for help. They were gearing up for their battle with the Titans. With an energy boost from our youth, they were able to increase their energy and power. In exchange for the adults guarding the Golden Fleece, in water where even the Titans couldn't tread, they would keep our young safe. We were foolish and naïve enough to believe that once the war was over, they would bring them back."

"Wait. That was a long time ago. Poseidon hasn't always had the uni's," Nerites said. "He only took over their care a hundred years ago."

"Where were they before that? That's a lot of lost time."

"From what we have been able to learn, they were held in caves and caverns. Starved of light and fresh air. Poseidon, for all his ill doing in keeping our children, did take pity on them and brought them to his home to be taken care of by you, Nerites."

"Oh," Nerites uttered. "He never told me why he brought them there. I didn't know where they were before. I'm so sorry."

"You have been a constant, kind, companion to our youth and they love you. You have nothing to apologize for," Spyres said, bringing his head down level with Nerites.

A tear welled and then dropped down Nerites cheek. I looked away, sadness taking me. The plight of the unicorns pulled at my heartstrings more than I wanted it to. I had to get back to Laya, but I was driven to help them. A part of me wanted to make it right for them.

"You've never been *really* free have you?" I asked, a wave of sadness washing over me. "If the Titans weren't hunting you to munch on, then the gods were taking advantage of your magic and kidnapping your kids."

"Yes. I had hoped for better for my children."

"Question," I said looking at the young playing in the water. It occurred to me that this would have been the first time they were able to do that. "If they were taken as children, surely they would have grown up by now," I said. "I mean; it's been a few thousand years."

"I can answer that," Nerites said. "Nothing ages on Olympus. Wherever they were kept before must have been under the control of Olympus, keeping the babies locked in their youthful state. They haven't grown at all since I started looking after them, just as I haven't aged. The gods might have thought that the babies were easier to bond with, but it didn't work out that way. They *are* easier to get an energy boost, though. The gods would pop in from time to time to get a boost. I never saw them feed, though."

"Jeez," I uttered, truly disgusted.

"When you have been around as long as the gods have, you lose sight of right and wrong. They function under their own set of values. Don't forget that," Spyres said.

"What's going to happen once they find out that all the unicorns are gone?" I asked Nerites.

"Well, as far as Poseidon goes I doubt he'll even report it. Quite honestly, he never seemed to be happy to have them. I always thought that it was because he hated the burden of looking after them; but, thinking back on it I don't think that he wanted any part of the bonding game. He isn't a bad guy," Nerites said, looking at me.

"Were there any bonds that were successful?" I asked.

"Unfortunately, yes," Nerites conceded. "Not as many as they would have liked, only a couple were able to bond with the uni babies. Two as a matter of fact, as far as I know."

"Who?"

"Zeus," Nerites answered. "No surprise there. But he actually made a bond with an older uni. As far as I could tell, he really earned the trust of that unicorn. Even took him to live with him. That was a willing bond. The other…well, it wasn't willing."

"What do you mean? A god forced a bond?" I asked, a chill spreading across my shoulders and down my back.

"Only an immensely strong god can force a bond, even with a young one. It takes a tremendous amount of power," Spyres said.

"Oh, it wasn't a god," Nerites answered darkly.

Spyres and I looked at Nerites. I didn't even know I was holding my breath until he spoke and I felt all the blood flee from me at his answer.

"It was a Titan."

KYLAYA

I WOKE in a dark room.

My eyes darted around, trying desperately to focus on anything. A sliver of light cracked into the endless darkness from around the door, sheading little light into the space. While my eyes struggled to adjust I could just barely make out what was around me. My fingers spread across the floor as I pushed myself up to a sitting position. Scraping against the hardness of the cold ground, my nails filled with dirt and grime. The air was chilly, but not cold. It, however, had a thick putrid stench; like rags that were left in milky water too long. The sourness of it grabbed the back of my throat and made me gag.

"Holy Hades," I whispered to myself.

"Really? I had harsher words than that when I got here."

I screamed.

"Well, glad you got that out of your system," the voice.

"Who's there?" I asked, trying to keep my voice even, but failing completely as it squeaked out of me.

"You have nothing to fear from me, child. My name is Persephone," she said.

"Persephone. Like the queen of the Underworld? That Persephone?" I blurted.

A light, pretty chuckle echoed around me. "Yes, though I'm not really feeling very queenly locked in this place."

"Where are we?" I asked, sliding myself up against a wall and feeling the rough surface bite through my shirt into my skin. There would be no comfortable sitting or sleeping in this place.

"I'm not entirely sure where we are," she answered. "I get flashes of power every once in a while. I've narrowed it down to somewhere *bad*. How did you get here?"

"I – I don't know," I said.

The last thing I remembered was Kronus waking and taking over my mind. His essence dominated me; pushing me out and locking me up. I had no idea how long I was a prisoner in my own mind before I woke in that room.

Days? Weeks? Months?

What had I done? What was done to me?

I needed to get out. I reached to my core, pulling on my power. No way was I staying there. If blasting my way out was my only option, so be it.

But there was nothing.

Not a flicker.

Not a spark.

I pulled again.

Nothing.

My powers were *gone.*

Tightening in my chest reached across my ribs and squeezed them. *I can't breathe!*

"You okay?" Persephone asked.

"No…I…can't…" I was gasping for air and having no luck getting any.

"You're having a panic attack. It's okay. Just try to regulate your breathing. You'll be okay," she said, moving to me and placing a comforting arm around my shoulders.

"No…he…took…them."

"Took what?"

"My…power."

"Who did?"

"Kronus."

Persephone's arm dropped.

"What?" Persephone blurted. "Kronus?"

I nodded and tried to breathe slower and deeper. It took several minutes of focused breathing before I could answer any of Persephone's questions.

"How is that possible?"

"I kind of…absorbed his essence. We were trying to find all of them…so we could kill him," I said between breaths. "It didn't work out so well."

"Is Kronus *awake?*" she uttered.

"Not completely," I pulled in a deep, long breath, finally calming down. "Parts of him are. He's not completely together, just yet. If he has my powers, though, it won't be long."

"This makes so much sense," Persephone said. "It explains why the underworld has been buzzing. They *knew.* Those damned dead knew!" she said. I could hear her hands smack against the hard ground, but I could just barely see the outline of her face in the dim.

"My powers…they're gone," I said.

"Yeah. There's something about this place that does that. I'm not the most powerful of goddesses, but I can blow a lock off a door. I can't summon enough to break anything."

"Can you feel your power? At all?" I asked.

"Yes, it's there. It's just muted."

"I can't feel anything. It's like, they've been taken away. I don't understand how that can happen!"

"I'm sorry."

She moved to me, and sat against the wall next to me. Her face turned and I could finally see her beautiful, delicate features in the scant light.

"How did *you* get here?" I asked her.

"I was kidnapped. Taken right out of my bed in the palace of the Underworld," she said with a sigh. "Hades will be out of his mind."

"Doesn't like it when his things are taken from him?" I asked, remembering all my teachings of their "love" story. How Hades tricked Persephone into staying with him. How he kidnapped her to the Underworld and took her away from her beloved mother. Great guy.

"Ah, yes," she said nodding once. "I'm guessing you're referring to that good old mythology tale," she said. Bitterness rolled off her tongue in waves.

"Yeah. Shouldn't I be?"

"No. You shouldn't be. That tale is a complete lie. All of it."

"Really?" I mumbled. "Why would…why?"

"To protect me," Persephone said. "Hades did everything to protect me."

"You sound like you love him."

"He is my *everything.*"

My breath caught in my throat as a glow formed next to me, right where Persephone was sitting. It took my eyes a moment to adjust, but when they did, I realized that the glow was coming from her.

"How are you doing that?" I gasped.

"It's him. Hades. My love. This light is the bond that we have. When gods fall in love…"

"I know," I said, thinking about the glow that Jett and I had created a time or two. A smile spread across my face as the memory of him in my arms flooded back to me. I closed my eyes and went with it. For a moment I could almost feel him next to me.

Persephone gasped, placing a hand delicately across her mouth.

"You? You have it too?" she whispered.

"Yes. It just started not long ago." I smiled.

"You know how rare that is? How special?" she asked.

"I might have heard a little about it."

"There are only a couple of gods that have had this kind of connection. You have to be careful," she said.

"Why?"

"With the love comes an obsession too. If you are prone to jealousy or trust issues, this connection can drive you mad," she said.

"Oh," I uttered. I didn't think I had a problem with either of those. I thought of Jett and the light formed again, brighter this time. My heart filled with love and hope.

He will come for me. I know he will.

"Stop!" Persephone called. I opened my eyes and the room plunged into darkness again.

"What?"

"He's coming," she whispered, grabbed my hand, and shuffled across the room pulling me with her.

"Who?"

She didn't get a chance to answer as the door opened opposite us. The light from the hall was blinding, but didn't last long as a towering figure stepped into the doorway, drowning the light in his frame. He stooped as he walked in. I couldn't breathe. It was as if the air in the room was sucked out the moment that he came in.

"You having fun with the newcomer Persephone?" a darkly deep voice sounded.

Persephone didn't say anything but levelled a glare at him that should have had him scuttling back under whatever rock he crawled out of out. But he didn't.

He laughed.

The walls shook. I gasped and held on to Persephone's hand harder.

"Who are you? Why am I here?" I said.

He looked at me and narrowed his deep set black eyes. His skin was wet and his hair hung in long seaweed green lumps past his shoulders. More a mountain than a man, there was little to his neck which disappeared into his broad shoulders. With arms as big as tree trunks, he looked awkwardly huge. Giant.

Titan.

"Don't you know the Titan of the seas when he is standing before you?" he thundered.

Before I could react his hand snapped out and cracked me across the face. I was lifted right off the floor and thrown across the room into the wall. Persephone was on her feet and at my side before the ringing in my ears subsided. I grasped my jaw, certain that it was broken.

Defenseless and powerless, and at the mercy of a Titan; I would have given anything for my daggers in that moment. I tried desperately to pull at my powers, but they weren't there. The emptiness, that had been there since I woke up, seemed so big and bitter now. Somehow *I* was there, but my *powers* weren't. How was that possible?

But, there I was.

I didn't even know where *there* was, or how I had arrived.

"You little shit will show some respect," Oceanus snapped. "You might be Kronus' prize, but that doesn't mean I don't get to play with you until he comes back." A slimy smile gleamed out from between his grease-streaked hair.

My jaw was ringing with pain and all I could think was the way that he said *play*. I looked over at Persephone and really saw her for the first time. Her cheeks were sunken, her blonde hair hung matted and filthy in dreaded clumps around her face. She had bruises lined up her neck, and across her shoulders. Her clothes were ripped and dirty. She had a black eye and a swollen lip.

Gods. What has he done to you?

I wanted to reach over and grasp her hand, but I knew that would just anger the Titan more.

"Speaking of *playing*," the Titan said, licking his lips and eyeing Persephone.

A spike of pure ice plunged into my heart and shattered through me, pinching and poking as it took my blood. She lifted her chin and glared at him, looking strong and stoic. Even in her state, there was no mistaking her beauty. Her creamy skin stood out in the darkness of the room like a beacon. Her longs legs were folded gracefully under her delicate frame as her hands balled in her lap. Her jaw tightened as she pressed her full lips into a line.

I waited for the fight. Surely, the queen of the Underworld would put up a fight that would make him regret looking at her that way. She had me convinced of it…right up until he grabbed her arm.

Her lip wavered, as she was jerked to her feet by her arm. Tears welled in her eyes and fell, cleaning the grime from her cheeks in salty rivers. He ran his hand up and under her dress. My heart clenched. He was going to…

"No!" I screamed. Launching myself at his hand, I quickly learned that Oceanus didn't need his powers to get his way. His arm was like grabbing one of the punching bags we used for Guard training.

Solid.

Thick.

Strong.

He batted me away, the way an adult would a child - with no effort at all. I didn't fly as far this time, recovering in a roll. I got to my feet and ran at him again as my training kicking in. This time I went for his head. The bastard might be big, but big was *slow*.

At least I thought so.

The room buzzed and Oceanus turned quicker than I could have anticipated. A great hand shot out, grabbing me out of the air as I jumped kicked toward his head. I screamed as he got a hold of me by my thigh.

"Kronus said nothing about keeping you in one piece. *Alive* was what he said"

I dangled in the air as his grip tightened around my thigh, cutting the blood supply off. I couldn't get a grip or hand hold anywhere. I flailed and yelled in frustration.

"Leave her alone, you monster!" I shouted.

"Oh, sweetheart. You have no idea how much of a monster I can be," he rumbled. He let go of Persephone and turned to me. She shrieked.

"Take me! Oceanus! Leave her! Leave her!" she yelled, and ran to him, pawing at him desperately.

Panic slammed into me seeing the desperation that Persephone showed. It gripped me as hard as Oceanus did, wrapping it's choking tendrils around my throat and sending my heart into spasm.

Oceanus turned me around in the air so that I faced him, still holding me by my thigh. My hip was near to popping out as he twisted me around. His eyes were black as night, but it was smile that slid up his face that really turned my insides to ice.

"Monster am I?" he said quietly as he drew a finger across my cheek. It scraped across my skin like a barnacle. I could feel the sting of fresh cuts as he drew his hand away. A long dagger flashed in the light. I didn't know where it came from, it didn't matter. I kicked out and squirmed with everything I had. I didn't know what he was going to do with that and I didn't want to find out.

Persephone threw herself at his dagger arm.

"Don't you worry, my pet. I'll be with you after. There's plenty of me to go around," he said and kicked Persephone with such force that she flew across the room. She hit the wall with a sickening thud and fell in a dead heap to the ground.

Gods…no.

She was a goddess and couldn't be killed. *She's alive.* I reminded myself.

The grip on my thigh shifted sending a new stabbing wave of pain through my body and I wondered if death would look like a friend before long.

The tip of a dagger drifted over my collar. I hissed against the line it cut into my skin. In that moment, I wasn't as scared as I was angry. How was he able to keep me? *I shouldn't be here. I should be in my body fighting against Kronus. Trying to break free of his power.*

The front of my shirt tugged.

My eyes refocused.

"That's right," Oceanus whispered to me. He dropped me to the ground, grabbing my hands and forcing them above my head, pinning them to the wall.

My heart was bashing itself against my ribs and panic filled my lungs. My breathing was shallow and fast as Oceanus ran a massive hand across my collar and down to the front of my shirt.

"Look at me," he said. I refused. His grip around my hands tightened until I screamed.

"Look at me!" he yelled, his voice shaking the room so much that stone dropped from the ceiling, clicking across the stone floor as they fell.

Another squeeze at my wrists and I could feel the bones bending. A scream cut out of me like nothing I had ever heard before. I brought my eyes to his.

"There," he said, a smile sliding up the side of his moist face.

The dagger flashed before me and I closed my eyes against in the pain I knew was coming.

But it didn't.

There was another tug on my shirt and cold air hit my chest.

In that moment, I knew – I knew I wanted the pain, not what was coming.

My shirt and bra dangled loosely open in front of me, exposing my bare chest to the chill in the room, and worse Oceanus's gaze. His tongue slipped out and ran across his lips as a low groan echoed deep in his chest. I could feel the vibrations of it on my skin.

His eyes didn't leave me as his hand reached out toward me. My skin looked like white marble against the darkness of his. When I opened my eyes, though, the massive Titan had disappeared. Before me stood a man. Just a man. His hand gripped my wrists together just a fiercely as Oceanus did. He must have seen the look of confusion on my face.

"Oh, believe me, there is nothing weak about this form. But I find that I get…more from my prey in it," he said, lifting a hand and looking at it. "I can really feel your flesh this way."

He drew a light finger across my check, down my neck, across my collarbone and toward my chest. I wriggled at the feel of his skin on mine. He might have been easier on the eyes, but he was no less evil than before.

"Don't fight it," he whispered. A low growl emanated from him, just as before. His hand slowly slipped across my chest as he grasped the soft flesh there.

I whimpered.

It was wrong. It was *all wrong.*

The feel of his touch was foreign and unwanted. The only one to touch me there had been Jett. He was the only one and was supposed to be the *only* one.

His hand circled me. Massaging. Groping. Pulling. Pinching.

I cried out.

"Stop!" I cried, unable to keep the fear from shaking my voice. Trying desperately to pull my arms across my exposed skin.

"No, I don't think so," he said, moving his hand slowly down. My eyes flew open and the blood drained from me.

One finger.

That was all it took.

One finger to run from the underside of my breast, down the center of my core, over my navel, and to the top of my pants.

One finger to shred the fabric like a knife through silk.

One finger to take what I didn't want to give. To scrape away at everything innocent within me. Every bit of what I was.

One finger to claim my body as something other than mine.

Just one.

Just once.

When he let go of my wrists, I slid to the floor, grasping what was left of my clothes around myself as I wept into the cold floor.

"You wanted the monster, love. You barely got a *glimpse*," he said, turning from me. He walked across the floor and grabbed Persephone's unconscious body off the floor and tossed her over his shoulder. "Hope you liked what you saw."

"No," I uttered softly. "Don't take her."

Oceanus laughed darkly and hoisted her higher on his shoulder.

"She's going to get more than a taste," he said as he morphed back to the monstrous form he was naturally. His massive figure shook the ground as he stooped through the door, taking Persephone with him.

I sank further into the floor.

Darkness took over the room once again and I welcomed it.

JETT

"WHAT DO YOU mean a Titan?" I asked.

"Oceanus," Nerites said. "He came and…took a young one. I tried to stop him, but there is no stopping a Titan."

"Why would Poseidon want anything to do with the Titan of seas?" Spyres asked.

"Poseidon didn't bring him. Apollo did," Nerites said.

"Apollo? What's going on here?" I shouted.

"I don't know, but Oceanus was able to force the bond. I – I was there for that," Nerites said quietly. "I'm sorry I couldn't stop him," he said, looking at Spyres.

"This is bad," I said, placing a hand on my mouth. A Titan with a power boost? *Great.*

"It will give him powers unlike anything we have seen before," Spyres said.

"Like what?" I asked.

"Who knows? He could be able to pull souls from bodies. Transport minds. Manifest a consciousness into physical form."

"Wait, you mean like pull the mind from someone and then give them a new body?" I asked.

"A little more complicated than that, but essentially, yes."

"So, if Laya had wakens Kronus and he takes over her body, Oceanus would be able to pull him out of it and give Kronus a new body?" I asked.

"It's a possibility," Spyres said.

"No, you're right," Nerites said. Spyres and I looked at Nerites.

"What?" I uttered.

"I saw it. He had to try it. He had to see if his powers worked," Nerites said, his eyes on the ground.

"What did he do?" I asked.

"He – he pulled from me," he said.

"But-"

"I can't explain it. One minute I was being held back by Apollo, because I was trying to save the uniborn; and, the next it was like my soul was being torn in two.

"The pain was like…oh, it was all consuming. When I came to, at least that's the best that I can explain it, I was looking at myself. This hollow shell was standing in front of me, but it was me. Like a giant doll of myself. Dead eyes and all. It was so creepy.

"I looked down at my hands. They were mine, scars and all. When I looked over at Oceanus he was smiling. Damned if that wasn't one of the most terrifying things I have ever seen."

"He did it. Recreated a living being," Spyres uttered. I looked at the beautiful unicorn and knew that this was beyond bad if he seemed scared.

"What does this mean?"

"It means that he will have the ability to multiply the Titans," Spyres said.

"Like make *more* of them?" Nerites squeaked.

"Yes," Spyres replied.

"How do we stop him?" I asked. "We really don't need a bunch of Kronuses wandering around."

"We would have to break the bond with the unicorn," Spyres said. Nerites looked at him like he was insane.

"You know what you are saying right?" Nerites accused.

"I do," Sypres said straightening up. *"Do you see any other way?"*

"Okay, what are you talking about?" I asked.

"The only way to break the bond between Oceanus and the unicorn is to kill the unicorn," Nerites said, his brow furrowing over his darkened eyes.

"Great," I uttered. I didn't want to go around killing unicorns.

"When a bond is formed, a unicorn takes on the personality and traits of the god that it bonds to. The unicorn that was forced to bond will be a horrible creature. Ending their life would bring them peace," Spyres explained.

It seemed better, but it still meant killing an innocent unicorn.

"Where does Oceanus live? Where would he keep the unicorn?" I asked.

"His realm is far away, in the depths of the sea, where not even Poseidon's powers reach. There he has remained, unseen and unheard of…waiting," Spyres said.

"Can you show me?" I asked.

"Yes, but it is a hard journey."

"I'm not new to the water," I said, glad that something was finally working my way.

"True and I have to say that you handled yourself well against my kind," Spyres commented.

"Thanks. I'm sorry Nerites, I can't bring you with me. It's too dangerous," I said, feeling bad for the guy. "I can take you back to where we are staying if you'd like. You can meet my brother."

"Sure…," he answered.

"We can protect him in the water," Spyres said. *"Our magic would keep him safe from the cold and give him the ability to breathe."* Nerites smile lit his face.

"Can I come?" he begged.

"You realize that this is super dangerous and you might get killed," I said to him.

"After all the years locked away on Olympus, this is just what I need to feel like I am living again. So, yes. Possible death and all. Yes," he replied.

"I guess that's a definite yes," I said to Spyres.

"As promised, for you, the Golden Fleece," Spyres said and bowed his head low.

There was nothing there.

"Where?" I asked, looking as hard as I could.

"The golden string," he said. I stepped closer and ran my hand along Spyres's neck. His hair was softer than anything I had ever touched before. As soon as my skin came across the string, it vibrated like a live wire. I jerked my hand away, accustomed to the instinct to drop anything that did that.

"It's a string?" I asked, looking, but not touching it.

"Isn't it supposed to be like a sweater or wrap or something?" Nerites asked, stepping forward and squinting at the tiny golden thread…more like hair.

"It can be, if you so wish. This is more practical for our purposes," Spyres said.

"What were you trying to protect when I was in the water with you? You acted like the fleece was in that one iceberg," I asked.

"Well, you would have just attacked me if you knew it was around my neck, now wouldn't you? And, if by some chance, someone was to get through us, they would find nothing in that ice cavern and the Fleece would remain hidden," he explained.

"Good plan," approved Nerites.

I agreed. Smart. Very smart.

I reached up and grasped the delicate thread in my hand. This time, when I touched it, it fell away from Spyres's neck and wrapped around my wrist like a gold bracelet. The material it was made of was so fine I couldn't feel it on my skin, even when I ran my fingers across it. It was like it was a part of my skin.

"Amazing," I whispered as I looked at my wrist.

"Can I try it on?" Nerites asked. I looked up at him and raised my brows.

"Just kidding," he uttered. "Not my style."

"I need to get to Laya," I said to them. "I will have to meet you at Oceanus's palace. I have to get this to Laya before Kronus wakes."

"You sure that can't wait? I mean we are talking about multiple Kronus Titans waltzing around. We could use some help if to destroy this uni that Oceanus is bonded to," Nerites said.

"I know, but it will be that much harder to find and destroy with Kronus around to protect it if he wakes in Laya," I answered.

"True," Spyres said. "You go. I, Nerites and the Herditim will go find the bonded unicorn. We can take care of it. We've been aching to stretch our legs for a long time. There are many forms that we can take other than this one," Spyres said and I could swear that I could see a sly smile on his face. Which was an odd thing to see on a horse face.

"I wish I could see it," I said, and I wasn't lying.

"I'll tell you all about it when we see each other next," Nerites said.

"It's a plan," I said and sincerely hoped that I would be able to see them again. They were doing a dangerous job, one that would be putting them at great risk.

"Good luck," I said, and placed my forehead against Spyres's, as I had learned from Nerites.

There was a flash and a crack, like a whip. A pulse of air shot from the spot we touched and struck out in a circular wave. Nerites was knocked off his feet and the other unicorns dove under the water.

I pulled back, touching the spot on my head where we had touched.

"What was *that*?" I shouted, looking up at Spyres.

The moment his eyes met mine, I knew. No longer was the power in the air a trickling buzz at the corner of my mind, it was a waterfall of energy cascading over me. I felt like a battery fully charged and trying to take on more.

My powers snapped to life across my hands. Lightning ripped up my arms, across my shoulders and down my back. In a flash my whole body was a current of white light.

"Whoa!" I uttered, looking down at my hands, which were almost impossible to see under all the light and white flame. "What's going on?"

"You bonded!" Nerites shouted, jumping up and down.

"No! I didn't mean to! I don't know how I did that! I was just saying goodbye!" I blurted. My stomach flipped and then took a great flop. I thought I was going to be sick. I forced a bond on the leader of the last unicorns. What kind of monster was I?

"No," Spyres said. "You forced nothing, Jett. I chose you."

My eyes snapped up to Spyres.

"You…you chose *me*?" I echoed in wonder. "Why?"

"There is a great battle to come. We can sense a change in the tides of power. You are a part of the new. The old will fight against you in any way that they can, but it is time for you to rise. We place our faith in you and your kind. May the pain of the past stay there and new friendships forge a safer future for us all," he said and bowed to me.

"Oh no, please don't do that," I said wanting to grab the great and beautiful creature and force it to stand.

"This is amazing," Nerites said.

"I didn't come here to get an energy boost from a bond with a unicorn. Quite honestly, I'm not sure that I want one considering that I'm not so great controlling the power that I already have."

"You looked like you controlled it just fine to me," Nerites said. "When Zeus bonded, he flattened half of the houses on Olympus with a giant bolt of lightning that shot out of him."

"Really?"

"Yup. You just…got all bright as the sun. Trust me, if you didn't have ultimate control over your powers, you would have exploded this place," Nerites added.

"It's just my ring," I said, pointing to my hand. "It helps dampen my powers so that I can control them."

"What ring?" Nerites asked.

"This one!" I shouted, pointing to my ring - at least pointing to the finger that once had the ring my mother had left me. The object left there was a tarnished, rusted out, circle, not the beautiful, vibrant piece that was there before. The moment I touched the ring, it disappeared into dust.

"Great! I just blasted my mother's ring!" I huffed.

"Seems to me like it was made for a purpose and, now, that purpose no longer exists," Nerites said. I glared at him. How dare he say something so logical when I was angry?

"It's more of a sentimental thing," I huffed.

Nerites shrugged, "Alright. Prove me wrong, then."

"Prove you *wrong*? How?" I asked.

"Well, do something. Use that bonded power you have. See what horrors you create," Nerites challenged. I looked at Spyres.

"I chose you for a reason. Show him why."

This time Spyres's voice was only in my head. A hum of energy let loose in my core, driving through my muscles as it fast tracked in my veins. Not wanting to destroy any of the land around me, or harm any creatures, I simply aimed for the sky.

I pulled.

Faster than ever before, my power exploded from my core and down my arms. A massive ball of white light and energy converged in my hands. I smiled. It was blinding to all around, but not me or Spyres. He stood tall beside me, watching and waiting. I could feel his encouragement and support. I lifted the ball above my hand and shot it into the sky.

Like a bomb going off, it exploded. A wave of power and wind hit the sky, clearing it of any clouds and downing a few birds. *Oops.*

The sky darkened for a moment, as if my power had absorbed all light from it. When I dropped my eyes down from the sky, I looked at my hands. I had never done anything like that before. I had never felt anything like that before.

A whoop and holler drew my attention away from my own awe. Nerites was cheering and jumping.

"Aww, man! That was awesome! Do it again!" he smiled.

"Umm."

"Ah, I'm kidding." Nerites was laughing and smiling at me as he placed a hand on my shoulder. "Zeus has nothing on you, my friend."

I placed my hand on top of Nerites. "Thanks, I think."

"It is time."

"Yes, I have to get this is to Laya," I said waving my wrist with the Golden Fleece wrapped around it.

"We will take care of Nerites and see you soon."

I nodded at him.

"Wait! Are you two communicating telepathically?" Nerites asked looking between us.

I nodded.

"Oh, that is awesome! Rude. But Awesome," he added.

I chuckled.

"See you both soon," I said.

"Stay safe," I said to Spyres.

Focusing on only Laya, I hoped that my new bonded powers would help me find her wherever she was.

With a *pop*, Spyres and Nerites disappeared and I was off to Laya.

I'm coming.

KYLAYA

I DIDN'T KNOW how much time had passed when the door opened again.

Light pierced my eyes and woke me from a sleep I had desperately needed – even if it came in restless fits. There was a loud smack, like a sack of flesh hitting the ground and the door closed again.

"Persephone?" I whispered.

No response.

I inched forward in the dark, making my way softly and slowly toward the body. The room was pitch dark, but for the thin crack of light under the door. I couldn't see much of anything. Concentrating, I focused on Jett. Centering my mind on his face, his love.

Slowly, a white glow formed in my chest. My eyes adjusted as the figure came into view.

Before I saw her face, I knew it was Persephone. I recognized her dress and the brilliance of her blonde hair; even through the grime that coated it.

"Gods! What has he done to you?" I gasped and shuffled closer, turning her over to assess the damage. Her face was battered almost beyond recognition. The sight of it made me turn away for a moment. She was almost unrecognizable. New and old bruises mixed together up her arms and down her legs. Her knees were scraped raw.

But, it was the drying blood on the inside of her thighs that turned my stomach.

A rage lit in me that I had never experienced in my life. I wanted to kill him. Oceanus deserved to die for what he had done to Persephone. I didn't even know how many times he had hurt her like that. The way he talked, this wasn't the first. I could only hope that this was the worst.

A muffled moan slid from Persephone's split lips and I reached for her.

"No!" she begged. Her voice was raw and ragged, like she had been screaming. My heart shattered for her. She tried to sit up to escape, but her weak body wouldn't allow it and she fell back to the ground. A sob broke from her.

"Persephone, it's me. Laya," I said softly. I placed my hand gently on her shoulder.

Her head swung around so fast I staggered back. Her eyes were glazed over, as she looked at me, maybe through me.

The moment her eyes locked with mine she broke.

Persephone's cry was more animal than human. I could feel her pain in every part of me. I brought my arms around her and pulled her to me. She sobbed into my chest, hard and rough.

"I'm so sorry," I said.

Over and over and over again.

. . .

I WOKE to humming.

Persephone no longer was curled up with her head on my lap. At some point I had fallen asleep while comforting her. I stretched out my legs and listened. Her voice was beautiful. Soft. Haunting. It echoed off the walls in our dark room. Filling the space with her song.

"That's pretty," I said when she stopped. Focusing on Jett, I let the light within me out, filling the space with a warm white glow.

She looked...

"Wow!" I gasped. "You've healed, like a lot!"

"Perks of being a goddess. Fast healing," she said bitterly.

"I'm so-"

"Don't apologize, Laya. Please," she said raising a hand at me. "You've done nothing."

"I'm sorry it happened to you," I explained.

"I know you are," she said, nodding sadly. She bit her lip when it wobbled slightly.

"Are you-" I stopped myself.

"Okay? Am I okay?" she finished. I looked down, ashamed of the stupid question.

"I didn't…I wasn't thinking," I said.

Persephone stood with a huff. She circled the room like a caged animal.

"I'm mad," she said turning to me. "I'm scared. I feel weak. I feel…empty."

I said nothing.

"I miss Hades. My heart breaks and mends back together every time I think of him. The only thing keeping me alive in here is the hope that I will be able to see him again. That I will be able to fall in his arms at the end of this and be home again."

Tears welled in my eyes. I hoped that for her too.

"Tell me about him," I said, wanting to help her focus on something positive.

A quiet smile pulled at her lips and I knew that, for the moment at least, her spirit was happy.

"Hades isn't what everyone thinks that he is. Lord of Darkness. Ruler of the Dead. King of the Underworld. To me he is just a man. A good man. Tender. Kind. Loving. Hades saved me from a life I would have been eternally unhappy in. His love saved me. I know what the myths all say. The kidnapping and trickery. It was nothing like that. Not at all."

Taking a quick step to me, she sat. Her eyes were open and wide and her smile brought color to her pale cheeks again.

"You know; he was too scared to talk to me?"

"No way," I laughed. "Hades, afraid of *you*?"

"Yup," she laughed lightly. "He would show up in the forest that I took my walks in. At first, I thought that it was some kind of forest spirit. Then, one day, I caught a glimpse of him. Oh, Laya," she gushed. "I had never seen a man as beautiful as he was."

She grabbed my hands as the light of her love lit in her chest filling the room with a bright glow.

"So, you can bet I started coming back there more often."

"I'll bet," I laughed.

"He was there every time, but he remained hidden - sliding among the shadows. I would sit and braid flowers in the meadow, hoping that he would come and join me. But he never did."

"Really? How long did that go on for?"

"Forever!" she said. I laughed. "Well, it seemed that way."

"How did he get the nerve to talk to you?"

"I told him to stop creeping on me and come sit with me."

I laughed hard. "Good for you!"

"Oh, from that moment on, he was my *everything*. The days were too long when we weren't together and too short when we were. You know what that's like."

I nodded. I did indeed.

"Oceanus doesn't understand love," she said, looking down at her hands. "He thinks that it's a weakness, but it isn't. It's a strength, Laya. Don't ever let anyone convince you that love is anything but the most powerful gift that you can share with someone."

She reached across and grasped my hands again.

"I won't last much longer here," she said softly.

"Don't – don't say that. You will. You have to," I argued. She dropped her head and shook it.

"I can feel it. My soul is slipping. Every time he takes me, forces himself on me, I lose a part of myself. I think…I think he's feeding off me somehow. I can feel my powers weakening. It takes more and more energy for me to heal. There will come a time where I won't be able to heal myself."

"But, you're a goddess. You *can't* die!" I argued.

"That may have been true at the height of our power; but, not now. Our powers have been dwindling for a long time."

"Is there anything I can do?" I asked. "What can I do?"

"There is nothing to be done."

"Apparently, I'm the reincarnation of Gaia. I have to be able to do *something* to help you! You can't die in here! You can't!"

"You're what?" Persephone said and stood up. "How is this just coming up *now*?"

"I don't exactly go blurting that out to everyone I meet," I said.

"Does Oceanus know who you are?"

"Yes."

"And he's still keeping you here?" She stood and started to pace the floor.

"What? What is it?"

"The reincarnation of Gaia. My mother talked about you," she said.

"Me?" I squeaked.

"Yes. She would talk about the second coming of the gods. A power to overshadow all the gods that came before. I used to be scared of it. I never…I never thought of it as a person," she said looking at me.

"Ugh."

"I'm not scared anymore. It's time for the gods to retire. We've been around…too long. It's a blessing, at least that is how I see it," she whispered. "I would love to go somewhere with Hades and just be together for a few hundred years. We don't need much. Just each other."

"That sounds really nice," I said.

"Every day I am in here that dream slips further from me," she said.

"We *will* get out of here, Persephone," I said, grabbing her hands and squeezing them tight in mine. "We will. We have to."

"I don't know," she hesitated with a shake of her head.

"Your mother talked about me and my powers. What did she tell you? Maybe you know something about them that I don't."

"She didn't say much about specifics," she said.

My shoulders sank. I could see it in Persephone's face. She was fading. Her wounds might have started to heal, but her skin was pale underneath it all. The goddess glow she had was fading. Whatever Oceanus was doing to her was working. She was dying.

And I will probably die here too.

The sadness was almost overwhelming as we sat there on the floor of Oceanus's prison.

I couldn't afford to let myself fall down that rabbit hole of despair. Instead, I focused on Jett.

I *will* see him again.

I *will* hold him.

I *will* kiss him.

I *will.*

I will.

I will…

JETT

THE SMELL hit me before the light did.

I nearly gagged. Even the scent in our interrogation room at the farm wasn't that bad. The Siren's torture room didn't hold a candle to it either.

Where am I?

Stone walls surrounded me, but Laya was nowhere in sight. The air was thick with moisture, and filled my lungs with a heaviness that weighed on me. It was hard to draw breath.

Where is Laya?

"Laya?" I called out.

No answer.

I didn't understand. My powers were new, but I knew that I had thought of her and only her when I disappeared. Why wasn't she there?

A stone hallway opened behind me. My shoes crunched over the gritty floor as I walked down it. Unlike the walls in Triton, these weren't polished or smooth in any way. Sharp and jagged, you would lose some serious skin if you scraped against it. My shadow danced across the walls in the dim light of the lit torches. Not a slit of natural light shone. I was certain that I was below ground in what looked like a dungeon.

When I had left Laya, she was still at Eurybia's. She was supposed to have been safe there. *Where am I?* Dark, dank and all kinds of creepy, I couldn't help the anxiousness that crept through me. There was something terribly wrong with this place.

The hall ended at a large wooden door. I reached out and grasped the massive brass handle. When I pulled, it didn't budge. I looked back down the hallway and knew, without thinking, that going back wasn't going to take me closer to Laya. Driven by an urge that came from my very core, I poured my power into the lock. It turned to liquid under my hands and fell away from the door.

Tugging on the door, it opened with a sick creak.

I was hit with a wall of stench and left me breathless. The room was completely dark, not a window or light illuminated the space. Pulling the door wide, I stepped through, keeping the door open with my foot.

As my eyes adjusted to the dim, they landed on two figures across the room from me. Sprawled on the floor, one laid in the other's lap. Greasy hair hung over their faces, and their clothes were filthy and torn.

Prisoners. Why was I taken here?

The light from the hall casted shadows around the gloom of the room.

"No!"

My eyes widened and my heart stopped. I knew that voice.

"You *won't* take her!" One of the figures stood up across the room, tall and strong.

I knew the curve of her hips, the sweep of her neck, and that stubborn stance anywhere.

I rushed in the room and threw my arms around her, lifting her clear off the floor. Arms and legs beat against me as I pulled her to me.

"Laya," I shouted. "It's me."

"Get off me!" she screamed, scratching at me like a feral cat.

"What's wrong? It's me! Jett!" I said to her, stumbling back when she landed a right hook to my chin.

Laya's eyes were wild. I could see the streaks of dirt across her face, mixed with blood. My stomach dropped and my insides turned to pins when I looked at her, really looked at her. She was sickly thin. Her hair hung in greasy chunks around her face, which was bruised around her mouth and cheek.

I reached out to touch her, but she nearly bit my hand when I did. Laya looked like a wild animal.

"What happened to you?" I whispered. My heart was breaking. She didn't see me. She saw something…evil.

Her eyes levelled with mine. Her glare cut right through me.

"Laya," I uttered.

"Don't," she yelled. "You're not *real!*"

"I'm right here," I said gently. "I'm here."

I took a step toward her, but she planted herself against the wall and looked at me with terror in her eyes. Her stringy hair waved in front of her eyes like a dirty mop when she shook her head at me.

"Not real. Not real. Not real," she repeated to herself.

"I'm *real*," I said gently, slowly grasping her bony fingers in mine and bringing them to my cheek.

"No. No, you're not."

My world was shattering in front of me. I didn't understand how she was there, or why, or what happened to her; but she was, and she was *not* okay.

And, I was going to kill whoever did this to her.

"Dream stopper," I said to her, looking her in the eye. She stopped mumbling to herself and looked at me.

"What did you say?"

"Dream stopper," I repeated, bringing my hand to her cheek.

Her eyes widened and tears filled them.

"Jett?"

I nodded.

"It's…it's really you?"

"It's really me."

She launched into my arms and hugged me fiercely. A solid thud hit my chest as I pulled her close.

"I didn't think I'd ever see you again!" she said.

"What happened?" I asked her.

"How did you ever find me?" she asked, placing her hands on either side of my face.

"I just thought of you and it brought me here," I said to her. She pinched her brow and looked at me.

"That's it?" she asked.

"Well, yeah."

"I don't understand. Why didn't you come sooner?"

"I'm sorry. I didn't know you had left Eurybia's until I ended up here. I didn't know."

"How could you not *know*?"

"I-"

"It's been *months*, Jett! Where have you *been*?" she said.

I felt like I had been punched in the stomach.

Months?

In that moment the door flew open. A great shadow filled the space in the doorway.

"What do we have here?" a low voice rumbled.

Laya shrank toward the wall and placed herself over the body of the other figure.

"Did someone bring me a new toy to play with and not tell me?"

"Excuse me?" I said.

"No," Laya uttered. "He's not a toy. No." She came out from behind me, placing me behind her.

"Oh, I think he is a beautiful toy," the man said and stepped into the room.

"Laya," I said, and pulled her back. "Who are you? What have you done to her?"

"I've been...*playing*," the man said. My blood turned to ice. The grin that spread across his face told me more than I needed to know.

My powers lit in my hands and up my arms.

"Stay away from her," I shouted.

"I don't think so. She's...*fun*."

Rage surged from my core, igniting the power within me. A shot of light burst from my hand and hit the man in the chest.

He stumbled back slightly.

A dark, deep, rumble of laughter filled the room.

"You can't hurt me," he said. Standing up full height. "No one can."

"Who is this guy?" I asked Laya, not daring to take my eyes off of him.

"Oceanus. The Titan of the sea," she whispered back. Her lips quivering and her eyes darkening.

That's when I knew why I couldn't hurt him. The unicorn was feeding his powers and making him stronger. So strong that my powers had almost no effect on him. All I could do was hope that Spyres and Nerites would find the unicorn and kill it soon. Really soon.

There was a crack of thunder and before I could react, the beast of a man shot a bolt of green light at me.

Laya screamed.

The room filled with electric green light.

And then nothing.

I had stepped in front of Laya, to shield her from Oceanus's attack, but the bolt was floating motionless in the air between me and Oceanus.

"How?" I uttered and turned around to Laya.

I wasn't prepared for what I saw.

KYLAYA

THE DAYS stretched into weeks and then months.

There was no sign of someone coming for us, and I had long lost hope that there would be. If Persephone, a freaking goddess, couldn't get out…there was really no hope for me.

There was a shuffle in the hall and the door creaked open. I shielded my eyes against the light as Persephone was tossed in. Catching her, I sent us both crashing back onto the hard ground. I quickly laid her down and assessed the damage.

She was still breathing, though too slowly and too shallow.

"Hey," I whispered, placing my hand on her cheek and tapping my thumb on her nose. It was a secret touch that we made up so that, even in the dim consciousness after a turn with Oceanus, we knew a friend's touch. It helped to bring us out of the darkness that came afterwards and into the arms of a loved one. Because that's what we had become to each other. Every time we were thrown back through that door, we brought one another back and comforted each other until the tears stopped and exhaustion took us.

She didn't move or moan this time.

"Shoot." I shifted her to my lap and shook her shoulders.

"Come on, Sephie," I urged, tears stinging my eyes. "Come on. Look at me."

She didn't stir.

"No. No. Come on! You have to live! Hades is waiting for you! You can't leave him."

Nothing.

"Please, Sephie! Wake up!"

For the last few weeks, it had taken longer and longer for her to come back to herself after Oceanus, or Sea Scum as we called him, took her. He was somehow sucking her godly ability to heal and she was fighting back less and less.

I brushed a mat of hair from her face. Her very pale face. There was little life left in it. I couldn't stop the rush of emotion.

The sob worked its way up my throat, cutting and bruising on its way, just to remind me of the hurt I was feeling. It burst from me with a ferocity that I didn't know was left in my shattered and torn body.

I dropped over Sephie's lifeless body and let out the hurt and fear and sadness in one long hollow scream.

. . .

I didn't remember fading off to sleep, but I must have. When the door opened I was woken. For a moment I forgot that Sephie was gone. I reached for her only to find a cold hand.

A dark figure stepped into the doorway and I knew he was there for her again.

Anger and rage flashed through me like wildfire. I pulled at my power, but drew up nothing, just like every time before. My powers were with my real body, not this duplicate that Sea Scum created. In the months I had been there, I had pieced together what had happened to me, one small piece at a time.

Kronus' essence woke in my body and pushed my mind so far down that it went to sleep. I don't remember a lot of that time, but somehow, just having me in the recesses of his mind I was messing things up for him. I would get glimpses of the outside world every once in a while and that turned out to be my mind pushing forward and taking over my body again. Even if it was only for a moment, he didn't like it. So, he got Sea Scum to pull my mind from my body and hold me prisoner. Why he was keeping me alive, I had no idea. There was no way that I was going to let them take Sephie's body to do – I couldn't let my mind go there.

"You can't take her!" I was on my feet before I knew it, shielding Sephie's body from whoever Sea Scum had sent to grab one of us.

The figure didn't move, instead it hesitated for a moment.

For a brief second I thought that I had somehow gotten through to one of Sea Scum's lackies. When he launched himself across the room and grabbed me, I knew I hadn't.

There was something different about this guard, though - his touch was softer, gentler. Instead of comforting me, however, it scared me all the more.

I didn't trust different anymore. It didn't challenge me as it once had. Different meant new pain. New ways to torture me. Different was terrifying and there was no way I was just going to let whatever fresh hell Scum-face had lined up for me happen without a fight.

I might not have my powers, but I still had some strength in me. I clawed and scratched like a wild animal. Kicking and biting and, yes, growling like one too. The guy held on tight, as they always did. He was yelling at me, but I blocked him out. I had learned not to trust voices, especially the voices of my loved ones. Too many times I had been lured by the sound of my father, Mazz, my sister and worse…Jett. I wouldn't let another lie trick me into bed only to be taken with a savageness that left me begging for death.

Never. Again.

Whatever trick this was, I wasn't falling for it. Not this time. Not when Sephie lay no more than a few feet from me.

He grabbed my face and I was forced to look into his eyes. For a split second I forgot my pledge not to trust, as my heart leaped for joy. Jett's beautiful, perfect face was before me. His eyes swimming in icy blues, locked on mine.

I was one of Scummie's cruelest tricks.

"Laya, it's me!" he said.

"Get away from me," I barked back. It wasn't him. I knew it wasn't. It couldn't be. I had long given up hope that Jett would somehow find me. It was a trick.

I dodged his hands again, ignoring his words. Usually by this point, Sea Scum got tired of the tease and just took, but he didn't this time.

It was *different*.

Different was *bad*.

He moved quickly, and yet with a gentleness that took me by complete surprise. I didn't know that Oceanus was capable of that. His fingers laid delicately on my cheeks. I wanted to look away. I wanted to fight, but I was locked in those eyes. The eyes of a man I still loved so much it hurt.

He leaned in and whispered, "Dream stopper."

I don't remember what I said or did, but my arms found themselves around him.

Jett.

My Jett.

The crash of the door against the wall blew a hole through the hope that had sprung free in my heart.

Scum Face stood in the doorway. I shrank back, out of habit, towards Sephie.

I couldn't let him take her. My fears were compounded when he turned his lustful eyes on Jett.

No, he can't take Jett.

Jett sent a charge of power straight at Sea Scum, but there was no effect. The Titan was near indestructible. Nothing in all the history I had read back home talked about a Titan that could withstand a blast like that. It didn't make sense, but Scummie stood tall.

A dark, deep, rumble of laughter filled the room.

"You can't hurt me," Sea Scum said. Standing up full height. "No one can."

"Who is this guy?" Jett asked me.

"Oceanus. The Titan of the sea," I whispered back. Saying his name out loud still shook me to the core. Sephie and I didn't say his name out loud. There was power to his name. He would make us say it when he…when he took us.

Jett's eyes met mine and I knew he could hear the fear in my voice. I had nothing left in me to mask it. I was raw; mind, body and soul. Jett's powers lit in his hands and shot up his arms. He wasn't about to back off, and neither was-

A crack of thunder sounded, shaking the room. My eyes widened as a green bolt of energy blasted from Oceanus straight for Jett.

"No!" I screamed.

In that moment, something inside me snapped. A tear, like muscles and flesh ripping away from bone, tore through my core. My body jerked in pain. Once.

In the echo of the agony that followed, I felt something I thought had been taken from me for good.

My power.

With nothing left of me to hold it back, I let it surge forward.

A torrent of white light collided against muscle and skin, healing, renewing, and energizing me from within. It streamed out of me in white beams of light.

Stop him. I commanded.

My power answered.

A pulse of pressure beat through my veins, like a heavy wave of warmth. It pounded beneath my skin and then, with a great rush, it broke free. Filling the room in a light that came from within me, I watched in awe as the green energy that The Scum had sent toward Jett, froze mid-air.

The Titan's eyes narrowed. His mouth tightened into a thin line, as rage built and broke out of him.

"No!" His guttural shout shook the room as much as his great hands did when they slammed against the floor. Jett turned to me with wide eyes and a smile pulling at his mouth.

I looked back at *Oceanus.*

"No. It can't be," Oceanus uttered.

I held tight to my powers, finally embracing them as they were - unending, all-consuming, life-giving...*power.* Not giving a second thought to what I was doing, I shot my power out at Oceanus.

Boom.

My energy collided with his, as he shot out at me. White light cut straight through his green, slicing into him and eliciting a gurgling scream that I would never forget.

The moment that he was hit, something changed. I felt a rush and flush of heat from the very center of my being. Placing my hand on my chest, I staggered back.

Jett's arms were around me instantly.

"What is it?" he asked.

"I don't know. I feel..." I couldn't put it into words. When I had been separated from my body and powers by Oceanus, there was this emptiness in me that I couldn't explain. As if my center, my core, my...soul, was gone. In the moment after I hit Oceanus, that emptiness filled again. I felt...whole.

I looked up at Jett, whose brow was furrowed with deep concern. I placed my hands on his face and smiled. Truly, whole-heartedly smiled.

Movement from across the room drew our attention. Jett pulled me behind him, but I stepped to his side.

Oceanus grunted and groaned as he tried to get to his feet. I planted my feet and summoned my power, ready for a fight. Jett's warm light lit next to mine. Oceanus's eyes turned to us. Green gooey blood seeped from his nose and ears. I couldn't help the spark of satisfaction I got seeing Oceanus in pain.

"You bitch!" he shouted as he staggered to a stand.

There was a blast from my right, as Jett unleashed on Oceanus. His brilliant white light cut through the air like a whip, slashing Oceanus across the face and sending him back to the floor.

"You will NEVER speak to her again. You will never *look* at her again," Jett shouted as he walked a direct path to the downed Titan.

I could feel his anger vibrating in the air. At least I thought it was his anger…at first. An echo at the back of my mind called forward to me. Like a trickle of cold water down the back of my scalp, a memory slid.

Kronus…

There was no mistaking the warning. Kronus was coming. I could *feel* it. Panic gripped me.

"Jett," I squeaked out. I must have sounded off, because the light of his powers dimmed and he flashed to my side.

"What is it? Are you okay?" he asked, lifting my face to his.

"Kronus," I whispered. The air was stolen from my lungs. I couldn't breathe. If I came close enough to Kronus again, would I lose myself to him? He took me over, forced himself into me in a way that was more personal, more invasive than anything that Oceanus had done to me. I couldn't-

"You're shaking," Jett uttered.

The walls shook and the earth quaked.

"I can't – he's coming." I was losing my mind. My thoughts were so scattered I couldn't form words. Jett took my hand. His eyes flitted to Oceanus and I knew he wasn't not done with what he wanted to do to him.

Oceanus sat up slowly. A low rumble echoed through the room, and I realized that he was laughing. Jett's eyes snapped to Oceanus. Flames ignited in his hands in a flash.

"Jett, please," I begged. My skin was crawling with anxiety.

Oceanus's laugh echoed off the walls and around us. Jett stiffened at my side. His eyes narrowed and his jaw clenched, but he took my hand firmly in his.

"Hold on," he said and pulled me to him. "I have you."

A great bolt of light struck the room. Like lighting that came from under our very feet, it blasted the floor out from under us, sending us toppling head over heels.

My back collided with a large sharp rock, winding me. I struggled to breathe as I sat up in the rubble. A shower of dust rained down in the room.

"Jett!" I called out, trying to get to my feet.

"I'm here!" he answered and a hand wrapped around my wrist in the dim light, pulling me safely to my feet. Jett brought me to his chest in a tight embrace. But, I couldn't focus on my relief.

Someone was in the room with us.

"Well, well." The voice was eerie. It was familiar.

It was…mine.

Jett and I turned as one. Where the lightning had hit, stood – well, *me*.

"Wh-" Jett stuttered, looking from me to the other me.

"Gods," I uttered, unable to look away from the other version of myself. She was me, or she was the other me. The one that I used to be, before Oceanus had pulled me out of the body I had before. She was the original, but she was an empty shell now. When I hit Oceanus, I fractured whatever he had done to me. I felt my soul, my very being come back. Safely inside me, my power hummed in my veins once again. I was more *me* than the Kronus one. She was a shell, nothing more.

And she was housing an evil that we were not prepared to face.

"Kronus," Oceanus grunted as he tried to stand.

"Don't bother," Kronus said through my lips. Kicking out, Oceanus went flying across the floor as Kronus' foot hit him square in the gut. A sick crack sounded in the room as his head hit the wall.

I stood my ground, as did Jett. My heart drop kicked my lungs when Kronus stepped toward us.

He looked like me but…warped. My features were stretched and uneven over bone. The word "skinsuit" came to mind with a shudder.

Jett shifted his weight, placing himself just ahead of me again.

"We didn't get a chance to meet formally before-"

"Before you took over my body and shoved me out of it?" I finished for him as he came to a stop in front of us.

"Yes," he said was a stretched smile that reached painfully further than natural.

I could feel Jett stiffen, ready to spring and strike. My powers were tingling in my palms, and glowing just beneath my skin.

"I can't say that I'm not sad about losing those powers of yours, my dear," Kronus said. His voice sounded like mine…if I were gurgling on blood.

"I can't say I'm sorry to have them back," I said and let the energy shine through my skin, igniting my body in light.

"Indeed," he answered, looking me up and down like a predator did its prey.

Jett stepped forward.

"Oh, my. You *are* the pretty one," Kronus said looking at Jett. Jett's jaw clenched as his eyes narrowed under his heavy lashes.

"He's taken," I replied.

"Pity," Kronus pouted.

"What do you want, Kronus?" Jett asked, his power licking across his fingertips.

"Oh, the usual, world domination and all that," Kronus shrugged.

Jett gave me a side look. I could tell he was thinking the same thing. Why wasn't he attacking us? What was he waiting for?

"I hear that you are looking for my essences."

I bit the inside of my mouth. Kronus knew more than I wanted him to. During the time when we shared a mind, he had access to my thoughts and memories. Not all of them, but more than I wanted him peeking at.

"You won't find them," he said.

"Oh yes, we will," I said. "And when we do, we'll destroy them. We'll will destroy *you*." I stepped up next to Jett.

Kronus' eyes narrowed. I didn't budge.

"*Really?*"

"Yes," Jett said, stepping to my side.

"I can sense your powers," Kronus said looking at Jett. "Old. Angry. You remind me of my father."

Jett didn't say anything, but kept his eyes evenly on Kronus.

"Don't particularly like my father," Kronus said, staring hard at Jett. His eyes then moved to mine. "Oh. I finally see it. The reincarnations." He nodded and shook his head.

I looked at Jett, but his eyes weren't moving from Kronus.

"Well, this is awkward. Here I was going to offer you a place at my side," Kronus said.

"She's not interested," Jett said back.

Kronus glared at Jett. "No, I don't suppose so. It is a shame. All that power." Kronus slowly walked a line parallel to us. His brow furrowed as he grasped his lip in his fingers. "No, there's no way around it."

"Around what?" I asked.

"I'm going to have to kill you. Can't have all that power walking around and getting in my way." Before we could respond, Kronus threw his hands out. Steaks of wicked light snapped from his fingertips and straight toward us.

JETT

THE FLASH of light ignited the room in a blinding white. I grabbed Laya and flashed.

Kronus' attack collided with the stone wall, showering boulders and dust over the room and Kronus himself.

My powers lit up my arms and down my back. I could feel them hum in my veins as I called them forward. A ball of energy formed in my hand; pink and white light dancing together seamlessly. I threw it hard.

Kronus' eyes widened as the ball flew through the air at him. There was still enough of Laya in his form that it felt wrong trying to hurt him. With the back of his hand, that now had talons instead of nails, he batted away the light. It collided with the wall and exploded.

"Shit," I hissed, keeping Laya behind me. The Fleece vibrated around my wrist, reminding me of its presence, of its protection. With a small flick, it unravelled and fell into my palm. Without Laya noticing, I draped it over her wrist.

She would be protected. She would be safe.

"There are others that will stand against you," Laya said. "This isn't over."

Kronus smiled through Laya's face. Her teeth grew, piercing through the flesh in her lower lip. I watched in horror as Kronus mutated Laya's form from within. Her features pulled tight; tearing and stretching grotesquely over ballooning bone; mutilating her beauty.

"I never got the chance to fulfill the prophesy where I got to kill my father. I suppose there is some beauty in killing his reincarnation," Kronus said, pulling his bone thin arms back.

"Jett!" Laya shouted, as Kronus struck out with his power. Green light flashed and hit me square in the chest.

There was no pain.

In the back of my mind I could hear Laya's scream. Her voice calling my name. But, I couldn't reach it. I couldn't get to her.

The floor came hard and fast for me, but I didn't feel when I collided with its stony surface.

The room dimmed, as if someone was slowly snuffing out the light.

She was there with me, but I couldn't fight through the darkness to get to her. It was swift and sure as it bled into the corners of my vision.

Anger coursed my veins.

Get up! Help her!

But nothing responded…

…and the darkness kept closing in.

KYLAYA

"NO!"

Ripping open a wound in his chest, so deep it tore past flesh and bone, Kronus' strike found its mark. Neither of us had time to react. Jett hit the floor hard.

I screamed.

Love.

Agony.

Rage.

It was all there.

"Jett! *No!*" I ran for him, but a light zipped off of the ground, exploding it in front of me. Kronus wasn't done.

I rounded on him in a flash. Never, I mean *never*, had I been that blindingly angry. I let my rage take me over.

Two long ropes of light stretched out of my palms. Like whips of energy and light, I shot out at Kronus.

"Finally! A battle worthy-"

I snapped out with an arm. The whip lashed, slicing a deep cut across his face, effectively shutting him up.

His face twisted sickly to the side with the impact. Drawing a hand across his face, he wiped the oozing black blood from his pale skin. I no longer recognized myself in him. He was more like a creature from a nightmare than any person I had ever seen. His skin, once my own, was torn and stretched like patches of flesh over muscle and bone.

I drew back my arm and struck out again. This time the whip caught him in the arm. His bulbous eyes turned to mine. A scream, like a giant beast gurgling on its blood, sounded in the room. Kronus, more a monster than a man, rounded on me.

I wasn't expecting him to charge me, but he did. His long fingers, topped with black talons, scaled the ravaged and broken stone floor easily as he ran at me on all fours. Flipping the whip of power in my hand, I pulled it back across my body and sliced a wide arch in front of me. A long wound cut into Kronus' back, but it didn't stop him. Before I could hit him again, he ploughed into me, sending me flying back, over Jett, and into the wall behind me.

My head smacked against the hard surface, spraying stars across my vision. Kronus didn't wait. Jumping on me, he slammed my head again. Stars took over my sight. I opened my eyes in time to see him open his mouth, revealing long jagged teeth, and watch as he sank them into the tender flesh at the base of my neck.

No sound came from my mouth. The pain was more than my voice could convey. I saw Jett laying on the floor through Kronus' legs and a fire lit within me. The whips of power came to life. Emerging from my palms, they slithered up Kronus' body. At their touch, his skin split open, revealing bone and tissue. My blood poured forth down my chest with every breath; it was getting harder to focus and fight.

Kronus reached up, drawing his hand back and showing off his deadly talons. I steadied myself for the hit. My power snapped up, wrapped around his wrist and squeezed. Rearing back, he fought the bindings. The more he fought, the more they tightened, cutting and searing his flesh and bone as they burned their way through him. I clamoured over the rocks to Jett's side, grabbing his hand in mine.

I had never used my power to travel before, but I knew I had to be able to do it.

There was a thundering from behind me and when I turned around, Kronus was racing toward me. His hand was severed off, which had freed him of my binds. I looked back at Jett and closed my eyes.

Sam.

Take us to Sam.

I closed my eyes and pulled at my powers, wishing to go to Sam. To go where Jett could be healed.

"Please," I whispered against the sound of Kronus coming for us.

There was light…

…and then there was nothing.

JETT

IN MY DREAMS, Laya was with me. Her face was next to mine as we rested on a feathery bed. The room was light and warm, it smelled of sweet grass. A breeze floated in through a window, blowing a strand of her beautiful blonde hair across her face. The feel of her skin beneath my fingertips sent a jolt right through me.

I ran my hand across her face again and the jolt came once again. Harder this time.

Ouch.

Laya turned to me. Her eyes bulged out of her head and her skin pulled tight. She looked mutated and grotesque. My blood started to pump hard in my chest. Another jolt in my core sent pain firing through me.

"Jett?"

Her voice was like needles in my ears and I couldn't stop from slamming my palms over them.

"Come on," she urged.

Her mouth moved out of time with her voice. Every time she opened her mouth, it revealed jagged teeth within her gaping maw. I drew back, but there was nowhere to go. I couldn't escape.

Another jolt.

A scream built in my throat.

Jolt.

The scream mounted…

Jolt.

And broke free.

The nightmare wouldn't stop and the pain just kept coming.

KYLAYA

"THERE HAS TO BE something you can do!" I shouted at Sam.

It worked. I had brought Jett back to Sam. Scared the crap out of him when we popped into the room in the middle of the afternoon while he was reading.

"I'm trying!" Sam yelled back to me, "Kronus' power is unlike anything I have ever seen! I don't know how to heal something like this! I'm doing everything I can."

I fell to Jett's side, grasping his hand in mine.

This can't be it. It can't be.

Jasper burst through the door.

"What's going-" he froze the moment that he saw Jett. He fell to the floor next to me. "What happened?"

"He was hit by Kronus' power. Sam can't heal him." I looked in Jasper's eyes and saw the same desperation that I had.

"I'm sorry, Jasp," Sam uttered.

"No," Jasper whispered, looking down at Jett. "No, he can't."

A sob broke free as helplessness set in. I didn't know what to do.

"Wait," Jasper muttered. He reached up around his neck. Out from under his shirt came the vial that his mother had given him. Her gift of healing.

"Yes," I whispered.

He popped off the stopper and took a breath.

"Please work," he whispered. I echoed the same prayer.

Silver shining liquid swirled within the vial as he tipped it over. A drop of liquid fell, landing in Jett's gaping wound.

Light surged from Jett. I squinted against the brightness, but couldn't take my eyes off him. The gleaming tendrils of power reached into him and started to heal. Fusing flesh. Mending bone.

Please. Save him.

A pulse burst from Jett; shooting across the room in a wide circle and shaking the foundation of Eurybia's home. Tearing from him, a rush of wind struck out, pushing me back. Another flash lit the room, and, with a snap, the light retreated into him in a great rush.

Stumbling up, I scrambled over the floor to Jett. I yanked his torn shirt aside. His skin glowed, smoothe and pink, fleshly healed over the horrible wound.

I smiled.

"Yes!" Jasper shouted. Sam smiled.

But Jett didn't wake.

He didn't stir.

"What's wrong? Why isn't he waking up?" I asked Sam.

"He's healed. The wound is gone," Jasper said. "Why can't he wake up?"

"I don't know. I've never heard of it not working on a wound before," Sam said.

"Jett's was a wound inflicted by a Titan. Are they different?" I asked.

"It's old power. Maybe," Jasper said.

"Almost…primordial," I uttered to myself. I pushed my way forward, suddenly knowing exactly what I needed to do.

Focusing, I pulled at the very core of my being. Where the knowledge of eons gone by rested. Where the heart of my power was. I could feel the warmth and love that resided within it.

A surge of warmth blossomed filling me with hope.

Love.

Light.

Life.

It poured from me.

Closing my eyes, I felt the pressure of my gifts flowing from me to him. To Jett. Riding the wave of my love for him, I felt my power reach into him - bringing life back to the darkness within his mind.

When he took his first deep breath, I dropped my head down to his.

An explosion of white light ignited from our touch. It filled the room with a brilliant, vibrating, glow.

When the light died away, it revealed the greatest sight in the world.

Jett was sitting up and looking at me.

"Jett?" I whispered, placing my hands on my mouth.

"Whoa, what happened?" he said, looking at his torn shirt.

I flashed right into his arms, pressing my mouth to his. He grunted in surprise, but took only a second to sink into the kiss with me. I felt his hand wrap around me, pulling me tighter to his chest. When I broke free, I grasped his face in mine and just looked at him.

"I just got you back. I wasn't about to lose you again," I said to him.

"I'm not going anywhere," he said, running his thumb down my cheek. I pulled him into a hug, resting my head on his shoulder. If I could have, I would never have moved from that spot.

. . .

I DON'T KNOW how long we sat on the floor together like that, but it didn't feel long enough. Jett's hand wrapped around mine and didn't move for the rest of the evening. Like a lifeline, his skin remained against mine, connecting us as we filled our friends in on everything. The feeling of his thumb moving back and forth across my hand, grounded and comforted me.

I smiled when he placed a warm kiss on my forehead as he slipped into the covers beside me later that evening. The others had made their way to bed, as did we. I fell into bed, in my room with Jett. Everything felt luxurious. I ran my fingers along the sheets and over my shower fresh skin. Sweet and clean. A scent I never thought that I would smell again. It was magnificent.

Jett's hand found mine again, and I squeezed it tight. There was no asking Jett to stay the night, as if he could read my mind, he knew what I needed and never left my side.

Thanks to Oceanus, I was now afraid of the dark - like a child. When the lights went out I full out panicked. Jett wrapped his arms around me and called his power to light the room in a warm glow. Just for me.

"What are you thinking?" Jett asked.

"I'm thinking that I'm lucky my boyfriend has a built-in nightlight," I said to him.

His smile was everything as it deepened the lines around his mouth and eyes.

"I will glow for you anytime, love," he said, lacing his fingers in mine. I turned in the bed and placed my forehead against his.

"I love you," I whispered.

"Love you, too."

After the time I spent in the darkness of Oceanus's lair, I was different. Jett's touch dragged forward the touch of a Titan. I shrank away from his fingers as they brushed my cheek. A hard knot in my belly tightened and squeezed me from within.

"You okay?" Jett asked, dropping his hand and watching me carefully.

"Truthfully? No. Not even close."

"Talk to me, Laya. Please. I need to know. I want to help you heal," he said softly.

I dropped my head. I didn't want to relive all of it. To think about all I had been through, all I had seen, all that had been done to me. I didn't want to think about Sephie. Her loss was still so raw it hurt.

"I don't know if I can, Jett. I don't think I have the strength to go through it all again," I admitted.

"It doesn't have to be tonight. Whenever you are ready. Whenever you feel that you can share with me what happened to you, I will be here."

I looked up to his eyes. They stared back at me with love.

For the first time in months, my heart was light and joyful; and, all the pain my soul had sustained started its long journey to heal. I knew that Jett would be by my side for every step of that journey and would be waiting for me on the other side. For that, I fell further in love with him than I could have thought possible.

My heart was his.

My soul was his.

Now.

Tomorrow.

Forever.

ABOUT THE AUTHOR

Emory lives in a world of mermaids and mythology. Escaping into the world of Mer is the best form of self-care she can think of. Who doesn't want to visit with Jett and Darrien? When she's not hanging with her book boys, she teaches Arts Education in Regina, Saskatchewan. Mommy to two adorable kids, she gets lots of hugs and snuggles from her favorite little people. She's lucky to have a hubby that supports her writing to the fullest. Emory dove into writing with the goal of finishing one book…now she cannot stop and doesn't plan on it.

You can find her on Facebook, Instagram, and Twitter! @emorygayle

Also by Emory Gayle

The Water Series:
Water: Book One of the Water Series
Mer: Book Two of the Water Series
Siren: Book Three of the Water Series
Tempest: Book Four of the Water Series

Celia's Journey: A Water Story
Volume One
Volume Two
Volume Three (TBD)

The Triton Series:
Triton's Daughter: Book One
Siren's Son: Book Two
Primordial: Book Three (2020)